CINDERS, STARS, AND GLASS SLIPPERS

A RETELLING OF CINDERELLA

BRITTANY FICHTER

WANT MORE FROM YOUR FAIRY TALES?

Sign up for a free no-spam newsletter and free short stories, exclusive secret chapters, and sneak peeks at books before they're published . . . all for free.

Details at the end of this book.

To Dad,
You taught me I was a princess, but you also taught me to be strong. From bruises to bullies, you were there, reminding me that I was created by God for a special purpose and that nothing anyone said or did could change who I am. Whenever I fell, you helped me stand back up. And when it came time to find my Prince Charming, you set the bar pretty darn high.

CHAPTER 1
AN AMBASSADOR'S SECRET

M iss Elaina."

Elaina quickly scribbled the rest of her note in the ship's log then looked up and smiled. "Yes, Lewis?"

"Your father would like to see you."

Elaina thanked the first mate and set off for her father's cabin, barely restraining her feet from doing a little jig as she went. The salty air was fresher than it had been in days, thanks to a new eastern breeze, and the ship rocked confidently beneath her as it charged forward to their destination. In spite of her excitement at finally being called to speak with her father, she regretted leaving the warm sunshine above as she climbed down the wooden steps into her father's cabin.

"There you are," her father called from his large wooden desk.

"I was beginning to think you'd never tell me." Elaina laughed as she flopped down in the chair across from him.

Her father kept his eyes on the maps before him, but a small smile lifted the corner of his mouth. "All in good time. But before I tell you who our secret ambassador is, I need you to have Johnston take inventory for our upcoming stop at Solwhind. This will be a quick stop, and I need our stores full."

"Done. I had him check this morning."

1

Her father raised his bushy black-and-white-peppered eyebrows. "Have the riggers check the sails then. Tell them I don't want a single rope out of place."

"Done as well." Elaina folded her arms triumphantly. She loved this game.

Her father finally shook his head. "I'm not even sure what I keep Lewis around for anymore."

"Nor I, Admiral," Lewis called out dryly from the doorway where he stood.

Elaina laughed again. "If you must know, I still need to visit with Simeon to finalize tomorrow's menu. Our ambassador's sleeping quarters must be dressed up properly as well. But other than that, I'm not sure how tomorrow's meeting with the ambassador could go wrong." She leaned forward, folding her elbows on his desk. "*Now* will you tell me who he is?"

"Not yet."

"And why not?"

"Because I am afraid that when you find out who he is, your excitement will make you completely worthless to me until he leaves." He glanced at her glare and let out a shout of laughter. "Very well, then. I will make you a deal. When everything is done and you're sure of the headwind tomorrow, come back here and I'll tell you who our secret visitor will be."

"It's not King Xander, is it?"

"No, nor is it the prince. Now get a move on those tasks."

Elaina bounced out of her chair to kiss her father before flying back up the steps to the deck. She had work to do.

Preparing the ship's largest guest quarters took longer than she expected. The two cabin boys assisting her had no taste in color or fashion, so it took them three attempts at bringing the right bedclothes, pillows, and curtains out of the correct storage chests before they managed to find any that matched, much less were befitting a guest of such high caliber. For though Elaina didn't know who their guest was, her father had never put so much effort into impressing a visitor before. Not even when the queen of Vaksam had asked to tour the famous flagship.

Much to her relief, Elaina's meeting with Simeon, the ship's cook, flew by more quickly. Of course, it wasn't as though Simeon ever cooked anything less than delectable. Her father had gone to great length to acquire him as their cook when Elaina was eight, and he had not disappointed since. She even began to relax a little as he described his plans for pecan-encrusted salmon, lemon garlic potatoes, and a dessert of crunchy apple tarts. Perhaps it wouldn't be as grand as full-course meals from wherever their guest hailed, but for a meal at sea, it would be a miracle.

She started back to her cabin, weaving her way around rushing cabin boys and busy sailors as she went. Her good mood faltered, however, when she noticed a heap of rope that seemed to have been tossed haphazardly onto the deck and left without scruple. Shaking her head, she lifted her skirts and stepped carefully over the mess of rigging to investigate, careful not to trip in the dark of dusk. Only when she squinted in the dim light did she see the two black boots sticking up from inside the pile. Elaina let out a huff and cleared her throat.

Nothing happened.

She cleared her throat again, louder this time.

A snort sounded from inside the messy coil, and the boots eventually moved. After a long moment of struggling, a young man finally poked his head out of the pile. His scowl disappeared, however, when he saw who had awakened him.

"Miss Elaina!" He scrambled to stand but succeeded only in falling on his face.

Elaina pursed her lips but helped him up.

"My apologies, Miss Elaina! I only meant to close my eyes to enjoy the sun's warmth for a moment, and then . . ." He ended with a sheepish shrug.

"That's the second time this week, Davies." Elaina put her hands on her hips. "I know you're new here, but if you wish to last more than a week on my father's ship, you need to do as you're told." She leveled him a hard look. "*Exactly* as you're told." Then she sighed as she bent down and began to gather the messy rope in her arms. "Just be thankful my father or Lewis didn't catch you. There would have been a lot more than a fall on the nose to greet you if it had been one of them."

He took the rope from her and began to wind it properly. "I will strive my best."

"You have to do more than try on a warship."

"But how?" He paused and grimaced. "It's difficult to maintain a sense of urgency when we're sailing out to the middle of nowhere." He looked out at the endless sparkling water that surrounded them on every side.

"So all of these sailors running about, older and younger than you, are no indication of the urgency of our mission?" Elaina gestured at the flurry of activity going on around and above them as men jumped from task to task. "I don't know if you're aware of this, but my father's ship doesn't just go to war. We also host a myriad of very important meetings between navies and kingdoms from all around the world, and have prevented a number of conflicts by doing so. Giving an impression that is less than our best could result in a perceived insult to one of our guests. And insults can turn to war."

"I said I was sorry."

Elaina picked up the ship's log once more. "Very well. But from now on, you must obey orders. Do you understand?"

"Yes, miss."

"Good. Now get on with your work so there's no more trouble." She had turned and begun walking when he called out her name once more.

"Yes?"

"I hope this isn't too personal, miss, but . . . why do you visit the crow's nest so often?" He paused. "I've heard on other ships it's not considered proper for a lady such as yourself. Why not have the men do it?"

She briefly froze, then donned a forced smile. "You might not guess it, but sometimes a woman needs a moment to herself on a ship full of men." As she walked away, however, Elaina couldn't shake the feeling that had followed her all week concerning their newest sailor.

True, any woman of seventeen would draw the eye of most men on ships that went out to sea for months at a time, even if she did have freckles and her hair was that nameless color between blonde and brown. For after all, a woman was a woman, even if she was shorter than most girls of twelve. But the men on her father's ship knew without question that Elaina was to be left alone. In fact, most of them were as protective of her as they might have been their own daughters or sisters. Most had either helped raise her, or if they were very young, had been raised in part by her. But something about Davies Tanner unnerved Elaina. She just couldn't decide exactly what.

Instead of heading to the very crow's nest he had alluded to, as she had planned to do, Elaina tarried restlessly in her room until the sky was mostly dark and the stars were beginning to twinkle overhead. Only when she was sure the night guards were on duty and that Davies was down in the galley did Elaina climb into her beloved crow's nest and tilt her head up toward the sky.

"Is everything still clear for tomorrow?" she asked. "No storms or pirates or strange winds we should know about?"

All is well, Elaina. They chuckled. *Go find out what you've been dying to know.*

Elaina smiled and nodded. After whispering a thanks, she climbed back down the ropes and headed straight for her father's study. As she placed her hand on the door, however, she felt a pair of eyes behind her. One glance showed a familiar shadow about twenty feet away. She opened her mouth to call out to him loudly so the guards might hear, but he slipped below the deck before she could speak. Shuddering, she turned back to the door and went in, letting the warm glow of candles greet her as she entered.

"What's troubling you?" her father asked before she could say anything. He was seated in his favorite chair by the little fireplace in the corner.

"What do you mean?"

"You're putting your thumb to your lip again, and your eyes are as big as clams."

Elaina pulled up a chair of her own and forced her hand off her lip and into her lap as she stared into the fire. "I caught Davies Tanner sleeping again today. And he seems quite interested in my personal time."

Elaina's father tugged at his beard and took off his spectacles. "That boy isn't going to last much longer if he can't learn to mind himself. I only brought him on because he's the youngest son of a friend. Let me know if he bothers you again."

She nodded, eager to be done with the conversation. "On a brighter note, all should be well for tomorrow. The only ships in sight are ours, and the weather should be superb."

"Excellent. Now," he leaned forward, his eyes bright, "are you about to burst, or should I tell you who our visitor is?"

Elaina clapped her hands. "Yes! Please!"

Her father leaned back, a mischievous grin spreading across his face. "I hope you saved your best gown for tomorrow, my dear. For our ambassador will be none other than King Everard of Destin himself."

CHAPTER 2
GLASS SLIPPERS

P lease, Miss Starke! Help!"
Elaina whirled around to locate the voice above, but
she knew already whom it belonged to, and it made her
want to cringe. Sure enough, nearly as high as her crow's nest,
Davies Tanner had caught his left arm in the ropes that should
have been untangled hours ago.

"Again?" She shook her head and took a swift look around the
deck. "Hold on, Tanner." Of all the days for him to need a rescue.
Elaina kicked off her slippers and hiked her fine skirts up, tucking
them into the billowy pantaloons she wore for situations like this.
She began to climb the rigging but glanced over her shoulder with
every few steps she took.

Most of the crew members wouldn't be able to see her, as they
were already in place for the receiving party, where Elaina was
supposed to be as well. Hopefully, her father wouldn't notice her
absence before she got back. But she couldn't very well leave
Davies up in the ropes. Besides, they had only just pulled up alongside the ship that was delivering King Everard. Surely she had a
few minutes before the king disembarked from his ship and
crossed over to the *Adroit*.

As soon as she was sure no one had spotted her, Elaina finished shimmying up the ropes to where Davies was standing. She could have climbed even faster, had her formal gown not been so heavy.

"What were you doing up here?" She hooked her arm through the rigging and began to work the knot that had formed around his wrist. "You're supposed to be with the others on the lower deck."

"I was supposed to repair a sail," he mumbled. "Forgot, though."

"So you did it now." Elaina shook her head. "This is a reconnaissance meeting with the most powerful king in the western realm. The sail can wait." She finished untangling the ropes and gave him an exasperated look. "And you never repair a sail like this. It needs to be done on the deck."

When the young man nodded, she gestured for him to climb down ahead of her. He was more than likely to get stuck somewhere on the way down, and she would have to waste more time rescuing him again. Then they would both get an earful.

She felt hope bubbling up within her, though, as she scurried down the ropes and heard Lewis still calling out formations to the sailors on the other side of the deck. Perhaps her absence hadn't been noticed after all.

"Elaina. Tanner. How thoughtful of you to join us."

As soon as Elaina's bare feet hit the deck, her throat went dry. Turning slowly, she found herself face-to-face with her father, Lewis, and a heavily muscled stranger.

It was him.

A gold circlet of leaves sat on the stranger's brow, and he held himself as though he were very aware of the position the circlet gave him. More impressive than his fine clothes and regal stance, however, were his fiery gray eyes, which watched her with such intensity that she felt they might indeed burn her should she meet them for too long. At first glance, he looked quite severe, but when she dared to look again, she noticed his mouth curving up at one corner.

Elaina forced her own eyes to the ground to prevent herself

from gawking more, but that only served to remind her that she was standing barefoot in the presence of a king. Could this first meeting have gone any worse?

Her father looked as though he wanted very badly to roll his eyes. Lewis, however, did not look surprised in the slightest.

"Elaina," her father finally said after she had put her slippers back on and managed a curtsy, "it seems you have been a bit preoccupied. Are you ready to join us now?"

"My apologies—" Elaina began to dip into another curtsy, but Davies interrupted.

"Please forgive her, Admiral . . . Your Majesty." Davies was mashing his hat into an unrecognizable shape. "It was my fault. I got stuck—"

"I don't remember asking you," Elaina's father snapped, glaring at the young man.

"My lady." The king stepped forward before any other awkward conversations could ensue. Elaina hadn't thought it possible, but even the two steps he had taken to close the gap between them made him seem even more . . . well, enormous. "It is good to finally meet the young diplomat I've heard so much of in my travels." He held out his hand.

Surprised at the humility of the gesture from the most powerful king in the realm, Elaina automatically extended her own hand. The king bowed to kiss it. But as soon as they'd touched, he stiffened, and a hot ripple of energy shot from his hand into hers.

Elaina started, and King Everard's head snapped up again. His gray eyes searched hers unabashedly, almost frantically. Actual blue flames danced within them, she realized. Could that have been what caused such a shock?

Her father cleared his throat. "I have had refreshments prepared for us in more private quarters. Does that sound pleasing to Your Majesty?"

King Everard straightened and turned to him, his face stern and composed once again. "That sounds excellent, Admiral."

Lewis led the way, and once King Everard followed with his

small entourage of two guards, Elaina's father turned to her and offered her his arm, which she took. Leaning down, he whispered, "What was that about?"

I don't know, she mouthed, relieved he didn't want to discuss Davies, although she was sure she would hear about that later.

Once everyone was seated for supper around her father's heavy wooden table, which had been bolted to the floor for safety in turbulent waters, Elaina found herself more relaxed and nearly wiggling with excitement. She had dreamed of this day for years. To hear the king of legend recount his adventures himself, rather than hearing them from fifth- and sixth-hand sources, was sheer delight. To make the eve even more perfect, she was seated just to his left. She would have to remember to thank her father for that.

As everyone else got settled and proper introductions were made, Elaina studied him as discreetly as she could. To her surprise, there was a bit more silver in his golden hair than she had expected, and more stress lines at the corners of his eyes and mouth. She had known him to be just a few years younger than her father, of course, so this shouldn't have come as a shock. But perhaps it was his massive arms and chest that had at first suggested more youth, for he was far fitter than any young man she had ever met. Either way, sitting next to such a man might have been disconcerting if she hadn't known him to be a man with a large heart as well.

He was also quieter than she had expected, asking questions of those around him that he seemed to know would take some time to answer. How had her father come to command Ashland's flag-ship at such a young age? As the king's favorite admiral, how did he choose his crew? What was Lewis's homeland? How had Elaina enjoyed growing up on the sea? Every question seemed carefully crafted to allow him as little speech as possible. With one hand on his chin and the other at his elbow, King Everard drew the life story out of everyone in the room without sharing a single personal detail about himself.

Elaina might have called him brooding, except that she could see him using his silence to study every inch of the ship and its crew. From the cook to the crewmen acting as servers, to her father and Lewis and anyone else who stepped inside the large cabin. And though he didn't openly stare at her the way he did the others, Elaina got the feeling he was watching her more closely than the rest of them combined.

But why?

All she could imagine was that it had something to do with the strange jolt that had passed between them when they'd first touched. She was tired of guessing, though, by the time the second course was served, so she put on her most diplomatic air and waited for a break in the conversation.

"I must admit, Your Majesty, I have done all I can to learn of your adventures and military exploits, but many of the stories seem incomplete." Why did she sound so shy? So girlish? Elaina wasn't shy.

"The young lady is interested in military politics?" King Everard turned his fiery gaze back to her.

"Politics are interesting, my lord, but your adventures intrigue me the most." Unable to help herself, she leaned forward. "Is it true that you have power over flame and illness alike?"

"I can create flame, yes." He turned his right hand palm up, and a small tongue of flame leapt into the air. "And my flame can be used to heal most illnesses."

Elaina thought she might pass out from pure elation.

"But flame is simply the way the Maker's power manifests in me personally. My eldest son has this power as well, though his flame is slightly different than mine." For the first time, he broke out in a grin. "My wife's power is completely *other*, though, and a good deal more terrifying."

"I had the pleasure of meeting Prince Henri not long ago in Maricanta," Elaina said. She wanted to ask him about the gifts of his other children but sensed that he kept such affairs rather private, as the two youngest Fortiers were well known for being hidden from the public eye.

13

"I was glad to hear it when he told me." He leaned forward and studied her again, the blue flame in his eyes dancing wildly. "But the Maker gives many gifts, and all can be fierce when used for the right reasons." He gave Elaina a sweeping glance from head to toe. "No matter what size the gift recipient."

Elaina rolled her shoulders back and tried to sit taller, daring a look at her father, who was staring uneasily at his supper. Was the king that perceptive? Or had Elaina's secret finally gotten out?

"Your Majesty," her father said as one of the crewmen cleared his plate. "I have word that no other ship is nearby save ours. My men will notify me if any others break the horizon. I suggest we begin our business while the sea is at rest."

King Everard nodded, and Elaina sighed. So much for getting to hear first-hand accounts of her childhood hero. King Everard was more of a mystery now than he had ever been.

As soon as the table was cleared and the crew members were gone, the cabin door was locked and a single candle was placed on the table. One window was left cracked open, but Elaina knew that Lewis had stationed one of their most trustworthy men just above it on the deck. Not that she would need to hear anything tonight, but it was best to not shut every window, just in case . . .

Or so she thought. As her father began to speak, Elaina felt the familiar nagging sensation begin.

Elaina.

No. She had waited her whole life for this. Whatever it was could surely wait. She tried to focus on what her father was saying.

" . . . behalf of my king, I am honored to hear what your endeavor has recovered. As you can guess, King Xander is most interested in locating the source of this rebellion and quelling it before it interrupts the lives of our citizens in Solwhind, much less the rest of Ashland."

"Whoever supposed darkness was at work in that city was correct," King Everard said, his eyes flicking to Elaina. "There is a surprising amount of evil in that city."

Come, Elaina, their voices called again. *We must speak with you. Now.*

Elaina gritted her teeth. The stars hadn't had anything important to report in over a fortnight. And they needed to talk now? She stayed firmly planted in her seat.

She had learned long ago that if she stayed quiet and still, most foreign dignitaries would forget she was present, and she could listen in on everything they told her father. A quiet young woman was easy to forget when it came to the matters of men. Then, after their guests departed, she and her father would discuss their findings. If she left now, though, her invisibility would be ruined, for King Everard would notice her leave.

"Were you able to track its source?" her father was asking. "Where is the darkness coming from?"

"To know that, I would need to be in the city for weeks longer —maybe months—which, unfortunately, I am not able to do. I do know, however, that whoever or whatever is responsible for this rebellion has sticky fingers and has spent much money and many years creating an intricate web of deceit and subterfuge."

"I am sorry to hear that," Elaina's father said. "But I thank you most sincerely on behalf of my liege for your time and assistance. My king has sent a gift of thanks to Destin. It should arrive by—"

Elaina!

Rolling her eyes, Elaina stood and excused herself. She slipped out of the room, squeezing her eyes shut in regret as the door closed behind her.

"Fine," she whispered up at the sky. "I am here. But I am quite put out with you right now."

You must know, was their only response.

Rarely were the stars so persistent. Whatever it was must be important. For such an interruption, it had better be.

Slipping her shoes off once again, Elaina tucked her burgundy gown into her pantaloon petticoat and scampered up the ropes to her own personal crow's nest. It wasn't as tall as the main crow's nest, but the half-barrel fitted to the second mast was just large enough for Elaina to sit comfortably inside. Sometimes her father joined her at night, but it didn't matter how high he went or how long he lingered with her. Only Elaina could hear the stars.

"What was so important that I had to come now?" She hauled herself into the crow's nest and nestled inside. "Couldn't it have waited one hour?"

No.

"Very well, then." She squinted at the ocean in the dark. "I see no great storm, nor do I see another vessel."

As the stars gave their answer, there was a sound from below, the click of boots on the deck.

Elaina frowned up at the sky. Surely she must have heard wrong. "That makes absolutely no sense at all," she told them. But as she was waiting for their reply, a head and broad shoulders appeared over the barrel's edge. Elaina had to stifle a scream until she recognized the silhouette of King Everard. And the glowing blue of the flames dancing in his eyes.

"Your Majesty . . ."

"My apologies, Lady Elaina," the king's deep voice rumbled. He did not move to get inside the nest, which was good, as it would have been too small, but positioned himself out on the ropes beside it. "I did not mean to startle you. I heard you speaking." He paused, as though that were explanation enough. Then he asked, "Would you mind sharing whom you were speaking with?"

"My, you . . . you are certainly direct, Your Majesty." Elaina laughed nervously. So this was why King Everard's enemies found him so terrifying. Could the man sense everything? She swallowed. "May I ask the reason for your curiosity?"

"You are gifted, young lady. Are you not?"

Elaina studied him for an eternal moment. Was there a way to avoid telling him? Her father, of course, knew of her secret. Her father's crew knew, too, though they never spoke about it outright.

She could see now in the king's eyes, however, that he would not be dissuaded. But truly, was there anyone who would understand more than he? After all, his gift was the reason she had idolized him for so long. She had innately known that he would understand what it meant to be different.

"My father has forbidden me from telling anyone."

To her surprise, the king nodded gravely. "Your father is a wise man." His voice softened. "I only know because I felt it when I touched your hand. Most would not be able to feel such power. I've simply grown sensitive to such things with time."

Elaina took a deep breath. "I wanted to stay in the cabin and listen, but their call was too strong."

"Their call?"

"The stars."

"The stars speak to you?"

"I can speak back, as well. We've conversed since I was small." She laughed a little. "I thought everyone else could hear them, too, until my parents assured me it was not so."

"And what kinds of things do the stars tell you?"

She paused. It sounded so ridiculous when she said it aloud. "My father believes they share messages from the Maker. They often warn me when the ships are approaching rocks or an enemy is headed for the fleet. Of course, my words to them are far less inspired. Though I . . . I sometimes speak to them when I'm lonely." She gestured down at the half-barrel she stood in. "That's why my father had this addition built on to the ship."

"And what was so urgent that they pulled you from the cabin tonight?" Did he sound amused? Or was it awed? Or perhaps disgusted?

"It's rather embarrassing, I must admit. You see, I don't always understand them perfectly. Sometimes their messages don't make sense." In fact, this particular message felt more than a little self-serving, something Elaina wasn't used to at all. She must have misunderstood them.

"And what did they say?"

She rubbed at the barrel's sanded edges with her fingers. "They said I am to accept your gift," she whispered.

By now, Elaina's eyes had adjusted to the dark enough to see the king's mouth drop open. He hesitated for a long moment before climbing down the ropes and going back inside the ship. Was he angry with her? Or with the stars?

But before she had too much time to worry, King Everard had reemerged and climbed up the ropes again. As soon as he was steady, he held on to the barrel's edge with one gloved hand while he reached inside his cloak with the other. He pulled out a drawstring bag and opened it. Carefully, reverently, he pulled out a pair of the most astonishing shoes Elaina had ever seen.

Two tiny slippers, so thin and clear that they seemed to be made of glass, sat in his hand. Swirls were etched on their sides, weaving in and out around the shoes like the wind over the waves. Elaina let out a little sigh as she reached out to touch the slippers. Just as she had imagined, their surface was cool and smooth. They were most definitely made of glass.

"Surely these would be fitting for Queen Isabelle or Princess Genevieve!"

"Ah, but you see, that's the strange part. I had forgotten I even owned these. They're relics from the past. I claimed them from an ancient glass castle in another world." He turned them slowly so that they sparkled in the light of the moon. "These shoes are no less than a thousand years old. The castle is gone now, but I took them in hopes that someone might one day have use for them."

"But wouldn't they break if someone wore them?"

"They were created by the glass queen, ruler of the realm long before our peoples ever inhabited the continent. She created all of her objects with special powers to aid individuals in need of help."

"But why me?" she whispered. "I need no help. I am in no danger."

"Not yet, perhaps." He held the slippers up and examined them more closely. "While I was preparing for this journey, the shoes somehow ended up in my pack. I hadn't placed them there, nor had the servants who were helping me." A small smile lit his face. "When I told my wife, she insisted I take them. She believed there would be someone who needed them along the way." Then he lowered the slippers and held them out to Elaina. "I believe that someone is you."

Elaina was speechless. She knew she should refuse the shoes. But before she could bring herself to do such a thing, they were in her hands. A strange vibration hummed through the glass. "What do they do?"

"I'm not sure. But I do know that no one has worn them before, for their power still courses strong through them, much the way your power courses within you." He straightened his cloak and glanced down at the deck. "Guard them, just as you guard your gift. Such beauty should never be flaunted."

She could only nod.

"You remind me of my wife," he said as he took a step down.

"You honor me, Your Majesty," Elaina murmured. Queen Isabelle of Destin was also gifted, and just as famous as her husband. From what Elaina had gathered, it was for good reason.

He paused on his descent, his brow furrowing. "My wife went through many trials of her own to become what she is today." The king's eyes fixed once again on Elaina's. "I pray these slippers will keep you safe through yours."

CHAPTER 3
BETRAYED

Sleep evaded Elaina for most of that night, despite the gentle rocking of the boat. She couldn't stop staring at the king's gift, wondering what on earth they could mean. Messages from the Maker were nothing new to her. Relaying warnings about approaching storms or pirates or hidden shoals was commonplace, even enjoyable. Elaina had never doubted her ability to use her gift in a productive manner.

Until now.

What in the depths had King Everard meant about trials? Life at sea was never predictable, but there was a rhythm to it that Elaina had grown accustomed to in her years on her father's ship. Like the constant rolling of the waves, there were good times and bad, and Elaina did what she could to enjoy the good and minimize the bad. But really, what could she need from a pair of glass slippers?

The call of the bugle woke her from the light slumber she had finally slipped into just before dawn. Groaning a little at the stiffness in her limbs, she rolled out of bed, washed her face with the fresh water someone had left in her wooden bowl, and dressed in her second-finest gown. Sleep or no sleep, a respectful send-off was just as important, if not more important than the welcoming of a dignified guest. And Elaina was determined not to ruin this last meeting with King Everard the way she had ruined the first.

Soon she was on deck standing beside her father, who was dressed once again in all his military finery. Gold and silver pins decorated the stiff, light blue uniform on one side, while thin bronze ropes decorated the other side, commemorating the battles he had won. He would need a bigger chest if they were to add many more.

Her father gave her an approving nod just as the king arrived.

"Admiral Starke," King Everard said, giving him a deep nod as he and his guards reached the deck.

"Your Majesty," her father answered with a bow. "I want to thank you again for the service you have done our country. Ashland is honored to count you as our closest ally. We hope such dealings will continue in the future." He presented the king with a sealed parchment. "Please never hesitate to call upon me should you need any seafaring aid. I am sure my king would be more than pleased to say the same for our land forces as well."

"I am honored as well, Admiral Starke." Then the king turned to Elaina. "I look forward to hearing of your many adventures, Lady Elaina," he said, a corner of his mouth turning up. "If you ever need assistance, my wife and I would be more than happy to do what we can."

Elaina had to remind herself to breathe. "I am honored, Your Majesty. I hope we have the pleasure of meeting again sooner rather than later."

All too soon, they were docked, and the king and his entourage were gone. Elaina wanted to mourn their absence, but she had no time to waste. They were in Solwhind, and she had a long list of tasks to complete.

"Father, I need to go to the fish market."

"What for?"

"I need to show Simeon's new galley boy where to find ingredients at the market. Simeon says he keeps confusing the spices."

"Why can't Simeon go find his own ingredients?"

"He's not feeling well."

But her father was already shaking his head. "After King Everard's report last night, I can't see the wisdom in letting you run about the city. Not while the rebellion is alive."

"Would you let me go if some of the men accompanied me? I only have a few stalls I need to visit, then three or four shops. Nothing that should take very long." She gestured back at the city behind them, so wide it was impossible to see from one end to the other. "I truly mean to be quick. I haven't forgotten King Everard's warning." And if she didn't have a few moments off the ship to clear her head, she might lose her mind.

Her father waved a hand at her. "Very well." Then he sighed. "I've some unpleasant business to attend to while you're gone."

Elaina's heart fell. "Davies Tanner?"

He nodded. "The boy just can't follow orders. Mistakes I can work with. Disobedience will get someone killed."

"I know." Elaina gave her father a half-smile and squeezed his hand.

"Well, be off with you now. We leave first thing tomorrow."

Soon Elaina, Lewis, two of the younger sailors, and the cook's new assistant, a boy named Joel whose voice hadn't even changed yet, were making their way to Solwhind's largest fish market. Elaina closed her eyes and sucked in a deep breath of air that smelled of brine, spices, and seafood. Hints of baked brown sugar floated in and out on the breeze as well. She led the men through the marketplace to the stall where the smell of sugar was coming from.

"Simeon likes his pecans baked with sugar," Elaina said, turning to Joel. "He loathes plain nuts. Make sure you only purchase from this vendor while we're in Solwhind. Simeon will know if you do otherwise."

"I don't see why it makes a difference," Joel muttered. "We passed two stalls much closer than this one."

Elaina smiled and simply handed him the pile of little brown bags to carry before turning to pay for them. After thanking the vendor, she opened one bag and popped a single nut into Joel's mouth. His brown eyes grew wide.

"See?"

He nodded vigorously, and Elaina had the feeling she wouldn't be hearing any more arguments.

As they started off toward their next stall, which was all the way across the wide marketplace, Elaina grinned to herself. She loved coming to port no matter where they went. There were exotic smells, new sounds, and clever wares to peruse. Colors changed by territory, and the foods themselves were always an adventure. But no matter where she went in the entire world, Ashland's largest city was by far the most impressive.

Surrounding this particular marketplace, which served the northwest wharf, countless cottages, inns, and manors lined the streets, snuggled between merchant shops, foreign dignitaries' dwellings, and public places of meeting, some even four or five levels high. At the center of the marketplace itself stood a glimmering fountain crowned by a statue of a mermaid, carved of marble with scales of mother-of-pearl. It glinted in the sunlight as they walked past it. Children hopped in and out of the fountain, chanting wishes as they did, while adults gathered around it to gossip and compare purchases.

Still, as much as she should have enjoyed a relaxing stroll, they could not linger today as she was accustomed to doing. Instead, she led her quiet band of men quickly down the line of stalls that edged the enormous marketplace. After a ten-minute walk, they came to their destination. This stall had walls of purple canvas covered by strings of fresh and dried herbs.

"Elaina!" A woman with weathered brown skin and warm brown eyes greeted her with an embrace. "You're back early!"

"My father had business to attend to, and our cook sent me to show his new helper where to find the finest spices in the city." Elaina turned to the boy. "Joel, this is Madhu. She sells spices from her family's farm."

"Do you have sugar pecans, too?" Joel looked hopeful.

Madhu's brown eyes sparkled. "I have something much better, young one." She turned and moved farther back into the tent to a little wooden table covered in herbs of every color imaginable. "What do you need, Elaina?"

"Basil, lavender, cinnamon, and black pepper."

Joel looked disappointed, but Elaina nudged him forward and had the satisfaction of seeing his eyes bulge as a gentle purple cloud covered the woman's hands. It turned and rolled around her fingers as they gathered, cut, ground, and mashed the different piles of herbs. Within minutes, Madhu proudly presented them with four bundles wrapped neatly in paper tied with ribbons.

"What did she do?" Joel looked back at Elaina in awe.

"No matter how long you are at sea," Madhu answered for Elaina, "your food will be just as flavorful as these seasonings are today. They will not dull, nor will they lose their potency with time."

"But how is that better than sugar pecans?"

Madhu and Elaina laughed.

"You might think differently, when you've been out at sea for months and all your other spices lose their—" Before Madhu could finish, a shout rang out from the center of the marketplace, near the mermaid fountain.

"I told you, I'll have none of that blood money!" a woman screeched. "You can take your filthy spoils and go!"

"My money's as good as the next man's!" a man shouted back.

"Not as long as you wear that vile mark on your arm! Until this city is free of that snake, I'll take no business from the likes of you! Or your fellow rebels!"

More men and women began to gather, and Elaina stepped closer to hear, but a hand grasped her arm and held her firmly in place. She looked back to see Madhu gripping her tightly. Her face was lined with anxiety.

"You need to leave. Now."

"But I only have a few more—"

"No." Madhu shook her head vigorously. "There have been too many kidnappings, particularly of visitors to our city, like you." She let go of Elaina and ran back inside her tent and fumbled to shove the little paper packages at Joel. Elaina tried to open her coin purse, but before she could pay her friend, Madhu shook her head again. "My gift. Now, you!" She turned to Lewis, who had drawn his sword and was glaring at the crowd. "Take her back to her father's ship. Get her out of here as fast as you can."

Lewis nodded once before taking the lead. The two other sailors walked behind them so that Elaina and Joel were sand-wiched in between. Whether it was Lewis's impressive size or the dangerous glare he leveled at everyone nearby, a small break in the crowd appeared before their party as they marched quickly back across the market toward the wharf.

"WHAT ARE WE DOING?" Elaina asked as loudly as she dared.

"We'll gather the others from the tavern. Then we'll do as she said and take you to your father's ship."

Elaina nodded. She had believed King Everard about the rebellion, of course. She trusted that there was indeed a group of traitors. But for some reason, when he had spoken of it, the evil had seemed small, young enough to still be hiding in the city's dark alleys while the general populace continued on with life uninterrupted. The gentle sun of that morning had only made her feel even more confident when they had set out earlier. She had felt sure it was safe. But feelings could be deceiving.

"How did she do that?"

"What?" Elaina looked down at Joel.

"How did she get that glow?"

"She's gifted."

"Oh." Joel's brow creased, then his eyes grew big. "Like you with the—"

Before he could finish, Lewis whirled around and caught the boy by the ear. "If you're going to be on our ship, you had better learn to keep your mouth shut. What Lady Elaina does or does not do is none of our business." He shook the boy by the ear once. "Understand?"

Joel nodded and whimpered, and they resumed their walk, only at an even faster pace.

The tension didn't begin to dissipate until they left the marketplace behind and had nearly reached the sailors' favorite tavern. Compared to some of the other taverns Elaina had seen, this one was really quite homey. Faded plaid curtains were visible through the windows, and the smell of baking bread was just as strong as that of ale when the door was opened and the little bell rang over it. She breathed a bit easier when they were all inside.

"Lewis!" The elderly tavern keep called out over the mild din of the large room. "You've come to join your friends, I see. They're over there." He waved at a familiar group of men in the far corner. A few of the younger sailors were brave enough to have serving maids in their laps, but Elaina knew it would go no further than that. Her father wouldn't allow such tomfoolery, and if he found out any had taken place, the guilty would suffer harsh consequences. Most of the men simply gathered around a few tables and laughed as they drank. Crews from other ships filled the room as well, each staying close to his own group while eyeing the others.

"Stay here," Lewis said. "This will only take a minute."

Elaina followed Lewis to the tables near the corner and sat at one of the tables, motioning for Joel to do the same. She'd heard it said that most presentable young ladies didn't show themselves in taverns. But Elaina was not most young ladies. She'd grown up around sailors, and there were few in the Royal Navy who didn't recognize the daughter of Admiral Starke. And as such, most kept their distance. Which was why it was such a surprise when she felt a hand lock itself around her waist and yank her from her seat.

"What—Davies! What do you think you're doing?"

But Tanner was far from the cowed young man she had seen

the eve before. This time his breath reeked of ale, and he wore a smug smile. Instead of answering her, he pulled her close against his body. Elaina struggled until she felt a knife pressed against her throat.

The room went silent, but nearly all of her father's men were out of their seats. Some had even managed to pull their own weapons.

"No closer!" Tanner called out, his words slurring. "Your admiral had the gall to cut me loose. The least you can do is hear me out!"

"We owe you no such favors," Lewis growled, taking a step forward, but Tanner pressed the knife tighter against Elaina's neck, making her wince.

"You see," he said, turning to address the dozens of other sailors in the room, "the flagship has a gift that they like to keep to themselves. It's why they're so special."

"Please," Elaina whispered. "Don't!"

"Hold your tongue, young man!" Lewis shouted.

"Well, I have a surprise for all of you!" Swaying slightly, he turned to the other men in the tavern. "You may think Admiral Starke is the mastermind commander of their . . . legendary vessel. But he's not! This girl can talk to the stars!" Tanner laughed hysterically. "Do you think your beloved Admiral Starke would be so successful without—"

Elaina took advantage of Davies's drunken laughter to slip out of his grasp. Smith, one of her father's oldest men, caught her and held her behind him as Lewis and the others swarmed Davies to gag and bind him.

"Pay no heed to a dishonorably discharged drunk," Lewis announced to the dozens of watching sailors. "The crown will have a say in what happens to this one. Spreading stories about the admiral's daughter." He shoved Davies hard.

"Don't you worry now," Smith whispered to her as he put an arm around her shoulders. "He was drunk. No one will give him credence."

Elaina managed a weak smile up at her father's old friend, but her thumb moved up to worry her lip as they walked. She hoped he was right. But the sinking feeling in her stomach said otherwise.

CHAPTER 4
YOU'RE NOT

Though Elaina was aware that she had done nothing wrong, guilt sat heavily in her stomach as she let Smith walk her back to the ship.

Usually, the sight of the *Adroit*'s deep blue hull with its yellow encircling stripe brought her a sense of peace and belonging. But for the first time in her life, the *Adroit* did not feel like home.

It seemed like hours that she waited in her cabin fiddling with her new glass slippers after Lewis had dragged Tanner down to face her father. Several times she could hear the younger sailors being called upon to run what Elaina guessed to be messages to and from the local naval office, but she continued to wait alone. Even the glass slippers and King Everard's words failed to distract her properly, only making her anxiety worse. So she glumly listened to the crew repair sails, clean the deck, and bring aboard boxes of supplies.

Though she couldn't see them from her lower deck, she could imagine the precise workings going on above. Each man fulfilled his task as though he had been born doing it. The king's flagship was not only known for its uncanny ability to avoid storms and outmaneuver its enemies, but also for its crew's ability to work as one. Each man had a purpose, and when a job went undone, all suffered. It was exactly the reason men like Davies Tanner couldn't be allowed to stay upon the ship.

"Elaina."

Elaina jumped at her father's voice. As she left her room and followed him to his quarters, Tanner was being dragged out of her father's office. It took two men to contain him as they pulled him toward the ship's ramp. Swallowing, she plastered a false smile on her face and marched in.

As soon as the door was shut, her father fixed his steely gray eyes on her. "He didn't hurt you?"

"No, Father."

He nodded but still came forward and gently took her chin in his hand, turning her head from one side to the other as he examined her neck where the blade had been pressed. Lewis must have been quite explicit in his recounting of the event.

He finally let go and folded his hands behind his back, going to stand and stare out the window. "It's an unfortunate thing, but our next mission will need to be delayed by several days."

"What do you mean?"

"I am afraid I have more than one man to replace. Smith, Canters, and Wiley have requested permission to retire."

"But I don't understand," Elaina said, glad not to be talking about the incident in the tavern but disturbed at the news all the same. "Smith has served a long time, to be sure. But he's still strong. And Canters and Wiley are barely thirty-and-five! They've only been aboard ten years."

"Unfortunately, my dear, we are rather spoiled on this ship. I take such pride in handpicking my men that many stay on much longer than they would on any other ship. It's an honor to serve on the king's flagship, and I hope my men are being truthful when they say I am a fair admiral."

"You are!"

"Thank you. But I'm afraid being on this ship has unfairly tinted the way you see the world of sailing." He turned and looked directly at Elaina. "As much as it is an honor to serve King Xander and Ashland this way, there comes a point in a man's life when he can no longer handle the rigors of life on a warship, when he wants to settle down and marry. To build a family. And living life on the seas makes such a life difficult."

"But you did it."

"And that turned out well, didn't it?" Her father's voice was hard, and Elaina regretted her choice of words.

"I'm sorry, Father, but . . . I'm still not sure what this has to do with me."

"You know I choose my men carefully. No one steps foot on this ship unless I have references for his references. I have done this since you came to live here with me, and until now, it has served me well. But it appears that I'm not always capable of choosing as wisely as I'd thought."

"He's only one man out of many, Father."

"Tanner, yes. But I have three men leaving and a handful of others preparing to do the same, if I can believe the rumors Lewis shares with me." Her father half sat, half fell into the chair behind his desk. "I have done my best to choose only the best men to surround you with, and I have done even more to keep them here. But a majority of my men have served faithfully for many years, and eventually, they will not all be here to protect you and your gift. A day that I fear is coming sooner than later."

"What are you saying?" Elaina took a step closer to the desk where she could reach out and stroke its scratched wood for comfort.

"I'm saying that it's high time I find a more appropriate living situation for you."

"You mean . . . leave the ship?"

"You're nearly eighteen, Elaina. Far too old to be gallivanting about the seas without proper instruction due a lady of your status."

"Father, it was only one incident! And he was drunk!"

"If this hadn't happened, something else would have."

Elaina opened her mouth to respond but found she had no

words. Instead, she fell into the seat beside her and focused on breathing.

"I have already sent word to your aunt that you will be returning to Rosington Manor." He picked up a quill and began to scratch away on a parchment before him. "You will live there with your Aunt Charlotte and cousin Lydia until you are old enough to inherit the manor of your own accord." His voice became gentle, though he still didn't meet her eyes. "You should enjoy it there. It's where you grew up, you know."

"Until I was five!" Elaina cried out. "I've grown up here! This is my home." She swallowed, trying to regain control of her voice. "I'm sure Aunt Charlotte and cousin Lydia are kind, but these men are my family. They've taught me about rigging and knots and winds—"

"And no one has taught you of fashion or courtship customs or even how to speak appropriately with young men of your rank."

Elaina opened her mouth to retort that she could care less about flirting with men of her rank, but her father silenced her with a fierce glance. Then he groaned and rubbed his eyes. For a long moment they sat in silence. Finally he spoke again, but this time, he sounded ancient.

"You have served the king well in your time on this ship, far beyond what many men do in their lifetimes."

"All the more reason to keep me."

"It's not worth the cost. The savage brute that killed your mother is still out there. And now that the public knows your secret, you could put the whole fleet in danger when he decides to target you."

Elaina squeezed the arms of the chair until her fingers hurt. "So you would have me fend for myself?"

"Hardly. You will be better protected than you've ever been. I've already sent word to King Xander, asking him to provide ample protection for you in the capital. He has said in the past that whatever I need he will give me, and I believe he will honor this request without hesitation or question."

Elaina's shoulders slumped as she took deep, measured breaths.

"Your mother's title passed to you last year, and in a few years, you will legally inherit Rosington," her father said in a quiet voice. "Many girls dream of such opportunities, but few have the rank or property and ensuing liberty to do it on their own. As you know, most families in Ashland cannot legally hand down titles to women at all, only a select few like ours. Use this to your advantage. Enjoy your life in Kaylem. Make friends, and find a young man worthy to kiss the ground you walk upon." His eyes brightened a little. "You will meet the prince. I hear he's an amiable fellow. Rather charismatic, actually, much like his father."

"I don't want to meet the prince." Elaina glared at the scuffed wooden floor. "I want to be with you."

"This is a man's world, Elaina. You have no idea what kind of a man killed your mother. Now if word gets out that—"

"Then what have you been raising me for?" She gestured up at the deck. "If I'm incapable of handling myself, why build me up with foolishness about my abilities to deal with the hundreds of men we've taken to sea? Why give me any responsibility at all?"

"Hang it all, Elaina! Why are you making this so difficult?" her father shouted, jumping to his feet. "I can't afford to nanny you all the time, putting my men and my fleet in danger! Now look at me. I am very serious about this."

She gave him the most dispassionate look she could muster.

"You are going to the capital. You will conduct yourself with grace and maturity, and you are going to stay out of harm's way. That is the end of this discussion. Lewis!"

Her father's first mate was there in seconds. From the grave look on his face, Elaina guessed he'd heard every word.

"We're setting sail for the capital. I want this ship moving in one hour."

"Aye, Admiral."

Gathering what was left of her dignity, Elaina slowly stood. As she reached the door, however, she shut it and turned back once more.

"You're serious about this then," she said, straining her voice so it wouldn't crack. "You really don't believe in me." She strode back over to him and took his hands in hers. "I can do this, Father," she whispered. "I am strong enough to make it on the seas."

"No, Elaina. You're not."

She fell back a step. "You don't mean that."

"Oh, but I do. I will not have you die because I was a fool and too proud to admit my own limits. And I'll not have you dead because you refused to acknowledge your own limits either. Now go with Lewis and stay in your quarters until I call you again."

"But I—"

"Elaina, once and for all, you are leaving this ship, and you will never be sailing on her again."

CHAPTER 5
DON'T FALL

E laina ran her hand lovingly down the polished blue rail of the *Adroit* one more time as the young sailor emerged from her cabin with her sea chest. The *Adroit*'s crew had formed a line on each side of her, their numbers creating a path all the way to the ramp, though Elaina knew her father had not instructed them to do so. He would have preferred the affair of her departure be kept as quiet as possible. But the men were here now, and she could see in their faces that they weren't going anywhere without a direct order. Perhaps Lewis had talked her father out of such an order.

Her throat thickened as the first mate himself stepped out of line and approached her. After bowing low, he held out a fist. When she put her own hand out, he dropped a little pile of wood that clinked softly into her palm. Elaina held it up to examine it more closely. As she lifted it, she realized that it wasn't a pile of wood at all, but rather, a bracelet with little wooden beads of all different shapes. Each seemed the work of a different carver, for no two were alike. Some were figures of people or animals. Others were little blocks with words or pictures scratched into them. Someone had been bold enough to carve a star.

"Made from a piece of the ship's hull we had to replace last week," Lewis said, his eyes not moving from the bracelet. "We were going to give it as a birthday present, but since this came sooner . . ."

Elaina threw her arms around him and hugged him tightly, inhaling deeply his familiar scent of salt and tobacco.

"Now, now, little lady." Lewis pulled out of the hug but held on to her shoulders, his eyes rimmed red. "Didn't think you could hang about with us old sailors your whole life, did you? Get out there and give a little shake to that royal court. I hear they need a good rousing from their comforts every now and then. If anyone can do that, it's you."

Elaina nodded and tightened her jaw against the stinging in the corners of her eyes. "I'll treasure it always," she said, looking in turn at each of the men, starting with old Lewis and ending with little Joel. "And don't look so grim." She forced a laugh. "It's not as though you'll never be in Kaylem again. And when you are, I expect to see you all as well and safe as ever."

"Elaina," her father called from the ramp. "Your aunt and cousin are here."

After giving the men one last brave smile, Elaina made her back ramrod straight and strode to join her father. Down the ramp and past the edge of the dock, she could see a carriage with yellow silk curtains pulling to a stop. A woman who looked to be in her early forties was peeking through the front window and a young woman about Elaina's age through the back.

Elaina turned back to her father. "It's not too late," she whispered, imploring him with her eyes once more. "We don't have to go through with this."

"I expect you to be strong." He motioned for the sailor carrying her chest to put it on the carriage. "The king's court is not for the weak of heart."

"And how I am equipped to handle this when I'm far too weak for life at sea?"

"Hold your tongue. You're being rude."

Elaina's annoyance burned deep but the pain cut even deeper, threatening to make her lose control of her breathing, and even worse, her tears.

Well, if he was determined to dump her off, she wasn't going to give him the satisfaction of crying and proving him right. So she kept her next retort to herself and focused on taking deep, even breaths as her aunt and cousin approached. After all, her father's betrayal wasn't their fault. So she put on her most diplomatic smile and turned to greet them.

"Elaina, this is your Aunt Charlotte and your cousin, Lydia." Her father gestured to each in turn, to which they curtsied. The woman was tall and willowy, and the girl was far more buxom than Elaina could ever dream of being, but they shared the same golden curls, flawless fair complexions. Most attractive, however, were their equally inviting smiles.

"How could I forget?" She returned their curtsies. "It's only been a few years since we saw each other last."

"We are so looking forward to having you back in the family home," her aunt said with a gentle smile.

Lydia nodded enthusiastically.

Elaina's father pulled her into a tight embrace, but as he did, he whispered in her ear, "Your aunt and cousin know your secret, but not another soul. Keep it that way." He roughly kissed her on the forehead and let her out of the embrace. Then he walked up the ramp without looking back.

Shouting accusations at his back was tempting, but Elaina was too well trained to allow her emotions to dictate her actions. So she took a deep breath and made sure her expression was one of cool confidence.

"Thank you again for greeting me here. It will be far more pleasant to make the journey with you than it would have been to travel alone in a hired coach."

"We wouldn't dream of such a reception," her aunt said. She held her hand out, and Elaina took it. For the first time, she realized how vaguely familiar her aunt looked, and not just because they'd met before. Foggy memories of another beloved face lay somewhere in her features. And against Elaina's wishes, that was comforting. "Now, come to the carriage, won't you? We have much to get done before tomorrow."

"Tomorrow?" Elaina asked as a footman helped her into the carriage. It was comfortable inside and even homey with patterned cushions on the seats and the yellow curtains softening the harsh sunlight that was trying to get in.

"Oh yes." Lydia clapped her hands and gave a little bounce. "Queen Ann is giving her annual Autumn Tea. The entire event is two days long, and being invited is a most gracious compliment. Not that we've ever been excluded, of course."

"Your mother and I attended the tea together before either of us were married," Charlotte said. "It was the first event that the queen hosted after her coronation."

Though Elaina was in the mood to hear about anything but royal tea parties, her mother's participation in this particular event made the prospect at least somewhat intriguing.

The carriage jolted as they began to move, but once it left the docks and moved onto a larger, busier city road, Elaina found that the bumping didn't bother her stomach quite so much. Rather, to her regret, she found that the distant green rolling hills south of the city were enjoyable to look at as they bounced along the road. A little familiar even. Colorful shops and houses moved by as well, and she was highly tempted to call them pretty.

No. She wouldn't allow herself to feel yearning or even curiosity for this life on land. That yearning had disappeared before she had turned eight. Instead, she tried to pay attention to what her cousin was saying.

"So who will be at this tea?" she asked after Lydia had finished explaining the queen's choice in linen color.

"Oh, everyone of consequence. Most of the court, several wives of the magistrates and their children, and about six or seven of the noble families, not including ourselves, of course." She paused and absently twirled a thick golden lock around her finger. "Oh, and I believe Prince Henri of Destin might be there as well. He's Prince Nicholas's best friend, you know."

"I've met him!" Elaina sat up straighter. Suddenly, the next few days didn't look quite so dreary after all. "A few years back when I was in port at Maricanta, he was there with his mother." Though she hadn't had the chance to meet Queen Isabelle herself, Elaina had highly enjoyed her time with Prince Henri. Maybe if she could get him alone for a moment he could help her understand why his father had been so cryptic when giving her the shoes.

Of course, to discuss that meant she would have to tell him her secret. Elaina nearly groaned aloud. She hadn't been off the ship for an hour yet, and her father's order was already making life difficult.

"You'll love the palace!" Lydia was still talking, her brown eyes bright. "It's not like other castles of dark stone and dreary moats and such. The palace has hundreds of rooms, but it looks more like one grand manor that stretches out in every direction. There are gates and walls and guards, of course, but even with them, you can see the palace for miles from the ground, for it's set up on a high hill. The walls are so white they nearly glow in the sunlight!"

"Lydia is an enthusiastic citizen of Kaylem, but I believe you will truly find much in the capital to keep you busy here," Elaina's aunt said in a more subdued voice. She smiled indulgently at her daughter. "The tea will take place on the front lawn, where there is also a rose garden your mother adored when she was young, as well as a hedge maze that's reshaped every season. You young people will have your own table away from the old women such as myself."

At this, Elaina had to laugh. Her aunt, though she had a few lines around her mouth and eyes, looked every bit as vibrant as her cousin of eighteen years. Elaina couldn't find a gray hair in her full head of golden curls, nor could she find the weariness that aged many women of her years. Only when she spoke of Elaina's mother was there any hint that her aunt had seen any of her own pain. And for that, Elaina was grateful.

Aunt Charlotte had loved her mother, too.

The knot in Elaina's stomach began to unwind itself just a bit.

"Elaina, please don't take this the wrong way, but is that the only style of gown you own?"

Lydia was studying her dress with a look of concern.

Again, Elaina laughed. "Unfortunately, yes. My father was always interested in representing the king to any ambassadors he met, so he took it upon himself to dress me as any respectable ambassador's wife might dress. He said the sea had no patience for frippery or gaudy frills. Every gown was designed with a particular kind of diplomatic meeting or event in mind, but never without practicality as well."

"And I'm sure all those respectable wives were older than my mother." Lydia sighed deeply. Then she rapped on the wall behind the driver.

The carriage came to a stop, and the driver stuck his head down by the window. "Yes, my lady?"

"We're not going home after all, Roland. Instead, we'll go to the seamstress's shop on Fourth Street. The second one, not the first one."

"What are we doing there?" Elaina asked.

"Getting you a new wardrobe, dear cousin! You'll have to wear one of my gowns tomorrow, as these won't be done in time, but I'm afraid your gowns just won't do." Then her eyes went wide. "Oh! I hope I haven't offended you! I don't mean to say you look—"

"I'm looking forward to it." Elaina put her hand on her cousin's knee. And in truth, she was. Then she inwardly cringed. How was she so quickly abandoning her vowed disdain for life on land?

"Oh good!" Lydia put her hand to her face dramatically. "Let's see. You're rather short, but my servant should be able to take up the hem and adjust the seams enough for you to wear my corn-flower silk day gown tomorrow. And maybe my emerald one the day after that? It should make your eyes look the color of the sea. I'm not quite sure what shade I would call your hair, but it will look darker if we put it up." Lydia's eyes locked onto Elaina's wooden bracelet. "And we'll need to find you something jeweled—"

"Oh, no." Elaina put her hand protectively over her wrist. "You may change anything else you like with me, but not that. Please, don't ask me to remove it."

Lydia pursed her lips for a moment, but then her eyes softened. "Very well. We will let that be. But everything else must go!"

Once that important decision had been made, Lydia continued to prattle on happily about which girl would wear what color gown and which boy would be flirting with which girl until they pulled to a stop in front of a little shop on a crowded street.

Elaina hadn't even realized they'd reached the market until the footman helped them down from the carriage, for Lydia had complained that the sun was hurting her eyes halfway through the ride and the second set of curtains had to be let down.

As Roland helped them out of the carriage, Elaina couldn't quell the curiosity bubbling up inside her. Though Kaylem wasn't nearly as large as Solwhind, there were people everywhere, bustling around as though they all had important plans pressing them for time. Shoppers bargained for food, trinkets, and household items, and the sound of hammers sounded from the roofs of newer buildings that were still being added at the ends of the main cross streets. Laughter rang out and vendors shouted out their wares. Women gossiped, toddlers tripped over themselves. Men that weren't at work on the many buildings squished in together raised their voices in friendly arguments about politics and pork prices. And though the scene wasn't as loud or busy as Solwhind's northern fish market, there was none of the animosity here either. Rather, a contentedness filled the air.

Elaina wasn't allowed to linger and look for very long, though. Her aunt excused herself to visit a friend she spotted ducking into a shop along the road, and Lydia practically dragged Elaina into the little shop behind them, where rich rainbows of fabric were rolled and piled up against each wall.

"Tabitha, this is my cousin, Lady Elaina Starke," Lydia told a short woman with graying dark hair. "She's been living with her father and needs an entirely new . . . appropriate wardrobe."

"I see." Tabitha nodded seriously as her dark eyes darted up and down Elaina's person. "Men have little understanding of such things. Well, no matter. We'll have you proper in no time."

As the seamstress brought from the back a vast array of fabrics in all shades and hues, Elaina began to feel as though bees were buzzing around in her stomach. Yes, she had been raised for diplomacy. But what did she really know of court life? Would she embarrass her cousin and aunt? In truth, she had never spent more than a few meals with people her age. What did they speak of? How did they pass their time?

Why had her father made her do this?

"So, Lydia," she said as the seamstress held up yet another bolt of blue cloth. Was it the third? Or the fifth? She couldn't remember. She simply needed a distraction before she really began to panic. "What is Prince Nicholas like? Does he have any scruples I should avoid discussing in order not to lose my head before tea?"

Lydia let out a laugh like bells. Elaina managed a tight smile as well, though she'd only been half joking.

"Of course not! Nicholas is utterly charming."

So Lydia and the prince were on a first name basis, were they? Interesting. "That's good to know."

"You sound nervous." Lydia paused for the first time and really looked at Elaina. "Whatever is the matter?"

Elaina drew herself up to her full height and stretched her arms out as directed by the seamstress. "I only wish to make a good impression." But silently, she berated herself. She had lived through sea battles, creatures of the deep, and a vast array of diplomatic meetings. And now a tea was sending her into fits of nerves.

Lydia put her arm around Elaina's waist and hugged her. "Worry about nothing of the sort. You are not only noble and the true heir of our family's estate, but you are my cousin. And when

Nicholas learns of this, he will make sure you are the most highly sought after luncheon partner of the day."

Was that what Elaina wanted? She didn't know anymore. All she did know was that tomorrow's tea was sounding more and more like a naval battle, and Elaina was heading right for it with a borrowed ship of blue silk and absolutely no strategy of any sort. She was sailing blind.

UPON LYDIA'S INSISTENCE, they visited not one or two but five more shops before Lydia pronounced Elaina's wardrobe finished. Not that Elaina minded having a new wardrobe, of course. But in the back of her mind, she had been dreading and anticipating the return to her childhood home more than she truly cared about which shade of cream was en vogue for petticoats.

The drive to the manor took longer than she expected. Kaylem was a larger city than Elaina had first thought, and the manor was on the far eastern side of the city away from the wharf. At least, that is what she thought, not that her memory could be at all reliable as she hadn't visited the home since she was five.

As the carriage rolled along, she peeked out of the windows to see the crowded, colorful shops and houses begin to give way to larger plots of land. The grounds were small enough to still see one's neighbors on all sides, but the houses were far enough apart that there was room on each piece of land for small barns, some livestock, and expansive gardens on each side and behind.

And to the north, just as Lydia had promised, sat a palace that gleamed even in the light of the moon.

"We're here!" Lydia called, snapping Elaina's attention back to the street they had stopped on.

As she stepped out of the carriage, she was greeted by a white stone arch three levels high, reflecting the moon nearly as brightly as the palace. To the left and the right of the entryway each level boasted six windows on each side, thirty-six in all. White molding lined the roof like frosting on one of Simeon's little cakes, and though the lawn itself was nearly too black to see, not a shadow was asymmetrical or out of place. Stirrings of a dangerous emotion moved somewhere in Elaina's belly, and she set her face into an expression of cool serenity as she walked up the white steps toward the grand blue door housed beneath the arch.

She paused at the entryway to run her fingers lightly over the white flowers carved into the doorframe.

"Peonies."

Elaina turned to see her aunt smiling sadly in the dim light of the lanterns hung on each side of the door.

"Theresa loved those. Actually, your mother never met a flower she didn't like." Charlotte came closer and traced the flowers as well. "I really do wish for you to be happy here, Elaina. When your father asked me to come and live here with Lydia, it was only ever meant to be temporary until you were of age to inherit the estate. As my husband had just died, it seemed a good opportunity to get a new start in a place that didn't remind me of him quite so much as our old home did." She finally looked up from the doorframe. "But it really is your home, and you deserve to feel as such."

"I certainly hope you have no wishes to leave anytime soon." Elaina summoned a smile, which somehow wasn't as hard as she thought it might be. "I would have no desire to live here without you." She paused. "You look like her. I mean . . . from the glimpses I can remember." She shook her head. "Remembering her gets harder and harder."

Charlotte opened her mouth to say something else, but Lydia bounded between them and grabbed Elaina by the hand. "Here I am ordering Roland about to put your new things away, and you can't seem to get past the front step! Come inside! You need beauty rest! We have much to do in the morning!"

Charlotte laughed and rolled her eyes. "You'd better do as she says," she called out to Elaina, who had already been dragged through the door and halfway up the stairs. "We'll have more time for a tour tomorrow."

"Little chance of that," Lydia muttered and shook her head, still pulling Elaina up the winding staircase. "We have work to do." They stopped on the third level, where Elaina was towed down the hall to the very last room on the left.

The door was already open, and the manservants were unloading not only Elaina's chest but also several dozen bags and packages all over the floor and the vanity. A bevy of maidservants had begun to unpack their contents.

"How much do I really need?" Elaina gawked at all the purchases. They didn't even include her gowns, which would be delivered in a few weeks.

"You're a marchioness, my dear cousin. I'm only an earl's daughter, which technically means you need to have a wardrobe even finer and larger than mine." She put her hands on her hips. "And that would be a difficult feat for anyone to manage."

Elaina gave an unladylike snort. "I think two or three gowns should do just fine. And perhaps two for formal events. But really—"

"Really you need to get your sleep."

When Elaina quirked an eyebrow, Lydia laughed, her round face dimpling adorably. "I know. I can seem a bit . . . overexcitable. But truly, I'm glad you're here. We won't be back at the country manor in the south, which I'm not sure you'd remember but in any case is far larger than this one, I can assure you, until summer, and my closest friend moved to Solwhind last year. It's been rather lonely here since."

"Very well," Elaina said. "Let me sleep tonight, and tomorrow you may do whatever you wish with me."

Lydia squealed and clapped her hands. "Oh, and I'm supposed to tell you that this was your mother's room before she and your father were married." She paused. "It was your room, too, when you were small. Mother says she would have given you the big one, but we didn't have enough time to—"

"This will do just fine." Elaina felt her chest tighten. She smiled as best she could and bid her cousin goodnight. Then she turned to the servants. "You may also go."

They paused in their work and exchanged curious looks.

"Truly," she said. "I wish to unpack my own things. But thank you."

As soon as they were gone, Elaina extinguished all the lights but a single candle. She carried the rest of the clothes and bags and boxes to a divan on the far wall and left them there to sort through the next morning. Then, once she had opened her sea chest to ensure her glass slippers were well, she rummaged through her belongings until she found her nightdress and bed slippers and put them on.

Her new room was large, much larger than she remembered. Nearly the size of the entryway downstairs, it was filled with all sorts of beautiful light pink furniture, chairs, sofas, a large vanity, and a four-poster bed near the door. But she had no wish to look further than she was required tonight. The smell alone was bringing back nearly overwhelming emotions, though Elaina couldn't tell exactly why or what those emotions even were. Like visions of shadows in a fog, she recalled fleeting pieces of familiarity. Happiness. Heartbreak.

She would explore the room . . . the whole house later. But the day had held enough change and trepidation to last her a week. She wasn't quite sure she would be able to handle anything more. So she kept her candle burning only long enough to eat from the plate of food left on her little bedside table, then she snuffed the candle out before she could see anything else that might bring back more unwanted memories, particularly the small portrait of a woman that sat on the mantel of her fireplace.

Before Elaina went to sleep, however, she crawled onto the window seat, where she opened the window and looked up into the night sky. A cool sea breeze blew in, and she drank deeply of its briny scent and closed her eyes. It was almost like being back in her little cabin aboard the *Adroit*. Almost.

"Are you still there?" she whispered out her window.

Where else would we be? They sounded amused. *It was at this window that you heard us first.*

"I know. It's just all so strange still."

We know. And we're here. As always.

"Thank you." Elaina smiled and began to move back toward her bed, not bothering to shut her window again.

Elaina?

"Yes?"

Tomorrow, when you meet the prince . . . They paused.

She walked back to the window seat and looked up. "What about it?"

Don't fall too hard.

CHAPTER 6
CHARMING

E laina didn't remember falling asleep, but morning came abruptly when she was awakened by girlish squeals.

"Get up, sleepyhead! It's tea day!"

Elaina groaned and tried to roll over, but Lydia somehow managed to yank her blankets off.

"It's breakfast for you. Then a bath. You have a ridiculous number of freckles, probably from all that time in the sun, so we'll need to scrub your face with lemon juice as well. Then to your hair and making sure my dress is hemmed to the proper length so you're not tripping on it. Then some rouge, and—"

"How about we start with breakfast?" Elaina yawned.

"Oh! Yes. Of course. Off you go now."

Elaina barely had time to finish her crumpet and fruit before Lydia had her off and running again. Only this time, it was to Lydia's room where three servants were already preparing baths, gowns, accessories, and a somewhat frightening number of cosmetics on the vanity.

How they managed to spend hours being bathed and scrubbed relentlessly, stuck in every direction by hair pins, and painted like dolls, Elaina had no idea. She had never taken more than an hour in her life to become ready for the day, and even that was when she'd fallen ill. And yet, somehow, Elaina looked out the window to find that the morning sun had waxed late when her cousin yipped to all the servants that they had no more time for primping. The women must be on their way.

Elaina was fairly shoved out the grand front door of the home she had yet to explore, but she found respite from her cousin's incessant chatter when they got into the carriage as Lydia seemed too excited to form coherent sentences. Elaina glanced at Aunt Charlotte, who simply shrugged and rolled her eyes, her smile amused.

The carriage wound its way through the lanes and up the gently sloping hill that the palace and its sprawling estate were settled on. The roads were well maintained, and the ride was impressively smooth.

According to her father, Ashland, though not large in land, was the second-most prosperous of kingdoms in the western realm, second only to King Everard's country of Destin. And thanks to their new trade agreements with the merpeople and the merpeople's sister country, Maricanta, Ashland's wealth had only continued to grow. Elaina could see now that King Xander's wealth hadn't been exaggerated.

Though Kaylem touched the sea on the western shore, north of the wharf, the palace was the closest building to the ocean, sitting on the northwest tip of the entire peninsula. Though Elaina had certainly never entertained thoughts of herself inhabiting the palace walls, as she was sure most girls of Ashland did, she had to admit that the palace couldn't have been situated in a more superb location. Rosington Manor was more than grand enough for her taste, but having a home bordering the ocean would be paradise.

If the land was ideal, the palace itself was just as appealing. Unlike many of the castles Elaina had seen in her travels, the palace was more like a vast manor, just as Lydia had described. Brilliant white walls were almost blinding where the morning light touched them. A tower crowned each of the four corners, but the rest of the palace was simple. Still, there was an elegance in its sprawling grandeur, five levels tall with hundreds of windows that reflected the sun even more brightly than the whitewashed walls.

And unlike most of the castles she'd seen, there were few walls surrounding the palace. A single white wall nearly twelve feet tall ran around the palace's perimeter on the southern and eastern sides that led to the city, but as their carriage moved up the winding road to the palace, she could make out that the palace's western and northern lawns had no walls, backing up to the ocean itself. Of course, that didn't mean the palace was without protection. Elaina knew from her time with her father that dozens of traps and other dangers lurked unseen beneath the shallow waves, should anyone try to sail up to the palace directly.

After being allowed entrance through a grand white gate that seemed nearly as tall as the *Adroit*'s tallest mast, Elaina and her cousin and aunt were handed down from the carriage and escorted to a short line of people that led up to a smaller open gate that seemed to open up to some sort of lawn. Elaina toyed with her wooden bracelet as they neared the elegant lady and tall young man greeting people at the head of the line.

"Marchioness Elaina Starke of Rosington Manor!"

Pulled from her musings, Elaina started when she heard her name announced. Yes, she was technically a lady by title. A very high one at that. But her title had never meant much to her out at sea. For out upon the waves, she was the proud daughter of Admiral Baxter Starke. And that was fine with her. But here, she was the lady of her own home, despite the fact that she hadn't yet walked its full length since she was five. Besides, holding the title that had rightfully belonged to her mother made her feel like an imposter.

But this was no way to present the Starke name. So she held her head high and put on her most practiced smile.

"Your Majesty. Your Highness." She dipped into her lowest curtsy.

"Elaina, I cannot tell you how lovely it is to see you again."

Then the queen put her hand over her mouth, her blue eyes widening a bit. "Oh! I do apologize for my familiarity. I was very close with your mother. It feels only natural to call you like the little girl I knew you as." She glanced up and down Elaina's person once. "Though I can see you are a little girl no longer." Her smile was wistful. "How many years are you now?"

"Seventeen. And there is nothing to forgive, Your Majesty. I am honored that you remember my mother so." *I wish I did.* But she didn't add that particular thought.

"You look so much like her," the queen whispered. But before Elaina could respond, the tall young man beside her cleared his throat.

"Lady Starke," he said, bowing and taking her hand. "I am glad to make your acquaintance again as well."

"Again?" Elaina echoed in confusion.

"Oh yes!" The queen clasped her hands and looked warmly at the young man. "Lady Theresa used to visit us often and bring you along with her."

"I believe the last time we met, you put a tadpole in my tea," the prince said, a gleam in his eyes.

Elaina's mouth fell open. Her father had never taught her how to recover from this kind of faux pas. But the prince just laughed. The sound was playful.

"It livened up a party that had been rather boring, if I recall." He leaned forward, smirking. "Quite a feat. Making a tea party enjoyable for boys of seven is next to impossible."

It was then that Elaina realized what striking blue eyes Prince Nicholas had, similar to the queen's but even brighter. How often had she wished for eyes like his, rather than her green-blue ones that couldn't seem to decide which color they really were. But really, he was quite striking in many ways. His dark brown hair, also the same color as the queen's, was cut short enough to stick out rebelliously in every direction, and his mouth was pleasant, quirking up as though he were enjoying a personal joke.

"So where have you been all these years?" he asked. The queen nudged him hard, but Elaina smiled.

"Traveling with my father aboard the *Adroit*, helping him conduct the king's business."

"Nicholas, no need to pry," the queen murmured.

"I would love to hear more about these adventures," he said, taking a step closer.

Elaina was tempted then and there to begin telling him all about life at sea, but a glance behind her at the growing line reminded her of propriety. Also, she noticed, Lydia's face was an odd shade of gray.

"I would be honored, sire." Elaina curtsied once more. "But I wouldn't wish to inconvenience your other guests."

"Oh . . . of course." Prince Nicholas finally seemed to notice the lengthening line as well. "But you will remember our talk?"

Elaina laughed. "I look forward to it."

She waited some yards away as Lydia and Aunt Charlotte paid their respects to their hosts as well. Lydia's brown eyes shone as she spoke to the prince in hushed tones. But their greeting was far shorter than Elaina's had been, and when they left the receiving line to join her, Elaina couldn't help feeling that despite Lydia's smile, something wasn't right.

They moved into the garden to mingle with the other guests who had already arrived. Aunt Charlotte went to speak with her friends on the other side of the lawn, leaving Elaina and Lydia to wander. Long rectangular tables, each nearly half the length of the *Androit*'s deck, had been already set with delicate plates and tea cups, robin's egg blue with painted orange leaves that wound their way around the dishes' rims.

Despite her momentary lapse of joy, Lydia proved to be a great help as she graciously moved Elaina from one group of people to another. Though Elaina was familiar with the key names of Ashland's political figures, names her father had required she memorize for meetings, she was introduced to more nobility than she had previously known existed. Some were warm and friendly. Others were reserved and seemed almost suspicious. Nearly everyone, however, was curious. So it was a relief when Elaina spotted a familiar face, one for whom she did not need an introduction.

"Prince Henri!" She beamed and curtsied.

"Lady Elaina." The young prince smiled back as he bowed, his golden hair falling in front of his eyes. "It is good to see you again. I hear you met my father recently."

"I did."

"And what did you think?"

"He certainly doesn't disappoint."

Henri let out a snort then began to laugh.

"Remind me again, how are you two acquainted?" Lydia asked dryly.

"Lady Elaina and I were privileged to meet when her father's ship came in to port in Maricanta. I was there with my mother on official business at the same time." Henri turned to Lydia. "It is good to see you as well, Lady Lydia."

"How have you and your family been?" Elaina asked, but he didn't get a chance to respond, for the bell for tea was rung.

As everyone moved toward the tables, Elaina didn't feel quite as wary as she had before the tea began. Lydia, however, stayed silent. Far different from the bubbling, bouncing girl that she'd prepared with that morning. Elaina meant to ask her if she was feeling well, but a servant interrupted her before she could find her seat.

"Lady Elaina, Prince Nicholas has requested that you be his partner for tea."

ELAINA LOOKED at Lydia in confusion, but Lydia's eyes were just as large as Elaina's felt.

"Very well," she finally managed to whisper. "I would be honored."

Her heart pounded as she was escorted away from Lydia to the center of the long table set for the young adults, as Aunt Charlotte had called them. Prince Nicholas was already at his seat, but he bounded over to Elaina when he saw her and relieved the servant by escorting her himself the rest of the way.

"You can't imagine how excited I am," he whispered as they reached the table. "I have read all I can of your father's excursions. I even hired a tutor to teach me the ways of maritime warfare. But to have someone here who has lived through it is quite a treat."

Elaina suppressed a ridiculous urge to giggle. He might look like a puppy—an adorable one at that—but she was determined to conduct herself with the poise and grace expected of a lady and admiral's daughter.

She hoped. He was unusually handsome.

As soon as everyone was seated and the tea was being served, the prince turned to her again. "So what is life like on the flagship?"

"Well," she paused and broke her scone in half. She would need to tread carefully. It wouldn't do to give away her secret by accident, particularly with so many around to hear it. "We traveled constantly. I think the longest we were ever in one port was three weeks, and that was only because a storm had damaged the ship."

"Did that ever get tiring? Always being on the move?"

"The ship was my home," she said, still staring at her scone, her throat suddenly dry.

"You miss it, don't you?"

She turned to see his eyes fixed on hers. His brow was creased, and the laughter had left his face.

She gave him a sad smile and nodded. "I do." Her eyes immediately went to her bracelet.

"Then why did you come back?"

"My father decided it was time I learn to flirt properly and ensnare myself a husband."

He stared at her, then let out a loud burst of laughter. "I see." He took a sip of his tea, still chuckling. "So among all those diplomats and princes you met, none were interested in helping you practice your flirting?" He quirked an eyebrow. "I somehow doubt that."

Elaina again suppressed the need to giggle. Instead, she nibbled a strawberry to hide her smile. "There were too many other interesting things to do." She looked down the hill at the scene before them. At the foot of the palace's hill sat the city. To its right lay the wharf, and past the city to its south and west sprawled countless manors, farmhouses, orchards, and fields.

"Every port had new food to try," she said. "New streets to explore and new customs to learn about. We attended festivals, banquets, and markets." She nodded at the orchards. "Where we have orchards here, others might have livestock or fields of flax or barley. Larger cities, like Solwhind, are too great to see the end of. But," she turned back to him, "it always came back to the sea."

He didn't answer immediately, just studied her with those striking blue eyes. Elaina knew he couldn't, but she felt as though he were able to see inside her soul. "I'm sorry," he finally whispered.

"How is your sister, sire?"

They both turned to see Lydia looking at the prince from her place across the table, several seats down.

"Which one?" the prince asked.

"Princess Daphne."

"Ah. She's doing well from what I hear. Already complaining about not yet being with child." He smiled mischievously and waggled his eyebrows at Elaina. "My eldest sister got married two full months ago."

Elaina smiled and started to reply, but Lydia spoke again.

"And Princess Sophia?"

"Constantly fretting about the impending wedding. I suspect she will continue doing so for the next four months." He faced Elaina once more. "So, did you ever visit the Albatross Shoals?"

"I have."

"And were they as terrifying as the stories make them sound?"

Elaina answered, but out of the corner of her eye, Lydia looked crestfallen. Guilt began to fill the pit of Elaina's belly, though she wasn't exactly sure why.

Not long after, the tea was finished and the shrubbery maze was announced. Nicholas stood.

"I know you boys are dying for a chance to meet her, but I'm going to show the new girl around today."

To Elaina's embarrassment and surprise, some of the young men groaned. A number of the girls also shot her withering glances.

"That is," he held out his arm, "if she'll have me."

Elaina paused, glancing once more at Lydia. But he looked so hopeful when she turned back to him that to deny him would have been utterly impossible. Elaina told herself to stop feeling so foolishly giddy as she held out her hand. He was just being kind to the new girl, that was all. And yet, as they left the table and began to stroll across the emerald green grass, she felt her heart thump unevenly when he pulled her a little closer and put his hand over hers where it rested on his arm.

Just before they entered the maze, Elaina looked back to search for her cousin. Other young men and women had begun to immediately couple off as well, but she finally spotted Lydia standing by herself, still behind her chair at the table.

"Do you think we might take my cousin as well?" She turned to the prince and gave him her shyest smile. "As you said, I'm still new here and am not familiar with where everything is."

"I think that's the point of a maze."

She laughed. "Yes, but suppose you should be called away on some urgent business while we're inside? Then I would be all alone and might die an old maid before I got out."

He studied her, for a moment looking quite ornery. But in the end, he merely bowed his head. "Very well. It would be my pleasure to escort Lady Lydia as well."

They walked back to the table and the prince held out his other arm, which Lydia eagerly accepted. As they walked back to the maze, however, neither one of them looked quite as satisfied as Elaina had hoped.

Still, the maze itself was an enjoyable challenge. The walls rose several feet above even the prince's head and were made of a grand assortment of flowers. Purple beauty berries, rust-red heleniums, yellow heliopsis, white iberis, and pink chrysanthemums surrounded them and lined the paths at their feet.

"You must have been a sight to see on that ship, Lady Elaina," the prince said as they met another dead end. "A beautiful young woman running around amongst the dirty sailors?"

"I'm afraid if you had seen me you wouldn't have found anyone as fashionably dressed as you see now." Elaina self-consciously tucked a lock of hair behind her ear. "I had always thought myself to be well turned out, but everything you see today is the artwork of my dear cousin."

"You have good taste." The prince turned and smiled at Lydia, who smiled back uncertainly. "That color really accentuates her eyes. Don't you think?"

"Yes, sire."

They made another turn, and Elaina was thankful to see that it was not another dead end. She wasn't sure how much longer she could stand to have her cousin and the prince in the same place. Whatever was going on between them was making the garden feel quite stuffy.

"My father can't praise your father enough," Prince Nicholas said as though nothing were amiss. "I've asked countless times to go aboard the *Adroit* for a few weeks so I may better understand the navy and its needs, but my father never allows it. He always says I'll just be in everyone's way."

"You would be welcome anytime," Elaina said. "I can safely say my father would have absolutely no objection to your presence, nor would you be a burden." Unlike her, apparently.

"Something just occurred to me. What did your father do with you during skirmishes or battles?" He frowned. "I can't imagine keeping a delicate thing like you on deck during such confrontations. Have you ever fallen overboard?"

Elaina smiled. "No. But when the fighting grew too severe, which was quite rare, I would go down and wait in my cabin."

The prince laughed, but Lydia sniffed. "It's not proper for a woman to be involved in such treachery as war."

"We really saw very little fighting. Some, yes, but in Ashland's navy, the flagship must issue commands. So we were often at the edge of the fighting, not in the middle of it. During dangerous battles, my father would have me stay in the cabin with a few casum balls of my own."

Lydia looked astonished. "Casum balls?"

"Earthen sod covering a ball of clay that explodes when it touches air," Prince Nicholas explained. "As soon as the ball is thrown, the sod falls off and everything around it is blown to bits."

"As I said, highly improper," Lydia muttered.

"Which is why I'm here now," Elaina said soothingly.

She felt mixed relief and regret when they finally found the maze's exit. Whatever was upsetting Lydia appeared to be getting worse by the moment. And yet, Elaina couldn't help being enamored by the very prince she had scoffed at only a few days before. Not only was he really quite handsome, but his intense interest in her father's work would have been enough to put anyone in her good opinion.

"I'm afraid the tea is ending soon," he said. Young men and women were moving across the lawn and back toward the entrance where the married ladies stood and talked. He looked down at Elaina, his eyes large and hopeful like a little boy's. "Do you think we might speak again of this? Perhaps tomorrow? I should very much like to hear more of your father's exploits."

"It would be my pleasure," Elaina said, smiling stupidly up at him.

"Until tomorrow then." The prince bowed low, kissing each of their hands in turn before going to join his mother. Lydia spotted her mother and both girls headed toward her. But this time, Lydia hurried on ahead.

Aunt Charlotte spent the ride home trying to coax details out of Lydia, but Lydia refused to speak more than a sentence or two. Elaina tried to make up for her cousin's silence, but she felt nearly too lost in her own thoughts to give many clear answers herself.

For the rest of the day, Elaina's head felt muddled. She tried to clear it by organizing her things in her room, but the maidservants continued to pester her about letting them help. As a result, her thoughts still hadn't settled by the time she took supper with her aunt and Lydia. The whole time she was at the table, Elaina did her best to smile and respond appropriately when asked a question, but she doubted her performance was very convincing. She simply wanted nothing more than to be left alone to drift in and out of thoughts about the prince and her new life in Kaylem. It wasn't until she was lying in bed that night that Elaina finally had time to think uninterrupted.

Perhaps her father had more wisdom in sending her away than she'd first thought. She certainly hadn't expected to enjoy her time with the prince. Many of the princes she had met were flighty and about as deep as a birdbath. But Prince Nicholas's sharp eyes and quick wit were signals of a deep intelligence, something she had learned to look for in many of her negotiations with her father. And not only was he intelligent, he was also handsome, attentive, and found life at sea enthralling. Really, if the Maker had ever created a man to her liking, Prince Nicholas would seem to be him.

"Is it possible?" she asked the portrait of her mother that now sat beside her bed. "Could the prince actually see something in me as well?" It sounded ridiculous when she said it aloud, but her mother's portrait continued to smile at her anyway. Elaina would take that for what it was.

The only blot of unhappiness on the entire beautiful canvas of her day was the emotional state of her cousin. Somehow, Lydia had transformed from an enthusiastic, squealing girl to a silent, miserable mess by the end of supper. What could she have done differently that might have made Lydia happier? What could she have done that was wrong? And though Elaina couldn't think of a single word that might have been out of place, she wondered if her cousin's silence was her fault after all.

CHAPTER 7
THE LOT OF YOU

E laina smiled as soon as she opened her eyes. She was going to see Prince Nicholas again.

Even as she basked in these happy thoughts, however, she was struck by how high the sun had already risen, quite a contrast to Lydia's exuberant start to the day before. The smells of breakfast were wafting up from below, and there was no sign that her cousin had even visited her room that morning. Not that Elaina minded sleeping in, as she certainly didn't feel the need to go through certain preparations—such as scrubbing her stubborn freckles with lemons—but where was Lydia?

Lydia had already gone to dress, Elaina was informed when she finally made it down to the dining hall for breakfast. She had awakened and eaten an hour before. Elaina did her best to smile graciously at this news, but her appetite somehow was lessened by it, and all she could do was pick at her cup of fruit until her aunt excused her.

When she opened the door of her room, she saw that a gown had been draped over her chair. Its material was fine silk, but the solid hue of mud was nothing compared to the vivid blue from the day before or the vibrant green Lydia had promised.

Was Lydia truly angry with her? And why?

They arrived at the palace after a long, silent carriage ride, but when Elaina finally made her mind up to confront her cousin, Lydia used the buzz of the garden's receiving line to step silently behind her mother. Elaina couldn't even make eye contact with her.

By the time she reached the front of the line, Elaina was more than ready to ignore her cousin and simply see the prince again. His easy conversation would be a welcome relief from Lydia's foul mood and her aunt's awkward attempts at coaxing harmony from both of them.

When it was her turn, Elaina curtsied and gave Queen Ann and Prince Nicholas a relieved smile. "Your Majesty, Your Highness."

"Lady Elaina, how pleasant to see you again. I hope you enjoyed yourself yesterday," the queen said.

"I was entertained most enjoyably." Then she looked at the prince, expecting his boyish grin again. To her surprise, however, Prince Nicholas was looking with bright eyes at something behind her.

"Nicholas." The queen nudged her son.

"Oh, Lady Elaina. I apologize." He smiled politely and bowed, though not as low as he had the day before. "I am glad to see you again. I hope you find today's activities as intriguing as those of yesterday." Then he promptly returned his attention to whatever was so interesting behind her.

She was being dismissed.

Forcing the gracious expression to stay on her face, she curtsied once more and moved onto the lawn, where she stood in the shade of a large tree to observe the line.

Something was different. The eagerness that had etched itself all over his face the day before had fled the prince's expression when he'd looked at her. But no, she realized as she continued to study him. It wasn't gone. It was just focused on someone else.

The girl behind her, the one whose family had separated Elaina from her aunt, was introduced as the daughter of an ambassador Elaina was somewhat familiar with. Full-figured in an adorable sort of way, much like a roly-poly puppy might be, the girl dimpled, blushing prettily as the prince gave her the same deep bow and smile Elaina had been given yesterday. His hand lingered on the girl's after he kissed it, and he took a half-step forward to whisper something that made her giggle.

Elaina had the sudden urge to look at Lydia. Sure enough, Lydia was staring miserably at the prince from where she was mostly hidden behind her mother. That's when it all made sense.

Lydia's first-name familiarity with the prince.

Her angry silence.

The prince's sudden interest in the girl who hadn't been there the day before.

Elaina smiled grimly to herself as she shook her head. *Don't fall too hard,* the stars had said. She'd been too distracted to really understand them then, but now the pieces fit neatly together.

The prince enjoyed his women.

How stupid she was, allowing herself to be swept away like a common ninny. How many years had her father spent training her to read the body for signals of untruth, nerves, and disingenuousness?

Admittedly, he was good. Even as she watched him from her place beneath the tree, she could honestly say she had never seen such a perfect performance before. His abilities were far above even the best diplomats. But she still should have known better.

Well, now she would. He would not be sneaking past her defenses again.

As soon as Lydia and her mother left the line, Elaina marched over to her cousin and grabbed her arm, placing it firmly in the crook of her own. Lydia looked rather perplexed, but Elaina was not about to allow the dabbling prince to separate her from her cousin again.

Her resolution didn't prove as easy as she had first thought, though, particularly when tea was announced soon after, and Elaina and Lydia were seated just across the table from the prince. Of course, the ambassador's daughter was given the seat that had been Elaina's the day before, the seat that Elaina guessed Lydia had previously occupied as well.

But that was all very well. Elaina could ignore him from across the table just as well as from down at its end. In fact, she could do better than ignore him. She could drive him mad.

Her best diplomatic skills on display, Elaina smiled and conversed with everyone within speaking distance. And though she knew many of the girls had harbored unfriendly feelings toward her the day before, turning their feelings around really wasn't that hard. Just as her father had taught her, she asked all the right questions, laughed at all the right places, and made sure to compliment others where and when she could. Everyone but the prince.

She had turned around to introduce herself to a new acquaintance halfway through the tea when she heard Prince Nicholas tell one of his friends that the Battle of the Reefs had been planned carefully by the admiral of his flagship as well as several other naval officers. She stole a glance at the prince, only to see that he was looking rather pleased with himself. It was impossible to miss such an opportunity.

"The Battle of the Reefs wasn't planned at all, actually," she said loudly as she stirred her tea. "In fact, the run-in with the pirates took the fleet completely by surprise."

The prince paused and looked at her, so she suppressed a smile and continued on.

"The flagship and several other naval vessels were merely out conducting scientific observations when the pirates turned around a bend and nearly collided with the flagship itself."

"In truth?" One of the young men crossed his arms and tilted his head.

She took a slow sip of her tea. "The pirates were fleeing from Maricanta's navy as well as a horde of angry merpeople. The Royal Navy simply happened to be in the proper place at the proper time to stop them."

The young man, whom Elaina thought to be an earl's son,

sneered at her. "And where would your ladyship have obtained such enlightening information?"

Elaina set her teacup down with a clink that was a little louder than necessary and fixed her gaze squarely on him. "Because I was there."

The chatter around them subsided, and at once, Elaina felt the weight of all their stares. But she merely continued gazing coolly at the young earl.

Unfortunately, her attempt at embarrassing the prince seemed to have failed, for he was chuckling quietly to himself.

"So you are telling me," said another young nobleman, "that you were on a warship during the most dangerous engagement with pirates our navy has seen in over fifty years?"

"Please don't," Lydia whispered. "I'm grateful for what you're trying to do, but please just leave it be."

Elaina squeezed her cousin's hand beneath the table but continued on. "Of course. My father was the one leading the charge."

The young men looked at one another in turns of confusion and indignation. Only two in the throng didn't seem completely appalled or condescending. Prince Henri tried unsuccessfully to hide a smile behind the pastry he was holding, and Prince Nicholas's attention was hers once more. He seemed to have all but forgotten the ambassador's daughter who still sat chatting away beside him. The intensity of the prince's gaze was no longer amiable, however, nor was it simply intrigued. Rather, he reminded Elaina of a hawk circling its prey.

"I think you're telling a falsehood," the earl's son announced above the gossip. He leaned forward. "I heard you tell someone you lived on the seas for twelve years. If you're such an expert on all things nautical, prove it."

"I wouldn't do that if I were you," Prince Henri muttered.

"Answer me this," Elaina said. "When leaving port in poor weather in a three-mast ship, which mast would you remove to capture the winds more favorably until the storm abates?"

The young earl scowled and opened his mouth, but paused. Elaina nearly allowed herself a smirk as the other young men around her began to confer with one another.

The prince did not confer. When his sharp eyes didn't leave her face, she finally allowed herself to meet their gaze. Then she allowed him one very small smile. She could play games, too.

Finally, the young earl stopped whispering with his neighbors.

"Are you ready to answer?" Elaina asked.

"The foremast," he said. "You would temporarily remove the foremast."

"And that answer goes for the rest of you as well?" Elaina looked around.

Prince Henri only scowled and stuffed his mouth with another pastry. Prince Nicholas rolled his eyes. The others didn't seem to have noticed their responses, however, for the rest of them simply nodded.

"Well." Elaina leaned back and folded her arms across her chest. "That answers that. One couldn't pay me enough gold in all the world to leave port with any of you."

"And why is that?" The earl had an unbecoming sneer on his face.

"Because the lot of you would sink the ship."

"Hold on now—" he began to protest, but Prince Nicholas interrupted him with a grimace.

"She's right, Appleby. You don't remove a mast, you idiot. If any of your masts are gone, your ship is in peril."

He studied Elaina once more with his hawkish stare, but she turned to her cousin and began a conversation about one of her new dresses, refusing to meet his gaze. She had said all she needed to say for the day.

Tea was soon called to a close. There were no activities to follow the refreshments, so Elaina was more than ready to go when her aunt began to approach them from the women's table across the lawn. Unfortunately, Prince Nicholas reached her first.

"I was telling the truth when I said I wanted to speak with you more about your father's ship," he said in a serious tone. He didn't even seem to notice the glare the ambassador's daughter was sending Elaina over his arm.

"But, sire, you have such knowledgeable friends."

And with that, Elaina walked away, dragging a wide-eyed Lydia along and refusing to cast even a single glance back at the prince she'd left behind.

CHAPTER 8
SHE HATES YOU

"A re you still up for practice, or did the tea tire you out?" Henri elbowed Nicholas once all the guests had been properly seen off.

"You know that these teas are not actually my idea." Nicholas shoved him back.

"But you can't pretend you don't enjoy all that incessant flirting. Speaking of which, what do you think of that new girl, the ambassador's daughter. What was her name? Lilac? Peony?"

"Clover," Nicholas said, nodding to the weapons room guard as he opened the door for them. "Throwing knives today?"

"Why not?"

"Miss Clover Belgrad is fair enough."

"But?"

Nicholas shrugged. "Not quite bright enough for my taste." The most in-depth conversation he could recall with the clingy young woman was something about the propriety of serving oysters at a dinner party. At least, that's what he thought she'd been talking about. He'd spent most of the morning . . . well, not listening. Not to her, at least. He smiled a little. "Lady Elaina, though . . ."

Henri shook his head as they headed out to the courtyard with their knives in hand. "I hope you're aware that she hates you."

"That can be remedied easily enough."

Henri snorted. "I doubt that."

The young men waited as a servant set up the large wooden target at the end of the courtyard.

"How well do you know her?" Nicholas asked.

Henri took aim and heaved his knife. It landed with a thud just inches below the target's center. "Not close enough to be on familiar terms, but we met briefly last year when our travels crossed in Maricanta. She recently met my father as well."

Nicholas threw his own knife. It landed an inch above Henri's. "And what was his impression of her?"

"I think he was ready to adopt her as his own, despite her already having a living father."

"And what do you think of her?"

Henri paused and studied him. "Why the sudden curiosity? You seemed to have tired of her fast enough this morning. Is this renewed interest because she made Appleby look foolish?"

"Anyone could make Willard Appleby look foolish, though I am in her debt for that. But really, what did you think?"

Henri watched him with cautious gray eyes for a moment before shrugging and aiming his second knife. "From what I know of her, she has a good heart, but she's also intelligent and as shrewd as a cat." He chuckled. "I wouldn't want to cross her." His knife landed just outside the center circle of the target.

Nicholas nodded. Then he yanked up his knife and threw it without pausing to aim. Chips flew out of the wood as it hit dead center. "Well, that answers that then."

"About what?"

"She's going to be my new tutor."

Henri looked at him as though he'd lost his mind.

"Look, my father refuses to let me even get close to the military."

"One of the reasons my father can't stand him," Henri muttered.

"He says men like Admiral Starke exist so royals don't have to be involved. But if I'm going to have any sense of what to do with our military, I need training. Good training." Nicholas ran his hand through his hair. "If my current tutor was wrong about a battle as important as the one at the Reefs, what else has he got wrong? And really, who better to teach me than the daughter of my father's best admiral?"

"I suppose I see your point."

Nicholas slapped his friend on the back. "Good. It's settled then." He went to pull his knives out of the target, but Henri blocked his way.

"You forget one very important detail."

"Which would be?"

"As I said before, she hates you. Apparently, you've never had to suffer a woman's wrath before." Henri shuddered. "I can tell you. It's not pretty. I live with two of them, and that doesn't even count the servants."

"You forget I have more sisters than you."

"But they're older, and they ignore you."

"Inconsequential. Besides, I know how to remove every reason a woman might think of to hate me." Nicholas bowed low with a flourish. "I am, after all, quite charming."

Henri rolled his eyes and pulled his own knives free. "I just hope you know what you're doing."

"Always the gentleman," Nicholas called over his shoulder as he turned to head inside. He had lessons to schedule.

CHAPTER 9

UNWILLING TUTOR

"Elaina, may I have a word with you?"

Elaina looked up from the book she'd been inspecting. Rosington had a much larger library than she remembered, which pleased Elaina more than she could say. From the sound of her aunt's voice now, however, Elaina sensed tarrying would be a poor choice. She put the book away and met her aunt in the front parlor, where a servant was helping Charlotte remove her outer wrappings from her social visit to their neighbors.

"Yes, Aunt?"

"Sit, please."

Elaina did as she was bid, a ball of unease growing in her stomach as the servant seemed intent on taking the entire morning to remove her aunt's shawl and gloves. When they were finally alone, her aunt spoke again.

"Elaina, you know I wish to make you comfortable here in every way. But while I was out calling on my friend Lady Appleby, I heard a rather disconcerting report of a conversation that transpired yesterday during the tea."

Elaina had been fidgeting, but now she went completely still as Lydia came bounding down the stairs and into the parlor.

"Oh, Mother. You're home early." She blinked at Elaina in the large chair then looked back at her mother. "What is going on?"

"Lydia, is it true that Elaina engaged in an argument with some of the young men yesterday?"

"I . . . wouldn't call it an argument," Elaina said before Lydia could respond. "More like a lively debate."

"Call it what you may, but is it true that you insulted the boy about his navigational skills?"

Nautical, Elaina corrected her aunt in her head but didn't dare speak it aloud. Instead, she took a deep breath. "He insulted me first. They all did."

"Elaina!" Her aunt looked exasperated. "Men of title do not like to be contradicted—"

"But they—"

"No matter how insipid they're being," Charlotte finished firmly. "Your mother left you in my care to prepare you for the life of a marchioness. Just because your father does not hold a title does not mean you can pretend that your mother held any small place in the court. In addition to management and stewardship skills, you also need to understand the proper etiquette that belongs to such a prestigious position!" She placed her fingers on her temples and rubbed them. "I have a headache and will be going to the kitchen for some of Gladys's lavender. When I return, I expect you to still be here, and we will continue this discussion."

"See what you've done?" Lydia hissed as soon as her mother was out of the room. "Look, I appreciate what you were trying to do. I . . . I know you were trying to make amends for the way Nicholas behaved but . . . Elaina, you just ruined your chances of marriage!" Her eyes hardened a bit. "And possibly mine! Men don't forget these things, you know! Willard already went home and told his mother. What do you think the others are doing with their friends?"

"Well, it's not as though I plan on marrying any of them anyway. Why should I worry about their offense?"

"I'm serious!"

Elaina sighed. "First of all, I doubt most of them will wish to admit to their friends that they were bested in naval warfare knowledge by a woman." She snatched up a fire iron and leaned forward to jab the coals in the fireplace with a vengeance. "That Willard would report it to his mother shows what a coward he is. Second, you forget something." She replaced the poker and leaned back in the oversized chair, sending Lydia a small, sly smile.

"What?" Lydia folded her arms and huffed.

"I am the legal heir to this home and will assume responsibility for it in four years. That means that when I pass in ten or thirty or seventy years, however long it takes the world to knock me off my feet, it shall go to my next of kin. Which would be you, dear. Now, while *I* might be sworn off by every eligible man in Ashland by the end of the day, you are not. You are lovely and sweet, and one day some man, many most likely, will recognize that and sweep you off your feet. And we shall all live here together, you with your man and eight children, and me as a crotchety old maid. And when I die, the estate shall be given to you and your family." She clasped her hands. "See? Problem solved."

Lydia rolled her eyes, but a small smile escaped her lips, which made Elaina smile even more broadly. Before she could tease her cousin any more about babies and men, however, someone knocked at the door.

The butler opened it, and a young man dressed in blue and white stepped inside. The colors of the crown.

"Prince Nicholas Whealdmar requests the presence of Lady Elaina Starke," the man said.

"I am she." Elaina stepped forward, ignoring the scathing look Lydia sent her that said *I told you so.* "What does His Highness want of me?"

"His Highness offers you the services of one of his coaches should you need assistance in attending his presence." He paused, his hand halfway to the bag he wore slung over his shoulder. "Will you be needing such a service?"

"Now?"

The courier looked at the floor. "Yes, my lady."

Lydia seemed frozen in place, her eyes the size of plums and her mouth open in a little *o*.

Fury, however, rippled through Elaina. He'd had the audacity to use her to betray her own cousin, and then had betrayed Elaina herself. And now he was summoning her like a child? A sharp response for His Royal Highness was on the tip of her tongue when Aunt Charlotte entered the room.

"An escort will not be necessary," Elaina said, clearing her throat. "I thank you, but I will take my own carriage and guard. You can tell Prince Nicholas that I shall be on my way within a quarter hour."

The courier bowed and left, leaving Elaina alone with her confused aunt and sobbing cousin. Over Lydia's cries about their destitution and the end of all hope for respectable marriages, Elaina informed Aunt Charlotte that she hoped to be back in time for the midday meal.

ELAINA MIGHT HAVE ENJOYED her first glimpse of the palace's interior if she hadn't been so preoccupied with the reason for her visit. She might have found herself in awe of the gold-veined marble floors or paused to study the life-size paintings of men and women that stared down at her from their silver frames taller than her bedchamber. But there was no time to gawk, as the servant leading her walked so fast they were both nearly running by the time they reached a set of large wooden doors on the third floor.

What little she had seen of the palace should have prepared Elaina for the prince's study. But when she was ushered through the doors, the sheer number of books inside was more than over-whelming. Indeed, it was the largest library she had ever imag-ined, let alone seen. All four walls were covered entirely in books from floor to ceiling. They made Rosington's library feel like a peddler's cart. Surely this collection couldn't belong to such a flighty man as the prince.

"Never seen books before?"

Elaina whirled around to see a man with wavy gray hair leaning against a large wooden desk in the corner. His scowl looked as though it had been carved into his face.

"Never this many at once."

He only sniffed and looked down at the open book in his hands.

Elaina shook her head a little to herself and turned back to examine the books more closely. She had been summoned by the prince only to be left alone with a cantankerous old man. This day certainly wasn't turning out the way she had expected.

After nearly fifteen more minutes of waiting and walking about the room, Elaina turned away from a tall window that faced the sea.

"You wouldn't happen to know what I've been summoned here for, would you?"

He threw up his hands and rolled his eyes. "Of course I do, because the prince explains his every decision to his tutor." He slammed his thick tome back on a shelf and pulled down another. "I haven't the slightest idea."

Just as Elaina was considering her own sarcastic retort, the doors opened and the prince strolled in eating an apple. His rebellious brown hair stuck out even more than it had the day before, and he looked smug.

Elaina curtsied stiffly, to which the prince shook his head and swallowed a large bite. "No need for such formalities in here. I told Dustin here to do away with such years ago." He paused then held out his apple. "Bite?"

Elaina could only stare. How on earth had she been enraptured by this infuriating man just two days before?

"That's an interesting one." The prince nodded at the bookshelf. Elaina looked back at the book her hand still rested upon.

"*Strategies of Taljlekin Warfare*?" She made a face. "The man

83

who came up with these strategies was a pig. Besides, his theories on defense coordination are weak."

"So you've read it, I gather."

She shook her head. "No, I've seen his strategies in action, and they turn out poorly every time."

The prince folded his arms and leaned back, that hawkish look in his eye again. "Do tell."

"Was the lady in a rowboat to witness such dealings?" the tutor called across the room, scowling.

Elaina ignored him and folded her own arms to match the prince. "The left flank is always left open."

At this, the prince gave her a wide grin. "So if you dislike his strategies so greatly, which would you recommend?"

Where was he going with this? She studied him for a moment before answering. "I'm more of the classical approach. It takes more ships, but provides a less penetrable position in case of pirates."

The tutor slammed his book down and came to join them. "And what qualifies you to make such judgments? What expertise have you in recommending naval strategies to our future king?"

Nicholas didn't take his eyes from her. "Master Dustin, I would like you to meet Lady Elaina Starke, daughter of Admiral Baxter Starke."

The old man sputtered. "Very well then, but what's that got to do with her?"

"She's lived on my father's flagship for twelve years. I think that should be qualification enough. So," he turned back to Elaina, "you must be wondering why you're here."

"Yes, sire." Obviously.

He waved his hand at her. "Please, desist with the pleasantries. In fact, you are free to call me Nicholas. I would prefer it even."

"Sire will do just fine."

Her curtness didn't seem to bother him in the slightest. He tossed the half-eaten apple on his desk and sat in the chair behind it. Then he leaned back and placed his hands behind his head.

"Have a seat." He jutted his chin out at one of the three overstuffed leather chairs before the desk.

Elaina sat stiffly.

"Yesterday, you corrected me on a somewhat major detail concerning one of our most significant naval battles," he said, giving Master Dustin a sideways frown.

The old man only straightened his coat, avoiding Nicholas's eyes.

"If I have brought you offense," Elaina said in slow, measured words, "I apologize—"

But he held up his hand. "I don't wish for your apologies." He gestured at Master Dustin. "I pay this man lots of money to teach me about naval battles and strategy. When I take the throne, I wish to be familiar with my fighting men and their needs."

This conversation was taking a turn Elaina had not expected in the slightest.

Unfortunately, the prince seemed to recognize her surprise because a satisfied smile spread across his face. "Apparently this man is teaching me incorrectly."

"I most certainly am not!" Master Dustin cried.

"Really? How many ships are in my father's navy?"

"Two hundred."

"Lady Elaina?"

She huffed. "Two hundred and forty-six."

Prince Nicholas's smile only grew. "I visited our shipyard this morning, and according to the keeper there, Lady Elaina is correct. We have two hundred and forty-six."

"I suppose this means you will no longer be needing my services then." Master Dustin straightened his jacket. Elaina felt pity for him as he trudged toward the door, looking even older than he had a few minutes before.

"I never said that, Dustin." The prince's gaze softened a bit. "You've been a good friend, and you've faithfully fed my appetite for knowledge for years now. I couldn't let such a valuable asset or friend go so callously."

The old man turned around, hope lighting his features. "What of the girl then?"

"Lady Elaina will tutor us both."

"Sire," she said, scrambling for words. "Surely you can't mean—"

"But she's a woman!" Master Dustin sputtered. "No, not a woman but a mere girl!"

The prince held his hand up. "Dustin, I have great respect for all the hard work you've given me over these last four years. But you've never been on a naval vessel. You might learn more than you think outside of books for once. And you." He turned to Elaina. "I ask you to consider the fact that my father will not live forever. When the Maker takes him to his eternal rest, loathe as I am for that day to come, I'm sure you will want the king's successor to know enough about the navy to keep it afloat with proper funds and sound orders."

Whatever Elaina had been about to say, she promptly closed her mouth. She did, however, hold the prince's piercing gaze for a long moment as his words rolled about in her head.

Unfortunately, he was right. Her father wouldn't be the king's admiral forever. He wasn't much younger than the king himself. But even without him on the seas, Elaina pictured the faces of her father's crew as well as the faces of all those sailors beneath him she'd met over the years. Even if her father were safe and at home by the time Prince Nicholas took the throne, the rest of the navy would be at risk without a king who understood them and their needs.

She sighed. "Very well."

"Excellent. Please arrive here in my study each morning at the ninth hour. Excluding the holy day, of course. Dustin and I will await your every word with bated breath."

Glancing at Master Dustin's face, Elaina doubted that very much, but decided it would be best just to remain quiet.

After that Elaina was given her leave. When she started for the door, however, she noticed the prince trying to smother a laugh.

"May I ask what's so funny, sire?"

"Oh, only that I've never seen such misery in a young woman who's been asked to spend every day in the confidence of a handsome bachelor."

She gave him a sweet smile. "Of course, sire. Master Dustin's face is handsome indeed."

Prince Nicholas's laughter ceased, but Elaina felt quite light on her feet as she walked out the door.

CHAPTER 10
FOCUS, NICHOLAS

Nicholas picked up the remnant of his apple and shook his head as Dustin followed Elaina out of the study. He had been correct about her holding valuable knowledge. As soon as he'd met her, something had told him she knew more than many of his father's military advisers combined, and now he was convinced more than ever he was right.

But good gryphons, the girl had a tongue like a dagger. Nicholas grinned to himself as he stood and walked over to peruse the new pile of maps Dustin had left for him. He hadn't stumbled upon such an interesting soul in ages, particularly not one willing to stand up to him. Henri had been right. She hated him with a passion. Of course, that wasn't a great bother. On the contrary, he loved a challenge. And Elaina Starke would prove to be a delightful one, he was sure.

A knock sounded at the door.

"Yes?"

"Your father wishes to see you in his study, sire."

Nicholas still didn't look at the servant, this time because he didn't want her to see the annoyance flash across his face. "Thank you. That will be all."

As soon as the servant was safely gone, Nicholas pulled in a deep breath through his nose and blew it out slowly through his mouth. He had known this conversation was coming. His return to the palace the night before had been far too late. Not that he'd meant to stay out so long, but circumstances had changed and had forced him to make a choice. Now it was time to pay.

As Nicholas approached his father's study, located on the highest level of the sprawling palace, the door opened. Out slipped a servant woman carrying a tray of goblets, a half-finished cluster of grapes, and dried, sweetened meats. This might not have bothered Nicholas, except for the fact that she was smiling just a bit too widely to have been merely collecting the king's half-finished midday meal.

She stopped smiling as soon as she caught Nicholas's eye, and immediately her face whitened as she hurried past him. Yes, she seemed like just his father's type. Buxom, with black hair and an excessive amount of rouge. Nicholas shook his head and took a moment to steady himself before knocking. It would do him no good to anger his father before they'd had a chance to start their usual argument.

Still, he couldn't help himself completely.

"I see lunch was quite appetizing," he said dryly when his father called him in.

"Always is," his father answered without looking up from his desk.

Nicholas folded his hands behind his back and waited for the usual tongue-lashing to begin, but this time it was a full ten minutes before the king even spared him a glance.

"You were down in the city last night."

"I was."

His father finally looked at him directly, but Nicholas kept his eyes on the shimmering sea outside the window behind his father's desk.

"I shouldn't need to remind you how inappropriate it is for a royal to be sneaking about the city at night unattended. For the love of all that's holy, Nicholas, you're of nineteen years! Danger aside, we have enough trouble brewing for us in Solwhind without you causing more in the capital."

Ah, an opportunity.

"Do we have any news of Solwhind from our contact?"

"We do." His father stood and handed him a parchment. "King Everard has finished his assessment of the rebellion."

Nicholas scanned the document but couldn't suppress his surprise when he came to a familiar name. "Lady Elaina was present for their meeting."

"So it seems she was. Anyhow, Everard has concluded that a dark power is at the heart of all our troubles."

"That would make sense." Nicholas frowned as he continued skimming the report. "We hadn't even heard of this rebellion five years ago. Usually natural rebellions take years to gather. This one seems to have sprung up overnight. It's as though—"

"While I appreciate the good king's attempts and have sent him a gift of thanks to compensate him for his time, I'm not sure I agree."

"King Everard is the most knowledgeable source of information about power of any kind on the entire continent! Why in the depths not?"

"He is very talented, yes. But, I'm afraid, too quick to see dark powers in every corner of the world." His father sat down again and pulled out a clean parchment and a new bottle of ink. "Sometimes reconciliation can be made through simple negotiations."

Nicholas stared at his father, unable to keep from gaping. He wanted to remind his father that Xander himself had yet to step foot in Solwhind in over five years. If anyone was qualified to draw conclusions as to the foundations of the small but quickly growing movement across the bay, it wasn't him. But Nicholas had another question, and angering his father further wouldn't get it answered.

"Have there been any more killings reported?" he asked.

Without looking up, his father handed him another parchment. Nicholas retreated to an open chair by the west window and sat down to study it.

"Did you read this?" he asked his father when he was done.

"Yes."

"And six more gifted citizens murdered doesn't bother you?"

"These killings have been going on for years. I have a rebellion to quell and business as usual to keep up for the rest of the kingdom, despite our largest city being in turmoil. For all we know, it's thugs marauding citizens who are simply in the wrong place at the wrong time. I can't very well drop everything for thugs. That's what we have bailiffs for."

"But they will continue unless we do something about them!"

"Focus, Nicholas!" The king was on his feet. "I admire your desire to protect our citizens. I really do. But if our kingdom decides to tear itself in two, there will be a great many more than half a dozen dead on our doorstep."

"I understand." Nicholas growled. "Now may I be excused?"

"Go." His father sat back down with a gusty breath. "But stay out of the city! Do you understand me?"

Nicholas understood. But ignoring the names of the dead on the list he clutched was the last thing he intended to do.

CHAPTER II
BEING VAGUE

He was here and he didn't notify me?" Elaina looked at the dock keeper in disbelief.

The dock keeper pulled at his beard and gave her a look of sympathy. "I am sorry, Miss Elaina. Said his business was right urgent. Oh, but he did leave this." The dock keeper darted back into his little shack, surprisingly quick for a man of his age, and emerged carrying a box just larger than Elaina's fists put together.

Elaina sighed. "Thank you, Chapman."

"Chin up, now, Miss Elaina." Chapman's green eyes were kind in his sun-weathered face. "Won't be the last time the *Adroit* comes to harbor. If I know ahead of time, I'll make sure to send you a missive."

Elaina pulled the old man into a quick hug then turned with her box to search for a place to sit that was out of the sailors' way.

She hadn't given up on convincing her father to take her back. Far from it, she had come to the docks every day for the last three weeks for news of him and his ship. Her plan was perfect. As soon as he arrived, she would tell him that with the prince interested in her knowledge, he might as well take her back so she wasn't tempted to share her secret. But it seemed her father hadn't given up his intentions either. He hadn't even seen fit to summon her on the one day his ship was in port.

Elaina yanked the string off the box and slid the wooden slat off the top. The note that had been folded over and sealed with her father's favorite blue wax raised her ire more than ever, but the little baubles in the box melted her heart. She didn't even have to read the labels to know who each was from. A bottle the size of her thumb, filled with her favorite molasses, a cloth bag of roasted seeds, a miniature pine cone, two seashells, and a single, misshapen pearl.

They must have gone south for a few weeks before returning to the capital. Elaina was tempted to keep the gifts and throw her father's folded note off the side of the dock but then thought better of it. If she couldn't live on her beloved ocean, perhaps she could at least glean a bit of information about it.

Elaina,

The crew is well. I found a replacement for Tanner. He's quite young but has an eagerness about him Tanner couldn't have dreamed of. We're leaving port soon to meet with a new ambassador from Staroz. I hope you are adjusting well. Charge whatever you need to the estate. I take full blame if your wardrobe is somewhat lacking compared to those in the royal court. Just get whatever you need.

Your Father

NOT A SINGLE WISH for her return or even an *I miss you*. Before Elaina could follow through with her original plan to throw the note in the water, however, a familiar voice reached her ears.

What was he doing out here on the docks?

Elaina stuffed the note back in the box and slid the lid shut just as Prince Nicholas came into view. Miss Clover Belgrad, the ambassador's daughter, was on his arm, and he was pointing excitedly to different ships and the cargo that was being loaded on and off them. Miss Belgrad, however, had wrinkled up her button nose and looked to be enjoying the outing far less than he.

Though the prince wore women as often as he wore cuff links, as Elaina had discovered over the past three weeks, she was a bit surprised he had dared to bring a proper little thing such as the ambassador's daughter to the shipyard. Clearly she was anything but interested.

When they began to walk closer, Elaina realized she had no desire to talk with him any earlier than she had to. Their lessons would take place in exactly forty-five minutes, and she was not in a rush to begin. Not after her father had abandoned her again. But before she could find a place to hide, he called to her.

"Lady Elaina!"

Forcing a smile, Elaina stood, turned, and curtsied.

"Your Highness. Miss Belgrad. How nice to see you again."

Clover's dark eyes darted up to the prince's face before meeting Elaina's briefly. "Yes, I suppose it is."

Elaina waited for more, but it seemed that was all the girl would be saying. So she finally turned to the prince, who was beaming at her.

"Lady Elaina, I told you, please call me Nicholas."

"And I told you sire would suit perfectly well."

The prince ignored Clover's gasp and grinned shamelessly. "Imagine meeting you all the way out here!" He patted Clover's hand. "I was just showing Miss Belgrad where I escape to every chance I get." He looked back up at the ships, his bravado momentarily gone, leaving him with the look of an excited little boy. Elaina nearly laughed until he returned his gaze to her. "And what brings you out here so early?"

"I was inquiring about my father's ship."

He nodded at the little box in her hand. "It seems you got an answer."

"Of sorts." She sighed. "It appears he was in port, but only very briefly. He left me a note, but that was all he had time for."

The prince's face straightened into a rare look of solemnity. "I am sorry to hear that you missed him." Then he brightened again. "But since you're here, you might as well come with us. I was just on my way to escort Miss Belgrad back to her home. It's only a few streets over from the wharf. Master Dustin is feeling unwell today, so we might as well have our lesson out here."

Elaina opened her mouth to protest, but then closed it again. While walking alone with the prince was hardly her idea of a dream morning, walking out amongst the ships and sailors was preferable to spending an hour alone in the prince's study, even if the door was open and a servant posted outside for propriety's sake.

"Very well," she nodded, hesitating only for a second when he offered her his other arm.

ELAINA ONLY HALF-LISTENED to Clover's idle chatter as they walked. While it was amusing that Prince Nicholas's girl of choice was possibly one of the silliest women Elaina had ever met, Elaina couldn't help dwelling on her father's note. Its contents had been so meager. She would have to ask the stars for more information that night. They had been rather quiet as of late, talking gently to her whenever she was lonely, but speaking little about what she really wanted to hear.

"Lady Elaina?"

"Pardon me?"

They had all stopped and were standing before a long, thin, two-level home on a busy street. Prince Nicholas was saying something, and Clover was looking at Elaina as though she were the daft one.

"I apologize. I was distracted."

"I can see that. I was asking if you wouldn't mind waiting here while I return Miss Belgrad to her mother."

Elaina watched as the prince walked Clover up to her door. Halfway up, he stopped and made a pleading face at the girl, holding her hand to his chest.

Elaina didn't miss the triumphant glance Clover sent her way before blushing and pecking the prince on the lips.

Elaina rolled her eyes. Had he no boundaries?

As soon as Clover was properly returned to her mother, the prince bounded back to Elaina. "Well, this is just grand. Where shall our lesson commence?"

"Perhaps back at the wharf?"

"Excellent." He offered Elaina his arm, and with a small inward sigh, she took it. As always, however, she began to feel more relaxed as they neared the smell of brine and fish.

He glanced at her then did a double take. "Why do you keep touching your thumb to your lip like that?"

She jerked her thumb away from her lip. "It helps me think. Unlike your prying questions."

"And what does a lady such as yourself have to think so hard about?"

"Lady Starke!"

She turned at the sound of her name. A nearby sailor dropped a deep bow. She returned his smile and waved before allowing the prince to lead her to a low wall overlooking the entire wharf.

"Do you know him?" the prince asked as she positioned herself on a barrel where she could see the goings-on below.

"No. Why?"

"Then I'm impressed!"

"At what?"

He glanced down at her dress. "First of all, most women of

your status would faint before they allowed themselves to be seen sitting on a barrel of fish."

Elaina laughed in spite of herself. "I'm sure that's true."

"No, truly. It's refreshing to be around a woman who doesn't mind . . ." He paused. "Living. In the real world, I mean."

Before the compliment became too enjoyable, Elaina asked, "And what is the second thing that impresses you?"

"They treat you like royalty here. Not that I mind, of course, but I don't think that chap even recognized me."

"Probably not." Unable to help feeling a little smug, she hastened to add, "I've grown up around these people. When you spend years with them . . . getting to know their struggles and being in a position to see their needs, it changes you."

"I see." He sat himself on the barrel next to hers, and they watched the ships in silence.

If she were honest with herself, Elaina found it rather enjoyable. It had only been three weeks since she'd left the *Adroit*, but it felt like a lifetime had passed since she'd had anyone to share her love of ships with.

"You see that man over there?" She pointed.

"The one with the yellow stripes on his coat?"

Elaina nodded. "That's Captain Vogel. He's one of the twenty-five captains who answer to my father."

Nicholas studied the man. "Why twenty-five?"

"Your father has six admirals. Five are advisers who run back and forth between the captains and your father to discuss the needs and wants of the navy and help him strategize. My father is the sixth admiral. His status is technically equal to theirs, but on the sea, his word is second only to that of the king." She gestured at the two dozen stationary ships. "My father has twenty-five captains beneath him because each captain is answerable for up to ten vessels of his own. The captains report to my father, and while your father is consulting with his advisers, my father is there to make snap decisions in the case of an emergency, particularly when orders from the crown aren't readily available."

Prince Nicholas looked at Elaina, his blue eyes sharp once more. "Your father certainly has a heavy load."

"Not only is he responsible for the entire fleet during battle, but he's also the king's ambassador when matters are too delicate to discuss on land, or when other parties insist on meeting in neutral waters. Sometimes other kingdoms ask him to mediate their disagreements so that matters can be settled fairly in a neutral place."

"That seems like an unwieldy job without much return."

Elaina gave him a sideways smile. "Ah, but it would astound you how liberal individuals can be with their information when they believe you to be a disinterested party. Your father has gained much useful information that way."

"You sound as if you've been present at quite a few of these sensitive meetings."

"I probably shouldn't tell you this, but I've run a few of them myself."

At this, the prince slapped his knee and let out a loud shout of laughter. Getting to his feet again, he held his arm out to Elaina, and she took it. He was still laughing as they resumed their walk. "Do you know how livid my father's magistrates would be if they knew an underage girl has been running their international affairs?"

Elaina bit her lip. Why had she shared that?

But the prince was still chuckling.

"Your father wouldn't mind, if he found out?" she asked hesitantly. Drat it all! She'd become too comfortable and said too much. Why did the prince have that effect on everyone? On her?

"Your father could get drunk and jump in the water chained to a boulder, and my father would think it brilliant." Then his face darkened a tinge. "My father's advisers, on the other hand, are largely a bunch of sniveling cowards who can't see past the ends of their own noses."

"Oh. I see."

He shook his head. "I apologize. Other affairs sometimes

distract me from the present moment." His face resumed its lighter expression. "So how was life growing up on the king's flagship? You know I'm quite jealous."

Elaina smiled as she stepped over a pile of dead fish someone had spilled. "Wondrous. My father insisted I learn all the graces of court life for meetings with important guests, but I also learned how to read the clouds for weather, how to climb rigging, tie knots, and follow maps."

"Can you use a cutlass?"

"Heavens, no! My father's first mate, Lewis, tried to teach me countless time. He always said it was imperative that I learn how to defend myself, should we be boarded by pirates. But I was hopeless." She held up a hand. "In a sword fight, I would be about as useful as a goat."

The prince gave her that disarming smile he'd charmed her with the first time they'd met, and Elaina averted her eyes as quickly as was polite. Her head was in charge this time. Not her heart.

They had walked to the end of the wharf and were starting back. Elaina noticed, however, that the prince's face was becoming more and more thoughtful as they went, and she found that this made her a bit nervous.

Finally, he turned to her. "Pardon me for prying into personal matters, but why was it that your father took a little girl onto a warship in the first place, then raised her there for over a decade?" He paused. "You were little, weren't you?"

Elaina struggled to keep her face passive. "Five years."

"You were only five years?"

Elaina stopped and turned to him. "When my mother was murdered, heartbroken doesn't even begin to describe the state my father was in. My relatives asked him to leave me with them when he went back out to sea. He had duties to your father and had to make a choice. Stay with me or fulfill his oath to the king." She shrugged. "Unable to leave me behind, he chose both."

Once again, the prince looked more like a bird of prey than the jovial flirt. After a moment of studying her, he stepped back and tilted his head. "You're hiding something."

"Pardon me, sire?"

"I don't know what it is, but you're keeping something from me. Something important." He raised one brow and gave her a little satisfied smile. "And though it may take me some time, I'm determined to find out what it is."

All the feelings of tolerance and distant amusement that Elaina had allowed during parts of their walk vanished. The prince might be more familiar to her now than he had been at the tea, but he was still just as dangerous as ever.

CHAPTER 12
NOTHING TO PRETEND ABOUT

E laina was decently proud of herself for finding her way to the prince's study. It had only taken her five weeks to learn her way through the never-ending maze of cavernous palace halls. Her elation dulled a bit, however, when she realized that Master Dustin was the only other person in the room. His joy, or lack thereof, was always infectious.

"Good morning, Master Dustin."

As she expected, he didn't even look up from the book he was reading.

Laying down her reticule, Elaina took up her usual chair, the one in the corner of the room farthest from the prince's desk. There she waited as she watched the shining waves through the narrow floor-to-ceiling window that created a gap between bookshelves. The silence grew heavier by the second, and after twenty minutes, Elaina concluded that if being alone with Prince Nicholas was undesirable, being alone with Master Dustin was possibly worse. Still, she waited.

And still no prince.

"Where do you suppose he might be?" she finally ventured to ask.

The older man shrugged his thin shoulders. "How am I to know?"

"Does he ever miss lessons completely?" If the prince wasn't going to show up, she had better things to do than sit around in angry silence with a grumpy old man.

Master Dustin drew a deep breath and let it out before closing his book with a thump. "The monarchs have their needs and their wants. Lessons are a *want* of the prince's. Sometimes other *needs* take precedence."

"Oh."

More silence.

"So," Elaina paused, hoping not to offend the old man again, "if you don't mind me asking, how did you become employed by the royal family?"

He scowled. "The prince sought me out when I was working as an adviser to a captain."

"So you were in the navy?"

"No. But I am a scholar, and my particular area of study was under a rather infamous explorer. I worked as his scribe for many years, during which time I was encouraged to seek and read of many historical battles and strategies."

Elaina nodded. This made sense. While Master Dustin knew much in theory, there was little about true life on the ocean or the navy's function that he really seemed to understand. Still, she could see how his knowledge of history could benefit a young man like the prince.

"So it wasn't the king who desired a tutor for his son?"

Master Dustin snorted. "The king approves of me about as much as I approve of you." He sent her a wry look, and Elaina laughed. "But the young prince is a headstrong fellow," he continued in a more subdued tone. "Trying to contain his enthusiasm for the military is like trying to hold back a storm. So his father allows him liberties here and there to keep him pacified." He looked down at the book in his hands, and his bushy brows drew together. "I suppose—" But then he stopped and just shook his head.

Elaina left her chair, daring to come a few steps closer. "What is it?"

"Nothing of public concern. Just an old man's musings." He began to straighten his clothes and looked as though he might walk out the door, but Elaina wasn't ready to let him go just yet. The prince was turning into more of a mystery than she had expected. There was more to the young man than unbridled flirting and fun. She had seen it in his eyes when they'd walked on the wharf and then several times since. With his sudden interest in her secret, she needed to solve his mysteries before he solved hers.

"Please." She put her hand gently on the old man's arm and gave it a little squeeze. "If I am to serve this prince as you do, I wish to know how to guard my words and my steps."

The old man grimaced at her for a moment as he toyed with his silver mustache, then he blinked a few times, as though surprised. "You worry about him?"

Praying he wouldn't rat her out, Elaina swallowed. "I think of him often."

"My dear," he said, his voice more passionate than she'd ever heard it. "It is not the prince's activities or interests that you need to be concerned about. I've been offered several positions since being employed by Prince Nicholas, positions closer to my family back in the southern hills. But I stay because I want him to succeed against the forces he is fighting."

"Forces?"

"Lady Elaina, our prince is far more interested in righting wrongs than our king, who will pursue peace at any cost. They both want what's best for the kingdom, but only one is willing to take the long, difficult road to get peace the right way." He shook his head, his thin face solemn. "I fear that if our prince is left all on his own, not only his father, but also the magistrates and other politicians will slowly eat him up, one at a time."

"You mean hurt him?"

"There are more ways to kill a man than by taking his life." He took a shaky breath. "In my time, I've seen strong wills crumble and souls reduced to remnants of the men they once were." He turned and walked to the door before pausing and placing a hand on its post. "Don't be so quick to judge him. Our prince is fighting a battle far larger than anyone in this court is aware of. And it's better if we keep it that way."

ELAINA TOOK her cue from Master Dustin and left the prince's study. When they parted ways, she felt a kinship with the old man she had never felt before. This would have been comforting, except for the new knowledge he had presented her with. Rather than clearing up the prince's mysterious stares and occasionally cloudy expressions, the tutor had only served to confuse her even more.

Did Nicholas's determination to find out her secret have to do with his own secrets? Or was he merely trying to turn her into another one of his conquests?

Elaina's head hurt by the time her carriage reached town. Though she had her guard—a gift from the king to her father at his behest—she now usually left him at the house when she went out. She'd grown familiar enough with her quarter of the city to know where she was going, and as many of the activities her aunt deemed proper involved sitting in the house, Elaina tried to walk as much as possible, slipping out while her relatives' backs were turned.

Today was especially nice for walking, so she left her carriage and its driver to rest just outside the square and continued into the market alone. Though the nippy air of autumn had indeed come, this late morning was deliciously warm. So much so that Elaina decided to tarry a little in the market shops and stalls. She had just ventured into a little shop that sold candles when she heard a familiar voice behind her.

"Elaina!"

"Lydia!" Elaina turned and smiled. "What a nice surprise."

"I thought you were meeting with the prince this morning." Lydia's mouth turned down just a hair.

"I was going to, but his tutor and I gave up waiting when he was twenty minutes late."

"Oh, that's a shame." But really, Lydia didn't sound as though it were a shame at all.

Elaina hurried to change the subject. "What are you doing here?"

"Oh." Lydia wrinkled her nose daintily and adjusted her sun hat. "Mother gets headaches from tallow candles. She needs the ones made of beeswax, so I was sent out to get some fresh air and fetch some for her on the way."

Elaina decided not to comment on Lydia's need for fresh air. Since the queen's tea, Lydia had hardly left the house. The bubbly, giddy girl that had greeted Elaina on her first day in the capital had never reappeared.

"After this, would you like to go to the ribbon shop with me?" Elaina asked instead.

"Of course. What for?"

Elaina gave her a sly smile. "I noticed Lord Devon eyeing you in that lavender gown at supper the other night. I thought I might get you a matching ribbon for when we see his family at the carnival."

"Really?" Lydia rummaged through a stack of candlesticks, but refused to meet Elaina's eye. "That's very thoughtful of you."

Elaina sighed. She, like her aunt, was running out of ideas.

As soon as they had chosen and paid for the candlesticks, Elaina and Lydia crossed the street to a slightly larger shop. Inside hung ribbons of all widths and colors. They fluttered as the girls opened and closed the door.

"So what do you and Nicholas do at your little rendezvous?" Lydia asked a touch too nonchalantly as they began perusing the ribbons.

Elaina headed straight for the purple section. "I think our

lessons could be called anything except rendezvous. They're nothing intimate, if that's what you mean. We discuss military strategy and organization. I mostly argue with his tutor, Master Dustin."

Lydia arched one perfect blonde eyebrow and peeked out from behind the green section. "You mean to say you spend two hours a day, six days a week talking about ships?"

"That is exactly what we do. Now come here and hold still." When Lydia did as she asked, Elaina held up two ribbons against her hair. "Hm, I think this one. But this one here might be a shade closer to your dress. What do you think?"

"I think you're telling me a falsehood."

Elaina huffed and tilted her head back to stare at the ceiling. "You can ask Master Dustin. That is really all we do, I promise." She looked warily at her cousin. "Truly, are you bothered so much by these lessons?"

Lydia's eyes tightened.

Elaina put her ribbons down and took Lydia gently by the shoulders. "I swear. I am only there because the prince insists upon it. Look, I wouldn't attend if it were up to me. You saw him summon me."

Lydia went back to looking at ribbons, moving to the yellow silks this time. "You are right. I'm sorry. I only . . . I only loathe the idea of seeing you hurt." She twisted a long blonde curl in her left hand. "I was foolish enough to believe he cared for me. But really, who can blame me? I mean, he's always been rather quick to move between his girls, but he spent three months favoring me. Three months, Elaina."

Elaina could only watch, her heart heavy.

"All that time he favored me, sought me out before all the others. And then the moment you showed up, all of that attention was gone. It was as if we had only ever been old acquaintances." Lydia held a ribbon up only to discard it. "I'll admit, I was horribly angry with you. I knew it wasn't your fault, of course. But seeing you with him, being drawn in just as quickly as I had been drawn in ... it hurt."

"What changed your mind?"

"Clover Belgrad. As soon as he left his new toy for an even newer one, I knew it wasn't your fault." She peeked wanly up at Elaina. "I suppose I was also a bit jealous at just how quickly you were able to recover. And ... how well you were able to push back."

Elaina chuckled. "My tongue is quick, but it will get me in deep trouble one day. Or so my father says. And," she stared hard at the two ribbons she was still holding, "I suppose I was a bit resentful of the fact that he had only been enamored for a day. I mean, he's still with her if that makes you feel any better. Apparently, I can't hold a candle to Clover Belgrad."

Lydia's eyes went wide. "Oh, I'm afraid you very well can hold a candle to Clover. Have you seen the way he looks at you even when we're in public?"

Of course Elaina had seen it. That look of hawkish interest never failed to appear at some point whenever they met at palace events or crossed paths when calling on friends.

"I'm afraid the prince is more interested in pursuing you than ever," Lydia said solemnly. "You've proven to be a worthy opponent. And if there's one thing the prince likes, it's a battle."

THAT NIGHT, as Elaina prepared for bed, she continued to hear Lydia's words echo in her mind.

"I believe she means well," she told the stars as she pushed open her heavy window. "But I can't help the feeling that she's still more than a little jealous as well."

She is. But is there truly anything you can do about that?

"No, there really isn't."

What was it her father often said? *There are often two sides to people. There's the side they want others to see and the side they wish wasn't there at all.*

"I am, however," Elaina continued to the stars, "going to do my best to appear as unattached to him as possible.

He might make that difficult. The farther you step back, the closer he comes.

"I know. But I like Lydia. I've never had a good friend like her . . . not a female one, anyway. Besides, it shouldn't be hard to convince her in time." She paused. "You wouldn't be able to tell me what he's hiding, though, would you?"

We see only what the Maker shows us. Now go to bed, Elaina.

Elaina obeyed and bid the stars a weary good night. But as she drifted off to sleep, she made two resolutions.

First, she would find out what the prince was hiding.

Second, she would convince Lydia that she was not in love with the prince. And she wouldn't even have to pretend, for there was nothing to pretend about.

CHAPTER 13
I DON'T CRY

"Winter is such an odd time for a carnival to come to town." Elaina looked doubtfully at the dusting of sugary snow that covered the dozens of lines of merchant tents.

"Winter came early this year," Lydia said after daintily licking her candied apple. "Usually autumn is at its peak at this time. Here, eat your apple before it falls off your stick."

"This is exciting, of course," Elaina said as she looked out at the hundreds of merchants and vendors that were calling out their wares, "but what exactly is the carnival's purpose?"

"About ten years ago, King Xander invited merchants, peddlers, performers, any tradesman that could travel to make money, really, and offered to pay their travel expenses. Winter is a poorer time for many, so he wanted a way to boost trade one last time before the slow part of winter came." Lydia shrugged, her green gown glistening even in the dull light of the cloudy day. "We've had it every year since. I think it was a brilliant idea."

"I have to agree."

Despite the white powder that coated everything, including the little boys that dashed past everyone and kicked up mud, Elaina found herself enjoying the carnival immensely. Nicholas had given her the day off from lessons, more so that he could attend the carnival, she suspected, than out of generosity to her, but that didn't really matter. In the two weeks since her discussion with Lydia in the ribbon store, she and Lydia had found themselves quite inseparable. Though she wouldn't trade her years at sea for anything, Elaina did wish she'd had the chance to enjoy the benefits of female companionship years sooner.

"How are your lessons with Prince Nicholas faring?" Aunt Charlotte asked. Their little trio paused to watch a man grow a flower by simply planting a seed and staring at the ground. As the crowd surrounding him clapped and cheered, Elaina found herself slightly envious. He didn't have to hide his talent so meticulously.

"Well, I suppose. His tutor doesn't resent me quite as much as he did at first, although we still argue at least half of every lesson. Oh, let us go look at that vendor. I should like to have some raspberry bushes in the garden next year."

"But how does the prince treat such lessons?" her aunt pressed. "Surely he appreciates the sacrifice of time you're making to give him such treatment."

Elaina groaned inwardly. One glance at Lydia's pale face was warning enough to tread carefully. "I think he enjoys seeing the debates as much as he does learning about ships."

"But is the prince—"

"He's a quick learner, though. And quite dedicated to ensuring the navy has all it needs. Oh, Lydia! Look at those reticules! Let us go see them."

As her cousin escorted her over to the merchant selling the reticules, Elaina breathed a sigh of relief. She hoped her aunt found her answer satisfactory and would allow her leave from any further discussion. Saying that the prince was a quick learner was an understatement. When he wasn't being impertinent, Nicholas was forever surprising her with new ways to consider strategy, and his appetite to learn was voracious. Getting his mouth to stop, of course, was the real trick.

But Lydia needed to know none of that.

Somewhere along the way, they lost her aunt to an old friend, so Lydia and Elaina continued on together. But their solitude couldn't last. Just as they rounded a corner to look at a cart selling unusually colored bottles of ink, Elaina found herself face-to-face with the prince.

Lydia's predicament was even worse. She was nose-to-nose with Clover's recent replacement, some girl from Vaksam who was distantly related to Willard Appleby. Behind the prince and his newest arm decoration stood a collection of young men and women.

"Elaina!" The prince looked much too delighted.

"Sire."

"Please, I've asked you to call me Nicholas."

"And I've told you that sire will do quite nicely."

Nicholas rolled his eyes and smiled down at the girl on his arm. "You see what my subjects think of me? This is the one I told you about, the one who grew up on a ship."

A look of panic passed over the girl's round face, so Elaina sent the girl her most reassuring smile. "It seems the prince believes all women share his affinity for sailing. I fear he doesn't realize just how odd I truly am for it."

The girl nodded, but the panic didn't quite leave her face. Nor did it leave Lydia's.

"How fares your father?" Nicholas asked.

"I'm afraid he hasn't yet been back to port. He's usually heading east this time of year. I hope to have some news from him soon, though." Perhaps if she could pacify him enough, he and his entourage would continue on and leave her alone.

"Lady Elaina!" someone from behind the prince called out.

Elaina wanted to cringe when she saw that it was Willard Appleby. "The prince here tells us that you learned to climb rigging when you were on the ship. Gown and all. That must have been quite a sight from below." His brown eyes were bright with an interest Elaina wanted to slap off his face.

To Elaina's surprise, however, she didn't have to set the young man straight, for it was Nicholas who snapped at him first. "Willard, enough!"

"Is it true, though?" another young man asked.

Elaina's annoyance melted a little when she recognized him as one of their neighbors. He was barely twelve and usually soft-spoken. "Can you climb rigging?" Unlike Willard's hungry eyes, the boy looked merely in awe.

"My father had special dresses designed for me so that in an emergency, I could do whatever I needed to do to stay safe."

"You wouldn't be wearing such clothes now, would you?"

Elaina turned back to Nicholas, who looked quite pleased with himself.

"Why?"

"Follow me." He set off, then paused and looked back when Elaina and Lydia stayed put. "Well, aren't you coming?"

Elaina glanced at Lydia and shrugged helplessly before starting toward him. Behind her, she heard Lydia sigh before following them as well.

After a few minutes of walking, they reached a stall with a surprising sort of structure standing beside it. Two poles had been erected in the center of the merchant's patch of ground where another tent might have stood beside the first. Ship's rigging, already tied into footholds, had been anchored to the ground with wooden stakes and stretched up to the top of the two tallest poles, where a bell hung from each. It looked just like the miniature rigging on a ship, the part that might lead up to the crow's nest.

"What is this?" Elaina asked.

But Nicholas only smiled. "What are the five most common sailing knots?"

"Really?" Elaina put her hands on her hips. "You gave me the day off."

Nicholas's smile only grew. "I'm not forcing you, am I? You're perfectly free to walk away if you wish."

Elaina rolled her eyes before looking back at the dangling

ropes. "The encasement, the snake, the noose, the moat, and the sheet bend."

"Girl's got a good sense of sailing knowledge there." A man with leathery skin and unkempt hair stepped forward.

"That she does," Nicholas said, reaching into his coat pocket. He held up two coins. "In fact, she's so good, I am willing to make a bet with her."

He had lost his mind.

Elaina tilted her head. "For what?"

"Beat me by climbing this rigging, tying every knot you just named, and ringing the bell first, and you win."

"What would I win?"

"What do you want?"

Elaina crossed her arms and studied him. Was he in earnest? There was only one way to find out. "Very well. I would want our lessons to take place five days a week instead of six." She paused. "But if you win?"

"I could ask for that curious bracelet you're always wearing. I have the feeling it would make for a good story." He looked smug as Elaina immediately covered her wooden bracelet with her hand. "But as I get the feeling you'll never part with it willingly, my prize would be that you allow me to be your partner at some formal event. A tea, a ball, who knows?" He gave her a ridiculous grin and waggled his eyebrows. "I get to choose."

Gasps went up from his entourage. The girls looked as scandalized as the boys looked excited.

"You don't have to do this," Lydia whispered, tugging on her arm.

"Absolutely not." Elaina shook her head and turned.

"Why not?" the prince demanded.

"You'd cheat." She took her cousin's arm and began to walk away. Before she got five steps, though, Nicholas called out behind her.

"You're just afraid you'll lose."

Elaina heard Lydia groan, but she whirled around anyway. "What did you say?"

"I said you're not going to climb because you know you'll lose . . . like a woman."

She should have seen it there in his eyes, that hawkish calculating look again. But Elaina was too far gone to care. Yanking off her fur wrap and shoving it at her cousin, she began hiking up her skirts as she marched back toward the little crowd, immensely thankful she had worn her special pantaloons that morning. Hopefully, her aunt wouldn't see her or the wrinkles this was sure to put in her new maroon dress.

But this was something she needed to do. For while Elaina couldn't punish her father for his hurtful words and lack of confidence in her abilities, she could surely beat the prince. And she could do it soundly, too.

"They're just trousers beneath," Willard whined. "Just fluffy trousers!"

Elaina sent him a deadly look before turning back to the prince. "You're on."

Nicholas swept into a deep bow before asking the girl on his arm for a kiss for good luck.

The man who had admired Elaina's knowledge of knots earlier seemed a little surprised when he found it was she who would be playing his game. But an extra coin from the prince quieted all of his protests about impropriety. Soon she and Nicholas were poised at the bottom of the rigging. Elaina's muscles were on fire already, yearning to do what they knew so well and had been denied so long.

She would win. She would get an extra day off. And maybe the prince and some of his obnoxious friends would learn to keep their mouths shut.

At the sound of a whistle, they were off. Elaina's fingers flew in and out of the rope without pause. Despite not having touched rigging in nearly two months, there was no hesitation. It was as though she had been born at sea.

To her surprise, however, out of the corner of her eye, she could see the prince keeping a steady pace as well. He wasn't quite as fast, but fast enough that if she made a single mistake, he would catch her in a moment.

Cheers went up from the group below. Elaina was pleasantly surprised to hear Lydia's voice as well, chanting her name in encouragement. Perhaps her request of less time with the prince had been the convincing factor. Determined to get that extra day off, Elaina pushed harder. She had only one knot to go. The sheet bend knot was the most complicated of all, but that didn't bother Elaina a bit. The knot was done in seconds.

Elaina's heart nearly stopped, however, when she reached the top of the rigging and tried to grab the bell. It should have been simple. She should have won by now.

But she was too short.

She couldn't even reach it, let alone ring it. She wrapped both feet around the knot she had just made and began to haul herself higher. Just as she pulled herself up to grasp the bell, however, the bell beside hers began to ring.

When she looked to her left, Nicholas stood steadily atop not even the highest part of the rope ladder, but the third rung down. And he was glowing.

Elaina closed her eyes and wanted to melt then and there. Before she could attempt to do so, however, her aunt called her name from below.

Could she have done anything more foolish?

Slowly, Elaina untangled herself from the ropes and climbed down the rigging, pulling her dress out of her pantaloons as stealthily as she could. Ignoring the cheers and laughs coming from the prince's group, she dragged herself up to her aunt. She could already hear the lecture. Her aunt wasn't her mother, but she had loved her mother very much, and it was only love for her that forced Charlotte to become strict with Elaina. The impropriety of a girl of nearly eighteen years hanging from suspended ropes was beyond shocking.

The imagined tirade continued in Elaina's head until she finally dared to meet her aunt's eyes. The pallor in her aunt's face, however, stopped her in her tracks.

"What is it?" she asked. Why was her voice so squeaky?

Elaina felt her stomach drop as, with a shaking hand, Charlotte handed her a parchment.

The broken wax seal was red. Elaina swallowed hard as she unfolded the letter. The writing was in the dock keeper's stiff hand.

~~Miss~~ Lady Elaina Starke,

I regret to inform you and your kin that the Adroit has failed to report as expected at port. No word or signal has been heard from Admiral Baxter Starke or his crew in two weeks. A search is underway now. I will inform you if anything is found.

Elaina put her hand over her mouth, but no sound came out.

"Elaina, I'm so sorry," Charlotte began to say, but Elaina could only shake her head.

"I . . . I need a few moments."

"I understand." Charlotte paused. "But we are here when you need us."

Elaina nodded faintly and walked away as though in a cloud. The crowds around her began to disappear into the sudden fog that filled her world. Without considering which way she was going, Elaina continued to move. She needed to get away. She needed to be alone.

It was not as though a missing ship was unheard of. Elaina had tracked a fair number in her days upon the *Adroit*. Some were found. Others were not. Storms, pirates, disease, there were an infinite number of reasons a ship might not come to harbor. That was the harsh reality of being a sailor in the king's navy.

But that was not what was eating her inside.

"Elaina!"

Elaina closed her eyes. *Just make him go away,* she prayed.

But the Maker did not listen. The prince came running up from behind her. He swerved around her and stopped so that he was blocking her path.

"I saw your aunt crying." He frowned. "What has happened?"

Not trusting herself to speak, Elaina handed him the note.

Upon reading it, he closed his own eyes and let out a deep breath. "I . . . I'm so sorry."

Elaina took the note back and began walking again. But the prince did not take her hint. Instead, he hovered beside her.

"Please, let me know if there's anything I can do." When she didn't answer, he took her by the shoulders and made her stop again. "In truth! You're the one who knows what to do in these situations! Tell me what we need to do so that we can find him. Say the word, and it will be done."

"You saw the message." Elaina's voice sounded distant and cold. "They're searching already. There's nothing more to do."

"Surely there must be something . . ." He let go of her shoulders and ran his hands through his hair. "I mean, it's acceptable if you want to cry even." He let out a sad attempt at a chuckle. "I won't tell anyone. I promise."

"I don't cry." She stared back down at the note. "I haven't cried since I was eight, on the third anniversary of my mother's death when I realized she was never coming back."

Nicholas gave her a long, strange look. "So you're just going to—"

"I just need to be by myself!" she cried out. "Is that so much to ask?"

He watched her a moment longer before slowly shaking his head. "No. It is not. But Elaina?"

Elaina stopped, but didn't turn to look at him.

"It's only human not to be strong all the time. You don't have to bear every burden alone."

Elaina had no more words with which to answer. The world had turned upside down, and it was all she could manage to stay upright and walk away.

CHAPTER 14
WHAT THE STARS SAY

The emptiness on Elaina's face bothered Nicholas for the rest of the day. The carnival lost all of its amusement, even with the new girl on his arm. And when he made some lame excuse to leave early, something about a stomachache from too many sweets, he knew no one believed it. Not even the somewhat simple girl from Vaksam.

He still couldn't get Elaina out of his head by the time dusk had fallen. And yet he had to, if only for a few hours. One misstep, and the day would get much, much worse.

"Four loaves, as usual," the cook murmured when Nicholas snuck down to the kitchens. She jerked her chin toward a dark blue bag on the counter, not looking up from the bread she was kneading.

Nicholas pecked her a kiss on the cheek. "You're marvelous."

Her calloused flour-covered hands finally paused. "You need to be careful. Your father was here this morning asking about you."

Nicholas stuffed the bag of bread beneath his cloak. "He's . . . occupied tonight. I should be fine."

The woman sighed, the dark circles beneath her eyes looking deeper than usual. She gave Nicholas a sad smile. "Even so. I'm not sure exactly what it is that you do out there, but I would hate to see you get caught."

Nicholas thanked her once more and slipped back out of the kitchens and into the stables. After saddling his horse, he waited until a cloud moved over the moon. The overcast sky had cleared earlier that evening, so he would have to rely on the shadows of random clouds until he reached the inner part of the city.

It was no small distance between the palace and his destination, past the market and the neighborhoods and smaller estates of his wealthier courtiers, past the prosperous homes of merchants and others who had come into money, to the small corner of the city that few of his class even knew existed. Still, he knew the route by heart, and there was no sign of his father's guards by the time he dismounted and pulled his horse into the lightless alley between two shacks.

"You're late," a voice rasped from the darkness.

"I had to wait until my absence would be unnoticed," Nicholas replied. "Now what's this about?"

"He took another last night."

"Where?"

"Not two streets from here. A woman named Casey."

"Didn't she work in the bakery on the—"

"That's the one. Found her this morning behind her shop."

"He's getting faster." Nicholas groaned. Then he sighed and squeezed his eyes shut, trying to remember his schedule for the next week. "Did she have any relatives?"

"A brother and an aging mother. Mother owns the bakery but can't run it much alone anymore. Casey and her brother did all the work."

"Blast. I won't be able to get out again for another three days. Think she would meet with me then?"

"I think her son would be more help. But aye, I can bring them both."

"Good." Nicholas pulled the bag of bread from his cloak and held it out. "Take this. And these." He dug into his pocket for a few coins. "Thank you again. Make sure your little girl gets a decent pair of shoes. Last I saw her, she'd grown another six inches."

Nicholas could barely make out the shadowed figure tipping his hat. "Honored, sire. Much obliged." And with that, Nicholas was alone.

He knew tarrying would be unwise, but Nicholas couldn't bring himself to hurry back to the palace. Instead, he directed his horse to the western outskirts of town that edged the water. The low roar of the ocean was soothing. It helped drown out the voice of frustration that was screaming inside his head as he slowly made his way north toward the palace.

A small sound interrupted his tumultuous thoughts. At first he thought himself to be imagining things. Sometimes the water's gurgles were deceptive. But the farther he rode, the louder the sound became. After a minute, he could distinguish a voice.

A familiar voice.

He stopped his mount and strained to hear. He'd reached the main naval dock, but there was no one to be seen. The only sign of life came from the distant glow of the dock keeper's lantern that hung outside his little shack.

But there. A movement caught his eye. Sitting on the dock's edge with her legs dangling over the water was a woman.

Nicholas jumped down and tied his horse to a post. Was she out of her mind? What woman went to the docks alone at night? His curiosity was answered, however, when he heard her voice again.

The dull ache of borrowed sorrow filled his chest as he took his cloak off and began to walk slowly toward her so as not to frighten the poor thing.

"Did I miss something?"

Nicholas froze. Was she speaking to him?

"I thought I'd listened every night," she continued. "But maybe I fell asleep . . ." Her voice faltered. "Sometimes I do that, and I don't hear." She paused, tilting her head. "Was it my fault?"

"You're going to freeze to death if you stay out here much longer," he said gently as he dropped the cloak over her shoulders.

Elaina's head jerked up. For a moment, panic filled her face, sharpening the ache in his chest. Then she closed her eyes and let out a deep breath.

"It's a bit late to watch the sunset, don't you think?" He sat beside her and dangled his own legs over the water. In the bright light of the moon, he tried to study her face without looking too conspicuous. Had her sanity fled her in her sorrow? Should he fetch her aunt? Had she *walked* all the way here? At night?

"After my mother died, my father never spoke of her."

Nicholas stared at her. When was the last time she had volunteered to speak with him? Had she ever?

She paused and tilted her head up to the sky again, seemingly oblivious to his shock.

Even in the darkness, Nicholas couldn't help but admire the graceful shape of her neck. There was an openness to her face, her posture, that he had never seen before. It was as though he was finally getting to meet her for the first time.

"But as long as he was alive," she whispered, "so was my mother in a way."

Nicholas found himself at a loss for words, something he was unaccustomed to. And he hated it. Finally, he forced himself to say the first thing that came to mind. "What are they saying?"

"What?"

He smiled and pointed back up to the sky. "You keep looking at the stars as though they speak to you."

She shook her head and looked back down at the water, shuddering delicately.

He tried again. "Sometimes we find words in places we don't expect. Are the stars talking to you tonight?" He chuckled. "I found wisdom in a turtle once. Of course, that was after I'd put it in my sister's room, not realizing my mother would be taking tea there with Sophia's friends." He paused when she didn't answer. "Elaina?"

"No matter where we sailed, I could see the stars. I suppose they make me feel close to him. Wherever he is."

Nicholas wanted so badly to take her hands. They looked even smaller than usual in her lap, vulnerable without gloves or a muff to cover them. It was a strange feeling though, for his desire wasn't to scoop them up the way he did the arms of pretty girls at parties. Not that she wasn't pretty, but . . . this time he simply yearned to comfort, to protect. He wanted to make her pain go away.

"I hate to be the one to say this," he finally said after she shivered again, "but isn't it about time you head home? The ninth bell just tolled."

She nodded wearily, and he hopped to his feet before reaching down to help her up. As soon as she was standing, he allowed her hand to drop. As much as it pained him, tonight he wouldn't press. In fact, his desire to flirt with her had evaporated entirely. He only wanted to help.

"Do you . . . do you mind if I walk you home?"

"If you wish."

The air was heavy, sounds of the ocean filling it like fog too thick for any of the questions he was dying to ask.

"What do you mean?" She whirled around and looked up at the sky.

"I didn't say anything. Who are you talking to?"

She stared at the sky for another moment before shaking her head and turning back to him. "No one."

"Elaina, who were you talking to?"

When she looked at the ground, he took her by the arms and held her there in case she decided to bolt. "There is no one here but us. And I did not utter a word."

She avoided his eyes, but the glance she let slip to the sky told him all he needed to know.

Why a father would risk raising his five-year-old daughter on a warship.

Why she was so defensive.

Why she was talking to the stars.

Without pausing to think about what he was doing, Nicholas grabbed her hand and sprinted toward his horse. Before he even untied the beast, he had her up and in the saddle.

"What are you doing?" she cried, but he hissed up for her to be quiet. As soon as his horse was freed from the post, he threw himself into the saddle behind her.

"Really! What is this? Let me down!"

"Shut up and hold on," he growled in her ear. Then he threw one arm around her waist and with the other sent the horse flying east. "There is someone out here killing people like you. Another one died last night. I'd like you not to be his next victim."

Elaina stopped fighting and turned as well as she could to look at him.

"Just hang on tight and lay low." Nicholas was nearly giddy with relief that he had placed his cloak over her shoulders earlier. It helped hide the shiny gown she was wearing as they cut through the black streets under the bright light of the moon.

Neither of them spoke again until they reached the east side of the city where the manors spread out across the plain. "Which one is yours?" Nicholas whispered. He was fairly sure her mother had lived on this lane.

"The one with the columns and blue trim. Two manors down." She wasn't fighting him anymore, but he could feel her body wound like a spring as he leaned forward to shield her with his own.

When they made it to the gate, Elaina called down for the star-tled gate guard to let them in. Nicholas didn't allow her off the horse, however, until they had rounded the manor and reached the kitchen door. As soon as they were stopped, he sat up and let her slide to the ground.

She straightened and dusted her gown off with some indigna-tion, but Nicholas didn't miss the trembling of her hands.

"Once you're inside, I'm going to have some stern words with your guard." He hadn't been aware that she even had a palace guard until just now, but he hadn't missed the white and blue uniform of the man leaning against a column as they had bolted past. Now that he understood the nature of her father's worry, however, he had a good idea as to why her father might have requested the extra protection. Not that such an idle guard would do her any good. "I want you to go inside now and stay there until I return and get you myself. Don't even go out with a guard. Only me."

"Your Highness! I am perfectly capable of looking out for myself."

"I don't care what you think you're capable of right now. There is an evil in this city that you don't know or understand. You are to stay here." She opened her mouth, but he cut her off. "That's an order."

CHAPTER 15
VULNERABLE

Elaina hardly slept at all that night. Instead, she tossed and turned in pointless, hazy dreams that hovered somewhere between unconsciousness and reality. Her father's disappearance mixed with the prince's anger until they created one miserable dream. Only when the sky began to gray was she finally able to rouse herself from the awful sticky fog that clouded her thoughts.

For lack of better things to do, Elaina dragged herself out of bed, washed her face, dressed, and pulled her hair up. Then she made her way down the stairs, where she met her aunt.

"Did you happen to hear that clatter last night?" Charlotte yawned. "I don't remember when, but it sounded like a stampede was running across our lawn." She shook her head as though to clear it. "When I looked, however, there was nothing. I suppose I should ask Jeffrey—"

"Mother!"

Before Elaina could answer her aunt, Lydia hurried down the stairs. She was unusually disheveled in her dressing gown with her hair still wrapped in rags. "Mother, last night I saw Elaina ride in with the prince on his horse—"

"Lydia!" Charlotte's tone was sharper than Elaina had ever

heard it before. "Get control of yourself!" She shot a look at the servants who had paused to watch the scene. "We will discuss this in private." She turned a fierce eye on Elaina. "And I expect the truth."

Elaina nodded and followed her aunt into the parlor, but she felt Lydia's eyes on her back the entire time. Her cousin's withering glare didn't lessen when she took up her place by the fireplace and Elaina sat in a chair.

"Now," Charlotte turned once the parlor doors had all been secured and the windows shut, "I would like to start at the beginning." She looked at Elaina. "Were you with the prince last night?"

"I never meant to even meet him," Elaina began, staring at her hands. They were still dry and chapped from her late evening out. "I had walked to the docks."

"You *walked* to the docks?" Charlotte's voice rose a level. "Without a guard?"

Elaina nodded.

"That is over an hour's walk! May I ask what for?"

"I needed to think. Being near the ships makes me feel nearer . . . nearer to him."

She was answered by silence, so it surprised her when Charlotte knelt before her, taking Elaina's hands in hers. Her eyes were brimming with tears. "Elaina, how could you do that to us? After what happened to your mother?"

"I didn't mean to—"

"I know. And I know this is hard for you, but . . . My darling, we cannot lose you as well. Not the way we lost her."

"How did Nicholas find you?" Lydia asked in a small voice.

Elaina took a deep breath. "He was out as well. I guess he heard me talking to the stars."

Charlotte's eyes somehow got even wider, but before she could speak, Lydia cried out.

"You told him?"

"No! No, he deduced it on his own! I swear, I didn't mean for anyone to—"

"Elaina!" Lydia ran to her and snatched Elaina's hands out of her mother's. "Do you know what this means?" Her face was white. "He can make you do whatever he wants! He can use this against you!"

"I really don't think he will."

"And how would you know that?"

"Because he was the one who dragged me home!" She yanked her hands away and went to stand by the fireplace. "He said it was dangerous. He even ordered me to stay here until he comes for me. Ordered!"

"Why did he order you to stay here?" Charlotte's voice was brittle.

Elaina immediately wished she'd left that part out. She slowly walked to the nearest chair and ran her hand along its purple-flowered covering. "He says there is someone out there who is killing . . . people like me. He said another one died yesterday." She looked at Lydia again. "I promise, I volunteered nothing."

"Killing?" Lydia whispered.

Elaina nodded.

Charlotte drew a deep breath in and then let it out slowly. "Well . . . if the prince has given you a direct order to remain here, then I am more than ready to help you obey." She arched her brows. "To ensure you obey. But even after this crisis is over, I no longer want you walking about by yourself. You are to remain with your guard at all times. And there will be no more of this leaving the house after dark, even with a guard, unless you're with me."

Elaina felt her freedom slipping away like oil through her fingers. But she knew she didn't have the right to argue this time. "Yes, madame."

When her aunt finally left, Elaina remained behind in her chair, appetite for the morning meal gone. Lydia moved to stand beside her, but it was a long time before she spoke. When she did, her voice was hesitant.

"I . . . I suppose I'm thankful that the prince was there to find you when he did."

Elaina could only watch her warily. Her heart and head were too muddled and twisted with every emotion imaginable to form a coherent response.

"But please, just consider your response to him after this," Lydia continued, staring at her hands. "I know he might seem heroic in what he did. And maybe he was. But . . . don't allow this one deed to blind you to who he really is. I know how easy it is to fall for his charms. He has so many." She looked as though she wanted to say more, but she finally followed her mother.

Elaina sat by the fire for a long while before she had the energy to return to her room. Aside from meals, she remained there for the rest of the day. It was in her chambers that she waited, watching through her window for the moment the prince's black horse might ride through their gate.

She was vaguely aware of the hole in her heart where her father had been. She even understood, to a point, that her beloved *Adroit* and all its men were gone, most likely forever. But she didn't wish to think of such things. Because thinking them made them feel more real, like they might actually be true. So instead, she thought about the prince.

Though she wouldn't admit it to anyone, particularly Lydia, there had been something oddly comforting in his behavior, angry as his command had made her. She was beginning to understand the secret side of the prince that Dustin had gone on about. He had certainly recognized her gift far faster than Elaina would have expected from anyone so pampered. And the way he had hovered over her as they'd raced through the black streets on his horse had sent more than fearful shivers down her spine.

Was Lydia right? Was Elaina falling for his charms?

No. This was more than charm. His charms were the little nuances that vexed her daily. This was something more. Something real.

Still, did that mean she was falling for him? Elaina refused to even consider that question. Instead, she continued to study the lawn. And wait.

And wait.

It wasn't until her third day of waiting, however, that Elaina finally spotted the prince. To her surprise, he was on foot this time. She was nearly ready to race down the stairs, when he left the path to speak with her guard instead of coming to the door. They talked for a few minutes, but Elaina couldn't read their lips. When they were finished, instead of continuing on to the entryway, however, Nicholas merely turned and began to walk back to the road.

Really? He'd made her wait three days, and now he wasn't going to free her from her prison? Well, she had held up her end of the order. Nicholas had come to her house in person, and now she was getting out.

Grabbing her cloak and stuffing it under her arm, Elaina prayed that no one would see her as she snuck out of her room. The midday meal had passed, and Elaina was relieved to find that her aunt and cousin had already retired to their rooms for their afternoon rests. In just a few moments, she was able to dart out the back door and press herself up against the wall, waiting for someone to notice her. There were no protests or objections, however, so she threw her cloak on and pulled her hood over her head. She edged her way into the garden then cut through to the other side of the property line, just in time to see Nicholas disappear around the distant corner of the lane, heading back into town.

She wasted no time in making chase to the end of the lane and then hurling herself into the crowds. Her height, or lack thereof, might have made following him difficult, for the streets were still quite full, except for the fact that he was so tall. Even with his head bent, he was a good six inches taller than everyone else. So through the crowds they went, the prince keeping his head down, and Elaina holding hers up as high as possible, nearly having to walk on her toes to keep him in sight.

They continued that way for what felt like miles. The shadows began to lengthen, but yet the prince walked on. Elaina began to wish she'd thought to bring her boots, but there hadn't been time in her haste to escape the house. She only hoped she would be back in time not to be missed at supper.

The streets around them began to narrow. The houses and shops grew smaller and closer together, many with uneven roofs and scraps of oiled cloth in the windows instead of glass. The people wore clothing that was patched and full of holes, and many of them jostled her harder than she was used to. After getting a particularly long look from an unsmiling man, Elaina jogged a little faster so the distance between her and Nicholas was only six or seven paces rather than the ten to fifteen she'd been keeping. She would rather the prince not see her at all, but if the need arose, she would prefer his wrath to that of a stranger.

She sent up a prayer of thanks to the Maker when Nicholas finally came to a stop. They were in a market square, though it was much poorer than any market Elaina had ever seen in Ashland. About a dozen tents in a little rectangle drooped with various materials that seemed as abused as their owners' clothes. Elaina darted to the side so he wouldn't see her. Just in time, as Nicholas looked all around before ducking into one of the tents and letting the flap close behind him.

When she was sure he was inside, she ran around to the other side of the tent and crouched where she could listen in. All four sides of this particular tent had heavy cloths draped down so no one could see inside. But to Elaina's delight, she found a hole just small enough to peer through.

Five people stood inside the tent, and in their center sat an old woman wrapped in all sorts of animal pelts. Elaina couldn't see her face, but her shoulders slumped and her white hair was undone. Nicholas knelt before her, reached in his cloak, and pulled out a small package wrapped in paper and string.

"I was told you like ham," he said kindly, holding the package in front of her. "Perhaps your son can make this into a warm broth for supper."

The woman didn't respond, but her whole body shuddered.

Elaina's eyes pricked as Nicholas took one of the woman's hands. "I can't tell you how sorry I am to hear about your daughter. I met Casey once. She was very kind."

This sent the old woman into more silent shudders, but her fingers visibly tightened around his.

"Thank you, sire." A large man took the package from Nicholas. "She hasn't eaten anything since it happened. Perhaps this will convince her. Honestly I don't know how she's lasted this long."

"What can I do?" Nicholas stood and faced the man, who Elaina guessed to be at least of forty-something years. He had a thick mustache and a round belly. His eyes were rimmed red.

"There's not much we can do, I'm afraid." He swallowed, his Adam's apple moving visibly. "Catch the one who did this?"

Nicholas's jaw tightened. "I plan to do just that. But here, before I forget." Nicholas reached into his cloak again and pulled out a small pouch. The clink of coins sounded as he handed it to the man. "Pay for the funeral and any other expenses you might have. That should be enough, but if it's not, talk to Smith. He'll contact me."

As the people in the tent began to thank Nicholas, Elaina realized he was about to leave. Scrambling up from the hole and back into the busy street, she spotted a shadowed corner where she might hide until it was safe to follow. Just as she took her first step toward it, however, a large woman brushed by her, knocking her sideways.

Right into Nicholas.

CHAPTER 16
GIFTED

An eternal moment of shock and embarrassment passed as Elaina stared into the startled eyes of her prince. He didn't look startled for long, though.

"What are you doing here?" His voice was hard, completely devoid of flirtation or teasing.

"I . . . I waited like you said. But you didn't come, so when you did, I followed you." Elaina felt more ashamed than she had in a long time, like a naughty child who had been caught.

"I've got one dead body on my hands here. I don't need another one. Now really, what suggested this might be a good idea?"

Elaina opened her mouth, but no answer came. Really, what had made this seem wise? All she could remember now was her desperation to escape the suffocating silence of the house, the endless reminder that her father was gone. "What happened to Casey?" she finally asked, unable to come up with anything better to say.

Nicholas glared down at her for another minute. Then he glanced around. "Stay close. It's not safe here."

For once, she didn't even consider doing otherwise.

He took her by the hand and began pulling her through the

streets. Unfortunately, they were already beginning to draw attention. While Nicholas's clothes were made of fine cloth, they were dark and nondescript. Meanwhile, her gray gown, though one of her more subtle outfits, was drawing looks, particularly as the afternoon was growing late and people didn't seem in quite as much of a hurry as they had been before.

Through alleys, under bridges, around similar little squares to the one they'd first stopped in, Nicholas led her. Her heart beat unevenly when they turned a corner and she noticed his hand briefly move to what she was sure was the hilt of a sword hidden beneath his cloak. Were they truly in that much danger?

After that corner, they hurried through yet another square. This one wasn't quite as impoverished as the place she had followed him to, but there were enough dirty, shoeless children running about to convince Elaina that they were still far from home.

A man in the center of the square caught her eye as they passed. Children and even a few adults surrounded him. Elaina paused as he poured a stream of water from a pitcher into his hand. As he poured, the water changed from clear to yellow.

"What are you doing?" Nicholas's impatient whisper made her jump.

"That man just changed water into oil!" Elaina pointed.

Nicholas glanced at him and his expression grew even darker. "And he's a fool for making it so public. Now come. We need to keep moving."

After nearly an hour of walking, the houses began to grow farther apart, and the street they followed led out of the city and through hills covered in orchards. Still Nicholas led them northeast through the lines of trees until they were at the foot of a hill not far from the palace grounds. Nicholas finally dropped her hand and went over to sit against the trunk of an apple tree. Picking up two of the apples on the ground beside him, he pulled out a small knife and began to peel the skin off one.

Unsure of what to do, Elaina followed suit and sank down

against the trunk of a tree across from his, willing herself not to think about how much her feet hurt. Birds chirped, and the sun sank low enough in the sky that everything began to turn a thin shade of gold. It could have been a scene from a painting, except for the roiling dread that was gathering in the pit of her stomach. She dared a peek at the prince every few minutes, but it wasn't until he'd completely peeled both apples and tossed one to her that he spoke.

"When I was thirteen . . . about six years ago," he said, staring pensively at the apple in his hand, "I was out running around the city, causing a ruckus with some of my less-than-noble friends. Someone mentioned that a new bakery had opened in the old town, and the baker made amazing tarts. Being of the age where boys follow their stomachs, I convinced them to take me.

"On the way, we decided to play a game. I had just darted into a back alley when I tripped over something." He wiped the knife against his shirt and put it back in its sheath. "It turned out to be a dead body." He looked directly at Elaina for the first time since leaving the square and pointed to his right temple. "The body had two piercings here, next to the eye. I thought it was strange, so I ran straight home to tell my father."

"What did he say?"

Nicholas let out a humorless chuckle. "When I got to the palace, my father was more upset about my exploration than he was about the dead body. He confined me to my room for a week. It didn't quell my curiosity about the dead man, however, so as soon as I was free, I began to search for an answer. I needed to know why someone would do that to a dead body."

"You were so young," Elaina breathed, but Nicholas just shrugged.

"I didn't learn much for about a year. My father was no help, as he thought the endeavor useless. But my unending questions of everyone I met eventually paid off when I began to learn of other bodies that had been found with the same marks." He rubbed his foot in the dirt. "I just wish my father would allow me to travel more to learn whether or not these murders are happening outside of Kaylem as well."

Elaina found herself trembling, but more from excitement than the horror of the story or the evening chill. This was the prince she'd seen traces of beneath the veneer. This must be the man Dustin had been talking about.

"After a few years of investigating, which was a slow and painful process, mind you, without the support of my father, I was able to deduce through the murder reports and stories from family members of the dead that everyone who died with the marks had been gifted in life." He stopped turning the apple in his hands and peered at Elaina. "What do you know of your kind?"

She blinked. "My kind?"

"Those with extra abilities. The gifted, like you, are more populous in Ashland than anywhere else in the world, at least that we know of. Being gifted is nearly unheard of in Destin, for example, outside of the royal family. There are gifted people in other kingdoms as well, but there are far more here in Ashland than all the other western kingdoms combined."

"Why is that?"

"We don't know for sure, but my guess is that it has something to do with Solwhind being the largest city in the western realm. Its opportunities for trade draw many to our borders."

"I met quite a few gifted people in Solwhind," Elaina said, thinking of Madhu and her spices.

Nicholas nodded. "Anyway, I began to track the deaths of the gifted. We try to take records of deaths, dates, and circumstances for civil records. Making friends with the healer who pronounces individuals dead helped, for he was able to inform me when bodies with those piercings showed up in the infirmary. I concluded after several years that someone was most definitely targeting them."

An image, long forgotten, flashed in Elaina's mind. It was a memory she had tried to banish, the one where her mother's body had been brought into the house for identification. And though the memory was fuzzy, she recalled with horrid clarity the two marks, like snake fang wounds, in her mother's right temple.

"What is it?" Nicholas sat up straighter.

Elaina shook her head to try and clear it. "I'm not sure. It was a long time ago."

Nicholas surprised her by standing and walking over to her, crouching just an arm's length away. "If you don't tell me what just made you squirm, I will go back to the royal records right now, and I will search for everything about you and your family until I find out what it was." He quirked an eyebrow. "Now, would you like to tell me, or should I find out myself?"

Elaina stood as well, ignoring how much her feet protested. "Why do you care? Why are you so insistent on being involved in every part of my life?"

"I don't know!" His shout echoed through the orchard as they stared one another down. "I only know," he said in a quieter voice, "that there's something different about you, Elaina. And something in my gut tells me that I can't let you die."

Elaina could only stare at him. He was the most utterly confusing man she had ever met.

When she remained silent, he shook his head and muttered to himself as he stood and began to walk back toward the road.

"You won't find what you're looking for in the records."

Nicholas stopped. Slowly, he turned. "What do you mean?"

"My mother was gifted."

He frowned. "I should have seen that in my research."

"You won't find it in the official records because we never told anyone." Elaina slowly went to join him. "Only my father, me, my aunt, and my cousin knew. My grandparents were already dead. My own gift had blossomed shortly before my mother's death, and my father was worried that whoever had killed her would come after me." She shrugged. "It was simply easier to let the family think he'd lost his senses with grief than to explain why he was actually taking his little girl to live on a warship."

"Who knows now?"

They stopped at the fork in the road. The road to the right led to Elaina's manor, and the road to the left wound up the hill to the palace.

"My aunt and my cousin. And most of my father's crew, though they would guard it with their lives . . ." Her voice faltered as she remembered the one exception that had landed her in this mess in the first place.

"What is it?"

He knew everything else. He might as well know this, too. "We were the ship that hosted King Everard when he made his report on the rebellion. After we were finished, we made a quick stop in Solwhind to gather some supplies. While we were there, a disgruntled sailor my father had kicked off the ship got drunk, and he announced in a small tavern, mostly full of my father's men, that I could talk to the stars."

His gaze softened a little. "That's why you're here now, isn't it?"

Elaina nodded and looked at the ground.

Fingers gently touched her cheek then moved under her chin to lift her face up to look into his. "Thank you for telling me this. I . . ." He frowned then let out a huff. "I don't think you understand just how important you might be. From now on, when you're not with me, you're to stay with your guards at all times. At least two. I'll make sure to send another."

"I really don't think—"

"So far as we know, your mother's murderer, if it is the same culprit, has never attacked anyone in public. The victims have always been out alone."

"You know," she said, attempting a smile, "I have managed to survive somehow for the last seventeen years. Almost eighteen."

Instead of looking amused, though, he just looked . . . tired. "Just promise me."

She sighed. "Very well."

CHAPTER 17

A BET LOST

I cannot comprehend how intervention might have been necessary beyond the border. They were out of our territory."

"So a ship full of kidnapped women is no longer our concern when they cross over another border?" Elaina stared defiantly up at Dustin.

"I never said *they* weren't a concern. I merely believe we should have hailed the Ombrins instead and allowed them to continue giving chase. It would have saved us a greater headache later on when they filed a grievance against us because your father trespassed in their waters." The old man closed his eyes and rubbed his temples. "Really, Lady Elaina, you give *me* such a headache sometimes."

"Well, I hope the women my father saved and returned to their families were worth your headache." Elaina smiled triumphantly. "And the grievance was dropped, if you remember, when an investigation was made as to the trespass."

"Really, sire," Dustin growled, "I don't know why you make a point to keep both of us. You can't possibly learn a thing with all of this . . ." He waved his hand at Elaina. "Interference."

"Oh on the contrary, I am learning much," Nicholas said, a

wide grin on his face as he reclined at his desk, boots propped comfortably up on his desk.

"I wish you wouldn't do that." Elaina walked over and stared pointedly at his feet.

"See what I mean?" Dustin threw his hands up and retreated to a chair in the corner of the room, where he would most likely remain for the rest of the lesson.

"Why not?" Nicholas asked, not moving a muscle.

"Because someone has to wax every scratch your filthy boots make on this glorious piece of furniture." Elaina pointed to the little indents in the wood as proof.

Nicholas sat up and leaned forward to look more closely. "Well, it appears you're correct. Fine, no more boots on the desk then." He made a mock bow from his seat. "Is there anything else then, my lady? Or can we get back to talking about ships?"

Elaina rolled her eyes but couldn't help smiling a bit. Though she had originally been loathe to admit it, as the first dreary winter month passed, she was finding more and more enjoyment in her daily meetings with the two men. Of course, she loved Charlotte and Lydia's companionship as well. Lydia, though still wary about the prince, had somewhat forgiven her since the carnival, probably because Lydia's old friend was still in Solwhind, and Elaina was the most convenient peer left to talk to.

But neither Charlotte nor Lydia shared Elaina's fervor for the sea. After several attempts at speaking about her former life and adventures with them, Elaina had gathered that her time aboard the *Adroit* was somewhat scandalous, and rather a moot point with them and their fine company. So she had reserved her passionate discussions about warfare and strategy for her daily visits with the prince and his tutor instead.

Really, Nicholas was proving to be an even sharper learner than she had expected. He had a strategic mind, and was quick to offer points of view Elaina had never considered. She would never admit such to him, though. It would make his ego even bigger than it already was.

There was also the relief that most likely came from the fact that Nicholas knew her secret. And with that relief came the even greater revelation that she trusted him. Not with her heart, of course. She knew better than that. Despite their time together in the apple orchard, he continued to flirt with her and every other woman within hearing distance whenever he got the chance, never fully returning to the serious young man she had followed through the city. Still, it was nice to have someone else who knew. Keeping her secret to herself, she realized, had been very lonely.

Snoring erupted from the far corner of the room. As soon as it did, Nicholas slid out of his chair. "Before we go on, I have two things to ask."

Elaina gave him a wary look, but he just shook his head.

"I think you'll like the first. My father has a contact who has been in and out of Solwhind in secret for a number of years now."

"A spy?"

"Precisely. And for the first time, he's meeting with my father's military advisers and a few of the magistrates to discuss his findings."

Elaina frowned. "Is the rebellion growing that bad?"

"I'm afraid so." For a moment, Nicholas's face melted into the grave expression she had seen in the orchard. "Anyway, I would appreciate it if you would come with me to the meeting. You've been to Solwhind more than many of us have recently, and I think you might provide some insight based on what he says."

"I would be lying if I said I wasn't honored to have such an invitation, but . . . why me?"

"You know things many of my father's advisers don't, and you've met people and visited places that should add some diversity to the group my father is planning." He searched her face. "It's in two week's time. Will you come?"

Elaina tried to swallow her excitement, but the answer was already on her lips. "Yes. I'll go." She paused. "What else did you want to ask me?"

A triumphant grin spread across his face, and Elaina immediately wished she hadn't asked.

"I've been trying to decide on how to make you pay up for your lost bet at the carnival."

"Really? I thought we'd—"

He held up a hand. "No. You are still in my debt. And I have decided that I wish you to accompany me to my sister's wedding and ensuing celebration in a month and a half."

"You cannot be serious."

"And why not?"

Elaina searched for a good reason to deny the prince his request, reaching for the first answer she came to. "I can't dance."

"You can learn. That's not a real reason to turn me down. Come, what's the real reason?"

Elaina could only shake her head in disbelief, so he took a step closer.

"Am I really so undesirable to spend a few evenings with?" This time, his voice was softer, and there was something, just a glint of earnestness behind the laughter in his eyes.

"Do you want a candid answer?"

He stood straighter and clasped his hands behind his back. "That would be nice."

Elaina hesitated, but when she saw he was telling the truth, she gave in. "When a woman is on your arm, she ceases to be a woman. She becomes your ornament and exists only to be admired and to bring you praise."

Nicholas's hands slid to his sides, and he looked as though she'd struck him.

Elaina looked down at the floor. "I am no one's ornament."

For once, he seemed to have nothing to say. He stared at her for a long moment, a dozen emotions flickering in his eyes. Elaina wasn't sure what it was in her words that had so visibly shaken him, but she felt a sudden pity in her heart.

"But," she forced a smile, "as I am a woman of my word, I will honor our bet." She gathered her reticule and walked to the door. "But remember, this is a bet lost. Nothing more."

CHAPTER 18
ALWAYS A CHOICE

Nicholas had planned to go for a run after his lesson, but instead he found himself walking to the opposite side of the palace after Elaina had gone.

Her words gnawed at him like a dog on a bone. Why was that? It wasn't as though he'd never heard of himself referred to as a ladies' man before. On the contrary, he had done his best to ensure his familiarity with all of the women his parents might choose for him, making sure never to get too close to any one in particular. Then his disappointment wouldn't be so great when his favorite wasn't chosen. For years it had seemed like a foolproof plan. Until now.

But there was something about the way Elaina had phrased his habits that made him more than slightly uncomfortable. And before he knew it, he was standing in front of his mother's door.

"Come in," she called in answer to his knock. A smile lit her face when she looked up from her writing desk. "Why, Nicholas! How nice of you to drop in. What brings you to visit at this time of day?"

"It's not so odd for me to visit you," Nicholas said uncomfortably, walking over to her window to gaze down upon the wharf in the distance.

"Enough with the nonsense." She put down her quill and turned to face him. "Something is bothering you. Now what brought you all the way up here to see me?"

"I heard something today that I can't get out of my head." Nicholas tried to think of a way to say what he wished without seeming insecure. He couldn't.

"Oh?"

"Someone said . . . I was told today that apparently I treat women as ornaments."

"Ah." His mother looked back down at her desk but didn't pick up the quill. "And who, if I may ask, told you such a thing?"

Nicholas stared hard at his boots. "Elaina. I mean Lady Elaina."

His mother nodded slowly, an expression he couldn't decipher on her face. It wasn't sympathy exactly. Understanding, perhaps?

"And you want to know if it's true?" she asked in a quiet voice.

Nicholas went back to staring down at the wharf. What he wouldn't give to have something highly urgent to do today.

His mother stood up and walked over to him, where she began to straighten his collar. "You are a very handsome young man." Her hands paused for a moment before starting again. "Much like your father was."

Nicholas wanted to yell, to shout at the top of his lungs. Of all the things he had striven to be in his nineteen years, like his father was at the bottom of his list.

Cool hands took his clenched fists and softly lifted them up. She kissed his hands the way she had done when he was a child. Unfortunately, her kisses didn't chase away the discomfort the way they'd once chased away the pain of a cut or scrape. "You have a good heart," she said.

Nicholas opened his mouth, but she held her hand up.

"I'm not done. Do you think I've missed seeing you escape the palace all those evenings with bread tucked under your arm?"

"How do you know I'm not just sneaking out to eat it?"

She rolled her eyes. "Your appetite is good, Nicholas, but I know that even you can't eat four loaves of bread in two-hour increments. Besides," she raised her eyebrows, "I'm your mother. I know everything."

"So you know then for sure I won't turn out just like Father?"

"Just because you're not walking the path you wish to be on now doesn't mean the Maker can't change you. The Maker changes all of us to be who we need to be." She moved over to her vanity and began to adjust some of her dark curls in the mirror.

"Do you love Father, even though he's not who he's supposed to be?"

Her hands paused, and her shoulders drooped just a little. Immediately, Nicholas felt guilty. But not guilty enough to miss hearing her answer.

She was silent, however, until she sat down at her writing desk again and began to sharpen another quill, forgetting, it seemed, the one she'd been writing with earlier.

"I always knew my hand wouldn't be mine to give, unlike your father who grew up under the impression that he would be allowed to choose his bride. So perhaps the marriage wasn't as much of a shock to me as it was to him."

"That's not really reason to love someone."

"No. But marrying your father did give me a beautiful home and an exceptionally luxurious life. It allowed me the chance to improve the lives of those who depend on my position. Most importantly, however, it gave me you three." She grinned up at him and gestured for him to come close. When he did, she took his hands again. "You and your sisters are the most precious gifts I could ever have asked for. And your father not only gave me the gift of children, but he has also done everything in his power to make sure you all are loved and cared for. And for that, I am grateful."

"But do you love him?" Nicholas pressed.

She twisted a lock of hair in her fingers, her eyes thoughtful. "Not in the way I had once dreamed of loving a husband. But in my own way, yes, I do love your father."

Nicholas knew he would regret the words as soon as he'd spoken them, but he had to know. "Even if he doesn't love you?"

Her face whitened a bit, but she took a deep breath and gave him a forced smile. "We all have a choice, Nicholas. No matter where we are in life, loving others is always a choice."

CHAPTER 19
DEEPER SECRETS

L ydia, that red brings out the apples in your cheeks," Elaina said as she helped fluff her cousin's skirts. "Or," she gave her a sideways look, "could it be because Lord Devon will be there that you're blushing?"

"I don't know what you're talking about." Lydia tried to slap Elaina with the end of her ribbon.

Elaina laughed.

"Well, I don't think you need rouge today either," Lydia said as she turned to fasten the pearl necklace around Elaina's neck. "You're fairly glowing."

"Am I?" Elaina sorted through her jewelry until she found her pearl earrings. She felt a pang as she held them out for her cousin to help her with. They had been a thirteenth birthday gift from Lewis.

"This wouldn't have anything to do with the prince, would it?" Lydia gave Elaina a sly smile, but Elaina sensed the trap. She turned and studied her mint green gown in the mirror, hoping to appear nonchalant. It was the first time she'd had the courage to wear the gown to a public event. Lydia had ordered it with sleeves made of gauze instead of silk, showing far more skin than Elaina had ever dared. Lydia had also seemed to forget that one might need proper dresses for the winter. Elaina would need to go back to the seamstress and remedy that soon.

"Of course not." She tried to sound careless. "I'm excited to speak with Queen Ann again. I have some questions about my mother I'm hoping she'll have time to answer."

"Or could it be that meeting with Nicholas you're planning to attend tomorrow?"

Elaina froze. "Where did you hear about that?"

"News gets around."

When Elaina turned, her cousin was no longer smiling.

"Particularly when the news is unusual."

"What's that about Elaina at a meeting?" Charlotte stepped in, still fastening her own earrings.

"Word has it that Elaina is attending a secret meeting of sorts with the prince," Lydia said, not moving her gaze from Elaina.

Elaina wanted to roll her eyes. It wouldn't be secret if tongues continued to wag like this.

"Is this true, Elaina?" Charlotte drew closer and frowned. "What kind of meeting is it?"

Elaina took a deep breath. "Prince Nicholas wishes for his father's advisers to hear me report upon my travels with my father. He thinks my report might help them better understand the rebellion in Solwhind."

Lydia looked somewhat deflated, but Charlotte looked more alarmed than ever. "I don't like this, Elaina. It's one thing to help the prince with his studies, but it's another completely to get involved in the men's world of war."

"I can't very well say no to the prince."

"Did he issue you an order?"

Elaina hesitated. "No."

"Then consider this. He is a prince, but you are a lady, and you are under no obligation to go to war for him. And that's exactly what attending this meeting will mean."

"But they need me, Aunt!" Elaina began to tie her slippers with a vengeance. "What I know might help save lives!" Ouch. That was too tight.

"He's changing you, you know."

"What?" Elaina looked up at Lydia.

Lydia shook her head. "The prince. You can deny it all you want, but you're different when you're with him."

Elaina looked at her incredulously.

Charlotte, who had been fingering a jeweled necklace on Elaina's vanity, sighed. "Just be careful, Elaina." She gave her a weak smile. "Your mother was my dearest friend in the world, and you're all I have left of her. Please don't be in a hurry to throw that away."

THE RIDE to the palace was thick with tension. Charlotte looked exhausted, Lydia looked indignant, and Elaina was livid.

She was nearly eighteen. What business did they have telling her how to use her knowledge?

Of course, Charlotte had posed a good question, though Elaina would never acknowledge it. Why *was* Elaina so insistent on going to this meeting? It surely wasn't to bring her aunt grief. Charlotte had been nothing but kind. And as much as Lydia could get on her nerves, Elaina had no desire to hurt her cousin. Their intervals of peace were truly enjoyable, brief as they could be.

I can do this, Father. I am strong enough to make it on the seas.

Elaina cringed at the memory. Had it only been three and a half months since she'd uttered those words?

No, Elaina. You're not.

That was why she had agreed to this meeting. Yes, it was good to feel useful again. And yes, she would enjoy meeting some of her father's old friends. But more than anything, she needed to prove him wrong. She was strong. She was a survivor. Even if her father hadn't believed it.

With her head held high, Elaina let the footman help her from the carriage. She turned in the usual direction to wait for a palace escort like the ones greeting her aunt and cousin. To her surprise, however, it wasn't a servant who bounded to her side but Nicholas himself.

She automatically accepted his arm, but leaned in as they began to walk toward the east gardens. "You seem to be missing something."

"And what would that be?"

"A woman."

"Ah, yes. Well, it seems I must have forgotten to find one in the midst of all my more important duties, such as brushing my hair and helping my mother and sisters decide which teacups would best match the green room. I suppose you could always escort me."

Elaina tried unsuccessfully to suppress a smile. "It seems I have already begun." She stayed facing forward, as she could feel Lydia's eyes boring a hole through her from behind. Still, it was hard not to laugh, for the prince didn't really look as though he had even tried to brush his hair. Its brown spikes were as unruly as ever. Of course, not in an unbecoming way. For all his faults, Elaina couldn't find one thing about his appearance today that was unbecoming. Not that she ever could.

His silver-buttoned jacket, the color of an evergreen tree, and his black trousers were cut to fit his form perfectly and made him look even taller than usual. Elaina would never have said it aloud, but standing so close to him made her feel strange, like there was a warm gooey slush inside her that threatened to burst loose in the form of a stupid girlish giggle. But this was nonsense. She shook her head slightly to clear her thoughts.

As if agreeing to her notion of nonsense, he leaned down as soon as they were a little ahead of her companions. "I don't want you out of my sight today." Elaina began to scowl at him, but he continued. "I've met with our spy and his assistant this morning. Our spy I have no misgivings about, but his assistant is a different story."

Elaina's wish to tease disappeared. Of course he didn't have a girl on his arm. He needed to make sure she stayed safe. That his kingdom's secrets stayed safe with her.

Elaina wanted to kick herself. This was all just business, of course. She had known that and even insisted upon it. But why, then, had it felt so good to think her arm was on his simply because he wanted it there?

They followed the line of escort servants and guests along the path that led through the eastern gardens, a short walk that was protected from the winter winds by thick foliage trimmed at a perfect angle to shield those within the hedges. This path wound all the way around the palace to the back of the palace, where a glass room was built against the bottom two levels of the palace like an elaborate, gigantic, transparent lean-to.

Despite her annoyance with herself and the prince, Elaina let out a little gasp. Walls of glass surrounded them on the east, north, and west and overlooked the ocean. Evergreens of every kind had been grown in giant pots and placed expertly around the soaring space. Other winter flowers, pansies and primulas and forget-me-nots, grew clumped together in arrangements around each table and walkway, every color of green and blue imaginable. Snowdrops bowed their heads at the center of each table, and purple irises lined the walking paths. Baskets of dusty green leaves and bright red berries hung down from above.

"Do you like it?"

Elaina looked up to see Nicholas watching her.

"Oh, it's lovely!" She closed her eyes and breathed in the rich scents of sweet flowers and soil. "If I lived here, I don't think I would ever leave!" She moved closer to the back of the green room and peered through the glass. "You can even see the entire northern beach from here!"

"This was my father's birthday gift to my mother the year I was born."

When Elaina turned to look at him, Nicholas's face was a

strange mix of anger and admiration. "I think he was excited she had given him a boy."

Elaina was tempted to dig deeper, but before she could ask, Nicholas took her arm again and drew her close, pointing to the center of the room. "There's our spy," he said in a low voice. "His name is Alastair Bladsmuth." Then Nicholas mashed his lips together. "Where his little assistant is, however, I'm not sure."

"The middle-aged gentleman speaking with Lydia?" She was surprised to see that Lydia had already beaten her there. She and Nicholas must have walked more slowly through the garden than she'd thought.

"That's the one. Here, I'll introduce you." He led Elaina toward the table where a man was speaking with her cousin. Lydia's face was brighter than Elaina had seen it in a long time, and the man, though definitely several decades older, looked no less enchanted.

"Alastair," Nicholas called.

The man immediately stood and bowed. Lydia curtsied as well, though without as much fervor. Elaina avoided her gaze and focused on him.

"I see you've met my partner's lovely cousin, Lady Lydia Tifft. Lady Elaina Starke, allow me to introduce Mr. Alastair Bladsmuth."

Alastair bowed again. "It is an honor, my lady." He leaned forward and took her hand.

Elaina smiled back. "Truly, Mr. Bladsmuth. I am delighted to meet you. And I'm glad you've met my cousin. She's a wonderful partner for conversation. Also highly skilled at the game of Skitkol if you're a brave soul."

To her surprise, Lydia sent her a grateful smile. Could she possibly have been flirting with the man? Already? Elaina wanted to laugh, but she managed with great effort to keep her face straight.

"Mr. Bladsmuth has shared his origins with me and my father of course," Nicholas said, pulling a chair out for Elaina then sitting in one himself and looking at Alastair. "But I was rather hoping you could share it with our new friends, too."

"Oh, it's nothing highly impressive." Alastair waved a hand. "Still, if these fine ladies don't think they would be too bored to hear from a commoner."

"Of course not!" Lydia gushed.

Elaina nodded eagerly as well, though she wondered just how much the spy would share. And how much would be the truth.

"Well, my father was a blade smith, hence my name, as was his father and his father and so on. But none of them were very good. When I was a lad, we rarely had enough to eat or proper clothes on our backs. So when it was my turn to learn the craft, I decided that I wasn't going to waste my days doing something I hated so much." He leaned forward and shrugged. "As soon as my father died, I sold the shop and set out to make my fortune in the world. Even joined a friend serving in the king's court for a while." He gave a dry laugh. "I learned a lot those first few years. Learning doesn't make much money, though, and it wasn't until I stumbled across a crime as it was being committed that I found I was of use to anyone."

"You saw a crime being committed?" Lydia fluttered her fan even faster.

"Well, it really was a sad sort of way to come about one's livelihood. But I saw one man trying to kill another, and I was able to chase him off. He ran as soon as he saw me, but not before I saw his face."

"What did you do?" Elaina asked.

"I did all I knew how to do. Went to the authorities. When the king caught wind of what I'd seen, he asked me to speak to his records keeper. The records keeper decided he liked me and wanted to use me to collect records from around the kingdom." Alastair shrugged his thin shoulders. "Been doing that since, and never for a day have I looked back."

Ah, so that's how he was hiding his true profession. Well, a spy was a sort of records keeper. Just not the kind Lydia was most likely picturing as she fanned herself dramatically.

Nicholas had been watching the scene with an air of contentment. His face tightened, however, when a younger man approached the table.

"Forgive the interruption, please." Alastair turned to each of them briefly, his eyes repentant. "This is my assistant, Conrad Fuller." He looked back at Conrad. "What do you need?"

While they whispered together, Elaina did her best to study the assistant casually, as though she were simply curious. Conrad was younger than Alastair, but Elaina couldn't tell by how much. His hair wasn't graying as his master's was, nor were there as many lines about his mouth and eyes. But Elaina could understand why Nicholas was so on edge about him. Conrad's dark eyes never stopped darting, even as he spoke with Alastair in hushed tones. He regarded each person at the table with what looked like wary resentment.

The air felt palpably lighter as soon as he was gone again.

"I am so very sorry," Alastair said as he stood. "I must excuse myself. Only briefly, though!" He looked at Lydia for a long moment. "Might I rejoin you when I am free?"

Lydia blushed. "Of course."

Alastair gave her a wide smile. "Good. I was hoping you would say yes." With that, he kissed Lydia's hand then Elaina's. After bowing to Nicholas once more, he began to walk away. He seemed to drop something, however, for he bent down just beside Elaina. As he stood, a small square of paper was pressed into Elaina's hand. Instinctively, she closed her hand around it, and before she could say anything, he was gone.

Nicholas had taken up small talk with Lydia, speaking more about Alastair and asking her what they'd discussed before he and Elaina had joined them, but Elaina didn't hear what Lydia said in return. Instead, she moved her hand ever so slowly under the table until she touched Nicholas's hand. Tingles moved through her as she passed the square of paper off. Of course, it was only to share whatever message she had received. But the touch still felt strangely intimate.

What was wrong with her today?

After a few more minutes of talk about nothing, Nicholas looked across the room as though he'd heard something. "I do apologize, Lydia, but I fear I have a parent who must see me." He glanced about and smiled. "But it appears Mr. Bladsmuth has returned from his errand. Would you allow me to steal your cousin while you speak with our guest?"

Elaina half expected Lydia to break into a baleful glare, but instead, she only tittered and looked about excitedly. As soon as Alastair rejoined them, Nicholas begged their leave and escorted Elaina away. Rather than moving toward his mother, who sat at the table in the center of the green room, however, he led them out of the green room entirely and into the palace. As soon as they were in a smaller room off the main hall, he ducked into a corner and ripped open the folded parchment.

"What is it?" Elaina leaned over his arm to get a better look.

"It appears the final member of our meeting tomorrow has arrived." Nicholas refolded the parchment and tucked it into his sleeve. "This particular guest is technically not supposed to be in the country right now, as his assignment is in the east, so his attendance is one best kept quiet."

"Where are we going?" Elaina asked.

He had taken her arm again and was walking deeper into the palace. "My father needs to know of this guest's arrival, and I would prefer to tell him myself."

As he spoke he began to walk faster.

"I'm afraid this meeting isn't going to be as secret as you would like it," she puffed in a whisper as she tried to keep up.

"What do you mean?"

"Lydia accused me of attending a secret meeting with you tomorrow."

Nicholas shook his head, but kept up his pace. "If the palace maids ever quit gossiping, I'm not really sure how they would occupy their time. Here. We'll take these stairs."

They moved up a set of shiny marble steps.

"I must say," Elaina whispered breathlessly after they'd climbed several more levels. "I am enjoying myself."

"Really?" Nicholas kept walking, but he gave her a little sideways smile. "I'm glad to hear that."

"It feels good to be useful again. But, I might enjoy it more."

They finally left the stairs and turned down another gleaming hall. "And what would make it more enjoyable for you?" he asked.

"If you would slow down. Some of us don't have legs the length of a mast."

At this, Nicholas let out a laugh and slowed his pace. "Is that better? Or are you just trying to get more time alone with me?" He waggled his eyebrows.

Elaina wrinkled her nose at him. "In that case, you'd better walk faster."

Three turns later, Elaina and Nicholas were standing before a set of massive doors.

"This is your father's room?" Elaina gawked at the sheer size of the doors.

"This is his study." Nicholas knocked once before opening the door for her.

Elaina stepped through, but immediately wished she hadn't. A little cry of surprise left her lips, and she turned away to hide her face.

A woman in servant's garb sat on the king's lap. One of her shoulders was bare, the neck of her gown hanging loosely down her arm, and she was entwined in the arms of the king.

Nicholas, however, did not seem so shocked. Nor did he seem confused. When Elaina dared a glance at him through her fingers, he was shaking. Yanking the message from his sleeve, he threw it on the ground and stormed out.

Elaina, not knowing what to do, kept her head bowed as she turned just quickly enough to drop a blind curtsy before chasing after the prince.

CHAPTER 20

NICHOLAS

I f Elaina had thought Nicholas a fast walker before, she'd had no idea how fast he could run. Or perhaps he wasn't running. Perhaps he was just walking as he usually did, not slowing so she could keep up. Maybe he was trying to get rid of her.

Well, he wasn't going to get rid of her that easily. Elaina pushed even harder, catching a glimpse of a coattail here and there as he rounded corners and flew down stairs. Sweat began to run down her back as she pressed on, and her feet strained as she pounded them against the slick marble floors in her thin satin slippers. What she wouldn't give to have her sturdy sea boots.

It wasn't until she had followed him out of the palace and down the lawn to the west bank that she found him on a little private dock with a rowboat. A boat that he had already climbed into and was furiously throwing things about in as he muttered incoherently.

Finally, he plopped down on the first plank seat and looked at her. "Well, are you coming or not?"

Elaina calmly lowered herself onto the edge of the dock and took off her slippers, dangling her feet over the water. "And where might you be going?"

"Anywhere but here."

"I don't think you're going anywhere."

His blue eyes narrowed. "And why not?"

"Because I have your oars." She held up one of the two oars that were still lying on the dock behind her.

He looked around his boat in confusion, then scowled even harder.

She went on in a softer voice. "But I don't think you really need to be out on the water right now anyway."

"Oh really?"

She shook her head. "I've seen too many accidents involving men who lost their heads at sea. Why don't I sit here instead, and you tell me what's going on?" She wasn't sure she really did want to know, but from the crazed light in his eyes, Elaina was afraid he might really do himself harm if left alone. If she had learned anything in her years at sea, it was that when men were angry, they could be unusually stupid.

Nicholas rolled his eyes but let his body slide down until he was sitting on the boat's floor. He covered his face with his hands so his voice was muffled when it came out. "That was my father's latest mistress."

Elaina felt the air rush out of her chest. "Oh, Nicholas."

He pulled his hands off his face and pushed himself up against the back of the boat. They were quiet for a long time, the slapping of the water against the dock and an occasional sea bird screeching from above the only sounds around them.

"Before my parents married, my father was in love with another woman. He was devastated, from what I gather, when my grandparents told him to marry my mother. He did as they asked, but his love for the first woman never lessened." Nicholas paused and his jaw clenched. "My mother caught them together not long after the wedding. She, being the merciful soul that she is, did nothing to embarrass or expose them. She even found a comfortable place for the woman as a lady-in-waiting in a neighboring kingdom, rather than publicly humiliating them the way they deserved."

"Your poor mother," Elaina whispered. She couldn't imagine marrying a man so desperately in love with another.

"My father never saw the kindness for what it was. Instead, he decided to fight back. He's kept a steady line of women for enjoyment over the years, but I've never seen him go that far . . ." His voice trailed off.

"Nicholas, I'm sorry. I . . . I don't know what to say."

He shook his head. Pulling a tart from his pocket, he threw it in the water and watched the gulls dive in after it. "I shouldn't be surprised by now. I've seen enough over the years. But . . . sometimes he does things that surprise us all. Like when he gives Mother those extravagant gifts. I used to think he was trying to win her affection again, but then I realized it was just his guilt eating away at him." He paused. "Did your parents love each other?"

Elaina felt a sad smile come to her lips. "They adored one another, from what I can recall. In fact," her smile faded, "my father refused to talk about her after her death." She studied the dark water beneath her feet. "I remember little of her, and what I do remember is good. But it would have been nice to *know her* instead."

Nicholas had pulled one knee up and was resting an arm on top of it as he stared up at the palace. His position made Elaina's heart twist in an odd way. It made him look vulnerable. There was no swagger, no bravado, and she had the sudden urge to brush the rebellious hair out of his face so she could read it more clearly.

"I don't want to be my father." His blue eyes grew wide. "But I'm afraid that's the very man I'm turning out to be."

"You won't be."

He gave her a hard look. "You accused me the other day—"

"I didn't mean—"

"And you were right."

Elaina could only stare at him miserably. Yet, somehow, she heard herself whisper, "But you won't be."

"How do you know that?"

She paused. How did she know that? She had accused him, it was true. But now that she was beginning to see the man beneath the mask, she didn't need the stars to tell her what she was beginning to see for herself.

"Because you care."

His eyes softened and his jaw unclenched. Just then, the clouds parted enough for a thick ray of late afternoon sun to burst through, making the towering clouds above and around them look darker than ever before. But there in the sunlight, with eyes the color of an azurite stone, he stared back at her, and for the first time, Elaina saw neither a prince nor a boy who played foolish games. He wasn't a spy, nor was he a scholar.

He was just Nicholas.

"I think we had probably better get back to the tea," Elaina mumbled, pulling her slippers back on and tying them carelessly. "They'll be looking for us."

She heard him get to his feet. "We can return through the gardens. That way it looks as though we've just been strolling." He got out of the boat and began trudging back up the lawn, his shoulders still slumped, but Elaina stayed put. After a few strides, he turned back. "Aren't you coming?"

"Aren't you going to be a proper gentleman and offer to escort me?"

The sorrow didn't leave his face, but a hint of a smile touched his mouth as he returned and held out his arm, which Elaina took with dramatic solemnity.

"I've enjoyed this afternoon immensely," he whispered in a sardonic tone, "but don't think this means I've forgotten our deal. You still owe me my sister's wedding."

"I wouldn't dream of it." She elbowed him slightly. "Someone has to keep you in line."

CHAPTER 21
CONFIDENCES SHAKEN

Nicholas had to plant his feet firmly to keep from pacing as he waited in the entryway of Elaina's manor. He'd been here before, of course, though that hadn't been since he was courting . . . His heart dropped a bit when Lydia walked into the room.

Nicholas bowed, and she curtsied, but the air instantly thickened. Ever since Elaina had laid his philandering out plainly so he could see himself for the dolt that he was, Nicholas had been followed by the anxious, longing eyes of girls everywhere, it seemed. How many women had he truly encouraged?

Why didn't you show me this earlier? He asked the Maker. But he already knew the answer. It had been there all along. He had just refused to see the pain he was leaving in his wake.

Just like his father.

"How do you do, sire?" Lydia asked. Her words were polite enough, if stilted.

"I've been better. Thank you for asking, though. And you?"

Before she could answer, footsteps sounded on the stone floor above them. When Nicholas looked up, he felt as though the air had become breathable again.

Far from the ethereal green gown she'd worn the day before,

181

the one that made her look like a fairy, Elaina now wore a practical dark red wool dress. The shape, with its long, thick sleeves and the way the skirt gently curved off her hips, was modest but comely as it flattered her petite form. The color brought out a few of the strawberry highlights in her honey-colored hair. It also made her freckles stand out even more than usual. Nicholas recalled his sisters going on once about freckles being unattractive on a woman, but he couldn't understand such talk. Elaina's freckles were adorable.

When she reached the bottom of the steps, she turned and bade her aunt and cousin goodbye, as though she were merely going for a stroll along the lane rather than attending a secret meeting with a spy, the king, and the king's most important military advisers.

They walked to the carriage in silence. What was she thinking? Her face was once again that cool mask of resolve and daring, the one he could read the least.

Even if he couldn't read her, she could probably read him like a book. Shame and gratitude rolled in as he recalled what she had witnessed the day before. Her gentleness had confused him, and her choice to call him by his given name only muddled his heart more. There was no way this young woman could have really meant all that she'd said. She was too good, and she knew his fickle ways better than anyone.

It wasn't until they were out of her house and into the carriage with the window shades drawn shut that she finally let out a breath and turned to face him directly.

"So where is this meeting?" Her blue-green eyes lit up like waves shimmering in the sunlight. "I have it from a good source that a few of my old friends will be there."

"This source wouldn't happen to live up in the sky, would it?"

Elaina just wrinkled her nose enchantingly.

What he wouldn't give to have this girl with him all the time.

What he wouldn't do to miss this meeting completely.

"Elaina," he began, already regretting what he was about to

say, "I want to apologize ahead of time for some of my father's colleagues. There will be some present that you recognize, but . . . unfortunately, some of my father's magistrates are required to be in attendance as well."

"I know many of the magistrates are also of noble blood," Elaina said. "But what exactly is their purpose in such meetings?"

"Magistrate is a position chosen by the people in local districts, though I'm afraid it's often bought in coin and favors, mostly by lords or earls who can afford it. They usually meet with my father to report the needs of those they represent, and they act as mediators between the crown and the people of their districts.

"Their purpose in this particular setting, however, is to balance the king's power in matters of war so that it's impossible for him to declare war without their express consent." He leaned back and rubbed his eyes with one hand. "Official law requires there shall be no meeting of the king and his military advisers without at least three magistrates present. Unfortunately for us, today we get the grand privilege of hosting five."

"Five? Isn't that a bit excessive?"

"Any magistrates who find out about the meeting and wish to attend are allowed, and as the magistrates play politics harder than anyone else in my father's court, they tell only the colleagues they like."

"Which means?"

"There will only be one magistrate in attendance tonight that I don't want to strangle on a regular basis."

"Ah." Elaina nodded politely, but her eyes were wide.

"But please," he hurried on, "I don't wish for you to be intimidated by them. They will do their best to make you feel out of place. They do it to all the additions to our parties that they didn't personally appoint. They even tried it on me once, though their efforts were not nearly as impressive with my father there as they might have been otherwise." Just thinking of the men made him want to punch something. He studied her. "But you're still nervous, aren't you?"

Elaina looked at her hands as she spoke. "My title is my own. My land is my own . . . or will be in a few years. But I have never represented myself in a meeting. It was always in my father's name and with his blessing. This is the first time I've ever come as . . . myself."

"Marchioness is a grand title. You'll technically be higher in rank than a number of the magistrates who will be present."

"I know that." Then she took a deep breath and drew herself up to her full height, which was not very impressive but quite dignified. "Title or no title, however, I have negotiated with kings and ambassadors, and I have seen monsters the average man wouldn't dream exist." She jutted her chin out. "I do not plan on being intimidated."

Nicholas nodded and grinned, but the shadow of doubt that remained in her eyes concerned him. He found himself hoping she'd seen snakes before, the scaled kind with fangs. Because if she had, she would be much better prepared for the men they were about to face.

NICHOLAS PAUSED ONCE MORE in front of the doors. Torchlight flickered on Elaina's face, and despite her bravado in the carriage, she suddenly looked young and vulnerable.

"I'm not going to offer you my arm this time," he bent down and said in a low voice. "I don't want them to see you as my companion. I want them to see you walking in on your own two feet as a respected confidante and reliable adviser."

She stared thoughtfully up at him and shook her head just a little.

"What?"

"You are probably the most confusing person I've ever met. One moment, you're requiring my presence as a dance partner at your sister's wedding, but the next you're treating me like a respected peer." She smiled a little and shook her head again. "I don't understand you, Nicholas Whealdmar."

"That makes two of us," he muttered, nodding at the servant. "All right. Let's go."

She stood at his side as the servant opened the door, but as they entered, she fell back a step, the closest to hiding that he'd ever seen in her.

The chatter that echoed through the cavernous room fell to near silence as everyone stared. In the dim light of the many torches, most of the admirals seemed impressed and pleasantly surprised. Several of the magistrates openly scowled. The king barely gave her a glance and a nod before turning back to the man he was speaking with.

Nicholas looked back at Elaina. Her eyes were wide, and the expression on her face made him want to wrap her in his arms and run back out the door with her. But that would benefit neither of them. So instead he strode over to a chair at the large stone table and pulled it out for her to sit on.

"My prince. Lady Elaina." Alastair hurried over and gave them both a quick bow. "I am glad to see you here. We can begin now that everyone has arrived." He shuffled to the front of the room and thumbed through the stack of parchments he was carrying. Finally, he pulled out what looked like a map and laid it on the table. Before he could say anything, however, a fat man reclining on the other side of the table spoke.

"I see our prince now needs a companion wherever he goes." His eyes moved down Elaina's figure slowly, hungrily. "At least she's decently appealing."

Elaina's face seemed to drain of color.

One of the naval officers, a burly man with a single gray streak through his dark hair, jumped to his feet. "You'll have some respect—"

"I find it a bit disconcerting, Lord Benedict," Nicholas cut in with a smooth voice, "that my father's top advisers have so little confidence in their own abilities as to be shaken when joined by a woman."

The admiral met Nicholas's eye. Nicholas wished he could express to the officer how much he would enjoy seeing the impertinent magistrate pummeled, but that wouldn't help Elaina in the slightest. Finally, the admiral gave Nicholas a small nod and sat back down, but not without knocking into Lord Benedict's chair with a loud thump.

"For those of you who are not familiar with Marchioness Elaina Starke," Nicholas announced, putting his hand on her shoulder, "Lady Starke has recently inherited her mother's title and is the daughter of our distinguished admiral Baxter Starke, High Commander of the Royal Navy. Though he was recently reported as missing in action, Maker carry his soul, we are privileged to have Lady Elaina's experience and advice here today. She has sailed with her father and assisted in his negotiations and ambassadorial efforts for the last twelve years." He bent his head toward her. "Lady Elaina, I don't suppose you need introductions to the admirals, but let me introduce you to the magistrates attending us today. Lord Stiles." He gestured to the bony, sniveling man in the corner. "Lord Hampton, Harvey Monger, and Lord Greyson."

Elaina nodded to each, receiving a smile only from the elderly Lord Greyson in return.

"And Lord Benedict." Nicholas fixed his eyes on the belligerent magistrate and imagined them boring a hole through Benedict's head. "You will treat her with respect."

"Tell me then, Lady Elaina." Lord Benedict leaned back and scratched his chest with a meaty hand. Nicholas resisted the urge to slap the leer from his puffy red face. "If you're so experienced in politics, which of the duchesses of Pembrose bore an illegitimate child in order to retain her family's lands after her husband died and left her childless?"

Elaina raised one brow delicately, suddenly looking quite

dangerous for being such a small woman. "Lord Benedict, you live in Solwhind, do you not?"

The magistrate frowned. "How do you know that?"

"I've seen you before."

"I don't recall that."

"You don't recall much, I'm sure. No, we've never met, but I saw you once at a meeting of the magistrates in Trent. My father was attending as a special guest."

"You're stalling. I don't see what this has to do with my question about the duchesses of Pembrose."

She smiled like a wolf moving in for the kill. "I find your question ironic, particularly considering what happened at Trent."

Lord Benedict was not a man of particular health, and Nicholas wondered if he might die of heart failure now in his chair. Even in the firelight, his face turned the color of a tomato, and he gasped for breath. One of his friends slapped him on the back, but all the admirals looked quite smug. Elaina merely smoothed her gown out and politely folded her hands on the table. Nicholas bit back a laugh.

"I think we've established Lady Elaina's qualifications to contribute," Nicholas's father finally snapped, glaring at Lord Benedict. "Let's get on with the meeting."

"Quite so, sire," Alastair said, fumbling with more maps. "Conrad, the sea one."

His assistant appeared from the shadows and flipped through the uneven stack of parchments until he found one, pulled it out, and then disappeared into the corner once again.

Alastair pushed the parchment to the center of the table. "I have been observing in Solwhind since before the rebellion, over five years now. From what I've gathered, the main group behind our rebellion is made up of the followers of a man who calls himself *the Shadow*."

"That's original," one of the admirals muttered.

Alastair glared at him for a moment then went on. "From what we can tell, from the very start the Shadow has been encouraging behaviors that the crown has long declared illegal. If it produces gain in Solwhind, it's lauded." Alastair thumbed some more through the pile in his arms. As he did, a few parchments floated to the table.

Nicholas and Elaina leaned forward to see them better. Each parchment had a drawing of some sort along with little notes scribbled in all the margins. The ones closest to them had pictures of plants.

"Extortion, blackmail, and all sorts of illegal items are being traded and imported by his followers," Alastair said, holding up a single parchment triumphantly before passing it to the admiral sitting to his left, "which is no small number of merchants and peddlers, among others, mind you. Most importantly, however, is the herb lithorium."

Nicholas heard Elaina suck in a breath.

"Pray tell, what is lithorium?" Lord Greyson asked, holding his monocle up to peer more closely at the paper.

"A deadly toxin that makes the mind weak and the body useless. But it's addictive and enjoyable when taken in all forms of the plant. Usually dried and crushed like tea. The plant comes from the far east before it's made into a purple powder. It's often sold to youths who don't know any better."

"It's expensive, isn't it?" one of the admirals asked.

Alastair nodded rapidly. "Oh yes! Highly! But it makes the dealers a lot of money. Many are selling everything they own to get their hands on it."

"What about people?"

Everyone turned to look at Elaina.

"I beg your pardon?" Alastair pushed his spectacles farther up his nose.

"Has there been a slave trade established in Solwhind as well? Perhaps one that's still mostly hidden from the public?"

"And how would this slave trade be carried out?" Lord Stiles asked, sniveling and dabbing his constantly running nose with a handkerchief. "Cargo is inspected before it is allowed to enter port."

"Precisely!" Lord Benedict slammed his fist on the table. "Lithorium is small enough that it's easy to smuggle in and out. It can be carried in a pocket or reticule. But humans?" He snorted.

"But the last time I was there—"

"I'm sure you found some lovely ribbons for your hair." Lord Benedict rolled his eyes.

For one brief moment, Nicholas wondered if Elaina was capable of leaping over the table and wrapping her tiny hands around his fat throat. It would serve the horrid magistrate right if she did.

"Benedict," Xander said in a warning voice.

"If you believe there is evidence to support such a claim, my lady," Alastair said in a rush, "then I will certainly do my best to look into it."

Elaina nodded back, still looking put out but somewhat mollified.

"Unfortunately, Lord Stiles," Alastair said, "the bailiffs are having a difficult time quelling the illegal activities, even at border searches. The Shadow has too many followers now, so many that it is difficult to know whom to trust. Some of the bailiffs have even been attacked. Others have joined the rebellion."

"Why weren't we told of this sooner?" Nicholas leaned forward.

"Unfortunately, sire, the situation has escalated very quickly. Ships are moving between the two main bay ports less and less, and many of the sailors are reporting little because they either sympathize with the Shadow and his followers or have been intimidated into silence." Alastair shrugged helplessly. "This movement has been going on for years, but for some reason, it's seen unprecedented growth in the last three months. I'm afraid the situation is spiraling far faster than we had anticipated, which is precisely why I requested that I come out of hiding to meet with you all personally."

He briefly searched the messy pile of papers until he found another map. Everyone leaned forward to see more closely as he pushed it to the center of the table.

At the map's center was a large bay. On the bay's west side lay the peninsula on which Kaylem sat. The capital city was marked at the peninsula's western shore with miles and miles of orchards and fields and smaller towns between the capital and the peninsula's eastern wharf. Across the gigantic bay from the eastern wharf lay Solwhind, which covered most of Ashland's eastern land, stretching right up to the kingdom's border. Elaina knew from experience how a carriage ride could take hours to move around or even directly through the city.

"The Sharyn Sea," one of the admirals muttered.

"Where is that?" Lord Hampton asked as he squinted at the parchment.

"It's merely the bay." One of the admirals scoffed. "Don't you ever leave that big house of yours?"

"Lord Hampton, the bay is so large that it often behaves more like a sea than a bay," Alastair said quickly, adjusting his spectacles yet again. "Therefore, many of the sailors call it the Sharyn Sea instead." He looked up at the king. "The bay is allowing them to become emboldened, Your Highness. We have so little land south of the bay itself that they know you will have to send your soldiers over the water if you wish to interfere. They believe that this gives them the advantage of cutting you off before your troops arrive, or before you can get word to your soldiers and naval officers already stationed near or in Solwhind."

"I've lost two ships in the last month," an admiral said, the one who had tried to defend Elaina's honor. "I thought the first was due to a storm, but the second disappearance was quite suspect."

"I lost a ship in a supposed storm last week as well," another admiral said.

Alastair nodded. "They have ships patrolling the entire coast, posing as merchants. My assistant and I believe that whenever they think a ship is carrying dangerous information or an unusual number of soldiers, they act as though their own ship is in distress. We haven't seen it ourselves, of course, but my assistant was told by a reliable source that there have been a strange number of distress flags thrown up in the bay lately."

A hush fell over the room, and every eye turned to Elaina. Her face remained calm, but Nicholas could see her jaw muscles tense.

"What are they doing with these missing ships, Mister Bladsmuth?" she asked in a quiet voice.

"I . . . I only wish I knew, my lady. It is just theory."

Elaina nodded.

Nicholas wished very much to pull her into a hug, but he satisfied himself with touching her shoulder instead. To his surprise, she reached up and, for a moment, allowed her hand to rest on top of his.

"What do you make of this?" The king leaned back in his chair and looked at his admirals. All five of them shared glances.

"As I said, I've lost two ships," the first admiral said. His name was Bordeaux, or at least that's what Nicholas thought. Thanks to his father, he never spent enough time around the officers to be sure of all their names.

"I've lost none for sure, but one of my captains was going out to investigate a ship that was late to port last night," another said.

One by one, as the admirals began to compare their losses, Nicholas had a sinking feeling in his stomach. How had they missed this?

"Is this normal?" he whispered in Elaina's ear.

"For one admiral to lose a ship every few months, perhaps," she whispered back. "But not all of them at the same time. No, something is wrong."

"You all live in Kaylem or in the country or in some nameless village. But I live in Solwhind!" Lord Benedict protested. "How has this been going on without me or my colleagues, servants, or family noticing any of it?"

Either Lord Benedict was the most oblivious man alive, or he was lying. And Nicholas was betting it was the latter.

"Lady Elaina," Nicholas said, glaring at the magistrate, "have you seen any signs of this the last few times you were in Solwhind? Or perhaps that King Everard mentioned?"

A few of the magistrates started at the mention of the foreign king.

She tilted her head and put her thumb to her lip. "The last time I was there," she said in slow measured words, "just a few months ago, I visited a friend in the northern fishing market, the large one near the northwest wharf. A riot broke out in the center of the square between a group of citizens. One accused the other of wearing a mark . . ." She looked at Alastair.

"Oh, yes!" He fumbled with the scattered papers until he found another drawing. He held it up for everyone to see. "The followers of the Shadow all have a knife symbol sewn into their clothing or tattooed on their arm."

Elaina nodded. "My friend begged me to leave immediately. She said it wasn't safe." She glowered at Stiles then Benedict. "As I was *going* to say before, she said people had been disappearing. Particularly visitors."

"That's rather bold," Nicholas said.

"I will meet more with my advisers after this, but for now, what is your recommendation, Mister Bladsmuth?" Xander asked. "How do I prevent trouble in my largest city from spreading like a plague to the rest of the country?"

"I would begin by taking this to *all* of the magistrates together," Alastair said gravely. "Ask what can be done on the ground level. If you try to weed this rebellion out by brute force, the people who are undecided as to whom they're following will see it as a stronghold of the king, and they will resent the crown even more."

"Surely there can't be that many followers." Lord Hampton yawned.

"There are enough," Alastair said, looking the thin lord in the eye, "that should we continue on this path unaltered, I'm afraid we will have ourselves a civil war."

CHAPTER 22
JUSTICE

Elaina hadn't realized just how much she'd begun to look forward to lessons with the prince until he was gone.

As soon as the meeting with Alastair was concluded, Nicholas had whisked her back home with a rushed apology for the behavior of some of the magistrates and a quick explanation that he would be gone for at least a week, maybe longer.

Elaina, understanding the sensitivity of war and missions, suspected immediately that his disappearance had something to do with wishing to see the rebellion for himself, but she knew better than to press for information.

Still, she'd been caught by a wave of unexpected regret when he had bid her goodbye. His eyes had lingered on her face even after he'd said the words, and she had found her own arm unwilling to unwind itself from his as quickly as it should have. His absence shouldn't be long, he'd promised, so why had it been so difficult to say goodbye? And why had she meant it so earnestly when she told him she would pray for his success and safe return?

To make matters worse, there was an emptiness that settled upon her daily routine when she was forced to content herself with ladylike activities all day, particularly considering the excitement of the meeting. Going to the docks now provided little pleasure and was full of unwanted reminders, as she was trailed by the two palace guards everywhere she went. She couldn't mourn the *Adroit*'s loss properly with them hovering about. Even the stars had been quiet. Every night they said only the same few words again and again.

Beware of the planted yellow seal.

As if that was something she was supposed to understand.

In her attempt to ignore the crawl of the minutes through the day, Elaina had just sat down to write in her journal, a habit she'd taken up to replace the routine of writing in her father's ship log every day, when Lydia burst into her room.

"Guess who's come to call!"

"Who?"

"Look out your window!" Without waiting for her, Lydia bolted to Elaina's window and looked down, clapping her hands like a little girl.

Elaina followed at a slightly slower pace. When she looked down, however, she had to admit her surprise as well.

Alastair was standing just outside a coach. The coach's door was ajar, and he was speaking intently with the driver.

"What do you suppose he wants?" Lydia giggled.

"I haven't the slightest idea."

"Well, let us go see! Or no! It would be more proper to wait until he is announced in the parlor. Then we can take our time coming down as though we were doing something of import, rather than simply waiting for him."

"Because simply waiting on a guest would be the height of impropriety."

But Lydia was already at Elaina's mirror. "How do I look? Is my hair curly enough? Do I need to add more rouge? Perhaps I should change."

"You look as lovely as ever," Elaina said, taking her cousin by the shoulders. "Now hold still. Let me adjust your gown in the back."

"Maybe it would be better if I just—"

"If I had your figure, I would feel confident wearing a shapeless sack." Elaina stood back and smiled. "And this is by no means a shapeless sack. Now, I hear the servant coming up the stairs."

As she'd predicted, a servant announced their visitor. Lydia squealed, and Elaina took her arm so that they would have to walk down the stairs together. She really did not have an idea as to why the spy was at their home, but it would be best not to allow Lydia to trample him in her excitement.

He was standing in the parlor, staring out the window into the fruit garden when they arrived. As soon as the door shut, he turned and swept into a bow nearly low enough to compete with Nicholas's. "What a pleasant surprise! I came hoping to find one lady at home, and I have found two!"

"And which of us did you wish to find?" Lydia giggled, but Elaina could see the strain beneath her smile. *Please let it be Lydia,* she prayed. *For the sake of the sanity of all who live in this home, let it be Lydia. I beg you.*

"I had an afternoon with little to do, so I volunteered to run a message to Lady Elaina," Alastair said, indicating to the two empty chairs by the northern window. "But I must admit that I was hoping to make your acquaintance again, Lady Lydia, if you are available to trade a few ramblings to help an idle man pass an afternoon."

Elaina let out a sigh of relief as Lydia's smile returned in full. "If you wish to hand over my message now, Mister Bladsmuth, I can take it and allow you two to enjoy your ramblings."

Alastair pulled a little folded, sealed square of parchment from his pocket and handed it to Elaina.

"Oh, Elaina," Lydia whined, "you must not go! I wish for you to stay here, too! The more, the merrier!"

Elaina stared hard at her cousin for a long moment. The last thing she had expected was for Lydia to want to share their visitor, especially with her. But when Lydia's eyes flicked back to Alastair, Elaina understood.

Lydia wanted her to witness them together and, when he had

departed, to tell her whether or not Alastair truly favored her. For Alastair's sake, Elaina certainly hoped he did.

"Is Conrad here?" Elaina asked, trying to sound nonchalant. "I thought I glimpsed him just a moment ago in your coach. Wouldn't he like to come in and have some refreshments?"

"Ah, that is very kind of you. But I'm afraid my assistant has an earache and will be resting in the coach for a while. You mustn't worry about him, though. I've left him with an herbal remedy from the royal healer. He simply wished to escape the sounds of the palace for a while."

"Of course," Elaina conceded with a smile. Disappointed that her attempt at getting to know more about the younger man had failed, Elaina settled in her chair and prepared herself for a very monotonous afternoon.

As it turned out, however, the afternoon wasn't nearly as dull as she had expected. Lydia asked surprisingly good questions, even in her besotted state, and Alastair gave even better answers.

"So how exactly did you conclude you did not wish to be a blade smith?" Lydia asked after tea and treats had been brought to the parlor.

Alastair studied his cherry tart. "Believe it or not, it was when my closest childhood friend showed an unusual talent for sensing poison, of all things. Without even touching a substance, he could look at it and know whether or not it had touched or contained any sort of poison.

"That's an odd talent to have." Lydia frowned at her orange scone.

Alastair shrugged. "Yes, but highly useful, particularly around people who are powerful and might have foes. The king, King Xander's father back then, eventually caught wind of his gift and wished to have him work at the palace. And he did." Alistair leaned forward in his chair, his eyes suddenly bright. "The moment he left was the moment I knew I wanted to do something greater than smith for the rest of my life."

"Oh, he was gifted!" Lydia exclaimed. "Just like—"

Elaina froze.

"Just like whom, my lady?" Alastair asked.

"Oh," Lydia laughed and began fanning herself at a rapid pace, daring a glance at Elaina. "Elaina and I saw a few gifted individuals at the carnival recently." She laughed nervously. "I find it fascinating that all gifts are so different. One was able to turn objects into clay just by touching them! Another woman was able to calm bees by singing to them so she could gather their honey without getting stung. Just so fascinating!"

Elaina thought she might pass out from relief. That had been a close call. Not that Elaina didn't trust Alastair. He had given her no reason not to. But he was associated with Conrad, whom Nicholas didn't trust in the slightest.

As soon as Elaina had recovered from her near heart attack and Lydia had continued on a different vein of conversation, Elaina had an idea. Nicholas might not be there, but Alastair was. Perhaps Elaina could do a little spy work on her own.

"So you were a blade smith by trade," she began when Lydia stopped talking long enough to sip her tea. "What was Mister Fuller's occupation? Was he a smith as well?"

Alastair's easy smile fell ever so slightly. "No." He paused to take a long drink from his tea. "No, I'm afraid Conrad's story is quite sad and far more pitiful than my story ever was."

"What happened?" Lydia asked.

Alastair studied his cup. "Most of his history isn't mine to tell. I will say, however, that I found the little runt trying to pick my pocket in Solwhind." He chuckled, his eyes growing distant. "He's been with me for fifteen years since. Doesn't speak much, but he's a good lad." He turned to stare up at the distant tops of the windows. "He's saved my life on more than one occasion, though," he said softly. "I'll give him that."

Elaina wasn't sure how much the term *lad* applied to Conrad, as he looked to be at least the same age as Nicholas. Still, she could see that Alastair wished to say nothing more on the subject, and she knew better than to push.

It was intriguing, though, to think how many secrets were floating above them like clouds as they all sipped their tea and chatted amicably. They were each hiding something. For Lydia, it was her desperation. Though she was only eighteen, Elaina knew she was worried about growing old and dying a penniless maid.

For Elaina, her gift was, as always, her secret.

For Alastair, it was Conrad. And the fact that he was a royal spy.

Too many secrets. If a romantic seed did eventually conspire between her cousin and Alastair, Elaina would have to make sure Lydia learned at least something about the true nature of his occupation. But for now, there was only today. Today, Alastair was the perfect gentleman, and Lydia the grateful recipient of any and all praise and adoration.

"I apologize." Alastair's words interrupted Elaina's thoughts. "But I am in need of the powder room. Where would it be? I'm afraid all this water in the air from the recent storm has me all sticky."

After Lydia had given him directions and he had gone, Elaina excused herself as well. She wanted to see the contents of the letter in her hand, but she wasn't entirely sure Lydia wouldn't demand to see it if they were left unattended by their guest.

On her way to her room, however, she ran into Alastair again.

"I cannot apologize enough," he said as she drew nearer. "But I seem to be lost."

"It is no problem at all. Follow this hall to the end, and you will find another powder room there. It is not as large as our powder room downstairs, but it should be adequate." As she turned to open her door, however, he reached out and gently put his hand on her arm.

"Before I go and while we're alone," he said, taking a deep breath, "I'm afraid there is something I must admit that is not quite appropriate for your cousin to hear, due to the nature of my work."

"Yes?"

"Prince Nicholas revealed to me some of his research concerning the deaths of the gifted."

"Oh?"

"And while I have been hired by the king to examine the rebellion and its cause, I must confess that I think I've discovered something on the subject that will interest our prince greatly."

Elaina turned away from her door, too curious to go in now. "And what is that?"

"I believe the Shadow and our killer of the gifted is one and the same!" he whispered, his eyes bright.

Elaina gaped. "What proof do you have?"

He shook his head. "Not enough to convince the king yet, I'm afraid. But I've seen too many coincidences to ignore the correlation completely."

"I am glad to hear it," she choked out, "but I'm not entirely sure what this has to do with me." Had he discerned her secret as well? Elaina prayed not.

"I'm sorry. I don't wish to upset you," he continued in a rush. "The prince just seems to trust you so much, and I will be gone when he returns so I thought . . ."

Elaina swallowed the lump in her throat and forced a smile. "I would be glad to relay any information you wish to share."

"As I said," he continued in a quieter voice, looking at the floor and moving one foot about in a half circle, "my gifted friend had great potential to rise high in the court. But what I didn't tell your cousin is that this mystery man killed my friend before my friend had the chance to celebrate his twenty-fifth birthday."

"I'm . . . I'm so sorry."

"You see, I pursue the killer not only for the prince's purposes, but for my own as well," Alastair said, his voice growing more resolute with each word. "I am going to see him to justice." With that, he turned and stalked away.

Elaina entered her room, though she didn't necessarily remember actually opening her door or walking in or closing it behind her. Moving over to her window seat, she absentmindedly cut open the seal and read the note.

Lady Elaina,
Though he did not tell me where he was going,
Prince Nicholas left a message that said he should be
back in the library for our lessons on the first day of the
last week of this month. If plans are altered, I shall
inform you.
Master Dustin

ELAINA BEGAN to fold the note back up to burn it, but a movement from outside her window caught her eye. Sitting up, she peered down into the rose garden beneath the window.

Just below her window, hiding in the bushes and staring up at her, was Conrad.

CHAPTER 23
THAT WRETCHED SHIP

When Elaina dared to peek out of her window again, Conrad was gone. Shaking, she left her room and went in search of Alastair. The house was large, though, and Elaina didn't find him until she returned to the entrance to see Lydia bidding him farewell from the steps. He was already in the coach.

"Was his assistant with him?" Elaina asked Lydia as the coach drove away.

"Who, Conrad Fuller?" Lydia shrugged. "I didn't see him. I assume so, since that's where Mister Bladsmuth left him."

Elaina went in search of her guards. Her trepidation grew when she found the front of the house empty. There was always someone within sight of the door. It wasn't until she moved to the back of the house that she found the two men in uniform. They were huddled together, speaking in hushed tones. The servants were gathered around them whispering amongst themselves.

"Gerard?" Elaina called. "Cameron?"

"Here, my lady."

"What has happened?" Elaina hurried to their sides, but came to a halt as she stepped on broken glass.

"Take care, my lady. It's all over."

"When did this happen?" she asked, peering closer at the jagged hole in the kitchen window.

"Just now, I'm afraid." Gerard shook his head and scratched his thick brown beard. "Good thing no one was standing by the window. They might have been struck by the stone."

"Did this happen about ten minutes ago?"

Cameron looked away from the glass for the first time. "I caught sight of someone rounding the corner about then. I chased him back here to find the glass already broken. Why?"

Elaina swallowed. She had always loathed the idea of having her two guards nearby, but suddenly, two didn't seem enough. "I looked down from my bedroom window and saw a man staring up at me."

Both guards stood upright.

"A diversion." Gerard looked at his companion. "Must've known we would stop to look at the broken window."

"Did you get a good look at him?" Cameron's hand went to the sword on his waist. "If we go now, we can find him before he leaves the grounds."

Elaina shook her head. "You don't have to. I know who he is. He is the assistant to the king's record keeper. His name is Conrad Fuller."

Both guards stiffened.

"What is it?" she asked.

Cameron and Gerard exchanged a look.

"Just how well do you know Mister Fuller, my lady?" Cameron finally asked.

"Hardly at all. I have only met him once or twice while at the palace. We haven't exchanged more than a single word." She eyed them suspiciously. "Why?"

"We're not really authorized to say—"

"Cameron," Elaina said, putting her hands on her hips. "I just looked out of my chamber to find a man in my roses. I believe I deserve a decent explanation." She lifted her chin. "Or shall I have to ask the prince for assistance when he returns?"

Cameron paled slightly, and Gerard held his hands up defensively.

"Of course you won't need to go to him. We can tell you enough." He rubbed the back of his neck and glanced about at the servants. "But first, may we move indoors where it's a little more private?"

As soon as they were in the dining room, Elaina ordered the doors closed. Once the room was shut off from the rest of the house, she turned and folded her arms. "Well?"

Gerard walked to the window and stared out. "Conrad Fuller has been spotted in a number of inappropriate places since arriving at the palace. It's really been putting the guard into a bit of an uproar."

"What kinds of places?" she asked.

"The chambers of other visitors. The servants' quarters. Even the armory once, though the fellow doesn't look strong enough to lift a javelin, let alone anything of value."

"Then why hasn't he been stopped?"

Gerard glanced at Cameron, who shrugged. "It appears he is taking advantage of his relationship with Alastair Bladsmuth. Every time evidence is requested, no one can prove anything. He doesn't take any objects. He's just . . . looking."

"Why he would be beneath your window, however, is beyond comprehension," Cameron muttered, gripping the edges of his sheathed knife until Elaina wondered if the leather would give away under his strong hands.

"I think this is a matter for His Highness," Gerard said slowly. "We will, of course, remain here, and if we catch him doing anything inappropriate, we will surely apprehend him. And when Prince Nicholas returns, you should speak with him about this. Perhaps his father will believe your word over ours. But until then, I think it wise that you remain close to home until the prince returns."

"My aunt should be home from visiting any time."

"As much as I am glad to hear that," Gerard said, "I'm afraid I mean permanently. Until the prince arrives home, of course."

Elaina took a deep breath and straightened her shoulders. "Thank you. I am grateful for your honesty . . . and your loyalty."

As soon as the guards had returned to their posts, Elaina began heading back to her room. On her way, however, she spotted a movement in the parlor.

Lydia was still sitting by the fire. She was no longer seated properly on her chair, but was draped sideways across its arms with her feet hanging off one side and her head leaning back against the other.

"What was that all about?" She pushed herself up on her elbows. "I heard something break."

"Someone threw a rock through one of the kitchen windows."

"Oh my! Was anyone hurt? Did they see who did it?"

"No, thankfully."

"But did anyone see who did it?" Lydia repeated.

Elaina took a deep breath. "Not exactly. But we have an idea."

"Well, before I grow old and die, tell me who it was!"

Elaina sat down in the flowered chair across from Lydia's and traced the nearly invisible stitching with her fingers. The sun had dulled the fabric's bright colors, making the room look much like the way Elaina felt. Sickly gray.

"Lydia," she began slowly, "did you enjoy speaking with Mister Bladsmuth today?"

"Oh, he is just delightful!" Lydia's beam returned in full. "I mean, he is a little older than I had always imagined a man I might find attractive, but really, he is intriguing!"

"Good." Elaina tried to smile. "When you were saying goodbye to him before he left . . . did you talk to him any more about . . . me?"

"Why would I do that?"

"It was just that earlier you seemed to be on the verge of talking about me." Elaina couldn't look her cousin in the eye. "And you stopped yourself, which was good. But I'm afraid you may need to be more careful with what you share with him."

Lydia sat upright in her chair. "And why would that be?"

"It's only that Mister Bladsmuth is a man of many contacts," Elaina said, hoping not to give too much away about Alastair's real occupation. "And should he unwittingly share some of that information, not knowing that it's personal—"

"Are you really doing this?"

Elaina looked up at Lydia in surprise. She had never heard her cousin shriek before.

But Lydia was not finished. "You cannot simply be content with stealing the prince from me. No, you have to go imposing regulations on my words with the first man who shows half an interest, as if I were some . . . some . . . sailor on your father's ship!" She picked up a pillow and threw it at Elaina.

Elaina blocked the pillow with her hands. "That's not what I'm saying—"

"You! The biggest hypocrite in Ashland giving orders!"

"Now what is that supposed to mean?"

"You think you can tell me whom to trust and not to trust, when I've been warning you about the prince all along. But no! You haven't listened to a word I've said! You've become inseparable from the most untrustworthy man in the entire kingdom!"

"Lydia, that's quite enough!" Now Elaina was shouting, too. "I have worked with the prince on the most professional of terms since he *ordered* me to train him!"

"Oh, of course!" Lydia rolled her eyes and waved a hand. "Because it's highly professional to disappear with a man for an hour during a luncheon thrown by his own mother."

"He needed to speak with his father!" Elaina stomped over to her cousin and yanked another pillow out of her hands. "Really! What do you want of me? What more can I do to appease you?"

"You can go back to that wretched ship from whence you came! You can leave my house and my life and never speak to me again!"

"I wish I could!" Elaina's breathing felt strained. "But I can't."

night."

"I know. And your position of the pathetic orphan is what makes this entire situation more dreadful."

Elaina's arms fell limply to her sides. She opened her mouth, but no words came out. Instead, her stomach twisted as hot shame washed over her, though she wasn't sure exactly why she felt guilty. She had anticipated an adverse reaction from Lydia, of course, but nothing like this. And the rejection hurt worse than she had thought it could.

With nothing else to say, Elaina turned and trudged up to her room. It was the last place she wished to be, after her earlier scare. But it was the only place she had left to go.

HOW ARE YOU FEELING? THE STARS' chorus of voices was gentle as twilight bled across the sky.

Elaina leaned against the window frame. "I was afraid you wouldn't come tonight."

We're always here. You know that.

"You don't always speak." Elaina toyed with the figures on her wooden bracelet. "It makes it a little difficult to feel like I'm being heard sometimes."

He always hears you. And we hear you, too. You need to trust us in this, Elaina. You're never truly alone.

"It can feel that way." Elaina's throat constricted. She cleared it again. "I only . . . I feel like the world is spinning faster than I know how to keep up with."

Are you speaking of Conrad Fuller?

"Yes. And no. My father is still missing. And now Lydia is angry with me. Really angry, I'm afraid. And Nicholas . . ." She stopped herself.

What about Nicholas?

Elaina got off her perch and stomped back into her room to pace. "Nothing. Forget I said anything about him."

You miss him, don't you?

"I shouldn't miss him." She rubbed her eyes with the palms of her hands. Lydia's words had haunted her all evening, and she had worked to convince herself otherwise. But the more she lied to herself, the brighter the awful truth shone before her.

"The problem is that Lydia is right!" She kicked a pillow that had fallen on the floor. "I *know* better! I know better than to allow him to get into my head." *Or my heart,* she added grimly to herself. "But sometimes, just sometimes, I glimpse a part of him that's so much more a man. It's as if he leaves his boyish foolishness behind, for just a few brief moments. But as soon as I pause to take a second look, he's back to his old games." She grabbed a pillow from the bed and returned to the window seat. Squeezing the pillow to her chest, she drew up her knees and let her head rest against them. "Also, my head aches."

The stars laughed gently like a thousand bells ringing over the city rooftops. *A good night of sleep will heal that. As for the prince, however . . .*

Elaina lifted her head to look up at the sky. "Yes?"

Have you seen no change in him since arriving?

Elaina ran her hand through her loose hair. She hadn't bothered to roll it into rags. Her head throbbed too much. "I've only known him for a few months. He changes so fast I can't keep up with him." When the stars didn't reply, she mashed her face into the pillow. "I just feel so alone."

Are you alone because you have no choice? Or because you've chosen to be that way?

"What do you mean?" Elaina pulled her face from the pillow to glare up at the stars.

You may object, but it already seems as though you've made the decision to trust the young prince with much. And yet you push him away.

Elaina started to reply, then stopped. They had a point. He knew her secret. Well, he had guessed that. But he had also proven faithful in keeping it. And the truth about her mother? Well, he had pulled that from her as well. But again, it had only made him more determined to protect her.

And yet, every time he tried to pull her closer, she pushed him back.

Still . . . Elaina's heart quickened a little as she remembered the feel of his hand gripping hers as he pulled her through Kaylem's crowded streets. The way he had leaned over her protectively when they'd raced through the streets on his horse, ready to take an arrow for her, should one have been loosed. The rough stress in his voice as he'd begged her to keep guards for her own protection. The esteem in which he'd held her opinion in the meeting room.

We've seen many humans come and go. And one thing we've learned through it all is that no human can make this journey alone.

"You wouldn't happen to also be able to tell me anything about Conrad, would you?" Elaina tried to sound teasing. "Or where my father's ship is? I could use a distraction, you know." Not that she expected an answer. She'd been asking that question every night since the *Adroit*'s disappearance.

Some things you will need to learn for yourself, little one.

"The Maker won't even let you give me a hint?"

Elaina, you know we speak only what he directs.

"I know."

Sometimes he has humans learn lessons easily. Other times, hard lessons are required to accomplish other purposes.

"What?" Elaina shook her head and gave a tired laugh. "Are you saying that the world doesn't exist solely for me?" She yawned and stretched. "Well, if you can't tell me where he is, then I suppose I shall go to sleep now." She paused, the memory of Conrad's face still fresh in her mind. "Would you stay with me while I fall asleep?"

We're always here. You needn't even ask. But Elaina?

"Hm?" Elaina asked as she pulled a blanket over her on the little window seat. For some reason, she had grown tired beyond comprehension.

Harder times are coming. You need to prepare yourself for the after-math of the hidden yellow seal.

But Elaina only half heard what they said. She was already slipping into the bliss of exhaustion.

CHAPTER 24
TURBULENT WATERS

"Well, that was bloody brilliant." Nicholas stormed out of the meeting room into the blinding afternoon light that reflected off the snow.

"Sire," Oliver called in a low voice from behind him. "We really should get back to the ship as soon as we can."

"No." Nicholas stopped and surveyed the market before them. It was just one of Solwhind's dozens of markets, a smaller one, he'd been told, that belonged to some of the more impoverished of the city. "I need to know more."

"It's not safe, sire."

"My father's refusal to come here after the rebellion began is partly to blame for this. I'm not about to let it get worse because of fear."

"Your father was only trying to protect you," Oliver said dryly. "As am I."

"And I appreciate your efforts more than my words will ever be able to express." Nicholas met his captain's gaze. "But I fear the absence of the crown has only driven this place into further chaos."

"And what do you propose to do about it here and now, sire? We are only a few men. The others are within half a day's walk, but not even they would be enough to protect you adequately should the Shadow's supporters discover you."

"I don't expect you to do that. I expect you to help me learn more about this place and these people. We will slip in and out after speaking with enough citizens to better understand the unrest."

"But, sire, that is what we have Alastair Bladsmuth for."

"Of the fifteen magistrates I was *supposed* to meet with in there," Nicholas jabbed a finger back in the direction of the stone building they'd left, "more than a third have either given up their loyalty completely or failed to show at all. At this rate, I'm shocked we haven't had an outright uprising already."

Captain Oliver sighed but gave a nearly imperceptible sign. Five more guards began to move casually in their direction.

Nicholas tried to look casual, too, as he pressed deeper into the market. His borrowed clothes were supposed to pass him off as a wealthy visitor, and the stubble he'd allowed to grow over his jaw made him look several years older, or at least that's what Sophia had said. But as he moved through the crowd, he still felt eyes trailing him everywhere he went.

He approached a stall without any customers and gave the man behind the table a deep nod. "My friend and I just arrived. I don't suppose you could tell me what the event is here."

"Event?" The man paused, knife poised above the fish he held against a wooden block. He looked Nicholas up and down warily.

"Aye. The marketplace is so busy." Nicholas smiled. "Haven't been here since I was a boy, but I remember this place. It wasn't so crowded then."

The man shrugged. "A rise in fish prices."

"Is there a shortage of trout elsewhere in Ashland?" Nicholas asked.

"You going to buy some fish or not? Got a line behind you."

"I'm sorry. I didn't mean to take up your time." Nicholas turned away and began scanning the crowd for other individuals who looked as though they might talk.

He finally pushed his way over to a woman two stalls down. Her tent was piled high with tarts, scones, and other baked goods. "These look delicious."

She looked up at him with the most enormous eyes he had ever seen. Her jaw trembled.

Well, that reaction was a little strong. Nicholas was tall, but he hadn't ever seen himself as horribly intimidating. "Do you make these?" He gestured to the food.

The woman nodded.

"Which do you think my sister would enjoy?" he turned around and asked Oliver loudly.

Oliver hesitated only for a second before answering. "The blueberry ones."

Nicholas nodded. "I'll take four of those and six of the lemon pastries. And throw in five of the red ones."

The woman began to wrap the morsels in thin sheets of brown paper. As she did, Nicholas leaned in just a little.

"Is there an event going on here to bring so many people? A carnival, perhaps?"

She shook her head and went back to wrapping the food.

Nicholas continued. "The last time I was here, there weren't nearly so many people in the market."

She finished wrapping the baked goods and tied their little package with string before handing it to Nicholas.

Frustrated, Nicholas dug into his pocket and pulled out a coin. As he handed it to her, however, her eyes darted to the right. Nicholas followed her gaze to a man standing a few tents down who was watching them with an unabashed glare.

On his sleeve was a crudely stitched knife.

Nicholas looked back and forth between the angry man, who was oddly well dressed, and the trembling woman before him. Then something bright caught his eye.

"That's a lovely bracelet," he said, leaning closer to study the thick gold band encircling her wrist.

The woman yanked her hand back and pushed her sleeve over

the bracelet where it had peeked out. "Good day," she whispered to the men before turning and moving to the back of the stall.

"This market is infested with the rebellion," Oliver whispered as they moved away. "You can hardly turn without seeing another knife patch. What is it you're trying to learn?"

"I want to know whether lithorium is truly the driving force behind this mad trading or whether it's a combination of all the illegal activities."

"Ashland's economy has grown steadily in the last ten years. Why should this be any different?"

"Have you been to Solwhind since the rebellion began?" Nicholas asked.

"Not since you have."

"And even as a boy, I remember none of this . . ." Nicholas gestured at the crowd as he searched for the right word. "Frenzy."

"Well, you've got treats." Oliver nodded at the package in Nicholas's hand. "Why not ask the best source?"

"Which would be?"

Oliver pointed to the closest edge of the market where a gaggle of children played in an alley, throwing snowballs and kicking slush at one another. "Children know everything. And their allegiance is often cheap."

"This is why I keep you nearby," Nicholas said, laughing and shaking his captain's shoulder.

"I thought it was because of my incredible good looks," Oliver muttered as they moved toward the outer edges of the crowd.

Just as Oliver had predicted, they had the attention of at least a dozen children by the time Nicholas reached the outer rim of the market. And all eyes were trained on the neatly tied package in his hands.

"Is that sweeties, mister?" A girl, barely taller than Nicholas's thigh, tugged on his trouser leg.

Nicholas crouched down. "It is."

Immediately, he had seven or eight children so close they were touching him.

"And they are for whoever can best answer my questions," Nicholas said, untying the package enough for the scent of baked sugar to drift out. He pulled out a lemon pastry and popped it in his mouth. "Can anyone tell me why the market is so busy?"

"The market is always busy," the first little girl said, her eyes never leaving the package.

"No it's not," a boy said. He was nearly a head taller than the girl. "It wasn't always so busy."

"And why is that?" Nicholas asked.

"My mum says it's because of the bad things they're selling now."

"Your mum's wrong!" another child called out. "My father says it's because of the bracelet people."

"Bracelet people?" An image of the woman and her gold bracelet flashed through Nicholas's mind.

"My mum says it's because a man has come in and is selling magics."

"Magics?" Nicholas asked.

The little girl rolled her eyes as though he were a simpleton. "She says he sells people's magics. If you want the magics, you buy it."

Was he hearing correctly? "How . . . How does someone know if you want to buy a magic?"

"People wear a knife on their shoulder, like this." She pointed at her own shoulder and traced a long shape into her arm. "That way, my mum says, when the Shadow is in town, he knows who wants to buy his magics." She shrugged as though the concept were quite simple. "Then they can get rich using whatever it is their magics make."

Nicholas glanced back at Oliver, whose grizzled face had hardened. "Do you know where I could find someone who has purchased one of these . . . magics?"

"I do!" A boy who looked about nine called out. "His name's Jackson. He lives in the big houses six streets up from here. He works for a magistrate, and he just bought something two days ago." He gave a sly smile. "I know because I was peeking through his window when I heard him say that the Shadow was going to come to his house."

After thanking the children for their answers, Nicholas not only handed them the sweets but gave out a few coins as well. The children squealed with delight as he and Oliver stepped away.

"And?"

"Theodore Jackson," Nicholas said grimly.

"Isn't he a wealthy merchant of sorts?"

"Yes, and an assistant to a magistrate."

Oliver sighed. "I don't suppose there's any chance you'll be able to pass up visiting this man?"

Nicholas shook his head. "We're going to visit an old friend."

NICHOLAS HESITATED for only a moment before knocking on the door. His guards were less than thrilled with the plan. Though dressed in common clothing to better blend in, they all grumbled about having the same feeling as Nicholas—that they were being watched everywhere they went.

A butler opened the door. He looked annoyed until Nicholas gave him his name. Then he looked absolutely terrified.

Ushering them in with a thousand apologies, he seated them in the drawing room and then snapped at one of the maids to fetch them some tea.

As they waited, Nicholas wandered the room. The house was large and well furnished. Embroidered tapestries hung on the walls, almost as masterfully woven as those in the palace. Vases with brightly colored ornamentation were scattered about the room, most without flowers in them, and several sculptures were on display as well. Nicholas leaned closer to look at one.

"Oliver," he called softly.

"Yes, sire?"

"What do you notice about the decorations in this room?"

Oliver squinted at a bust on the mantel. "It's not very good."

"No, look at the material itself. And then look at these vases." Nicholas picked one up, slowly turning it over in his hands. "No dust. None whatsoever."

"The man is rich enough to keep a decent household staff," another guard suggested, but Nicholas shook his head.

"This is different. Smell the paint. They're all new. They must have been purchased within the last week."

"I'm confused," the younger guard said. "He's obviously wealthy. What's so odd about that?"

"To own vases like these, one is not merely wealthy," Nicholas said, putting the vase back. "These vases are made by a particular potter and his wife, and they're sold only in one of the bigger markets. The artists are originally from the east." He looked back at Oliver. "My mother loves their work, but because of the cost of the gold and silver paint, even my parents have purchased only a few for the palace. But this man has at least a dozen. And all brand new."

"My prince!"

Nicholas turned to find a heavyset gentleman standing in the doorway. His words were slightly slurred, and his arms outstretched. When he bowed, his arms stayed aloft.

"What an honor to have you in my home! I must admit, I did not expect it! I'm delighted, though! I hope you will stoop so low as to allow your servant to feed you luncheon."

"It would be my pleasure," Nicholas replied.

Jackson snapped two thick fingers, and a young girl dressed in a maid's uniform came running. "Tell Fanny that she will be cooking for a prince today! Make sure luncheon is superb."

The girl turned and stared at Nicholas, her mouth falling open. Nicholas gave her a small smile, hoping to remind her of her duties before her master lost his patience. Though he'd only met him once, Nicholas didn't recall his host being a very patient man.

"I will admit that I am a bit surprised to see you in Solwhind, sire." Jackson turned to sit on the couch, stumbling slightly as he did.

Nicholas waved his hand. "It was meant to be quiet. I wanted to speak with some of the magistrates, and royal proclamations would have impeded an honest, quiet conversation." He took a sip of his exceptionally sweet tea. "Your employer was there."

"I hope I do not offend you, sire, but might I express how impressed I am with your person. I have not seen you since you were small, and here you are now, a man in every respect." He picked up his teacup and peered into it, as though expecting to find something at the bottom.

When Nicholas dared a glance at Oliver, his captain's frown confirmed what he suspected. Their host was acting somewhat strangely.

"I greatly admire your decor," Nicholas said, walking over to the nearest vase. "The Zhus are accomplished craftsmen."

"You know them?" Jackson smiled pleasantly and leaned back into his seat, although there was the barest hint of hesitation in the big man's eyes.

"We have some of their work at the palace. I've never seen their like in skill." Nicholas paused. "Or in price."

"Ah . . . Yes. Well, I believe art is an investment." Jackson chuckled uneasily and scratched his nose. "I put all my extra coin in trying to turn investments when I can." He stood, stumbling again as he did. "Would you like to see the garden? It is particularly lovely."

Nicholas looked over at Oliver, who seemed less than thrilled with the suggestion. Still, he followed Nicholas dutifully out the door.

A thin layer of icy snow crunched beneath their feet, another reminder that a walk in the garden was an odd idea. "This red pine tree is one of my favorites." Jackson was shouting now, though Nicholas couldn't understand why. "I collect things from the far east, you know!" They walked over a little wooden bridge. "The koi in the pond were brought in all the way from—"

Nicholas didn't see the blow coming, but Oliver did. In a second, Nicholas was on the ground and Oliver was standing over him, sword in hand.

Nicholas jumped to his feet and drew his own weapon, but the fight was already over. Oliver's blade was at Jackson's thick neck, and Jackson was pinned against his beloved red pine.

But rather than giving up, Jackson let out a guttural scream and slid down the tree, flailing his large arms in all directions as he tried to roll away. Another guard tried to pin his arms down, but before his wrists could be properly bound, Jackson grabbed one of the guards' knives and pulled it from his belt.

A crackling sound filled the air. Nicholas gasped with the others as the knife shimmered for one long moment before turning to a single solid diamond.

The shocked guard was too slow. Jackson sliced through his shirt and across his chest. The guard fell to the ground with a sharp cry. Oliver shouted orders to the other guards as they tried to gain control of Jackson's swinging dagger. But Jackson proved an unusually strong man, and their metal weapons had no effect on his new knife.

In another thirty seconds, the three other guards had been injured as well. Only Oliver remained standing as he and Jackson faced each other down. Every time Nicholas tried to get close, Jackson would start swinging wildly again and Nicholas would be forced back. Nicholas was tall, but Jackson had him outweighed at least twice over.

"Get out of here!" Oliver called over his shoulder. "Find a bailiff!"

But Nicholas had no such intentions. He darted around to the back of the red pine. Looking around frantically, he finally found a rock just the right size, buried in a thin layer of snow.

He said a little prayer, pulled his arm back, then brought it forward with all his strength. The stone cracked on the back of the big man's skull.

The younger guards looked up at the prince in awe as Jackson collapsed between them, but Oliver only scowled.

"I told you to run."

"You also taught me to throw."

"Something I'm sure I'll regret forever."

"I want him to come with us," Nicholas said. "According to that child, he's dealt with the Shadow directly."

It wasn't long before Jackson had been double-bound tightly by his wrists and ankles. To Nicholas's great relief, his other guards were going to be quite well. They had only surface wounds, as Oliver called them. Nothing a good bottle of ale back at the palace and a few days' rest wouldn't fix.

As soon as they had Jackson in his holding cell back on the ship, Nicholas ran to his cabin where he had hidden his leather satchel. He yanked it out and dumped its contents onto the floor where he could sort through them easily. It felt like a lifetime later, but eventually he found what he was looking for.

"Oliver," he called as he raced up to the deck, taking the steps two at a time. "Look at what I found."

Oliver took the parchment from him. "A list of the recent dead? I saw this the other day."

Nicholas tapped on the bottom of the page. "Right here. Look at the second to last entry."

"Paulina Taylor. Forty-two. Found dead on the second day of the new year. Gifted."

"What was her gift?" Nicholas asked, nearly breathless.

Oliver looked up at him, his face filling with disbelief.

"I think," Nicholas said, "we need to have another chat with our guest."

Nicholas was glad to find Jackson awake. He hoped the man's

headache would last a lot longer than the period of unconsciousness.

"It's simply miraculous," Nicholas said, leaning against the bars of the holding cell. "You've never shown any signs of a gift. But now, just a week after her death, you discover that you're gifted. Even more peculiar is that you have the same ability as a woman who was found brutally murdered last week."

"I don't know who you're talking about," Jackson slurred, rubbing the back of his head.

"Her name was Pauline Taylor. She was a mother of six and had her first grandchild on the way." Nicholas squeezed the bars until his fingers hurt.

"I had nothing to do with her death. I didn't even know her."

"But you were willing to buy her gift?" Nicholas slammed his fist against the bars.

Jackson fell backward.

"Now, are you going to make this simple and confess? Or shall my guard beat it out of you?"

Jackson pulled in a deep breath through his nose and got to his feet. He stared at Nicholas for a moment before he began to laugh. It began as a chuckle but grew into guffaws. "I have no fear of you," he finally hollered, still doubled over in laughter.

"If you haven't noticed," Oliver stepped closer, "you're now on *our* ship."

Nicholas crossed his arms in front of his chest. "And if the threat of bodily harm doesn't change your mind, consider this. You're already going to be under the death sentence for your attempt on my life." He shrugged. "But if you can help us, I'm sure my captain of the guard here might be able to get you life in prison instead."

But Jackson kept laughing.

Nicholas and Oliver watched as the man doubled over so hard this time that he fell on the ground again, his laughter still unceasing.

"He's growing madder by the minute," Nicholas whispered.

"You think you're in charge here." Jackson chuckled as he pulled himself into a sitting position, still panting from his outburst. "But you know nothing!"

"Would you care to enlighten us?" Oliver hefted his weapon to his shoulder, but Jackson only made a face at it.

"He gives wonderful gifts." Jackson leered up at them. "But to give those gifts, he must do terrible things." He leaned forward, pressing his face between the bars until it had to hurt. "For a gift to go into you," he pointed at Nicholas, "so must darkness, too!" Then he began chortling again as though he was very clever. "But come here and I will tell you a secret!"

Nicholas ignored Oliver's warning glance and crouched beside the bars. Jackson's hands shot out and grabbed him by the collar, pulling him so close he could see the red and black veins beginning to spread throughout the whites of the man's eyes.

"I cannot tell you who the seller was because I don't know," he whispered.

"I suppose you prefer your death to be quick then," Oliver said, suddenly inches from them with weapon drawn, but Jackson stuck his tongue out at the captain.

"I cannot tell you because he never took off his mask!" Then he turned back to Nicholas, whom he still held. "I can only tell you that I paid him ten thousand pounds in gold."

Nicholas felt his jaw drop.

"But if you want to get really rich," Jackson began to sing, letting go of Nicholas's collar, "here's what you must do! To get it back tenfold, you must deliver the goods!"

"Which would be?" Nicholas grabbed Jackson by the collar this time and slammed his face up against the bars. "What does he want to find?"

Jackson smiled beatifically and whispered, "The girl who talks to the stars."

CHAPTER 25
YES

N icholas! It's so good to have you home!" Nicholas's mother pushed her chair back from the table and ran to wrap her arms around him.

"I was only gone for a week, Mother." Still, Nicholas smiled and hugged his mother back, kissing the top of her head.

"So, how was your meeting?" His father dabbed another slab of butter on his biscuit. "I see you made it back in one piece."

"Thanks to Oliver," Nicholas said as he walked to his seat, nodding his thanks to the servant placing a plate in front of him. "This looks delicious."

"Your father wanted to welcome you home with a good meal." Nicholas's mother beamed at the king as she sat down again. In the warm glow of the morning light that danced in through the windows, one might have fancied them in love.

Nicholas studied his father anew. "Did you miss me that much?"

"I know how awful ship food can be. Sit, sit." His father waved him down. "Your mother was just telling me a delightful tale of the day your sister managed to sit on a cat. Now how did your mission fare?"

"The meeting was awful," he said as he sank into the chair to his father's right.

"Oh?" For the first time, the king's face betrayed a hint of displeasure. He stopped buttering his biscuit and made a slight gesture at one of the servants. Immediately, the room cleared until it was only Nicholas and his parents.

"Where is Sophia?" Nicholas asked.

"Out with several of her ladies-in-waiting, perusing fabrics for the wedding," his mother said.

"So what about the meeting went wrong?" Xander asked.

"Everything. We have traitors galore who openly support the Shadow and all the *improvements* he's made to the economy. We have spineless rats who are too terrified to remember their fealty." He shook his head and took a sip of juice. "Some didn't even turn up, and those who were loyal were bullied by those who weren't."

"I suppose I should go and see if Sophia needs some help." His mother began to stand.

"Actually, Mother, you might be able to help me. Have you seen Lady Elaina since I've been gone?"

His mother looked surprised but sat back down. "Elaina Starke? Yes, actually. I had tea with her family a few days ago."

"How was she?"

"What does this have to do with the rebellion?" Nicholas's father frowned.

"Believe it or not, it does. Now, Mother, how was she faring?"

"She looked a little uneasy, but when I asked after her health, she claimed only to have a slightly upset stomach. Nothing alarming." She sighed. "I can only suppose it had something to do with her father being gone. Poor girl." She put down her cup and studied him. "Why?"

Nicholas took a deep breath. The colorful arrangement of fruits and pastries before him looked suddenly far less appetizing than they had. "Because I think she is in danger."

"Danger! How in the depths could Elaina be in danger?"

But Nicholas turned to his father instead. "Father, when was the last time you spoke with Theodore Jackson?"

His father leaned back and scratched his beard. "I couldn't say for sure. Several years at least. What about him?"

"After the meeting, I decided to visit the market nearby and see how business was progressing, to see if what Alastair said about the illegal trade was true."

"And was it?"

"No one would talk to me at first, so I can only assume so. The environment was far more hostile than I've ever encountered. Eventually, though, we did receive a tip that Jackson had spoken with the Shadow himself."

The king's eyes grew large. "What did you find?"

"I went to visit Jackson at his home. While I was there, I discovered that he had somehow acquired a great deal of wealth very recently."

But Nicholas's father was already shaking his head. "You can't go conjecturing about such things, Nicholas. The man likes to play cards—"

"When I asked him how he had gained it, he tried to kill me."

"Xander!" Nicholas's mother shot out of her chair and faced her husband. "You promised he wouldn't be in any danger!"

"I didn't expect him to be a fool and run headlong into dangerous situations." He turned back to Nicholas with a grimace. "Well, if it was worth risking your life over, I hope you found something important."

Nicholas reached down to his belt and pulled the diamond knife from its scabbard. He tossed it onto the table with a loud clank.

Nicholas's parents gaped at the weapon. Gingerly, his father reached out and took it.

"Where did you get this?" he whispered.

"It seems the Shadow is not just selling lithorium." Nicholas leaned forward. "That belonged to one of my guards before Jackson touched it."

"But Jackson was never gifted," the king said, still stroking the knife.

"Father, it is my belief that the rebellion and whoever is targeting the gifted are linked."

To Nicholas's dismay, his father's expression went from awestruck to one of disgust. "And there you go again, Nicholas." He shoved his chair back and stood. "For once, can you not leave this obsession behind?" His voice grew louder with each word.

"I don't see how the proof can get any clearer! It's in your hands! Literally!"

"Who was your informant that Jackson saw the Shadow?"

Nicholas hesitated before letting out a huff. "A child in the marketplace."

"You gleaned your information from a street brat?" The king threw the knife. It clattered onto the floor, leaving a dent in the marble. "What does that have to do with the rebellion? What does any of this have to do with Elaina Starke?"

"When we interrogated Jackson on the ship, he said the Shadow is offering one hundred thousand pounds of gold for a girl who fits Elaina's description exactly!" Nicholas shouted.

For a brief moment, he considered telling his father of Elaina's gift but decided against it. At best, his father would forbid him from seeing her so she wouldn't encourage his obsession. At worst, his father would try to use her himself.

At the mention of the reward, Nicholas's father stopped pacing. His face lost some of its redness, and he looked at his wife, who was white as a sheet. He finally sighed and rubbed his hand over his face.

"Look. I can send more guards to her home if it makes you feel better. The girl does have a great deal of knowledge, and if word has spread about her father's disappearance, there's a chance someone might try to capitalize on that. I can understand a reward on her head, so I will honor your concern in that area. But," his eyes darkened again, "I expect you to stop this nonsense with the gifted and focus on the rebellion. You've seen it for yourself. Now I need you to start acting like a king. Not some spoiled boy with too much time."

Nicholas wanted to tell his father just what he thought of Xander's performance in the role of king, but as his father had already agreed to grant more soldiers for Elaina, he held his tongue.

The king sat down, picked up his spoon again, and heaped a large serving of cranberry glaze on his cheese. "I have one other request of you as well."

His voice had become pleasant again, but Nicholas wanted to snort at the word *request*.

"King Quinton from Ombrin will be at your sister's wedding. I would like you to be especially attentive to his daughter, Princess Monique."

"I'm sorry, Father, but I have already requested that Elaina come as my partner, and she has accepted." Nicholas glanced at his mother, but her answering glare was rather frightening. He looked back at his eggs instead.

"Elaina can be your partner, but she will just have to share."

"I cannot—"

"Ombrin is likely to be our greatest ally, should a civil war break out, seeing as they are our neighbors." His father's voice remained calm, but its volume ensured Nicholas wouldn't get in a word edgewise.

Nicholas resisted the urge to bang his own head on the thick mahogany table.

"Well, it appears I have a prisoner to help interrogate." The king wiped his face and strutted off as though nothing had happened.

Nicholas stared after his father in disbelief, but it was the razor edge in his mother's voice that snapped his attention back to her.

"Nicholas, I want to know exactly why Elaina Starke has become an international target. And don't tell me it's because her father was a famous admiral."

Nicholas stood and walked uncomfortably to her side. If his

father's wrath was bad, his mother's could be ten times worse. "I invited her to attend a meeting with one of Father's informants and some of our military men."

The queen's face went from rage to horror. "Why on earth would you do that?" she whispered.

"She's quite knowledgeable in political and military ways. I swear, I only thought she would be—"

"No, you failed to think at all, Nicholas! You put her life in danger!"

"She's as intelligent as any man!"

The queen got up and went to the window. "I'm not arguing that point. Any dimwit who spent five minutes with the girl could tell that." She turned and faced Nicholas again, fingering the jewel around her neck. "But you are a man. If you are captured, as much as it would kill me, you would most likely face torture and we would be sent a ransom. It would be simple."

"I'm glad you think so." Nicholas folded his arms across his chest.

She took one of his hands. "But she is a woman," she whispered, shaking her head. "And a young, beautiful one at that. Do you have any idea of what happens to women who are taken for ransom?"

As Nicholas stared back into his mother's eyes, he felt the blood drain from his face. "I never meant to put her in harm's way," he croaked out, his throat suddenly parched.

His mother closed her eyes and bowed her head. "She is the only daughter of my closest friend in the world," she murmured. "It nearly destroyed me when her mother lost her life. Don't put Elaina at risk of suffering a death worse than her mother's." She opened her eyes and looked up at him, imploring. "Promise me you'll keep her safe."

"I promise." Nicholas gritted his teeth. Yes, he would do that. If nothing else in this world, he would keep Elaina safe.

After his mother left, Nicholas wandered over to his study. He would gather a few things and then set out for Elaina's home to explain the extra guards. She would probably be upset, but he would have to tell her the truth. She deserved that at least.

Though it might kill him to tell her that he was the reason she was in danger in the first place.

To his surprise, however, two extra guards stood outside his study. Peeking in, he was even more surprised to see Elaina in deep conversation with his tutor. From the looks on their faces, they were actually enjoying one another's company.

"Your Highness!" Dustin noticed him first and swept into a bow.

Elaina's face lit up with the widest smile Nicholas had ever seen her wear. As she curtsied, he also realized that instead of the practical knot she usually wore on the back of her head, she had pulled her hair up into an intricate braid coil with ringlets that hung down to frame her heart-shaped face. He was also fairly sure that the light pink dress she wore was new.

More than anything, though, she was safe.

Before he knew what he was doing, Nicholas had closed the distance between them, and he did what he had been longing to do since Jackson had uttered the words. He pulled her into his arms and buried his face in her hair. As he inhaled deeply and closed his eyes, he prayed more earnestly than he had prayed in years.

Thank you. Thank you for keeping her safe.

"Um . . . Your Highness?" Her voice was muffled.

"Oh, I'm sorry." He let her go, but wasn't able to look away. "I'm just glad you're safe."

CHAPTER 26

EVERY SHIP

Elaina tried to keep her thumb away from her lip as she neared the prince's study.

It was only the exhaustion, she had been telling herself for the last day and night, that had made him so emotional the day before. He hadn't even had the ability to focus on the lesson, so she'd called it short just five minutes in. He'd just needed sleep. That was all.

And yet, she couldn't shake the feeling of his arms wrapped around her as he had hugged her to his chest. His shirt had still smelled of sea salt, and for one brief moment, she had felt safe.

But what had changed? Had he? Or she? Had they both gone mad?

She didn't get to ask, however, for when she arrived at the study she found it empty and a note on the desk.

I gave Dustin the day off. Please meet me down at the ballroom. Ask any servant and they will escort you.

Even with the help of a maid, the walk to the ballroom was longer than Elaina had expected, but after about a dozen more twists and turns, she began to hear music. What was Nicholas up to this time? She frowned a little as they neared a set of wide, nearly ceiling-high glass doors. When the doors were opened for them, however, she gasped.

Even her greatest adventures to exotic lands hadn't prepared her for the splendor of the royal ballroom.

Hundreds of arches edged in gold raised the distant ceiling higher than Elaina had even imagined the palace was tall. The rounded squares of ceiling between the arches were painted a deep cobalt blue, and each held a different constellation.

"How long did it take them to paint those constellations on the ceiling?" she called out over the cacophony of the orchestra as it warmed up.

"That's not paint, my lady," the maid escorting her called back. "Those stars are made of diamonds."

This ballroom might as well have been made for her.

"A bit ostentatious, I know." Nicholas left the musician he'd been speaking with and greeted them. "When my father was young and our economy really began to grow, he had this ballroom designed for my mother."

Elaina noted the prince's physical improvements with satisfaction. The circles beneath his eyes were mostly gone, and the bounce was back in his step.

"Going somewhere special after this? Perhaps to woo an unsuspecting maiden?"

"What?"

Elaina brushed the shoulder of his stiff gray coat with her finger, trying to ignore the way the coat accentuated his broad shoulders. "Gold buttons, even. I can't imagine this formality has anything to do with our lesson today."

Confusion, annoyance, and pain flashed across his face before he once again donned his usual mischievous grin, the emotions gone so fast Elaina wondered if she'd really seen them there at all.

"Actually, we're going to take a break from lessons today."

She crossed her arms. "Well, it seems I'm hardly dressed for whatever escapade you plan for us to strut about at."

"Nonsense. My sister is getting married in a month, and I plan on dancing."

"I told you, I don't know how to dance."

"And that, my dear Elaina, is why we're here." He gestured to the orchestra, which had quieted from its earlier din. "You see, I like to dance, and I intend to do so at my sister's wedding."

"Are you sure you don't wish to bring two girls?"

He didn't look amused. "Look, I am bringing one partner to this wedding. And she is going to dance. So stop being a coward about it and stretch yourself a bit."

"Fine." She straightened her shoulders and held her arms out toward him stiffly. "But not because you say so. Simply because a lady should know how to dance."

He grinned, and she narrowed her eyes.

"And because no one calls me a coward."

"Oh, stop whining. Now, when I ask you to dance, you allow me first to bow." He demonstrated. "And now you curtsy. Good. When I hold my hand out like this, you take it with your right. Correct. Place your other hand on my shoulder like this. Now I will take your waist."

Elaina's breathing hitched a bit as he placed his large hand gently but firmly against her waist. She had danced reels, of course, with the crew on her father's ship, and jigs with the children in village squares sometimes. But never anything this intimate. Never anything that required so much . . . touching. His hand was warm on her side even through her bodice, and the way his other hand wrapped around hers sent a shiver down her back.

"You all right?" He looked at her in surprise.

"Of course." Why did she sound so nervous? "Just trying to memorize everything so I don't make a fool of myself at the wedding."

"You could never look like a fool." He had begun to turn her slowly as the musicians started to play. It was a slow song, and with Nicholas's help, Elaina began to find that the little bounces and sways were quite relaxing in a way. There was something freeing in being twirled to a rhythm.

"You're a quick learner," he said after they had been dancing for a little while.

Elaina laughed. "When you grow up on a ship, you learn to keep your steps light and your knees bent, or you fall in the water. What is this one called, anyway?"

"The Montelaid. It's one of the slower dances we'll learn. Tomorrow I'll teach you a quicker one called the Quintup. It has only five steps, but the music grows faster and faster until you're forced to make a mistake."

Elaina turned again, enjoying the brief feeling of weightlessness that came whenever she spun. "I like the sound of that one." She almost added that she was looking forward to it already, but stopped, surprised at herself, dually ashamed and awestruck.

She knew better than to encourage him, knew better than to allow him to draw her in. But every part of her heart yearned for . . . well, this. The contentment of laughing at his jokes. The ease with which she could tease him. The freedom of talking about her old life at sea without feeling ashamed.

The feeling of complete security that came in those brief moments of the dance where he pulled her into his chest.

With thoughts of safety, however, came the recollection of the danger she'd tasted while he was gone, and her peace melted away.

"What is it?" He stopped dancing and raised his hand for the musicians to pause.

She took a deep breath and glanced around. "I don't know if it's a good thing to discuss here . . ." She looked pointedly at the servants walking in and out and the musicians behind him.

Understanding lit his blue eyes. He released her, much to Elaina's regret, and walked over to the maestro. After a few words that she couldn't hear, he returned and took her hands again. They began to dance once more, but this time the music was noticeably louder.

"As long as it's not too revealing," he said in a low voice, "we should be able to keep our conversation decently private."

She nodded, but still hesitated, not quite sure where to begin. Admitting weakness was difficult. It was like admitting her father had been right. But what other choice did she have? Her guards had been upset with her the night before when she'd admitted to them that she hadn't told Nicholas about Conrad's intrusion immediately upon his return.

"When you were gone," she began slowly, "something strange happened at my home."

His brows knitted together. "You weren't harmed, were you?" His voice had an edge to it that sent a shiver up Elaina's spine. And not in a romantic way.

"No." She shook her head and looked at the ground.

The floor here was flecked with red and blue. She hadn't seen that anywhere else in the palace.

"Elaina?"

She sighed and continued, though she couldn't bring herself to look him in the eye. "Alastair came to visit Lydia and bring me a note from Dustin about when you would return. I remembered what you'd said about Conrad, so I asked Alastair where he was. Alastair said he was in the coach feeling ill and had wanted to stay there to lie down, so I said nothing more about it." Her words were coming too fast now, all rushing out of her like a flood. "But when I went up to my chambers later on, I looked out the window to find Conrad just below it."

Nicholas's grip tightened around her hand and waist. When she dared to glance up at his eyes, they were dark, burning with a wrath she'd never seen there before. For the first time since she'd known him, he looked . . . dangerous. "Where were your guards?" His voice was flat.

"We think he threw a stone through the kitchen window in order to distract them. They said they would have requested more guards immediately, but it seems Conrad has been up to other mischief in the palace. Whenever the guards try to take action, he threatens them with his relation to the king through Alastair."

"My father needs to hear about this," Nicholas growled, but Elaina shook her head.

"He has, according to Gerard. But since Conrad leaves no proof of his snooping, your father refuses to charge him with anything."

Nicholas's face was hard, jaw flexing and eyes like icicles as they stared down at her. When she involuntarily shivered, however, he seemed to remember himself.

"I'm so sorry, Elaina. This is all my fault," he said, bowing his head. "I never meant to put you in danger."

"What do you mean? *You're* the one who insisted I keep guards nearby. I wanted nothing to do with them." Elaina shuddered again as she imagined what might have happened if there had been no guards.

"I mean I didn't stop to think about what was at stake for you when I asked you to get involved in this mess." He shook his head, somehow still leading them through the dance.

"But I wanted to be involved!" She laughed humorlessly. "Do you know what torture it is to sit at home and sip tea and *sew* after living the life I left behind?"

"The Shadow is looking for you."

Elaina's feet stopped working and became rooted to the floor, but Nicholas forced her to keep turning.

"Try not to look so alarmed," he whispered. "They can't hear us over the music, but we don't know who's watching us now."

It took her a moment to collect herself, but somehow, Elaina made her feet move again. As she did, shame warred with fear. She had lived through battles and sea beasts. This one man, whoever he was, shouldn't frighten her. And yet, he did.

"How do you know?" she squeaked.

"Apparently, the Shadow is also connected to the attacks on the gifted."

Something in Elaina's dull brain lit like a match. "Alastair told me he believed the same thing!"

Nicholas nodded grimly. "While I was in Solwhind, I was attacked by a man who had recently purchased the gift of a dead individual. Then, when we were interrogating him on the way back here, he said the Shadow is offering one hundred thousand pounds of solid gold in exchange for the girl who talks to the stars."

Elaina took deep breaths to steady herself under the watchful eyes of her dance partner. She wanted to deny it, or at least to shout that she wasn't afraid, that she was unaffected by such a threat. But the trembling in her stomach and the sudden desire to draw closer to Nicholas kept her mouth shut. As they slowly turned in circles, Elaina warred with herself. She would be stronger than this. She had to be.

"I don't understand it," he said.

Elaina looked up, hoping her fear wouldn't be visible in her eyes. "What's that?" Ugh. Her voice was warbling.

He was watching her carefully. "You're so determined to do it on your own, to be strong. You push yourself to the limit, and you run headfirst into danger." This time, it was he who stopped dancing and stood still. But he didn't let go of her. "What is it that you so desperately want," he whispered, "that you're willing to give up everything for it?"

If he'd asked her that question when she'd arrived that morning, or even yesterday, Elaina would have been able to tell him. She would have told him how she wanted to prove her father wrong. She wanted to return to her life at sea. She wanted to live for the mission and her father's beloved navy.

But now, as she stared into his blazing blue eyes . . .

"I'm not sure anymore."

He swallowed hard and bent until their faces were nearly touching. "While I was in Solwhind, I saw things." He cupped her jaw in his hand, and for the first time, Elaina didn't pull away. "And I kept seeing your face. When I found out that the warlord himself is looking for you, it nearly killed me to realize I was the one who had put you at risk. But," he paused, his face becoming resolute once more. "I learned something about myself in the process."

"You did?"

He leaned forward until his forehead was resting against hers. "I can't lose you."

"Why?" she breathed.

He took both of her hands in his and cradled them to his chest, tracing her knuckles with his fingertips. "I have been blessed with everything I've ever had. All I ever had to do was utter the word and it was mine. As such, I've spent my entire life floating from one desire to the next, and until I met you, I never knew what I *needed* the most."

"What is that?" she whispered, not trusting herself to speak aloud.

"Every ship needs an anchor, my lady." He tightened his grip on her hands. "I've been drifting for a long time now. And I wish to never drift again."

Elaina had to remind herself to breathe.

The prince might have just declared his love.

And possibly just asked her to marry him.

And to her shock and horror and joy and relief, she found herself wanting nothing more than to stretch up on her toes and kiss him.

Instead, however, she cleared her throat several times, willing her heart to beat steadily again. When she finally did glance up at his face, she nearly laughed and cried at the same time. He looked more anxious than she had ever seen him.

"I think," she finally said slowly, "that you've given me much to think about."

He didn't say anything, just stared at her with hopeless eyes.

"I also think," she said, pulling her hands free and dropping into a curtsy, "that my family will be wondering where I am soon." The hopelessness lingered on his face until she added with a hesitant smile, "I am, however, quite looking forward to tomorrow's lesson."

Nicholas blinked, then broke into the biggest grin she'd ever seen.

CHAPTER 27
PLAYTHINGS

Nicholas tugged at the sleeves of his coat. His mother had ordered it made specifically for the wedding just two months before, but in those two short months, he'd needed the blasted thing altered twice. And now the sleeves were too short. Again.

"My prince."

Nicholas turned to find Alastair bowing low.

"You're back already." Nicholas was glad to have a reason to ignore his coat.

"Aye." Alastair came to stand beside Nicholas and looked over the railing at the royal chapel below. Though the wedding was in an hour, servants beneath them were still scurrying around to finish last minute details. "So everything is going as planned, I gather?" he asked.

Nicholas snorted. "The rebellion takes over Solwhind and declares war, and my father refuses to change a single detail of my sister's wedding."

"Do you think he should have canceled it?" Alastair looked at him with wide eyes.

"No." Nicholas scratched his freshly shaven chin. "Not canceled. I just think a thousand pounds of flowers, two dozen baskets of turtledoves, and a three-day feast seems a bit excessive right now. It's not as though her vows would be any less finished in the eyes of the Maker if the festivities were a bit . . . scaled back. It just sends the wrong message." Not to mention the number of people from Solwhind who had been invited and were still confirmed guests.

And as Elaina was to be partner to the brother of the bride, at one point or another, they would all be looking at her. It was too many people too close. Of course, he didn't speak this worry out loud.

"But I'm sure you didn't seek me out to discuss my sister's purple rose garlands."

"Ah, yes." Alastair's eyes lost their gleam. "I wanted to let you know that I have sent Conrad to look into a possible traitor as we speak."

"Someone here in the capital?"

Alastair nodded, his wary eyes never leaving Nicholas's face.

"Splendid!" Nicholas's heart suddenly felt as though it could fly. Wedding or not, Conrad would be out of the way for the day. Maybe even two. When Nicholas had spoken earlier to Alastair about the young man, Alastair had promised to put an end to his snooping, but any time Conrad was out of the way completely, Nicholas was happy.

"Let me know the moment you learn anything." He glanced down. A familiar figure lingered in the doorway. "I'm afraid I am needed below now, but you know where to find me."

Nicholas nearly tripped down the chapel steps as he ran to the first level, his heart thumping out of rhythm. As soon as he saw her, though, his trepidation melted away. She was a vision.

Her sky-blue gown was light and airy. Gossamer sleeves revealed her lean, sun-kissed arms. Dozens of layers of similarly thin material made her skirt look like a snowdrop flower. She might as well have been a flower fairy herself. And like the beautiful green dress she had worn to his mother's garden tea, this dress was completely unsuitable for the season. Of course, knowing with whom she lived, Elaina's wide array of lovely but impractical dresses was probably the fault of her fashion-obsessed cousin. Nicholas wanted to both thank and rebuke Lydia at the same time.

As Elaina handed her outer wrap to a servant, keeping only her white shawl, she looked around the chapel. Her eyes grew large as she wrung the shawl in her hands. Thin, honey-colored curls were piled on top of her head, and her blue-green eyes were luminous as she took in the scene around her, slowly turning like a wind-up doll. Her pink pearl lips parted slightly, and Nicholas had to work hard to pull his eyes away from them.

No need to stand there and gawk, though. She would be on his arm all day long, where he could keep her safe and bask in her beauty from up close.

Of course, if everything went as planned, he intended to do more than that before the third feast was concluded.

"The servants just lit the fire, so this room won't be warm for another half hour." Nicholas removed his coat and laid it over her shoulders. He half expected her to object, but she didn't. Instead, she pulled it more snugly around her and gave him a regretful smile.

"Thank you. My cousin assured me it would be warm enough for a dress such as this, but really, it looks as though it might snow outside." She glanced back at the door, where her cousin and aunt were talking with a few of the other early guests.

"I'm sorry for the chill, but I can't say I'm disappointed in her choice of dress." Nicholas cast an eye at the way the gauzy layers of blue cascaded off her slight hips and down to the ground.

Elaina gave him a warning look, but he just grinned back. Reading her was becoming a little easier by the day, and behind her scowl he thought she might just be slightly blushing. He knew better to tell her that, though.

"But truly, you look lovely."

She turned away, but he didn't miss her cool little smile. "You clean up nicely yourself. If I didn't know better, I would be fooled into thinking you a respectable gentleman."

"Now where would the fun be in that? Then you would have no one to order about all evening. You'd be like a captain without a ship." He held out his arm, and she took it, shaking her head and laughing. Her laughter was like the sound of the chimes the servants hung in the garden at spring. "Come," he said. "Let me show you where we'll be standing and walking for the procession."

An hour later, Nicholas stood in the back of the chapel with Elaina beside him, surrounded by his family and all the other individuals who were participating in his sister's ceremony. They were supposed to be lined up in an orderly fashion, but his mother was crying, his eldest sister was crying, and all of the bride's maidens were trying to comfort them, though half of them were crying as well. He couldn't even see the bride to know whether or not she was in tears.

The men huddled in their own group, a few safe feet away from the gaggle of women where they wouldn't be called upon to stop any of the weeping.

Nicholas, of course, did his best to hug his mother and remind her that Sophia and her husband were staying in Ashland, unlike Daphne, but even his words did little good. He soon gave up in frustration and shoved his hands in his coat to make his retreat.

Elaina, however, was as calm and collected as ever and somehow managed to wander from the men's group to the women's and back again, sharing kind words wherever she went. Soon even his mother was laughing, despite the tears still running down her face. Everyone Elaina spoke to ended their conversation with a smile, even some of the bride's maidens that he had once entertained as partners at other parties. At one time, they'd been considered conquests of his own.

But not anymore. Now there was only one beauty outshining all the other women in the room. And as much as he loved his sister, the true beauty wasn't the one in white.

Nicholas felt something change inside him as he and Elaina

began their slow walk down the aisle preceding the bride. He had been drawn to her more and more in the months since she'd arrived, but he'd never felt anything as strong as this, and it was all he could do to focus on the red carpet down which they walked. Longing like starvation filled him, making him wish more than anything for this day to be their own.

For all his life, Nicholas had worried he wouldn't find the right one. Hopping from pretty face to pretty face, he'd continued to move on, hoping not to make the same mistake his father had, marrying one when his heart belonged to another.

But in these small moments, as they turned and walked to their respective seats, Nicholas felt in his bones that if he could keep Elaina, he would be perfectly satisfied for the rest of his days.

As his sister and her groom, a higher lord from one of their southern territories, said their vows, Nicholas watched Elaina. She wore a small, contented smile. The freckles scattered along her nose and cheeks made her eyes look playful and bright, and the way she leaned forward slightly in her seat made her look . . . hopeful?

The power of his stare drew those eyes, however, and she turned and met them steadily. And for once, she didn't look away.

His heart caught in his throat. Did he dare hope that she was feeling the same things?

I'm sorry.

The prayer was so spontaneous that for a moment, he didn't even realize he was praying. How long had it been since he had truly prayed anything more than a short request or complaint?

I don't deserve anything you've given me. And I truly don't deserve her. But, Maker . . . she makes me want to be better, to do what's right. Please don't take that away from me. Let her be my anchor in the dark.

After the ceremony had finished and the time to return to the ballroom and mingle with guests and nibble on light refreshments had begun, he and Elaina said little. The change between them was palpable, and Nicholas was nearly afraid to know exactly what that change was, except for the fact that she seemed to stand closer to his side as they greeted other guests, and she glanced up at him more than he could remember her ever doing before.

He reached into his pocket and fingered the silver band. Of course, it wouldn't be prudent to propose in the middle of his sister's big day. But sometime during the course of the celebration, he would get her alone. Then he would ask what someone like him had no right to ask, in the hope that he could be given what he could never in his lifetime deserve.

He felt somewhat lightheaded at the thought of it.

"Nicholas, come here!"

Nicholas turned and couldn't help the small groan that escaped him. Elaina glanced up at him in surprise, but said nothing as he led her over to his father. Pasting a false smile on his face, he bowed to his father, then inclined his head to the man beside him. He had forgotten all about his father's assignment.

"This is—"

"King Quinton." Nicholas bowed his head again. "It is an honor to see you again." He gently nudged Elaina forward. "Let me introduce you to Lady Elaina Starke."

The king bowed, but Nicholas didn't miss the way his eyes lingered on her figure for a moment longer than they should have. It took every ounce of self-control not to grab the tomato-faced, oversized king by the collar and teach him a lesson.

King Quinton didn't seem to notice Nicholas's glare, however, for he only laughed and turned back to Nicholas's father. "Took us longer to get here than usual, what with your little war going on and all. How is it that you haven't been able to extinguish the rebellion yet?"

"As you can see, my daughter has kept me fairly busy," Xander said dryly, gesturing to the festivities around them.

"That I understand. Speaking of daughters, Monique. Come here. Nicholas, you will remember my daughter, Monique."

Nicholas certainly remembered Princess Monique. She had been one of the few young girls Nicholas had never even contemplated chasing, for not even adolescent Nicholas could imagine spending time with her wheedling laugh or constant whining. If there was one woman in the world he could trust himself not to flirt with, it was Monique.

But as a young lady pulled herself from a gathering of women nearby, Nicholas felt his confidence crumble and his blood run hotter. *I told you I'm trying to change. Are you determined to make me fail?* he pleaded silently to the Maker.

Princess Monique wore the same petulant pout that she had the last time they'd met, but that was really the only thing about her that remained the same. Dressed in the most provocative gown he had ever seen on a noble lady, her bodice was cut so low that it barely managed to cover any part of her ample chest. The dress lines alone were enough to distract nearly every male in the room, but as if its design wasn't enough, her dress had been sewn far too tight. Where Elaina's gown draped down over her gentle, petite curves like feathers on a sleek little bird, Monique's gown gave her curves their own curves.

"Princess Monique." Elaina dropped into a graceful curtsy.

Nicholas was immensely grateful for the interruption to his thoughts.

"I don't know if you remember," Elaina continued in her smooth, confident voice, "but we met a few years back when my father's ship docked in your royal city. It is good to see you again."

"Of course," Monique muttered, hardly sparing Elaina a glance. How was it possible for a beautiful, voluptuous woman to so greatly resemble a hyena stalking its prey, smiling at them all the while?

"Nicholas, why don't you take the princess for a stroll in the rose garden?" His father turned to him.

Nicholas clutched Elaina's arm closer, as though she would protect him from his father's schemes. "It would be my honor," he managed to choke out, "but Lady Elaina is my partner for the day, Father."

"Fah! Lady Elaina can stay here and entertain two old men. I believe King Quinton here was a great admirer of her father. She can regale us with old sailing stories for a few moments while you show Monique around."

Nicholas and his father shared a very long look. He did not wish to take Monique off alone, and he wanted to leave Elaina with Monique's father even less. But at least they were in public, so hopefully her father would behave with some decorum. That, and Nicholas knew that not even he could challenge his father in public and hope to come away unscathed. There were limits, even for the crown prince.

Finally, he broke off the look with his father and turned to Elaina, trying to apologize with his eyes. She gave him a slight nod. But there was a tightness in her eyes that betrayed her look of serenity.

Swallowing hard, he let her arm fall from his and then held it out to Monique, who accepted it and immediately pulled herself closer to him than Elaina ever had.

Standing as straight as he could, keeping his body rigid, Nicholas walked woodenly toward the open ballroom doors. One quick turn around the path of roses. That was all he would do. Then they were coming directly back into the ballroom. Surely he could keep his eyes away from her for that long.

They left the ballroom and started down the path of roses without saying much. Nicholas pointed out the different colors in what he hoped was the most boring tour she had ever been given. After rounding a few bends, however, the pressure of her arm disappeared. Looking back, he barely had time to see her disappear.

Nicholas started after her, not sure what to make of her odd behavior, when he was yanked backward and shoved against a thick hedge. Before he knew what was happening, warm lips were pressed against his.

EVERYTHING in him shouted for him to get away, but he couldn't concentrate as she pressed herself against him. Escape was necessary, but his body wouldn't respond to his mind's desperate commands.

Finally, he was able to free himself from her grasp. He stumbled sideways, panting, staring at her in horror and backing away until he was at the other side of the hedge.

Too many girls. Over the years, Nicholas had kissed too many girls. And because of it, his reaction to Monique had been exactly that . . . a reaction. He hadn't meant to kiss her back. But she'd taken him by surprise, and all the years he'd spent giving and receiving simple pecks and then slightly longer sentiments in secret had taught his body to never say no or even to protest.

And now that lifetime of indulgence had betrayed not only him but also the beautiful girl whose hand he had pleaded with the Maker for just an hour before.

Nicholas swallowed hard and fumbled to straighten his coat, as though fixing his appearance would wipe away what he had just done. "We . . . we need to return." His voice squeaked like a youth's. "We're not yet betrothed and shouldn't be found in such a situation."

She arched one perfect black eyebrow haughtily. "It would only make our own vows faster for fear of scandal." Then she laughed. "Come, Nicholas! When did you become such a killjoy?"

He held his arm out as far as it would go.

Rolling her eyes, she took it but pouted the entire way back.

When they arrived, Elaina was still with his father and the other king. She said something Nicholas couldn't hear, and both men burst out laughing. Elaina herself smiled, looking as though she entertained kings every day.

"There you two are. That was a fast walk. Did you have fun, my darling?" King Quinton asked Monique.

"I don't find Prince Nicholas at all eager to join in any sort of negotiations, Father." Then she sniffed before returning to the group of girls she'd been standing with earlier.

Nicholas thought he would feel better after she left, but the nausea didn't leave. It only grew worse as Elaina took his arm again.

He and Elaina took their seats soon after, when toasts were made, but none of the merrymaking was enjoyable. The food was dry and tasteless. The choir that sang the blessing over his sister and her husband was off-key, and he had no desire to address the well-wishes of the hundreds of guests who came to his table to greet him.

As usual, Elaina came to his rescue, but he could feel a new hesitance in her glances and in the way she moved. It wasn't until the ballroom floor was opened for dancing, however, that they had any chance to speak privately.

He placed his hands on her hand and waist as he had so many times during practice. The way her small fingers fit into his had seemed so natural before this, so right. But now they burned feverishly against his skin.

"How did negotiations with the kingdom of Ombrin fare?" she asked as the first slow dance began.

It was all he could do to give her the slightest shake of his head.

"I see." She pursed her lips together and took a deep breath. "May I ask who attempted negotiations first?"

He could only stare at her miserably, barely managing to complete the turn the dance required.

"Then I suppose," she said, her voice husky, "I don't need to ask what that red lip powder is doing on your face."

Without thinking, Nicholas let go of her hand and reached up to touch the edge of his mouth. When he looked at his fingers, they were tinged with a hint of rouge. It was the same shade of red the princess was wearing.

Nicholas steeled himself for the biting lecture he knew he deserved. The knowing glare that said she had been right about him all along. The silent treatment she had been so good at doling out when they had first met.

But nothing prepared him for the single tear that rolled slowly down her face.

Self-loathing devoured him as he realized he had broken the heart of the girl who refused to be broken.

Her remaining hand loosed itself from his shoulder, and though the dance wasn't done, she stepped back.

"Please, Elaina. I . . . I'm sorry. I never meant to—"

"Lydia was right," she whimpered before turning and walking away.

Nicholas followed her as she pulled her shawl from the chair where she had left it and headed for the door.

"She pushed herself upon me!" he called out as they left the ballroom and headed down the main hall.

Elaina walked faster.

Nicholas ran until he caught her on the palace steps. There were a few people milling about the entrance and the guards near the door, but Nicholas didn't care who heard him. He would get down on his belly and grovel if that's what it took for her to forgive him. "Please!" He stood in front of her, hands raised cautiously. "You have every right to hate me, but at least hear what I have to say!"

"Fine." She sniffled, crossing her arms and setting her little chin stubbornly. "I will give you one chance to answer my question truthfully. Suppose she did set herself upon you. Did you resist? Or did you kiss her back?"

Nicholas wanted with all of his heart to say he had resisted. But it wouldn't be the truth.

"I'm not a plaything, Nicholas." She turned to stare out at the sea, swiping at her cheek with the back of her hand. "For one brief, glorious moment, I thought you had changed." She turned back to him. "But for one brief, glorious moment, I was a fool." She stepped around him and began again to descend the steps.

"Where are you going?" he called out. "You arrived with your family."

"I am walking."

"At least let me walk you home!" He began to run after her again. "It's not safe—"

She whirled around, fists clenched at her sides. "Then get me a guard!"

All Nicholas could do was to nod and stumble back up the steps.

CHAPTER 28

THE ACCUSED

L ady Elaina!"
   Oh, so it was *Lady* Elaina now, was it? She kept
   walking.

"Lady Elaina, wait!"

Elaina nearly ignored the command until she realized that it wasn't Nicholas calling after her at all.

She looked up from the ground to glare at the four guards hurrying to her side. "Oh good, you're here." The words tasted bitter as she spoke them. "You will escort me straight home. Once we're there, I will hear no missives from the prince, understand?"

"We're not here to escort you home," the guard standing closest to her said, hand on the hilt of his sword.

Elaina frowned at that hand. "Then why are you here? Because if you're here on the prince's behalf, you can just go back to the palace and tell the prince that if he's man enough to—"

"We are not here on behalf of the prince," another burly guard cut in.

"You're not?"

"His Royal Majesty King Xander Whealdmar has summoned you."

Elaina looked back at the palace. She hadn't even left the

palace grounds yet. Why would the king be summoning her? There was no way he could know what had transpired between her and Nicholas in such a short period of time. When she looked beyond the guards, Nicholas was standing in the same place she'd left him, looking just as confused as she felt.

She turned back to the guard. "Has the king told you why he wants me?" Had there been a sighting of her father, perhaps?

"Yes, my lady. On charges of high treason to the crown."

ELAINA'S KNEES were numb from kneeling and her wrists sore from the shackles by the time the charges were read.

How long had it been since she was publicly humiliated, arrested right on the palace steps? It felt like days, but judging by the sun outside the window, it could only have been an hour or two. In that time, it seemed the entire kingdom had managed to squeeze itself into the throne room to witness the proceedings. Elaina wouldn't have supposed anything could have pulled people away from the wedding festivities, but apparently arresting one of the court's highest ladies could do just that. Elaina could hear her aunt weeping from somewhere in the back, but she kept her eyes focused on the small square of blue tile in front of her. It kept her from looking up at the man standing beside his father's throne.

This was a nightmare. It had to be.

"The charges against Lady Elaina Starke of Ashland are these: conspiring against the crown by fraternizing with hostile kingdoms, divulging secrets to foreign interests who would see Ashland fall in its civil war, and receiving payment for such fraternizations."

"And who is my accuser?" Elaina glared up at Alastair after he finished reading the charges.

Alastair nearly dropped his scroll, but he wouldn't meet her eyes. Whispers went up all around, but Elaina gave him her fiercest look. "It is my right by law to know who has accused me of such rubbish."

The king nodded and waved his hand, though it was without his usual pomp. "Tell her." His voice sounded ancient.

"Will Conrad Fuller and Miss Lydia Tifft step forward?" the man called.

Conrad stepped to the front of the dais from the shadows. His round, chalky face betrayed no remorse or regret. Lydia, however, cried piteously as she walked to the front of the room, tripping several times along her way.

Elaina couldn't breathe. She had known Lydia was jealous. They hadn't been close since their argument about Alastair. But Elaina had never dreamed her animosity could reach this extent.

Alastair cleared his throat. He had dark circles beneath his eyes, and he moved as though he were seventy instead of forty. His eyes were rimmed red, as though tears might start rolling from them at any second, and he avoided Elaina's gaze. Looking back down at the parchment in his hands, he took a deep breath, briefly closed his eyes, and then began to read.

"Elaina Hope Starke, Marchioness of Rosington Manor and all its corresponding grounds, is hereby accused of accepting payment from the Tumenian government in exchange for secrets stolen from the crown—"

"Tumen! I would like to see what proof there is to sustain such charges!" Elaina forced her voice not to crack.

Alastair gave her a sad look before nodding at someone to his left. "Bring it in."

A soldier entered the room, carrying her sea chest. Elaina looked back at Lydia, pleading for some sort of explanation, but Lydia only cried harder. Her mumbled words were difficult to understand, but Elaina could gather something about her not meaning it, and misunderstandings. As if apologies would help now.

"If you would be so kind as to open it, Lady Starke."

Elaina hobbled to her feet and walked forward, her chains

scraping the ground. Pulling the key from a hidden pocket in her dress, she opened the chest, only to feel her heart sink like a rock. Inside lay not only her glass slippers, the gifts from the *Adroit*'s crew, and a few other baubles, but a purple velvet bag as well.

Alastair stepped forward and lifted the bag, holding it up for everyone to see. As he did, the distinct clink of coins could be heard.

"I have never seen that bag before in my life!" Elaina cried, but for the first time, a man who stood near to the king called out,

"Silence!"

It only took her a moment to recognize Lord Benedict from the secret meeting. The other men standing around him, Elaina realized, were other magistrates, most of whom she didn't recognize.

Alastair bent down again and picked up a parchment that had fallen to the floor when he'd taken the bag. It was closed with a bright yellow wax seal.

"Your Majesty," Alastair held up the parchment and turned back to the king where he sat on his throne. "It's a Tumenian seal."

Gasps went up from the crowd, but Elaina could only hear the stars' words in her head.

Beware of the planted yellow seal.

Some help that caution had been.

Desperately, she began searching her memory for the last time she had opened her chest. It had been days. Weeks, really. In fact, the last time she recalled opening her chest was the day . . .

"He planted it!" She jabbed her finger at Conrad. "The last time I opened that chest, I found him hiding beneath the window of my bedchamber. I have never even met the king of Tumen!" She turned, finally willing herself to make eye contact with Nicholas. For by now, she knew he was her only hope. "Ashland doesn't have dealings with Tumen." Her voice cracked.

He met her gaze, but his face was hard and his eyes remained distant.

"Quite a charge you bring against the assistant of the king's personal assistant." Lord Benedict snickered. "As you asked earlier, what proof have you to lay such claims?"

"Ask my guards!" Elaina said. "They can witness that he was there that day!"

"Standing in a bush and planting false evidence are two very different charges," Lord Benedict said, shaking his head. "Nay, I believe you found a kingdom that was quite interested in Ashland's fall, should the rebellion win, and you decided to use those negotiation skills to benefit yourself."

Elaina had the desire to hurl some of her father's curses of choice at the fat, old baronet, the ones her father saved up for the worst of situations, typhoons and krakens and such. But instead, she turned to Nicholas once more, pleading with her eyes for help.

But his face did not melt into the teasing, friendly expression she had come to know so well, or even the injured, frustrated one that he'd worn on the palace steps. Instead, they were hard as flint.

CHAPTER 29

MISTAKEN

F ather," Nicholas murmured, still holding Elaina's gaze. "I request permission to discuss this hearing privately. With you first and then the magistrates."

The king nodded gravely before standing and leading the way out of the throne room, flanked by the magistrates. They made their way into a smaller antechamber behind the throne room, but instead of stopping there, Nicholas continued on into an even smaller room behind that. Once he and his father were alone and the door was shut, Nicholas let out a gusty breath.

"This whole hearing is a farce. Conrad Fuller planted that evidence."

His father slumped into a chair and leaned forward, elbows on his knees. "You know I like her, son. She's been as helpful to us as her father. But I really don't know what to do in the face of such proof."

"But the proof is a lie!"

"And you know that how?"

Nicholas tugged on his stiff formal collar, feeling desperate for some air that the confining legal robe did not allow for. "Elaina told me about Fuller snooping around her home, how he was standing just below her window at one point, just like she said. That also happened to be the day Bladsmuth was delivering a note to Elaina, and Fuller had accompanied him." Nicholas leaned over the table toward his father. "He had to have taken advantage of his master's distraction."

"But we've established that only Lady Elaina has the key to that chest."

"Perhaps she left it open."

Nicholas's father shook his head and rubbed his eyes. "And how do you plan to convince the magistrates on such circumstantial evidence?"

"I don't need to convince any—"

"You forget that I am not the only one responsible for her sentence! The decision is not solely mine!"

Nicholas wanted to throw something through the little window above him. Perhaps the sound of shattering glass would make him feel better. "Do you think she's guilty?" he asked instead.

His father's face looked haggard in the small window's weak light. "Knowing what I do of her character, my heart tells me no." He looked up at Nicholas. "But that will not convince the magistrates."

They sat quietly for a long time, each one staring at his hands. Nicholas wanted so badly to shout at his father and demand they let her go. But for the first time in his life, he knew his father wanted the same thing he did. And they were both powerless to get it.

"What is the punishment for such a crime?" Nicholas finally asked.

"Execution."

Nicholas closed his eyes. In his heart, he asked forgiveness for what he was about to say. But it was the only way he could think of that might save her life. "Father, do you know why Elaina is being hunted by the Shadow?"

"I assume it has to do with her familiarity with secret information."

Nicholas shook his head. "She's gifted." When he looked back up at his father, he finally saw the expression of horror that he had been waiting to see for years. "She used her gift often to save our ships while at sea. Hundreds of lives have been spared since she was a little girl. And now we're going to execute her," he finished helplessly.

"You really love her, don't you?" His father stared at him, his mouth hanging open.

Nicholas pulled the ring from his pocket and turned it in his hands, pausing when the gems caught the light and cast their sparkles all around him. "I was going to make her queen."

Nicholas's father stared for a long time at the ring. Then he stood and leaned against the wall and cursed. "There must be something we can do," he said, pounding his fist against it.

Show us, Nicholas prayed. *I beg you, do not allow innocent blood to be shed. Don't let* her *blood be shed.* If they had to sentence her to death, Nicholas didn't know how he would ever be able to live with himself, let alone face his mother or sisters or Elaina's aunt or any of his own friends—

Nicholas stood so fast his chair nearly tipped over. "I want her exiled."

"What?"

"If we can convince the magistrates to exile her instead of putting her to death, I can send her to Destin." Nicholas's excitement began to build as he paced the room. "King Everard adores her. She'll be safe there, and I can find a way to clear her name here and allow her to return home!"

"Slow down, son." His father put his hands on Nicholas's shoulders and held him in place. "I understand your plan, but convincing the magistrates won't be easy. Some of them haven't forgiven you yet for insulting them during the meeting with Bladsmuth."

"Father." Nicholas grasped his father's arms and held them tightly. "We have to try."

His father stared down at their clasped arms. How long had it been since they'd touched, Nicholas wondered. He couldn't recall the last time, nor did he care. He only waited.

Finally, Xander nodded. "Very well. I suppose it can't hurt to try."

Nicholas pulled his father into a quick embrace before straightening his shoulders and walking back into the antechamber.

"So," he said to the men piled into the little room, "is it safe to assume that you've made your decision unanimously?"

Lord Benedict rolled his eyes. "Did you really need to ask us that?"

"Not unanimously." Lord Greyson called out from the back. When several of the magistrates turned to glare at him, he only shook his head. "I am not convinced. Lock or no lock, it seems to me as though planting evidence might have been a rather easy task." He adjusted his spectacles. "Particularly with a girl of eighteen years. They're not known for taking care with secrets." He chuckled darkly to himself. "I should know. I had seven."

"The rest of us," Lord Stiles said in a thin voice after glancing at Benedict, who nodded vigorously, "believe she is guilty."

"Really?" Nicholas looked around, staring at each magistrate until he made eye contact. Most just looked down at the floor. "Well then," he said. "I have spoken with my father, and we agree that exile would be an appropriate sentence."

"But public hanging is the norm!" Lord Benedict cried out.

"Yes." Xander spoke for the first time, though he stayed seated behind Nicholas. It seemed as though the day's strain had taken most of the life out of him. "But if Elaina Starke truly did deal with the Tumenians, who would love to see us fall and our trade routes collapse, then who better to examine her than the Fortiers? Destin is Tumen's greatest enemy, and if anyone is to understand what brought one of our finest ladies so low, it would be they."

"I believe," Lord Greyson said, his thin face brightening a bit, "that Queen Isabelle has a gift that might be helpful in determining the truth. Perhaps she might even be able to discern whether the girl is truly guilty or whether something deeper is afoot."

Nicholas nearly allowed himself to smile at the old man. As Greyson's words sank in, the looks of relief on the majority of faces around them revealed that many had truly not wanted to send the girl to her death after all.

"So it is settled then," Nicholas said. "If you agree with a majority, I will send for a courier bird at once."

Everyone but Benedict and Stiles raised his hand. Nicholas wanted to jump and shout for joy until he realized what he still needed to do. This sobered him instantly.

The walk out of the antechamber to the front of the dais was one of the longest and shortest journeys Nicholas had ever taken.

Elaina was still on her knees before the throne. It galled Nicholas to see her looking so submissive. So defeated. And to know that he had played a part was even worse. Only a few hours before, he had betrayed her heart. Now he was ruining her life. He masked his feelings, however, with resolve. This was going to save her life, even though it would cut his own heart like a knife.

But Elaina would live.

He went to stand at the front of the dais until he towered over her small huddled form. "Lady Elaina Hope Starke, the magistrates and rulers of this land have found you guilty." His voice cracked on the last word. But he had to go on. "You are hereby sentenced to exile from Ashland," his voice grew quieter, "until you are either proven innocent or the Maker leads your soul into eternal bliss. And if you ever return to Ashland's shores without a complete pardon by the crown and his men . . ." He paused, but knew he had to say the words anyway. "You will die."

For the first time since he had begun speaking, Elaina lifted her head. Her face was wet and her eyes were red.

And the look she gave him pierced him to the bone.

As soon as Elaina had been dragged away and her guards notified of her final destination, Nicholas turned and stalked out of the throne room. In moments, he was in his chambers, yanking the infernal court robe off and throwing his travel belongings into a bag.

"And where do you think you're going?"

Nicholas paused, but didn't look up to answer. "Elaina was just declared guilty of—"

"I know. I was there."

"I'm getting on that ship with her, and I will accompany her down the river and through the continent to Destin. I have to explain everything."

His mother left the doorway and came to stand beside his bed, where he was still feverishly tossing legal documents and an assortment of weapons into his bag.

"Your father risked much with the magistrates today by allowing you to declare that sentence on your own. If he angers them too much, they have the power to call a hearing to express their doubts about his ability to reign." She took Nicholas's hands and turned him to face her. "Are you sure you want to run off like this without consulting him first?"

Nicholas gave his mother a quick hug, then closed his bag. "Give Father my thanks and respect. I will be back when I get this mess sorted out."

"I know I should stop you . . ." She shook her head.

"Then why aren't you?"

"I can't help feeling that this is part of the Maker's way of answering your prayer."

"So you're not going to tell Father?"

"Leave your father to me. Now go."

NICHOLAS STOLE AWAY in the shadows of the late afternoon. He really wanted nothing more than to leave immediately, but his mother had cautioned him to wait until she gave him the signal that all was clear. Once he knew his father was occupied with trying to restore the good spirits of the wedding feast, Nicholas made his escape. Covered in his darkest cloak, he slipped through the servants' passageways.

Every little noise startled him, making him sure the entire palace must have noticed his absence by now. Still, the few servants he did run into hardly spared him a second glance, and within fifteen minutes he was in the stables. He didn't breathe easily, however, until he was on his horse and beyond the palace gate, making his way to the eastern wharf.

Help me, Maker, he pleaded. *I am doing my best to make this right.*

The ride to the eastern wharf, across the valley and hills to the other side of the peninsula, would be quicker for a single rider on a fresh horse than it would be for a group of five men and one woman. But Elaina's party had left before him, and they would waste no time getting to their destination. They had been trained to move quickly and discreetly, and no doubt would be under orders to stop for no one.

For a while, Nicholas entertained the idea of catching them sometime during the night, but as the hours wore on, he had no such relief. The guards would switch mounts several times throughout the journey. They would stop at the royal stables scattered along the road for such purposes. Nicholas had to switch mounts as well, but whenever he stopped, there was never a horse ready as quickly as he wanted it, as the guard party had already taken the freshest, fastest ones.

It was late morning by the time he spotted the thin line of water in the distance, and afternoon when he actually reached the boats. His backside ached and his thighs felt like they might never work again. Still, Nicholas pulled his horse to a halt and called out to the nearest sailor he saw. "Captain Stein?"

"Four from the end." The man pointed up the wharf.

Nicholas pushed his horse south until he found the vessel and its captain.

"Captain Stein?"

"That would be me." But the grizzled captain turned nearly as white as his beard when Nicholas removed his cloak. "Sire!"

"Shh. I need you to keep my presence here quiet. I must speak with your prisoner below. It must be absolutely private."

"Aye . . . of course. You'll find her in the hold down there, under that flap."

"I wish to come with you. Do you have room?" Not that he would take no for an answer. "And I need my passage to be discreet."

The captain rubbed his chin thoughtfully. "If you want privacy, wait in my cabin until we set sail. Then you can sneak down to the hold quietly."

Nicholas thanked the captain and went to wait in the dingy little cabin. He couldn't help wondering at the security of hiring such a ship to carry the crown's most reprehensible prisoner. If Elaina had been a truly heinous villain with information pertinent to the enemy, it would have been quite easy to slip in and out with her and have no one be the wiser. He could only guess that most of the navy was busy with Solwhind and this had been the next best option.

Setting sail took an eternity, but he eventually heard the captain's call. Nicholas bolted from the cabin, threw open the hatch to the hold, and pulled it shut behind him.

A single candle lit the dark room, making it barely light enough to see his hands in front of his face. Not that the light mattered. She just had to hear him. He just needed her to know that he was sorry. Sorry for everything. Sorry for his waywardness and his inability to keep her safe. Sorry for putting her in danger in the first place and then allowing Conrad the freedom to do something so heinous.

When he turned around, however, Nicholas found the door of the prison cell hanging open.

The hold was empty.

CHAPTER 30

SOLD

"Ａll right. In you go." The sailor tossed Elaina into the hold of the ship. She missed the stairs, however, and landed hard on the wooden floor, smacking her head on the edge of a bench in the process. Before she was able to stand up, she heard the hatch slam shut above her.

She groaned as she pressed a palm against her throbbing temple and used her other hand to pull herself up onto the bench. The hold was nearly pitch black, the only light coming from a few holes in the hatch above.

But the darkness wasn't so bad compared to the smell, which made her gag. The scents of fish and salt had never bothered her, but then, her father had always insisted on keeping the *Adroit* spotless. This boat, less than a third of the size of her father's vessel, had looked nearly ready to sink from the outside. And though Elaina couldn't see much of the floor beneath her, she was sure she didn't want to. The spot where she had fallen was clear of debris, but she could feel a thin layer of sticky goo beneath her slippers as she sat on the bench.

The first ship had been frightening enough, with its human-sized metal cage in the hold and the fierce-looking guard who had watched her every move. But at least that ship had been clean. Not ten minutes after being thrown into the cage, another guard had come down. His navy uniform was rumpled and patched in at least ten different places, making him hardly look like a naval officer at all. But he had handed the protesting guard a parchment and then proceeded to pull Elaina from the cage, and no one had stopped him.

She had been elated at first. Perhaps Nicholas *had* believed her and had somehow convinced the guards to let her go. Or maybe the king himself had intervened.

But when she'd been freed from one horrid ship only to be dragged to this one, Elaina's hopes of Nicholas coming to her rescue died.

The hatch above opened again. Elaina squinted in the sudden light as three more people descended the steps, a woman, a man, and a young boy. Unlike her, however, they were not thrown. The man who had tossed her down held the hatch for them as though they were royalty.

"Are you sure we couldn't have afforded a better journey there?" the woman asked as she reluctantly stepped from the steps onto the dirty floor.

"Lilly, I told you," the man said. "With the rebellion, the only ships sailing between the harbors are local fishing boats and merchants. And if you had wanted a merchant to take us, you should have sold some of those necklaces that you keep stashed away, like I told you to."

"They were my grandmother's! And no. We'll not go through that again." She grabbed the young boy, who looked like he was about to leap off the fourth step. "It's only a two-day trip," she said as she pulled him close and began running her fingers through his black curly hair, as though that would calm her. "We'll make it through—Oh!" She put a hand over her mouth, then her heart. "I'm sorry, dear." She looked at Elaina, who had slid down to the darker end of the bench. "I didn't see you there. Did you hire them to take you to Solwhind as well?"

Before Elaina could even consider an answer, the hatch above opened again. This time, a girl around Elaina's age entered. Then she turned and held her arms out. Another woman, wrinkled and gray, followed slowly, allowing the girl to lead her carefully down the steps.

Lilly turned to greet them as well, seeming to forget Elaina in the process, which suited Elaina just fine. It would do no good to attempt escape, not now, anyway. Setting foot back on Ashland's soil would mean her immediate death. Lord Benedict would see to that. The best Elaina could hope for was to make it to her new destination, wherever that was, and pray another way of escape presented itself.

Before the ship left the harbor, they were joined by two young men, twin brothers who Elaina couldn't have told apart if her life had depended on it. From what she could gather from the excited chatter, which mostly came from Lilly, and the occasional comment from one of the other six, everyone but Elaina had actually paid the captain of this ship to take them to Solwhind, civilian travel between the two sides of the bay having been outlawed by the king.

Lilly, her husband, Drake, and their son, Elton, were going to live with Drake's brother, afraid the war would split the family up forever if they didn't move soon. Aspen, the girl Elaina's age, and her aged grandmother whom she called Gram, were going to live with Gram's eldest son, Aspen's uncle, so he could help care for her while Aspen found work. The two brothers didn't give their reasons for traveling, but then, they didn't really speak at all.

"What about you?" Lilly turned back to Elaina just when Elaina was hoping she would be forgotten in the corner where she'd placed herself. "You're dressed rather well to be traveling like this. Couldn't you have at least hired a," she glanced around at their grimy surroundings, "a *decent* fisherman to take you?"

Elaina did her best to smile. She knew from all the time spent on her father's ship that the less her enemy knew of her, the better. These people in the hold seemed harmless enough, but Elaina knew better than to trust anyone at first sight.

"We're all going to the same place." She looked around to find every pair of eyes on her. "I've never tried to travel through a civil war before." She shrugged. "It seems this was the best I could do."

Lilly sniffed and rolled her eyes, but Elaina gave a sigh of relief when the woman turned her efforts back to learning more about Aspen, who seemed just as reluctant as Elaina to divulge information. It wasn't until the ship had set off and small suppers of hard bread and cheese had been handed down from above that Lilly stopped asking questions long enough to eat.

While they ate, Elaina puzzled over her new situation. These people certainly weren't criminals, and none of them seemed to know what she had been charged with. But why had her change in ship taken place at all? Sending a convicted spy with intimate knowledge of the king's plans into the heart of the enemy seemed irrational and unlikely. Even if Nicholas had believed the charges, which she was beginning to think more and more that he must have, it would be unlike him to take such a strategic gamble. She knew too much.

Elaina's food tasted even staler than it had at first, and her chest began to physically ache. Tears threatened to spill down her cheeks as she recalled the ice in his eyes as he'd declared her guilt and punishment.

She had thought her heart hurt after he'd kissed Princess Monique. Now that pain seemed nothing but a whisper compared to the biting, clawing betrayal that threatened to consume her. All their talks and walks and teasing and scheming . . . Had it meant so little to him? She had believed at one point that despite his flirtatious ways, he had come to know her in a way no one had before, and she him. It seemed now that she had been mistaken about them both.

And as for Lydia? Elaina felt a wave of bitterness wash over her. Of all the ways to find revenge—

Elaina.

She wanted to sing with relief and shout in anger. Trying to look as though she were merely trying to see the sky, Elaina walked casually to the foot of the wooden steps and tried to peer up through the hatch holes. She couldn't answer, not with so many people around. But oh, how she wanted to! *Why couldn't you be more specific?* she wanted to yell. *Why didn't you just tell me to open my chest?* Since she couldn't talk back, however, she simply listened.

Don't try to run, Elaina, they said. *It's all for a purpose. Someone needs you.*

Elaina couldn't see any possible purpose in being publicly humiliated and charged with the worst crime imaginable. She couldn't see any purpose in her father being lost at sea or her mother being brutally murdered. And the stars had the audacity to tell her there was a purpose?

I may not be able to talk to them, she told the Maker silently, shaking as she prayed. *But I can talk to you.* She paused, the hurt and anger washing over her again. *I don't understand. I've done all I can to serve you and my kingdom. I've promoted peace and tried to prevent war. I've listened to everything you've said. But this?* She grasped the edge of the step railing and squeezed it in an effort to keep herself from crying. *What have I done to deserve this?*

For a long time, all she could hear were the soft sounds of Lilly singing her son to sleep and the gentle slapping of the waves at the boat's sides. But eventually, the stars spoke once again.

Take courage, Elaina. Someone needs you.

But in that moment, Elaina put her hands over her ears and sat down on the wooden steps, letting the sharp corners of her bracelet poke painfully into her cheek.

If anyone needed help right now . . . it was she.

"WHEN CAN we leave the ship, Captain?" Drake asked, hefting his wife's large sack up on his shoulder. "We've been docked for over an hour!"

The old captain spit on the floor before shaking his head. "I know you're all anxious to disembark. But before you go, I have a gift for you. We'll start with the ladies."

Elaina tried to stay in the shadows as two burly sailors climbed down into the hold with bags hanging from their wrists. Each one began to pull something out of his bag. The objects they held gleamed, even in the poor light. One walked over to Aspen, but before Elaina could see what he was giving the girl, the other stepped right in front of her, blocking her view.

"Your wrist." He held up a gold bracelet. The bracelets had bands nearly the width of two of Elaina's fingers, and a purple gemstone in the middle, as large as a thumbprint.

Elaina put her hands behind her back. "No thank you."

"Ah, but it'll look so lovely on such a delicate wrist as yours." Before Elaina could reply, he had grabbed her arm roughly and shoved the bracelet around her left wrist. She cried out and fought him, kicking and punching with her right hand, but the captain was at their side in a minute, holding her down as the guard took out a small key and locked the bracelet into place.

In less than a minute, the deed was done, and Elaina could not remove the bracelet no matter how hard she pulled and pushed and yanked. The other passengers put up fights as well. Drake had to be bound by hand and foot when he threw himself on the man attempting to put a bracelet on Lilly. The two brothers succeeded in knocking one of the sailors unconscious and breaking the arm of another before the crew was able to subdue them.

But in the end, they all wore the hateful bracelets. Lilly whimpered and her little boy cried. Aspen tried to comfort her grandmother, who was so distraught she began speaking gibberish. Elaina was very close to kicking a few of the guards in the knees when all was said and done, for good measure if nothing else, but decided that helping the brothers sit upright off the floor would be a better course of action.

"My brother will hear of this!" Drake shouted, his deep voice reverberating off the wooden walls. "You'll have the bailiffs down your throat in an instant! Your license to fish will be revoked entirely!"

"Well, that would be terrifying now," the captain grinned down from the steps, "if the bailiffs were still here." He disappeared through the hatch.

Most of the crew encircled the two brothers, who were beginning to stand once again. As soon as she was sure no one was looking in her direction, Elaina darted up the steps. She was nearly out of the hatch when a man she hadn't seen caught her by the arm and jerked her back down the stairs, smacking her head on the railing in the process. Elaina reached up and felt a warm, wet trickle running down her face. When she pulled her fingers back, several drops of bright red blood covered them.

Before she could try to stop the bleeding, however, she was pulled to her feet. Her hands were bound with rope in front of her, and her heart sank when she saw which knot they had used. She wouldn't be getting out of that binding until someone cut her loose.

Soon they were all gagged and bound in a row. Somehow, Lilly's little boy ended up between Aspen and Elaina, and he sobbed for his mother through his dirty cloth gag. When none of the sailors responded to his cries, he began to thrash.

Elaina threw her tied arms around him and pulled him close. If he struggled with the ropes too much, they would begin to cut his wrists.

The boy fought her, but when one of the sailors walked by and raised a hand, he buried his curly little head in her stomach and began to whimper. Elaina did her best to comfort him silently, for she was gagged as well, but all too soon they were being yanked forward.

The journey up the stairs and out of the hold was full of falls and muffled cries, but eventually they reached the deck. And if Elaina could have gasped, she would have.

The city before her was definitely Solwhind, but Elaina had never seen it looking so dirty. A thick brown haze that had never been there before covered the rooftops. Waste and filth lined the streets, and the harbor smelled of rotten fish. None of the passersby merely strolled; they all skittered like frightened birds. This was not the Solwhind Elaina knew and loved.

"Down you go." Elaina was shoved at the ramp so hard she nearly fell again. After turning to briefly glare at the short sailor who had shoved her, she started to walk. So did everyone else. Lilly hollered through her gag the entire time, something about her best dishes being left behind.

Two muscular men met them at the bottom. One led them at the front, and the other fell behind. Elaina's feet longed to fly as soon as they hit solid ground, but she knew better. They were all tied together with the most secure knot known to sailors. Elaina was a fast runner. Drake, Aspen, and the two brothers might be as well. But they had a small child, an old woman, and Lilly, who might have been fast had she not been blubbering on about her dishes.

Dark began to fall upon the city as they took to the streets. Elaina considered lunging at the first person she saw to beg for help. But every time she met a passerby, he only lowered his head and hurried on.

Someone needs you.

Elaina's ears perked up, but she immediately put her head down again and continued walking. She wasn't in the mood to listen.

Someone needs you, the sky whispered again.

Elaina ignored them, focusing instead on memorizing their route from the harbor. After walking east for a few minutes, they turned left and went north into a well-to-do neighborhood. Soon, they were stopped before a thick wall, at least nine feet tall, and a grand gate covered in elegant vines. The man leading them produced a key and unlocked the gate.

The gates opened up to a large courtyard filled to the brim with every sort of flower, bush, and vine, though many looked over-grown and nearly dead in the weak yellow light of the street lanterns. Birdbaths were scattered around the patches of grass, and climbing ivy hung from all four walls surrounding the property, casting phantom-like shadows on the already claustrophobic walls.

Nothing was as impressive or as imposing, however, as the house.

Really, it was a manor. Though it lacked the grand respectability of Elaina's house, which had been built hundreds of years before by her ancestors, this house was no smaller than Elaina's, nor was it lacking in opulence, despite the small piece of land it had been stuck upon.

Before she could examine the house further, the doors opened and a brighter light spilled out onto the front walkway. A feminine silhouette, tall and thin, filled the door. Slowly and meticulously, it made its way along their line, stopping to examine each individual the way Elaina had seen cattle examined before auctions. Then it stopped before Elaina.

"Turn your head," a woman said in a deep voice.

Elaina sent the woman her most hostile glare.

"I said turn."

Elaina enunciated her answer very carefully around the gag. "No."

"Hm," was all the woman said before moving on to Lilly.

Finally, when the woman got to the end of the line, she turned to the ship's captain, who Elaina realized must have followed them. Handing him what sounded like a coin purse, the woman nodded. "They will do."

"My brother will know my family is missing!" Drake called from the front of the line. He had somehow managed to loosen his gag. "He will set out to find us! He lives right here in this city!"

The woman turned gracefully, and in the light emanating from the open door, floated along the overgrown stone path back to Drake.

"If your relatives care to double my contribution to the Order of the Dagger, I will be happy to turn you over to them. And before you tell me to beware of the bailiffs," she said coolly, "know now that they are gone. All of them. They've either joined the Shadow, forfeited their titles, or fled the city. So," she leaned in and ran one finger down Drake's cheek, "the only ones who will hear you scream will be the servants of the Order. And as the Shadow is the one who so graciously allows me to invite people such as your-selves to experience my hospitality, I highly doubt either the Shadow or his followers will find any reason to help you."

"What does she mean?" Lilly's muffled whimper came from behind Elaina.

Elaina leaned back. "I think," she said through her gag, "we've just been sold."

CHAPTER 31
YOUNG AND STRONG

E laina stood in line with the others in the kitchen, where they had been herded. A fire roared in the hearth, and there were several candles lit as well, so Elaina didn't have to squint as much to make out the sharp, severe features of their new hostess. One of the guards began taking their gags off. As he went down the line, the thin woman stood back and began to speak.

"My name is Matilda Winters, but you may all refer to me as Madame or Lady Winters."

Elaina kept her face straight, though she wanted to retort that she highly doubted Matilda Winters had been born with or ever married into such a title.

"I have brought you here because as you can see, my house is large, and recent . . . infelicities have disrupted my regular household staff. Thanks to the Shadow's new laws, however, I have been lucky enough to have you all come to stay with me. As happy as I am to have you, though, I expect my home and its routines to remain uninterrupted. When I tell you to come, you will come. And when I give you a task, I expect it to be done to perfection."

She paused and made eye contact with everyone, her gaze

lingering on Elaina longer than any of the others. "And if any one of you feels the desire to try and run, Felix or Ivor here will make sure you come back. And I will make sure that you never feel the desire to ever run again." She looked hard at Elaina. "Understood?"

A few of them nodded their heads, but Elaina held hers straight.

Matilda looked at her for a moment longer before walking to the end of the line. "You." She stood before Drake. "Name and age."

He glanced down at his wife and son before grudgingly answering. "Drake Shofeld . . . Madame. Thirty-seven years."

Matilda looked down the line to where he had glanced. A slow smile spread across her pinched face. "It seems I'll be having little trouble with you, Drake."

She moved on. "And you?"

There was no answer.

Matilda's dark eyes went flat. "I expect to be answered when I ask you a question, old woman."

"She cannot answer, ma'am."

Matilda's head snapped over to Aspen. "I do not recall speaking to you."

"I . . . I'm very sorry, ma'am . . . Madame. My name is Aspen. But that's my grandmother, you see. Gram. She doesn't speak. Hasn't in five years. But she does sew quite well."

Matilda looked back at Gram. "Very well. But I won't be taking on a charity case. It's either work here or live on the streets for her."

"Please, Madame! She won't survive!" Aspen moved closer to her grandmother, despite her hands still being tied. Elaina wanted very much to step between *Madame* and the two women, but she knew that would probably only make matters worse for them.

"Then you'd better make sure you do enough work for both of you."

"Of course, Madame!"

"Good." Matilda moved down the line, stopping before the little boy. "Who are you?"

The boy shrank back toward Elaina.

"Answer him, boy," Drake said in a tired voice.

"I would do as your father says," Matilda added. "Now tell me your name."

Still, the boy shook his head.

Matilda had reached her hand back, and Elaina was nearly ready to yank him behind her, when Lilly called,

"That's Jacob. And he is five."

"And you are?"

Lilly puffed out her chest and jutted her chin out, staring straight forward at the kitchen wall. "I am Lilly, and I am thirty-eight."

"What about you?"

Elaina returned her gaze to Matilda to realize she was staring right at her.

If you're ever taken prisoner, remember this.

Elaina blinked as her father's voice echoed in her head. It was the same speech he gave to every new recruit on his ship.

Share as little information as you can with the enemy. Knowledge is power, and withholding knowledge from the enemy is keeping power for one's self.

"Your name?" Matilda took a step forward, stopping so close that Elaina could smell the garlic on the woman's breath.

"I'll not tell you."

Matilda's eyes shot up. "Oh, really?" She stepped back and addressed the other captives. "This one thinks she's better than you, it seems."

Elaina straightened her shoulders and kept her face impassive.

"You're dressed in more finery than I was expecting any of my guests to arrive in. Not very fitting for the season, though." Matilda pinched a bit of Elaina's gauzy blue skirt and rubbed it between her fingers. "I was going to provide everyone with a cloak, should he have needed it. But it appears you don't want any cloak, as then you wouldn't be able to show off your fine clothes."

Elaina wanted to scream. This impractical gown might have been a worse punishment than Lydia's betrayal.

"You're young and strong. You'll work in the kitchens, along with my cook and Aspen. Cook will show you what to do." She tilted her head. "And because I can only gather that you've been raised decently spoiled, you'll also wait on me and my two daughters for tea and meals."

She moved on, but the last glance she sent Elaina made it very clear that she hadn't forgotten Elaina's disrespect. Nor would she.

In the end, they were all assigned some burdensome task, despite the late hour of the evening. Elaina wondered how many servants Matilda had been forced to employ before the war. Not that it mattered now. Leo and Luca, as it turned out the brothers were named, were to clean out the carriage house, care for the animals, and tend to the many gardens and flower beds that covered the grounds.

Gram was assigned to mending and sewing clothes. Aspen and Elaina were in the kitchen. Lilly was set to cleaning the house. Drake was told to make repairs, and little Jacob was ordered to help his father.

Elaina turned woodenly toward the stairs, as they were ordered to head to the attic and sleep there, waiting for further instructions in the morning. Before she'd taken two steps, however, Matilda called for her to wait.

She turned to find Matilda standing behind her, hands clasped together in front of her and a patient look on her face.

"I do not know where you come from, but I can tell fine breeding when I see it. Even without your fancy . . . foolish clothes, I would have recognized you as someone of title in an instant. The set of your shoulders, the arch of your neck, your posture gave you away the moment you stepped onto my property." She took a step closer, close enough that Elaina could see the lines of white in her dark hair.

"I must admit I am a bit curious as to your upbringing. You

look stronger than most girls of title. But," she smiled thinly, "we can save that story for another day. What I am interested in is your will. We'll have to break that before long. You see, there is only room for one will in this house, and that is mine."

Elaina merely held the woman's dark gaze. It was easy to keep her countenance cool when she pretended Matilda was an obstinate politician. She knew how to deal with those.

"It is very well that you won't share your name," Matilda continued in a low, melodic voice. "We'll just have to find a new one that's more fitting." Matilda turned and waved her hand slightly as though she were bored. "Go get some sleep. You'll need it in the morning."

Elaina briefly considered darting for the door, but a glance through the window showed a guard's form hovering in the garden. Promising herself that she would one day be free, Elaina turned instead and slowly climbed the stairs.

On the second and third levels she passed halls with numerous rooms, luxurious carpets, and tall, ornate windows and doors. The house itself was quiet enough that she began to feel the effects of the day beginning to wear on her even as she climbed. Her head still throbbed from its earlier injuries, and Elaina felt that if she stopped, she might not be able to take another step. It was all she could do to keep climbing the stairs.

Odd noises greeted her, however, when she reached the fourth level. Thinking that this must be where the captives were to sleep, Elaina trudged down the bare hall and lifted the latch on the only door at its end. But it was locked.

Elaina placed her ear to the door. Sure enough, muffled sounds were coming from the inside, though in her exhaustion, Elaina couldn't tell what they were. She thought about running back down to the empty kitchen and retrieving something to pick the lock with, but her need for sleep won out instead. Shaking her head, she turned back to the stairs and continued the ascent. It was probably just another pitiful individual Matilda had managed to get her claws on as well. Perhaps someone else who also had a will.

Elaina finally found the attic above the fourth level. When she opened the door, she could dimly see the others huddled in little groups on the floor, all but the brothers, who stood looking out the single window that faced north. They glanced back at Elaina, but made no move to include her in their conversation. The Shofeld family sat curled up against the wall, Drake with his long arms wrapped around his son and his wife. Aspen had Gram in the only chair in the room, which looked to have a broken arm, and was leaning against her legs with her head in the old woman's lap. Elaina felt her way along the wall, bumping and tripping on objects piled up the floor. Though the room was large enough, perhaps larger than Elaina's own bedchamber at home, it seemed to have been stuffed with so much clutter that walking in a straight line was nearly impossible.

After searching for several minutes, Elaina finally found a clear spot in the darkest corner of the room to the right of the door. The floor was hard, and as Elaina found, full of splinters. Wishing again that the guards had given her time to grab the thicker wrap she'd left at the wedding, Elaina wrapped her thin shawl even more tightly around her and found a dusty book to lay her head on.

What kind of woman threw something so precious as a book up in this kind of junk pile? But then, what kind of woman kidnapped people and put the elderly and young children in attics during the winter?

As much as it killed her to know that Nicholas had ordered it, Elaina had at first thought her exile a possible path to salvation. She would find some sort of work in Solwhind, enough to earn some money. Then she would travel south to Destin as soon as she was able. She was strong, and she knew that King Everard would at least *listen* to her side of the story when she arrived, regardless of what he had heard. He was too wise not to.

Only now she was a slave.

But no. She would escape. It didn't matter what the stars had said. Perhaps someone needed her, but not like this. She would sleep now, and possibly work for several days or even several weeks. But somehow, she would find a way out. Matilda would not break her spirit. And most importantly, Matilda would never see her cry.

CHAPTER 32

AGREEMENTS

T ell my father I need to speak with him." Nicholas was off his horse and sprinting up the steps before the servants could take his horse or bags.

"Yes, sire!" The palace steward, who had come out to greet him, bowed then began barking out orders to the servants.

Nicholas stopped briefly in his own study to gather a few important documents. Then he stalked up to his father's study, not waiting to see whether or not the servant had yet announced his return. He banged on the door. "Father, we need to talk."

No one answered, so Nicholas pounded on the door again. "Father!"

A young servant opened the door just enough to stick his head out, his eyes large and his face pale. "Your father says he cannot speak with you now, sire."

"Oh really? Would it interest him then," he called through the crack in the door, "to know that I've just spent three days searching every ship in the eastern harbor for the exiled traitor that disappeared?"

The servant disappeared inside the room again, but not for long. "My apologies, Your Highness," he said, peeking out once more, "but he says he will not see you now."

For a long moment, Nicholas toyed with the idea of barging in and telling his father what he really thought of such a petty delay, but he knew already that such an intrusion would only end in a fight. And Nicholas didn't have time for a fight.

Elaina, wherever she was, didn't have time for a fight.

Alastair rounded the corner looking deep in thought. Leaving the servant to deal with his father, Nicholas grabbed Alastair by the sleeve and yanked him close. "My study. Now."

Alastair nodded frantically before turning and falling into step behind him.

As soon as they reached his study, Nicholas addressed the guard standing outside the door. "Not a soul is to enter or be within ten feet of this door unless it is my father."

The guard gave him a sharp nod, so Nicholas slammed the door shut and turned to face his captive. "I suppose you know why you're here."

The spy's thin face was even more drawn than usual, and he seemed to have grown more white hair overnight. He fumbled with his hands so much that Nicholas was tempted to feel sorry for the man.

But he didn't.

Alastair nodded quickly once more, staring at the floor. "I do, my prince."

"Then you can start by telling me exactly where she is."

"Where she is?" Alastair's head shot up and his eyes grew sharp. "Don't you know where you exiled her?"

"*I* exiled her to Destin," Nicholas said. "But when I arrived at the boat that was to take her there, she was nowhere to be found."

Alastair gaped at him. "You mean you don't know where she is?"

"Well if you can't tell me," Nicholas roared, "then why don't you start by telling me how she got into this mess in the first place?"

Alastair rubbed the salt-and-pepper stubble on his jaw and went to lean against one of the chairs by the fire. "I knew Conrad was investigating her, but I didn't want to say anything until we had evidence." His voice sounded ancient. "I thought he was only going to question her family and neighbors. He told me that a girl had informed him of a possible traitor who had been talking with Tumen. I didn't think anything would come of it."

"And you had no idea the girl you've been practically courting was his witness?"

"She said nothing! He said nothing! How was I to know?" Alastair threw up his hands helplessly.

"We are going to make one fact about this matter perfectly clear." Nicholas yanked the other chair out and turned it so he could face Alastair. Sitting in it and leaning forward, he said, "We both know that Elaina is innocent of these charges."

Alastair nodded miserably, staring into the fire.

"Good. We also know that your assistant has been a thorn in her side for over a month now. In fact, I'm convinced that he is the one who planted that evidence. This, of course, puts me in a terrible position." He glared at Alastair. "I cannot imprison a man when I have no proof of wrongdoing. But I *do* have multiple witnesses who can attest to his mischief." Nicholas leaned back and crossed his arms. "I cannot arrest him and I cannot let him run about freely with the knowledge he holds. So what do you suggest I do?"

"I know." Alastair let out a quiet sob. "I've allowed my love for the boy to blind me to his actions." He shrugged and looked at Nicholas through wet eyes. "But he's like a son to me." He wiped away the tears with his sleeve. "I will restrict him to his quarters until I can get sorted out what he has and hasn't been up to."

That was far from what Nicholas wished to do to the young man, and not nearly as violent, but without proof, there was very little more he really could accomplish . . . legally.

"As to Lady Elaina, however," Alastair sniffled and pulled a folded parchment from his coat, "I might be able to shed some light." He handed the parchment to Nicholas.

Nicholas opened it and began to read. Before he was even

halfway through, however, he felt as though he'd been kicked in the chest.

"Slavery?"

Alastair nodded. "After Lady Elaina raised the question of disappearing travelers, I investigated. Most of those in Solwhind don't approve of it, of course, but it seems that the Shadow is also encouraging this trade in order to bring in revenue."

"Revenue?" Nicholas stared in confusion at the paper in his hands.

"Whenever individuals pay for a . . . person . . . people, they must pay a monthly tax per head. The tax goes directly to the Shadow himself, as do the taxes on lithorium and other formerly illegal objects of trade."

"And the bailiffs?"

"No longer have authority. It is the rich who have authority now. The Shadow seems to be in desperate need of funds, so the rich are the ones who direct many of his steps." The side of his mouth twitched unhappily.

Nicholas went to the window. Leaning against it, he closed his eyes. "What could such a man need so much money for?"

"Waging a war, particularly with hired swords, is expensive."

Nicholas felt as though he'd aged a decade in the last three days. "So you think Elaina was *sold*?"

"When I saw the speed and small contingent with which she was being sent to her ship, I was concerned that it was too little too fast, if I may speak honestly. A mercenary could have easily slipped in and posed as someone else if she was being handled by a number of unknown persons. All one would have needed was a uniform."

"King Everard was right."

"I beg your pardon, sire?"

"King Everard told Elaina that he believed there was a deep evil in Solwhind. The kidnappings, the deaths of the gifted, the lithorium . . . This kind of evil goes far beyond general greed. Something dark is at work here."

"What do you intend to do?"

"I'm going to find it. And I'm going to destroy it."

Nicholas felt a hand on his shoulder. He was tempted to shrug it off but for the soft words that followed.

"Your Highness, I know you probably have little respect for me at the moment. But please know, I will do everything in my power to help you find her. You have my word." His voice fell to a whisper. "We will find her."

ALASTAIR'S PROMISE WAS COMFORTING, but it didn't protect Nicholas from the madness that threatened to take him while he waited for his father to speak with him privately. Not only did Xander bar Nicholas from his study for the remainder of the day, but when he finally summoned Nicholas early the next morning, it was to inform him that they were making an impromptu journey to the eastern shore of the Sheryn Sea, the same wharf from which Nicholas had just returned.

This would have pleased him immensely except for his father's insistence on keeping all of their attending servants and soldiers with them every step of the way. This many people, of course, took twice as long to cross the peninsula. And every time Nicholas begged and pleaded and threatened to have a private audience, his father brushed him off like a pesky child. It wasn't until two days later as they were inspecting naval vessels preparing to set sail for the war that Nicholas was finally alone with his father.

They were in the cabin of a warship when his father paused to examine some of the captain's log entries, and Nicholas saw his chance. As soon as their hosting captain stepped out to search for something, Nicholas took the opportunity to shut and lock the door.

"Really, now what's this about?" His father glanced up at him, then back down at the log.

"I have needed to speak with you privately for three days now, and you've brushed me off repeatedly."

"Children run off without telling their parents where they're going. I'm only treating you the way you've acted."

"This is an issue of national security!" Nicholas slammed shut the captain's log.

The king finally straightened and crossed his arms. "Fine. You have my attention. What is it, Nicholas?"

"Elaina was abducted!"

His father's mouth twitched, but he held steady. "I am sorry to hear that." He looked down and opened the log again. "You'll need to send word to King Everard that she's not coming."

"This is serious, Father! Forget that the woman I want to marry has disappeared. If nothing else, focus on the fact that a young, beautiful woman who knows more than half of the kingdom's secrets has disappeared."

The king looked up. "Do you have any idea as to where she went?"

"That is what I was trying to find out when I came here five days ago!" Did his father listen to nothing? Nicholas ran his hand through his hair. It was greasier than he usually let it get. Not that he'd had a proper chance to bathe in several days. "There was a mix-up with the boats, it seems. She was delivered to the right one, but then someone snuck her off. I spoke with Alastair, and we believe she was probably . . ." He had to swallow. "Probably sold into slavery."

His father stared at him blankly.

Nicholas put his hands on the table and leaned forward. "In Solwhind."

The king closed his eyes and let his head hang for a long moment. "Isn't the Shadow trying to—"

"Yes, the leader of the rebellion is searching for her. And do you know why he's searching for her, Father?"

"Because she knows our secrets." He paused. "And she's gifted, you said."

"Because Elaina can speak to the stars."

"The stars?" His father looked at him as though he were mad.

Nicholas nodded. "I saw her do it once. They talk to her, but no one else can hear. Apparently, they would warn her of storms and pirates and other dangers."

Xander opened his mouth as though to speak but closed it again. Shaking his head and muttering to himself, he pinched the bridge of his nose. "So . . . you're saying the Shadow wants her gift? But Nicholas, why didn't you tell me?"

"Because you were always so sympathetic to the plight of the gifted before."

"I don't need your sarcasm. I need you to be absolutely truthful with me." He leaned over the table. His words were a whisper. "Are you absolutely sure the Shadow wants her for her gift? Because if it's for our secrets, those will change soon enough. They always do in war."

"No. He wants her for her gift."

"How do you know this?"

"Because Jackson never said the Shadow wanted Elaina. He said the Shadow wanted the girl who talks to the stars."

His father fell back a step. "So he won't stop looking. But . . . what could he want with a girl who talks to stars?"

"Use your imagination, Father." Nicholas stomped over to a little porthole window. "Whatever it is, I can assure you that it will be nothing beneficial to the rest of our kingdom or to Solwhind. But I am not about to sit around and wait to find out. I'll set sail on a local fishing boat tomorrow and travel to Solwhind myself. There, I'll—"

"No."

Nicholas turned. "What?"

"No." His father shook his head. "You'll not be going anywhere. I've apparently lost an asset I never even knew I had. I'll not be losing another in search of it."

"I am going," Nicholas said. If he had to search every corner of the sprawling city, he would.

"You are going to return to the palace with me. I will speak with Alastair. We'll go about this rationally, and I'll send out the proper men in search of her." He met Nicholas's glare. "But you're staying put. And if you even think about disobeying me, I'll have you arrested and locked in your chambers."

Nicholas gaped at him. "You're willing to entrust the kingdom to me, but you threaten to lock me up?"

"I will entrust the kingdom to no one who insists on disobeying my orders. We will deal with this properly. Remember that tonight, when you're tempted to sneak away again. You'll do her no good locked in your chambers."

Nicholas threw the door open and stomped outside.

It was growing dark by the time he reached the place Elaina's intended boat had been docked. Sitting down at the empty spot, he dropped his legs over the side and let them dangle the way he had seen Elaina do anytime they were near water.

As tempting as it was to jump up and board the first ship that was headed to Solwhind, for he knew that despite his father's orders, boats were still slipping in and out between harbors, he knew better. Elaina wouldn't benefit at all if he got himself in trouble with his father. He might be the prince, but against the king's word, he stood no chance of escape.

"I seem to be destined to fail right now," he said as the stars appeared above him, one by one. "And I can't deny that I deserve it. Still . . ." He paused, closing his eyes. "I'm trying to do the right thing. But I could really use some help."

CHAPTER 33
TRUTH IN THE STARS

E laina had just closed her eyes, it seemed, when someone was in the attic shouting for everyone to wake up. She tried to stretch, sore from sleeping on the hard wood floor, but that hurt even worse.

"Which one of you is the girl with no name?" the strange woman snapped. Without waiting for an answer, she clumped over to Aspen and grabbed her by the wrist. She yanked her up to her knees. "Are you her?"

"That would be me." Elaina pushed herself into a sitting position.

"Huh." The large woman looked down at Aspen. "Are you Aspen then?"

The girl nodded quickly.

"You're both coming with me." She lumbered over to Elaina and grabbed her by the arm as well.

It took a lot of effort on Elaina's part not to wince as the woman pulled them down the stairs, her grip as tight as a vice. By the time they reached the bottom, it was a miracle that neither Aspen nor Elaina had fallen and broken bones.

"My name is Penelope, but that's just for Madame. You may call me Miss Penelope. You, nameless one." The woman picked up a broom and shoved it at Elaina. "Sweep. And while you do, watch the water and lard. Take it off the fire when it starts to simmer. And Aspen, scrub these plates until they shine." The woman shuffled over to a table in the center of the large kitchen, where she began to beat a lump of dough, muttering about what a poor state those ungrateful servants had left the place in.

Elaina glanced at Aspen, but the other girl quickly ducked her head and began to scrub the dishes vigorously. Elaina looked back down at the broom in her hands somewhat doubtfully. She knew how to scrub the deck of a ship until it shone, but she had never used a flimsy broom like this one before.

"Well don't just stand there gawking at it." Penelope called. "Start sweeping!" Then she paused, her eyes getting wide. "Don't tell me you've never swept a floor. What were you before? Some sort of high and mighty noble?"

Elaina gritted her teeth and began moving the broom back and forth. At first her movements were choppy and succeeded only in stirring up dust and making Penelope cough and curse at her. But as she continued to work, Elaina found a more comfortable rhythm and better movements that actually moved the dirt over the stone floor, rather than just throwing it up into the air.

"You lazy little oaf!"

Elaina jerked her head up to see Penelope snatch up a rag and wrap it around her hand. With the rag, she pulled the pot from the fire. "You let the lard burn!" Penelope set the pot down then grabbed Elaina by the shoulder, making her bite back a cry as the woman's nails dug into her flesh. She had to bite back a groan, too, when she saw the burnt mess inside the pot.

"Now I'll have to make it all over again, and Madame will be cross. Here. If you can't do anything else right, take the cinders out back. Felix will show you where to put them." She handed Elaina a bucket of ashes and nodded at the side door. Elaina took them grudgingly and turned to march out. However, she didn't see the broom that had fallen to the floor when Penelope had grabbed her, and she tripped. Ashes filled the air. Elaina coughed and choked and gagged as they filled her mouth and nose.

When the air had cleared some and Penelope's curses had ceased, Elaina was finally able to open her eyes.

Matilda was standing before her with a smirk. "I think we're found a fitting name for our nameless girl," she said softly.

Elaina looked up at her miserably, still unable to speak for the dirt in her mouth.

"And what would that be, Madame?" Penelope asked, crossing her arms with an equally smug expression.

"Cinders." And with that, Matilda turned and glided out of the room.

THE REST of Elaina's day was little better. Exasperated, Penelope gave her a cleaning rag and told her to go outside and beat the skirt of her dress with it so Elaina wasn't sending up puffs of cinders every time she moved. Elaina did her best, but she knew the shade of blue would never be the same.

For some reason, this saddened her more than she would have thought appropriate for a dress.

During tea, she failed to leave the parlor fast enough and had the privilege of being laughed at and taunted by Matilda's two daughters, Alison, a little mousy thing with a grating voice and nervous hands, and Dinah, a tall girl with broad shoulders and a mean backhand, as Elaina quickly discovered. After the three ladies had enjoyed their tea, Elaina was politely informed that when everyone else got their meals that night, she would be receiving half of hers for her laziness.

It wasn't until the sky had long been dark and everyone else had been sent up to the attic that Elaina was handed her single roll of bread. Too tired and hungry to think about decorum, she started to shove it half into her mouth until she saw Matilda watching her from the doorway. Holding the woman's gaze, Elaina deliberately held the bread away from her mouth and broke off a small piece and chewed it slowly. Matilda watched her for a minute then moved on without a word. Elaina waited until she was gone, then crammed the rest of the roll in her mouth.

It was good timing, too, for no sooner had Matilda gone than Penelope was back. She held out the broom once more.

"You'll sweep once more for your mess this morning. I've been stepping on ashes all day. Then you can go to bed, and I wouldn't suggest tarrying. If you thought today was hard, wait until you see what I have for you tomorrow."

Elaina took the broom but waited to begin until Penelope had gone. Sweeping was agonizingly slow compared to all the other work she had ever done, even net mending. But then, Elaina had done those other jobs all her life. She couldn't recall the first time she'd swabbed the deck or patched sails. And none of those jobs were light labor. Why then, was housework so hard?

By the time Elaina finished sweeping, the clock had struck, and only two hours were left until midnight. She pulled herself up the stairs without the slightest idea as to how she was going to do such work for another day, or even a week. When she reached the fourth level, however, her ears picked up another sound.

Exhaustion temporarily forgotten, Elaina went again to the single door. Once again, it was locked. But this time, there weren't merely whimpers coming from the other side. This time, there were cries.

Rebellion seized her. Anger at Matilda and anger at the Shadow prompted her to run back down the stairs. The kitchen was empty, so Elaina sorted through the dishes until she found a long thin pick of some sort. Taking it back up the stairs, she put the pick inside the lock and moved it around until she heard the lock click, thankful that Lewis had taught her to pick locks when in curiosity she'd once locked herself out of her own sea chest.

Elaina pushed the door open a few inches. "Hello?"

The sound of crying greeted her, along with several smells that made her stomach turn. Before walking any farther into the dark room, she darted back down the stairs to grab the first lamp she could find. When she returned, Elaina pushed the door open wider and searched for the source of the crying.

Inside was a large room, about as large as the attic above them. It had once been grand, with dyed carpets in reds and blues. But the reds had faded to pinks and the blues looked gray. A giant four-poster bed had been pushed into the far corner next to a window that faced the wharf. Several dusty trunks lay in different parts of the room. But none of that was what caught Elaina's attention.

An old woman sat in a chair. She moaned and her head rolled back as Elaina ran to her side. It was obvious from the state of her hair and the stench of the room that no one had tended to her in days.

"What can I do?" Elaina asked, kneeling at her side.

"Water," the old woman croaked.

Elaina jumped up and ran back down the stairs once again. Her legs protested, but urgency pushed her on. She took a ladle of water from the water bucket, but then thought better of it and grabbed the whole bucket instead.

When she was back up in the room again, Elaina tried as gently as she could to ladle water to the old woman's lips. Getting her to drink was difficult, though, as the woman continued to moan about how someone named Atta had never come.

"I . . . I don't think Atta lives here anymore," Elaina said, pressing the ladle to the woman's dry, cracked lips. "But drink this, please."

By the time Elaina had calmed the woman enough to get her to drink and eat a little of the bread she'd found in a cupboard in the kitchen, wash her face, change her clothes, and help her into the bed, the clock had struck one hour until midnight. Elaina's vision spun with exhaustion and hunger, but she knew she wouldn't be able to sleep until the woman was properly cared for.

From the former finery of the room, and from the decently stylish nightdress Elaina found for the old woman to change into, she could only surmise that this was Matilda's mother. There was a proud arch to her brow and just the touch of an accent Elaina couldn't name that were too similar to ignore.

And if Elaina had thought Matilda cruel before, nothing had quite prepared her for the horror of finding the woman's own mother locked away in a forgotten part of the house.

As Elaina finally lay down in her little corner of the attic, she hurt more physically than she could ever recall hurting in her life. Her bones felt hollow, and they ached as though someone had beaten them with a shovel. Muscles she hadn't known existed felt stretched and bruised, and her stomach made her nauseous with hunger. But deep down, there was a slight calm.

Not enough for her to sneak to the window and admit to the stars that they were right, of course. But enough for her to smile a little as she fell asleep. She hadn't escaped, but she had defied Matilda. The stars had been right. Someone needed her.

TWO YEARS LATER . . .

CHAPTER 34
DIFFERENT

I'm about to take a great gamble with your daughter today." Elaina sang as she began to brush Cynthia's hair.

"Oh?" There was a smile in Cynthia's words. "And pray tell what that will be."

"Well, last night she was boasting to a friend that there is only one cart in the market that sells tolerable peaches. And, she said, she would know that cart's peaches from any others should they touch her lips."

"I can guess where this is going."

Elaina laughed and put the silver filigreed brush back on the vanity before draping a heavy jade and silver necklace around Cynthia's neck. "After her little speech, I was sent to the market for some sugar for your granddaughters' upcoming tea, and while I was there, I noticed that Matilda's beloved peach cart was nowhere to be found." She turned Cynthia to face the mirror on the vanity. "So today, should the cart be gone again, I will be forced to find her precious peaches somewhere else." She wrinkled her nose at the two women in the mirror. "I might have to find the one that sells peaches with worms."

"That shouldn't be too hard since the crown has managed to cut us off from the world. But don't be too flippant now. The last thing you need is another switching." She glanced up and down Elaina's figure with her milky blue eyes. "You just recovered from the last one."

"I've had worse." Elaina bent and pecked the woman on the cheek. "Now, what do you need today?"

Cynthia fidgeted in the chair. "Unfortunately, as fine as my silk stockings are, even those get holes."

"Very well. I'll give them to Gram and see what she can do with them. Anything else?"

"Try to stay out of trouble." Cynthia caught Elaina's hand as she started for the door. "I mean it. Don't make me watch my daughter abuse you again."

Elaina glanced down at the bruise on her hand. "That one was actually Alison."

Cynthia's grasp tightened. "What for?"

Elaina rolled her eyes. "A young gentleman who had come calling on her addressed me. I dared to raise my eyes to respond to his question." She felt indignation rising in her throat but pushed it back down. It would not do to start the day in anger. "I suppose she was a bit jealous." Then Elaina forced a smile and leaned in for a hug. "But worry not about me. I will get your stockings done by tonight if I can."

She had just closed the door when a large shadow blocked her path to the stairs.

"Good morning, Dinah." Elaina adjusted the load of laundry on her hip. "What can I do for you?"

"You gave Alison my gown."

"I'm sure I don't know what you're talking about. Now if you'll excuse me—"

But Dinah reached down and grabbed a handful of Elaina's hair. Elaina had to restrain herself from shoving the wench down the stairs. Instead, she forced herself to look demurely at the ground. Alison's bony fists left bruises, but Dinah's thick forearms could break bones. She'd done it to Aspen once.

"I know she put you up to this," Dinah said, pulling Elaina's face up to hers. Elaina tried not to breathe in the pungent perfumes the young woman wore. "If it happens again, I'll make sure you hear of it." She shoved Elaina onto her back, and Elaina didn't move until Dinah's thick black hair had disappeared down the stairs. Then she stood, dusted herself off, and continued her journey to the kitchen.

In the two years that had passed since Elaina had come to live under Matilda's roof, she'd eventually settled into a routine. And though at first Matilda had not been happy in the slightest to learn that Elaina had strayed into a part of the house to which she had not been invited, she'd quickly realized that Elaina would be much more useful there than not. So taking care of Matilda's aging mother had become Elaina's responsibility along with the rest of her chores.

Cynthia had complicated Elaina's plans far more than she had ever dreamed possible. Escape had continued to linger in the future, just out of her grasp, but every time she thought of leaving, she knew in the back of her mind that the old woman probably would not survive more than a week in her absence. Her granddaughters never went to visit her, and Matilda acted as though her mother had already died. And though Cynthia had hardly been warm to Elaina's attentions at first, they had eventually found a kinship in the common knowledge that Matilda despised them both.

Still, when the brothers had escaped during that first month of captivity, Elaina had promised herself she would follow. Several months ago, on her twentieth birthday, she had even gone so far as to store away enough food for a few days in one of the empty wardrobes in the attic. But every time she saw a chance to go, there was Cynthia.

There was no denying, of course, that her time with Cynthia at the beginning and end of each day was what made her life bearable. The other slaves had one another, but Elaina had never been accepted into their circles. Not really. Now and then, Lilly would try to sneak her an extra blanket, and Gram had pieced together a cloak out of scraps when the last winter had made Elaina so ill she'd nearly died. But there was an emptiness inside that Elaina tried not to think about, just as she tried not to think about the one who had left it there. And in pouring all her efforts and love into the old woman, Elaina had found some respite.

"Come, Jacob. You can help me carry the peaches," she called as she reached the kitchen. Grabbing a basket, she didn't even stop to call for Ivor, who stood by the door waiting for her.

The market was scant today. Still, Elaina did her best to trade smiles and greetings with the vendors as she passed them. The smiles she received in return were about as sparse as the thin, lonely vegetables sitting in the bottom of nearly empty stall boxes, but many merchants still were at least polite enough to nod in return.

"Good morning, Mrs. Rosse." Elaina put her basket on the woman's stall.

"A blessed morning to you, Cinders." The heavyset woman gave Elaina a broad grin and wiped her hands on her apron. "The usual?"

"Yes, please. Jacob, don't touch those. We're not supposed to buy cherries today."

"I'm afraid I've less than I did yesterday. What with the siege and all."

"Whatever you have will do," Elaina assured her. "Penelope understands." In truth, Penelope would probably give Elaina an earful for bringing home such a small hunk of pork. But there was little Elaina or Mrs. Rosse could do about that, and Penelope knew it.

As she waited for the butcher's wife to wrap the meat, Elaina didn't miss the troubled looks the older woman kept sending at her bracelet. She said nothing, though. No one had in the two years that Elaina had been coming to the market. With Felix or Ivor always hovering nearby, or the possibility of someone breathing a word of treason to the Shadow and his men, Elaina had learned the worth of a mere sympathetic smile and an extra slice of bread when the guards weren't looking.

It wasn't as though she was the only person in the market with a gold bracelet. Others came and went, each with his or her own color of gem, but few came from households with as many slaves as Elaina. There was too much to lose should the war turn sour.

"They're coming!"

Elaina and Mrs. Rosse looked over toward the wharf to see a young man leap off a boat onto the dock, breathless.

"The Shadow's fleet returns!" He continued to pant, sweat clumping his hair and running down his face.

"Jacob, come here." Elaina reached out and grabbed the boy's arm, pulling him tightly against her even as he squirmed and protested.

But when he saw the ships, even Jacob froze.

Out of the morning fog they came. Dozens of ships, many in flames, appeared from the gray. Watching them was like seeing the ghosts of a fallen navy emerging from the depths of hell. Elaina put the package of wrapped ham in her basket and clumsily dropped a few coins on the table, but Mrs. Rosse just shook her head slowly as she stared open-mouthed at the boats.

"They've never had a battle like this," she whispered.

Elaina unconsciously moved forward, and for once, her guard didn't rebuke her. He instead followed suit, as did many others. Some cried out for sons or husbands who had been on the ships. Others ran away. But Elaina could only watch, mesmerized.

"What happened, Cinders?" Jacob whimpered.

Elaina rubbed his fuzzy head. "I don't know."

"Doesn't matter how much the Shadow offers next time." One man jumped off a ship, stumbling when he reached solid ground. He looked to be in his forties, seasoned enough to have seen more than one or two voyages. "I won't be going back. Not for all the gold in the world. He can find himself other boats for hire. Mine is done with this bloody war."

"What happened?" Ivor called out.

"They must have amassed their entire navy. The prince himself was there."

Elaina's heart stumbled, and it was a long moment before she could breathe normally again.

"Fought like a devil was in him, he did. Calling out orders like there would be no tomorrow."

Despite the tangle of anger and pain that still sat in a charred lump at the bottom of Elaina's chest, she said a prayer for Nicholas and his men.

"The Shadow isn't going to like this," a woman behind her said.

"You might not get a choice about going out again," someone else told the sailor. "Remember what happened the last time a captain disobeyed him."

The crowd that had merely gathered on the dock out of curiosity started to grow more agitated. Shouts rang out that didn't belong to sailors, and arguments broke out as to whether or not this war was worth fighting at all. Whether it ever should have been fought in the first place.

"Come."

Elaina jumped when someone nudged her shoulder. She looked back to see Ivor frowning around at the crowd.

"We need to go."

Gripping Jacob's small hand, Elaina followed him back through the crowd toward the manor. For once, she and the guard were in agreement.

ELAINA MANAGED to burn the pastries, spill a bucket of milk, and drop an entire supper plate on Dinah's lap. The fuss that the young woman made might have been amusing, had Elaina not had her hands whipped and been denied her supper for the mistake. Lilly and

Aspen traded glances over her several times throughout the day but said nothing. Elaina saw and knew they were curious, and possibly concerned, yet nothing she did could keep her mind on her work.

"Put that down and sit before you hurt yourself."

Elaina looked up from the teapot she was trying to fish the spoon out of. "Pardon me?"

Cynthia waved a hand dismissively at the teapot. "You're so distracted that you're going to drop that pot, cut yourself on its shards, and bleed to death. Now sit." She pointed to the chair beside her bed. When Elaina sighed and obeyed, the old woman took her hands and held them. Elaina closed her eyes and basked in the sensation of human touch.

"Is this about Dinah? I heard her confront you in the hall."

Elaina shook her head. Her clashes with the girls were commonplace enough, but none had been able to upset her like this.

"Then would you like to tell me what has you so muddled?"

Elaina glanced at the window. Though most of the fires were out, the evening had come fast as the sky had filled with blackened smoke that made it nearly impossible to breathe outside.

"You can't possibly be upset at the Shadow's great loss." Cynthia smiled wryly. "Unless . . . you have someone who was out on that water today."

"It's not like that." Elaina shook her head and withdrew her hands. "I mean . . . I suppose you could say I was thinking of someone, but I'm quite sure he wasn't thinking of me." She stood, cleared her throat, and brushed off her apron. Returning to the teapot, she searched for the right words.

It was easier to push away the anger and hurt when she was working. And as she was rarely outside at night, she didn't have to worry about the stars trying to encourage her about her present state, telling her to persevere and not lose faith as they always did on the few occasions on which she got to hear them. But when she was with Cynthia in the quiet of the evening, it was harder to ignore the thoughts that were assaulting her like a barrage of casum balls.

"My father raised me after my mother died," she began slowly. "He caught me crying once when I was eight, and he told me, 'Let someone else make you cry, and you've given them power over you. Allowing someone to overpower you means a lost battle every time.'" She shrugged, turning back to the pot and trying to reach the spoon once again. "I was good at it for a long time." She half smiled.

"But there was someone who did," Cynthia said.

"The hard part is that I knew better. He'd broken so many hearts before I came along. I even watched him! But there was a time where I was convinced he had changed . . ."

"Ah. And he wasn't repentant, I take it?"

"Oh, he begged, pleaded his repentance. But as soon as the tide turned and I was at the mercy of the crown, falsely accused of a crime I didn't commit, he banished me from the kingdom and sent me to this hell!" Elaina stood and started to gather up clothes that needed to be washed, throwing them furiously into the basket.

"Do you mean to tell me that you were in love with the prince?"

Elaina froze.

"Well, Matilda was right." Cynthia let out a sad chuckle. "She thought you came from aristocracy, but I had no idea . . ." She sighed. "What a shock that must have been for you to come live here like this."

Elaina threw the rest of the clothes into the basket and tossed it into the corner. "I've worked hard all my life. It's the betrayal that's eating me alive." She felt her eyes begin to prick, so she blinked furiously and cleared her throat. "I begged my father to let me stay with him, but he decided to send me to live with *proper* female relatives."

"What happened?"

Elaina shrugged. "I was angry, but when I met them, I thought

I might actually have found a place with people who loved me. I thought I might have even found a man who—"

But she couldn't finish. Every joke. Every annoyance. Every look. Every touch.

Every idiotic, loathsome, hateful hope she had ever entertained pounded down on her like a typhoon. Against her will, tears were streaming down her face and her body racked with sobs. "He broke me, Cynthia. I was stupid enough to let him in. And he broke me. And it still hurts!"

"Cinders, I—"

"But do you know what the worst betrayal of all was?"

Cynthia watched her, silent tears running down her own wrinkled face as well. Slowly she shook her head.

"Growing up," Elaina sniffled and wrapped her arms tightly around herself, "I *knew* the Maker would fix everything. He would make it all right. He promised he would in the Holy Writ." Elaina went over to the window to glare out at the smoke-filled sky. There were no stars visible tonight. "But every time I thought things were getting better, he *let* them hurt me. He let him break me. He let them *sell* me." Her throat ached so badly that it hurt to talk. "I've been reduced to cinders and ashes. And he's only stood back and watched."

Soft arms wrapped themselves around her, and Elaina let her head fall onto the old woman's shoulder. For a long time they stood that way, slightly rocking back and forth.

"Iron must be sharpened to be useful, you know," Cynthia finally said.

Elaina brushed the rest of the tears away from her eyes. "What?"

"You're being sharpened here, whether you know it or not." Cynthia smiled sadly. "Maybe your time here is what you need to serve someone one day who's actually worth serving."

"Oh, Cynthia! I didn't mean I wanted to leave you—"

"Stop that right now," Cynthia snapped, and for a moment, Elaina could see a frightening resemblance between the old

323

woman and her daughter. "Do not think for one instant that I'm trying to garner pity. Now help me back into bed, then sit while I drink my tea, and maybe you'll see what I'm talking about."

Elaina, too tired to argue, obeyed, seating herself on one of the many trunks.

"I was not always a helpless, frail old woman, you know." Cynthia sat up straight. "I was a woman of power and influence. I could catch any man's eye and have any life I wanted, thanks to being the daughter of one of the wealthiest traders in Solwhind."

"What happened?" Elaina asked.

Cynthia merely shrugged her thin shoulders and took a sip of her tea. "Time stops for no one. Matilda grew up and married, and my own husband died. He was my third, you know." She sighed. "It all started out with a harmless cold. Matilda had lost her own husband by then, so when I fell ill, she brought me into her home to live with her and Dinah and Alison. Before long, however, she was sure their home was too cramped, despite having lost her husband recently. So she insisted that we all move back into my home."

"Where was your home?"

Cynthia gave her a hard smile and gestured to the walls. "This *is* my home. By title, I am mistress here."

"Oh."

"Don't look so forlorn. Maybe if I had been sharpened a bit more in my youth, instead of getting everything I ever wanted, I might have learned the value of having a softer edge. And maybe," Cynthia grimaced, "I might have raised my daughter to have a kind bone somewhere in her body, and we wouldn't all be in this dreadful situation."

"How do you do it?" Elaina blurted out. "How do you keep your sanity, stuck in this room day after day knowing what was taken from you?"

This time, it was Cynthia who looked out the window. Her sharp expression softened a bit, and she gave a little smile. "I've had a lot of time to spend with the Maker since then. And, upon reflection, have found that I've been treated much better than anything I deserve. Particularly when he sent me you." She smiled at Elaina, her milky blue eyes warm. "In my youth and beauty and prime, I had little in mind but to see just how far I could spread my reach. It wasn't until I became a prisoner in my own home that I began to realize how many years and resources I had wasted in pursuing pleasure. But you." She held her hands out.

Elaina came forward and took them.

"I don't know why the Maker has allowed so much pain to come into your life, but don't ever think it in vain. It may not be visible right now, but sometimes . . ." She took a deep breath. "Sometimes you just have to wait and see."

"But I—"

"No. You are the kind of person to push and push until you either fall off a cliff or you die trying. I know because I've seen you nearly do it here. All you can do is your best. Then the best you can do is trust and let go."

Elaina put her thumb to her lip. "I don't like letting go."

Cynthia laughed. "I can tell. But you are not the Maker, Cinders, and the more you try to be, the harder your life will get. Now," she lay back against her pillows, "I think we should both get some sleep. But Cinders?"

Elaina paused, her hand on the door. "Yes?"

"About that prince."

Elaina's throat was suddenly too tight to answer.

"I've been around power enough to know that sometimes those who seem the most powerful of all are often those most at the mercy of everyone else. Your prince might have been as much in control of the situation as you were."

CHAPTER 35
ABSOLUTELY NOT

Nicholas rolled over, but before he even opened his eyes, he sensed another presence close by. Rubbing the sleep from his eyes, he blinked a few times to find not one, but two people in his bed.

The morning light was warm as it streamed through the windows. Its golden rays made the two bodies beside him glow like angels, and Nicholas's breath fled.

The little girl snuggled between them was the most beautiful creature he had ever laid eyes on. Hair the color of honey stuck out in every direction as she breathed, her little chest rising and falling peacefully. Her chubby little cheeks were rosy in the late spring sun, and though her eyes were closed, Nicholas recognized the shape of his own.

How was it possible to love someone so much only a second after laying eyes on her? And yet he somehow knew in his heart of hearts that he would gratefully give his last breath for the child.

The woman lying beside the child was a vision all her own. One arm was tucked under her head and the other was wrapped around the little girl. She sighed in her sleep, and a small smile lit her face.

A gleam caught his eye. The silver band on her finger reflected the sunlight, its gems casting a net of sparkles around the room. Without thinking, he looked down at his own left hand.

He was a husband.

A father.

Everything in him longed to lean over and kiss them both. More than anything in the world, he wanted to gather them both in his arms and hold them close, to protect them from the world.

And for them to protect him from the silent and lonely hell he'd been living since she'd disappeared. Since he had sent her away. He paused then looked more closely at the little girl, trying to discern her age. Was it possible? If everything had gone as he had once hoped, could they have a child by now? Could she already be old enough to have such thick curls?

Slowly, tenderly, he leaned down to place a soft kiss on her head.

The pounding on his door was so loud that Nicholas's whole body jerked. He thrashed around, trying desperately to reach out, to grasp them, but all he found were empty sheets. Elaina and the little girl were gone. Nicholas put his head in his hands, nearly overwhelmed with the need to cry.

It was just a dream.

The pounding, however, was not, for it came again and again.

"Nicholas!" his father called through his door. "Get up and pack. I've got an assignment for you."

Muttering a string of words he'd never have dared breathe in front of his mother, Nicholas pulled on his robe and stumbled to his door. By the time he answered it, however, his father was already walking away. The man that stood guard outside his room handed him a sealed parchment.

Still blinking the sleep from his eyes, he broke the seal and began to read.

"Must be a dangerous mission for him to leave you with such heartfelt sentiment."

Nicholas looked up from the parchment in surprise.

Henri Fortier stood facing him, hands behind his back and an ornery grin on his face.

"When did you get here?"

"Well, hello to you, too. I thought you'd be glad to see me."

Nicholas rolled his eyes. "Get in here, you idiot." He shoved the parchment at his friend, ignoring the questioning look his guard gave him. "Give me five minutes to get decent and read that while you're at it." He left his friend in his receiving room and went into the next room to change out of his nightclothes.

"Not having the servants help you anymore?" Henri called through the door. "Glad to see you've learned to dress yourself. Bravo."

"We're at war. The servants have better things to do. Besides, at least I know how to shave properly." He imagined Henri running his hand over his blond chin stubble self-consciously. "Now, did you come here for a reason, or was your purpose just to annoy me?"

"Well, if you must know, my father had business just south of your border, and I thought you might enjoy seeing me."

In spite of himself, Nicholas smiled smugly as he pulled a shirt over his head. "Meaning it was dangerous and he wouldn't let you help."

"Precisely." Henri paused. "But it seems your father has no scruples about sending you into dangerous places. Care to trade for a day?"

Nicholas splashed some water on his face before returning to his front chamber. "My father has never suffered the loss of a single night's sleep for sending me anywhere. His main concern was always that I not make bad situations worse. And now that I have proven myself to be at least somewhat competent in his eyes, I have become a convenient errand boy of all sorts." He held his hand out and Henri gave the parchment back.

"At least he relented with the military. From what I hear, you seem to be as involved as you ever wanted to be." Henri frowned. "Why are you being sent to look for Willard Appleby?"

"It seems the dolt finally fell prey to his own stupidity. His father reported him missing yesterday, and they think he might have been kidnapped by slave traders while visiting the eastern wharf."

Henri's smug expression darkened. "Isn't that what you think happened—"

"Yes." Nicholas squeezed the parchment so tightly his thumb went through it. Crumpling it up and throwing it at the wall, he returned to his dressing room and began pulling clothing from a wardrobe. Henri followed.

"But your father didn't allow you to—"

"No." Nicholas began shoving his clothes into a satchel. "Appleby's father, however, has been an important financial contributor to the war effort, and thus, his precious son is a top priority."

Henri was quiet for a long moment. When Nicholas finally looked up at him, he had moved over to the southern window and was staring out with a solemn expression. "My mother cried when we received your message," he said softly. He turned and looked at Nicholas, his gray eyes no longer teasing. "They would have done everything in their power to find her if you had asked. All you had to do was utter the word."

Nicholas closed his bag and leaned on it, closing his eyes. "I know." He shook his head. "But if my father had caught wind of their interference, he probably would have gone out of his way to make it more difficult for them." He shook his head. "Everyone would have been hurt, including Elaina."

"I know. My mother said the same." Henri kicked a pillow that lay on the floor. "But not a day goes by where she doesn't think about Elaina and how they might have helped her."

Nicholas shook his head to clear it of the dark thoughts. "Well, I'm sorry you've come just to see me gone."

"Are you taking that spy you told me about?"

"I don't think so. He's already in Solwhind on another

mission." Nicholas paused, then looked up. "Unless you wish to join me. Would your father approve?"

"Of course I want to go. And would he approve? Absolutely not." Henri grinned. "I'm only here because Eloy is escorting my brother and sister to some event in the east. Mother is going with them, and Father didn't want to leave me alone. Eloy's already annoyed because I'm with you."

"Why?"

"He thinks you're a bad influence on me." Henri pulled an orange from his pocket and began to peel it.

"Does that mean you want to stay here?"

"No, you loon! Let's go."

HENRI, Nicholas, Captain Oliver, and the three soldiers accompanying them rode hard, arriving at the docks just after midnight. It wasn't long before they had located the small vessel posing as a trade ship that was to take them across the bay.

As soon as they boarded, Nicholas and Henri retired below deck to their cramped quarters while Captain Oliver stayed with his men.

"What's wrong with you today?"

Nicholas looked up from the stick he'd been whittling.

Henri leaned back and shook his head. "I visit you for the first time in six months, and you haven't heard a word I've said since we pulled anchor, have you?"

"Your sister has been rubbing off on you. You haven't shut up since we left."

Henri leaned forward. "I mean it. What's wrong?"

Nicholas stared hard at the stick he was whittling. No shape was appearing, despite the hundreds of wood shavings that were piled up on his boots. An hour of work, and Nicholas had succeeded in whittling . . . another stick. He threw the knife and the stick on the ground.

"Fine then. Suit yourself." Henri lay back on his cot and kicked his boots off.

"I had a dream the night before last."

Nicholas pulled his hat over his face. "About?" His voice was muffled.

"Do you remember how I wrote to you and told you I was going to ask Elaina to marry me?"

"And steal all the glory of Sophia's big day for your own? Yes, I recall something like that. We couldn't go because my brother was unwell."

Nicholas's throat went dry. "Did you know that if she had said yes . . . if none of this had happened, we could have been married by now?" His voice fell to a whisper. "Our daughter might have already been old enough to walk."

Henri sat up on his elbow. "Daughter?" He leaned forward. "You know most dreams are simply that, Nicholas. Just dreams."

"I know that," Nicholas snapped. Then he shook his head and ran his hand through his hair. "This one was just so real. It was . . . what could have been."

What could have been if he hadn't been a fool.

If his father wasn't so obstinate.

If Nicholas had had the courage to defy the magistrates.

When Henri didn't answer, Nicholas looked over at him. In the dim light of the single lantern, he could see his friend staring pensively at the ground. Finally, Henri nodded.

"If that's the way you feel, I just have one question."

"And that is?"

"How are we going to find her?"

Nicholas felt a ridiculous grin spread across his face. "I was hoping you would ask that."

After about an hour of planning, they decided to retire in preparation for their early morning. Henri, however, took him by surprise when he said,

"She's changed you, you know."

Nicholas had lain back in his cot and was glad his friend couldn't see his face. "What makes you say that?"

"I may not often be around, but I've seen you enough to know that you haven't worn a woman on your arm since the day she disappeared."

Nicholas rolled over, the lump in his throat growing. "We've got an early day tomorrow. Might as well get some sleep."

But rest really wasn't what Nicholas wanted at all. As he closed his eyes, Nicholas prayed desperately that the Maker might give him the dream once more. A few more minutes with what should have been.

CHAPTER 36
SIGNS

Nicholas and Henri kept their heads down and their eyes sharp as they made their way through the marketplace closest to the wharf. Blending in was harder for Nicholas than it was for Henri, of course, as he stood a good head taller than everyone around them, so Nicholas was relieved when he spotted the stall. Signaling to his guards with a casual gesture, he stopped and pretended to browse the selection of bread at the stand. Henri stood behind him, keeping watch while Nicholas did the talking.

"Not a wide variety," Nicholas remarked to the stall's owner.

"Not many supplies getting in and out of the city," the owner said, hardy glancing up at Nicholas from the knife he was using to clean his fingernails. "King's got us cut off on nearly all sides. Only a few ships get in and out, and those who do charge heavily for what they carry. Same goes for the land borders, too." He finally put his knife down. "You must be new here."

"As you said, some ships do get in and out." Nicholas lifted a loaf and examined it. "Last I saw your city, it was much cleaner, too. And your people better fed." He rapped his knuckles on the bread, which made a hollow sound.

The man shrugged and scratched his dirty mustache. "No bailiffs, no rules." He squinted at Nicholas. "What of it?"

Nicholas lowered his voice. "I'm looking for someone." Glancing around to make sure they weren't being watched too closely, he pulled a gold coin out of the wrist of his glove. The coin had a small circle of stamped wax on one side, so small one might mistake it for mere grime.

The man's eyes widened just a hair. He quickly snatched the coin from Nicholas and shoved it beneath the table.

"And?"

Nicholas leaned forward and pretended to examine another piece of bread in the corner. "Willard Appleby," he whispered before straightening again.

To his surprise, the man looked puzzled. "Why that one?"

"His father believes he was abducted at the eastern harbor several days ago."

"Aye, he's here." The man paused. "But I'm not sure you'll find him as helpless as you think."

"Why is that?"

Before the man could answer, Henri bumped him from behind. They were running out of time.

"Just tell me where to find him."

The man nodded and whispered an address.

Henri bumped him again, but Nicholas had one more question. "Are there any pockets of slaves here? Somewhere I might find those forced into servitude?"

"Any still here are with the wealthy, but it would be impossible to find them all. Most are only daring to keep one or two whilst the war is going on." He paused and scanned the crowd, then pointed subtly. "But you see that girl over there? The one with the gold and purple bracelet? She belongs to the largest group I've seen yet. Her owner keeps six. Used to have eight before two got away."

Nicholas turned and looked at the young woman, his breath speeding up. His heart fell when he saw her, though, for even though she was about Elaina's age, the girl was taller and far more full-figured than Elaina had ever been. Still, she was a lead. And that was the most Nicholas could ask for.

Nicholas turned and nodded his thanks to the man, handing him another coin and taking one of the stale loaves with him. Henri followed close behind. Henri's sword remained in its sheath, but the crease between his brows told Nicholas exactly how Henri felt about the marketplace. And Nicholas didn't blame him.

They made their way through the dirty children, beggars, and nearly empty stalls to the alley where the girl stood, trying to bargain with someone selling shawls. Her shoes had holes in them, and her clothes were threadbare. Messy red hair was pulled into a thick braid that was wound carelessly around the girl's head.

Nicholas prayed Elaina's lot was better than that of this girl.

As they drew closer, Nicholas realized she was accompanied by a very large man. Though not as tall as Nicholas was, the man was about three times as wide, with arms as thick as Nicholas's legs. Nicholas glanced back at Henri, who nodded slightly without looking away from the large man. They needed a distraction.

Henri swerved to the left and stumbled into a woman pushing a cart of firewood. Calling out apology after apology, he attempted to help her pick up the mess, but only succeeded in spilling more of the wood. Nicholas prayed quickly that Henri would escape unscathed as the woman's husband began jabbing a finger at Henri and shouting at the top of his lungs.

Nicholas owed his friend a very large mug of ale when they got back to the palace.

As he had hoped, the large man's attention was set on the scene Henri had created. Nicholas slipped up beside the red-haired girl and pretended to look at shawls as well.

"I apologize for my forwardness, miss, but would you happen to have a name?" he murmured.

The girl turned and looked at him warily. Her initial look of suspicion, however, turned to wide-eyed shock. "You're—"

"Please don't."

"Oh. Yes." She nodded and went back to sorting through the shawls, but her hands shook. "Aspen is my name, Your—um, sir."

"Do you belong to a household of other servants as well?"

She nodded. "Matilda Winters."

"Do you know a girl about your age named Elaina?"

"No, sir."

He had known that asking the question was like loosing an arrow into the dark. Still, when she said no, he felt all the air rush out of his chest. He hadn't realized he'd allowed himself to hope until now.

Nevertheless, this girl and her fellow servants were his people. His responsibility. Elaina might not be with them, but that didn't mean he shouldn't help them.

Elaina would have done it.

"I don't have much time." He glanced back at the large man behind them, whose gaze was still on Henri's ruckus. "Don't tell the others who I am, but . . . could you get out of the house tonight? All of you? And make it to the fourth dock on the wharf?"

She glanced at him, eyes wide. She looked terrified, but she nodded. "I . . . I think so."

"Good. Have them there no later than midnight." He glanced back at the guard, who had turned and was staring right at him.

"Be there," he whispered. Nodding, he flipped the stall owner a coin and handed the girl the wrap he had randomly picked out.

"She's delectable," he said loudly, nodding to the big man as he left. "I'm surprised you haven't swept her off her feet."

The big man rolled his eyes, and Nicholas quickened his step. Hopefully the man had believed his act. Though Nicholas was loathe to play the flirt again, he knew that if she got in trouble, it would be a more forgivable sin for her to get caught talking to a flirt than a spy.

Nicholas was relieved, when he returned, to find the cart upright again and Henri placing the last log back on top of it. He caught Henri's eye, and Henri apologized once again to the couple before falling into step behind Nicholas.

As soon as they had rounded a corner and could no longer see the market, Henri caught up. "You owe me."

"I know."

"Honestly, do you know how much trouble I would be in if my father found out I nearly had to knock someone unconscious just so you could talk to a girl?"

Nicholas sent his friend a sideways grin. "Your father does realize that you're of twenty-two years, does he not?"

Henri snorted. "You try telling that to the Great King Everard of Destin."

Nicholas laughed, but his humor died quickly. "That girl was a slave. We're taking six of them back with us on the boat tonight when we're done with this errand."

Henri gave him a look of disbelief. "First of all, we have no guarantee this debacle will be finished by tonight, particularly if Appleby is up to more than his father thinks he is. Second, have you forgotten that our little boat only carries twelve at most?" He glanced around at the four men walking with them at varying distances. "They make four. You and I are six, and if we succeed in getting this fool back from his kidnappers or whoever helped him get here, that makes seven. We can only take five more."

"We'll figure that out when we get there. We'll think of something. We always do."

Henri rolled his eyes.

"I mean it. The Maker has given us a chance to free six people from enslavement. Do you think I'm going to let the size of a rowboat ruin this chance?" After all, it was what he hoped someone else would do if they found Elaina . . . wherever she was.

"Nicholas, in two years you have gone from being one of the most wayward reprobates I had the pleasure of calling friend, to the most annoyingly pious and faithful."

Nicholas refused to look at his friend. "It's just like you said. She changed me. Now shut up. Here we are." He stopped before a tavern. "We'll stay here until the evening. Once it's dark, we'll look for Appleby."

As they went inside, Nicholas drew in a deep breath. They would figure out the sailing details later. First he had to find Willard. Then he would find Elaina.

CHAPTER 37
STOLEN GIFTS

Nicholas squinted down the street in the deepening of the evening light. He could barely make out Oliver motioning toward the big storehouse.

Either the foolish young man had really been kidnapped, or he was up to no good. Because the Willard Appleby Nicholas knew wouldn't be caught dead in a common fish house. Particularly an abandoned one.

Nicholas motioned back to Oliver, then he and Henri darted across the street to the fish house while his soldiers fanned out.

Hoods pulled down over their faces, Henri and Nicholas flattened themselves against the rough wooden wall and peered through the single window beside the door. Several candles had been lit inside, but not enough for them to make out any details through the dirty window. Aside from the flames' flickers, no movement was made. But surely someone was inside. Only a fool would leave behind lit candles in a warehouse made of wood.

They waited there for much longer than Nicholas had hoped. Suppressing the horrid urge to kick off his boot when he felt something crawl into it, he had just begun to wonder if their contact had been wrong when a shadow crossed in front of the window. Before passing by completely, it seemed to stop and look out the window, leaning into the pane to stare outside. After muttering something Nicholas couldn't make out through the glass, the figure began to pace again.

"Doesn't look like a hostage to me," Henri whispered.

"There's only one way to find out." As Nicholas left his hiding place to stand at the door, he had the sinking sensation of familiarity.

Because the last time he'd knocked on a door in Solwhind, everything had turned out so bloody well.

Nicholas glanced around once more before rapping on the door to ensure his men were where they were supposed to be.

Willard Appleby opened it. His look of utter surprise answered any lingering doubts Nicholas had as to the young man's intentions. He didn't even need to glance at his friend to know that Henri was thinking the same thing.

"My . . . Nicholas." He cleared his throat and glanced at Henri. "Henri." After dropping into a bow so deep he nearly stumbled, he gestured inside to a few crates pulled up beside a small hearth. "I certainly didn't expect to see you here. Won't . . . won't you come in?"

Nicholas walked in, keeping his hand on the knife at his waist. He didn't like leaving Oliver and his men outside, but he really couldn't have asked for a better ally to have at his side than Henri.

"Please, come stand by the fire," Willard said. "It is spring, but the nights still have quite a chill to them here by the water."

The building was tall enough to fit three levels inside. Wooden crates were piled up against every wall, and there was the distinct smell of fish in the air. No proper floor covered the ground, only dirt. The windows were small and placed high enough that from the outside, peeking through any except the front window would have been difficult, even for someone as tall as Nicholas.

Nicholas stopped beside the fire then turned and folded his arms. "Would you care to explain?"

"Explain?" Willard stared at him blankly. "Oh, you mean my presence here. Yes, I suppose that does need some explaining."

He began to pace, toying with his clothes and constantly twitching his fingers. Nicholas couldn't help noticing the vast difference between the arrogant young aristocrat that so often visited his court and the agitated boyish man before him.

"Well?"

"Well," Willard laughed nervously, "I . . . I was told about a new kind of treasure that could be sought here in Solwhind."

Nicholas felt his blood simmer. "You don't mean slavery?" The thought of someone like Willard Appleby owning Elaina threatened to ruin his already tried calm.

"What? Oh, of course not." Willard traced a long crack in the wall, but his fingers continued to twitch so badly that he could hardly keep his hand on the wood for more than a second or two. "No, this treasure is quite expensive, but far more rewarding." He let out a short laugh and looked at Nicholas then Henri. "You both look so suspicious! Here." He held out his shaking hand, palm up. "Let me show you."

Before they could respond, a thin layer of sand began to grow in the palm of his hand. The layer became a little mound, then a pile, growing until it began to slide off his hand and onto the floor.

Nicholas closed his eyes. Why couldn't these encounters ever go smoothly? He'd never had so much trouble with gifted folk until the non-gifted had begun to help themselves. He started to walk back to the door to call for Oliver, but what he hadn't counted on was Henri.

Henri was on top of Willard in an instant, using one of his powerful hands to hold the young man still while his other hand pressed his sword against Willard's throat.

"Where did you get such witchcraft?" Henri shouted.

"What do you mean?" Willard squeaked.

"I have had the misfortune of knowing you for most of our lives, and you have never had that power!"

"I bought it!"

"It had to come from somewhere!" Henri bellowed. "The only

way to transfer that kind of power is through an evil like you have never imagined! Now where did you get it?"

Nicholas stared at Henri, unsure of what to do. Interrogation had always been a possibility, of course, but Nicholas hadn't imagined it escalating quite like this. Henri was supposed to be the calm one, the one with a cool head, but Nicholas had never seen him so enraged. Nicholas needed to regain control of the situation. He also needed to get Willard back in one piece, preferably alive.

"I bought it! I swear! That's all! See?" With a shaking hand, Appleby pushed his unkempt hair out of the way for Nicholas and Henri to see the two scars in his temple.

Before Nicholas had decided what to do, Willard flicked his hand, and gritty sand filled Nicholas's eyes. They burned so intensely he dropped his knife as he tried unsuccessfully to clear his vision. But the sand continued to swirl around him, biting his skin like thousands of little gnats. He stumbled and struck his shin against something sharp. As he tried to get up, still unable to see, he felt hands grab him around the shoulders and drag him along the ground. Nicholas rolled and kicked, but every time his vision started to clear, more sand filled his eyes. His backside hit something hard. Then again. And again. Were they going down steps?

"Henri!" he called.

"I can't see a blasted thing!" came Henri's reply.

Before he could use Henri's voice to find his bearings, the hands let go, and Nicholas was dropped hard onto something metal. It clanged shut as footsteps ran away.

He must be in another room. But where?

Nicholas got on his hands and knees and began to feel around until a few moments later when his eyes began to clear. Henri's shouts continued from above, sometimes punctuated by a cry from Willard. But steps eventually approached again, as did the sounds of a struggle and more of Henri's curses and threats.

Nicholas squinted at Henri's blurry form as it was shoved into the cage with him. But by the time he could focus enough to stand, the gate was shut and locked. His eyes continued to blink and tear furiously as he tried to make out their surroundings. From the look of the earthy, windowless room around them, they were in the cellar.

"Henri?"

"I'm working on it." Henri, still blinking hard with tears rolling down his face, had summoned a ball of blue fire that hovered over his hands and was pushing it against the lock.

"How did he get you down here?" Nicholas could understand someone with a new gift taking advantage of him. But Henri?

"Goes to show what happens when your father never lets you out of the training room," Henri growled. "Now let me focus."

It hurt to stare at Henri's hands directly, as the flame was full of what looked like miniature lightning strikes. But Nicholas couldn't help peeking. Though Henri had shown him the gift a few times when the boys were younger, Nicholas hadn't seen it in several years, and Henri's ability to control his gift had magnified significantly.

Unfortunately, as powerful as the fire was, it wasn't strong enough to melt the lock. At least, not with the urgency they needed.

"Willard, what are you doing?" Nicholas called out. The young man was sitting cautiously on one of the dirt steps that led up into the room they had been dragged from. "Do you think a few days in an abandoned fish house is going to give you what you need?"

"It's unfair for a few to have all the power," Willard said, staring at the ground.

"So you're buying yourself some. But at what cost?" Nicholas really wasn't sure where he was going with the conversation. He just needed to get Willard talking. He had a bad feeling about their location. Down here, several dozen candles were lit and placed on the dozens of crates that edged the cellar. Why would Willard have several dozen candles lit already? And why did he have a cage? He couldn't have known they were coming.

"Who owns this place, Willard?"

The young man just shuffled his feet.

Nicholas took a calming breath and suppressed the heat boiling up within him. Twenty-one years was far too old to be acting like a sullen child, but there was little Nicholas could do about Willard's behavior from the cage.

"Too bad my mother's not here," Henri muttered.

Nicholas opened his mouth to ask Willard again, but he could hear the door in the main room open, and Willard scrambled to his feet to greet the hooded, masked man coming toward the steps.

HALFWAY DOWN THE steps the figure froze then immediately reached up to tug the cloak further down its face.

"Your Eminence," Willard said, "I used the gift you gave me to trap—"

"I can see who they are!" the hooded figure shouted in a whisper. "What possessed you to think you should imprison King Everard's son? Or the Ashlandian prince, for that matter?"

Why was he whispering? Was he afraid of being recognized?

"I . . . I know he isn't the girl who talks to the stars," Willard stuttered, "but perhaps you might have a use for the Destinian prince." He suddenly looked hopeful. "I could help you harvest his gift. Then perhaps purchase it?"

Nicholas felt sick as the hooded figure turned to examine Henri once again. Not only was Elaina still being hunted, but now he had put his best friend in mortal danger.

"First let's do what we came to do. This gift will be no good to us at all if he's dead."

Willard nodded, and the hooded man hurried back up the steps. When he descended again, he was dragging a very large, heavy sack. As soon as he had placed it in the center of the little room, just out of reach of the cage, he opened the top to reveal a dirty, disheveled man with a fresh wound to one eye and blood all over his nose. The man moaned a little as he curled up in a ball on the floor, his eyes shut and his breathing shallow.

"That cage won't hold them for long," the cloaked figure whispered to Willard. "You'll have to help me if we're going to get this done in time to keep them subdued."

Henri continued to press his blue flame against the bars, but Nicholas watched the two men outside the cage. He got the feeling a lot of questions were going to be answered very soon.

The hooded man pulled out a dagger. It was an odd-looking thing, unusually short for a dagger, but it had an opaque ball the size of a marble attached to the end.

Only then did Nicholas make the connection. This weapon must have given the Order of the Dagger its name. This man must be the Shadow.

The Shadow used the dagger to carefully cut two slices into the unconscious man's temple, about an inch long each. The man on the ground moved a little, but Willard held him in place as the hooded man kept working. The Shadow held up a little clay jar about the size of Nicholas's fist and removed its cork.

"Hold his head to the left," he told Willard. Willard obeyed, and the hooded man tilted the jar until a single drop of viscous black liquid, much like ink, oozed out and disappeared into the man's first cut. He repeated the process with the second cut. "Keep him still," he ordered.

"I know." Willard said, a bead of sweat running down his face. "I remember from last time."

"Did you empty yourself the way I told you?"

Willard grimaced. "I tried."

"What do you mean, you tried?" the Shadow asked. "I told you, for the Sorthileige to work without driving you mad, you need to first empty yourself of all your preconceived notions about—"

"I tried! All right?" Willard cried out. "You had years with enchanters to teach you! I got one hour with *you*."

"For your sake, I hope you were successful." The Shadow shook his head before muttering, "They never believe me about the madness."

The two men positioned themselves on the unconscious man's body just as he began to twitch.

Henri's fire had ceased, and he stared open-mouthed as the man's twitches turned to convulsions.

"Nicholas, we need to get him out now!" he shouted.

Nicholas knew his friend was right, but he couldn't help watching for a second longer as the Shadow grabbed his victim's head and twisted it so that the cuts were facing down. He held the dagger's orbed end beneath the unconscious man's head as blood began to drip out. As the blood hit the orb, it disappeared into the knife itself.

Henri was once again trying to use his fire to melt the bars, but Nicholas had seen enough. He grabbed Henri by the sleeve and yanked him to the back of the cage. Leaning back, he gave the door a good solid kick.

Henri's fire must have weakened the lock because it snapped and the door flew open.

Willard let go of the thrashing man and began to summon more sand, but Nicholas was expecting it this time. Throwing his cloak over his face, he blindly rushed at Willard and knocked him to the ground. When he turned to look for Henri, however, he saw the Shadow dart up the steps. Henri was right on his heels.

"Henri, no!" Nicholas let go of Willard and dashed up after his friend.

Thankful that his legs were longer than Henri's, Nicholas caught him at the door and grabbed his arm. When Henri turned to face him, however, Nicholas felt his confidence waver.

Henri's eyes were glowing with the Fortiers' legendary blue flame, and his face was twisted into pure rage. Nicholas could feel him trembling through the sleeves he was gripping.

"Let me get him!" Henri shouted. "I can stop him!"

Nicholas, praying for the strength to overpower Henri, should the need arise, shoved his friend up against the wall. "I need you to help me save the man downstairs!"

Henri continued struggling, so Nicholas shoved him against the wall again.

"Listen to me!"

Finally, Henri blinked a few times. The fire in his eyes began to die down just a little.

Nicholas silently thanked the Maker. "Henri, I need you to save that man. You know about whatever it was that the Shadow put inside him. I don't. If you don't stop it, he will die."

That, and it was the last thing Nicholas needed for the Destinian prince to get involved with his rebellion's warlord. Forget Nicholas's own father. King Everard would be the one to have his head.

After what felt like ages, Henri nodded and numbly began to walk back toward the cellar steps.

Nicholas followed. Willard was gone when they reached the cellar, but he was the least of Nicholas's worries now. When Nicholas began to kneel across from Henri on the other side of the dying man, however, Henri shook his head.

"Go sit on the step. I've never done this before. I don't want to hurt you while I try."

Nicholas wanted to argue, but decided to obey. Henri seemed to know what he was doing. "What was it he put into the man's temple?"

"Sorthileige."

Nicholas shuddered. He'd heard of the dark substance of pure evil, but had never seen it with his own eyes. "What are you going to do?"

"I need to get rid of it." Nicholas took the man's head in one arm and placed his other hand beneath the still bleeding temple. He held the man's head for a moment and closed his eyes. When he opened them he shook his head. "My father can put his fire into blood to devour sickness. But I don't think I can burn it without killing him. It's too thick."

351

"Is there anything you can do?"

"I think . . ." Henri drew a shaky breath, sweat clumping the blond hair on his forehead. "I think I might be able to draw it out, though."

The unconscious man's chest moved less with each breath, but still Henri hesitated. Nicholas shuddered again. What kind of evil was this? He said another prayer for his friend.

Finally, Henri took his palm and held it against the two incisions. Blue fire began to emanate from his hand and move into the man's head. At first, it merely looked as though Henri was waiting for the bleeding to stop. But the longer he held his hand to the man's head, the more Henri's whole body began to tremble.

"Henri?"

But Henri's eyes were squeezed shut, and his lips were turning a ghostly shade of white. A groan escaped him. Blood trickled from one nostril down to his mouth.

Nicholas was off the step in a second and at Henri's side. He didn't care what Henri had told him to do. He had brought his friend into this mess, and he wasn't going to leave him alone now. Placing his hands on Henri's shoulders, he tried to hold him upright as Henri began to lean forward. As they touched, a burning, nauseating, sickly sweet sensation began to move through Nicholas's hands and up into his arms and shoulders, and Nicholas had to fight the sudden desire to collapse. Instead, he gritted his teeth and tried his best to hold Henri upright.

It was impossible to tell how long they crouched like that. Nicholas's whole body protested, trembling with the effort. His mind protested as well, begging him to separate from the darkness. It was all he could do to support Henri as he prayed like he'd never prayed before. His prayer was simple.

Deliver us.

A lifetime later, Henri let out a cry and dropped the man's head on the floor with a loud thud. A burst of blue flame shot out from his hands, its momentary glow like that of a casum ball. Nicholas strained to keep his friend from falling as Henri slumped sideways into his arms.

Don't let him die, he begged the Maker. *Don't put his blood on my hands. I beg you.*

After several long moments of shallow breathing, however, both Henri and the man on the ground began to gain back some color.

"Why didn't you listen to me, you idiot?" Henri wheezed.

"Last I recall, you're not my mother. Are you all right?"

Henri swallowed and nodded, but it was a long time before he was able to stand on his own.

"You say you've *never* this that before?" Nicholas asked, bending to inspect the man on the floor.

"No. My father is usually the one to deal with Sorthileige. My mother hates it." He tried to give Nicholas a smile. "But it seems I survived."

CHAPTER 38
SUCH A PRICE

S ire!" Oliver was at Nicholas's side as soon as he and Henri
had dragged the man from the cellar out of the building.
"Right before our eyes, all of the doors to the storehouse
disappeared! There were no windows, not even a hole big enough
for rats to get in! They only reappeared just now with you!"

Nicholas glanced at Henri. "Another gift from our captor."

"Captor?"

"A long story, Captain. For now, suffice it to say that the
Shadow himself graced us with his presence. We're alive, though,
and that is what's important. Now, I need you to send two of the
men to look for Willard Appleby—"

"No need, sire," one of his men called from the shadows. He
dragged a struggling, protesting Willard behind him. "We caught
him trying to climb a wall. Couldn't see how he escaped, but we
could see him fall off the wall plain as day."

"Good work. You and Angus take him back to the ship. Oliver,
you and Hardy will accompany me and Prince Henri to the nearest
inn."

"Inn, sire?"

Nicholas nodded at the limp body between him and his friend.

"This fellow needs rest and a good swig of ale, but I think he might be able to help us."

As soon as they were on their way to the nearest inn, Nicholas gestured for Oliver to fall back a few feet so he could have a few private words with Henri.

"Do you think he'll recover?"

The man they shouldered between them was all but unconscious.

Henri grimaced and tried to pull him up higher, though the effort obviously still strained him. "Hopefully, but I have no way of knowing. I think I was able to draw out most of the poison, but I'm not as skilled as my father."

"What about Willard? What do you think made him act so strange?"

Henri arched an eyebrow.

"You know what I mean. More so than usual. He's usually flippant and conceited, but not nervous like that."

"I can only guess that he's taken in too much Sorthileige. If the Shadow uses evil to remove the gift, I suppose he must use it to put the gift into someone as well." He shook his head. "He did say some nonsense about needing to be emptied before taking in the darkness."

Only then did Nicholas remember Jackson's speedy descent into madness and ultimate death after dragging him back to the palace two years before.

"Sorthileige," Henri continued, "is the vilest form of tangible evil in the world. I've never seen any as pure as that. I wonder where he gets it."

"If it's hard to get, it would make sense that he needs so much money," Nicholas said. "He must be buying it to use on his victims, and he's been taking victims for decades. Turn here. I think it's down this street." They paused and readjusted the man's weight before walking toward a distant lantern that Nicholas remembered spotting earlier that day. "But what I don't understand is his motive. Surely it would be more lucrative to use such . . . skills the way he's been doing for years. Why start a war?"

"He's been forced to keep quiet for a long time. Do you think he would have a reason to need so much Sorthileige all of a sudden, one that would require massive amounts of money produced by . . . I don't know . . . taxes, perhaps?"

Something niggled in the back of Nicholas's mind, and though he couldn't put his finger on an exact answer to Henri's question, his thoughts turned to Elaina. The Shadow wanted the girl who spoke to the stars. Could the extra Sorthileige be meant for her? Would she need more than other victims for some reason? What was her role in the Shadow's schemes?

As soon as they were admitted to the inn, they were shown upstairs to a room at the end of a dark hall. Laying the man in the filthy bed, Nicholas did his best to wipe the grime off the man's face as Henri called the innkeeper for some ale and tea.

"I'm sorry to rush you," Nicholas told the man as his eyes fluttered open for the first time, "but we're in a great hurry and must be gone soon. I need to know, though, everything you can remember about the man that caught you."

After a few long swallows of ale, the man stiffly sat up on his elbows. "He got my twin brother first. I saw it all." He shuddered. "I tried to stop them, but they tied me up. Would've got me that first day, too, except that I escaped. But not before I saw them cut his head open just like they did me tonight." He reached up and touched his own temple. "Put the black drops in him and everything."

"What was his gift?" Nicholas asked. "And what is yours?"

"He could summon sand."

Nicholas looked at Henri. Nicholas had never liked Willard much, but it was hard to imagine a childhood peer committing such atrocities. "And yours?"

"I can summon water, sir. Out of the air."

"What did they do after that?" Henri asked. He had moved to the window and had his arms crossed. His face was taut.

"After all the . . . black stuff had gone into that man's dagger, he just rolled my brother over and left him there. Then he started to cut open that young man's head, the one that took my brother's gift."

"I'm sorry," Nicholas said as the man wrapped his arms around himself and began to sob softly.

"The black liquid from the knife dripped into the young man's cut," he said through his tears. "And before I knew it, he had my brother's gift. That's when they turned on me . . ."

Nicholas frowned. "I don't understand. How can it be so simple? Drops of blood in and out with this . . . Sorthileige?"

"It's not," Henri said from the window.

"How?"

Henri closed his eyes and pinched the bridge of his nose. "It's a bargain. You get the gift, but you also get the darkness. You trade a piece of your soul, your humanity for it."

"But people who are gifted don't have to pay such a price—"

"Because the Maker has given it freely. Evil must have its share in order to make such a deal." Henri sighed. "That's why people die if the gift is removed. If they die while they still have the gift, like you heard him say, the gift is forever gone. If it's taken from them, I suspect it runs out with use and time. He needs live victims to prey upon because the gift is a part of who they are. It's embedded in their souls. In fact," he added in a quieter voice, "it's a mercy of the Maker to take them after the attacks, really. They can live in bliss with Him rather than walk around on earth without being whole."

Nicholas frowned. "Didn't someone try to steal your mother's gift once?"

"Yes, but it was different. He tricked her into sharing it. He didn't steal it from her, putting poison in and then bleeding her out the way it's being done here. And she was able to recover her power since she was the one who gave it up in the first place." His jaw tightened. "This is worse."

Nicholas drew in a shaky breath as he sat back on his haunches and tried to comprehend what Henri was telling him. Because if it was true, if the Shadow worked that way, he was still on the hunt for Elaina. He was on the hunt for her soul.

Henri let out a heavy breath and returned to staring out the window at the streets below, and Nicholas got the feeling that they needed to leave before his friend got any ideas about hunting down justice. So he swallowed his nausea at the gruesome description, and they paid the innkeeper in advance for several days' stay for the man. Then they joined Oliver and Hardy down at the inn's door.

Nicholas was deep in thought as they started their trek back to the wharf, so it surprised him when Henri interrupted his thoughts.

"Have you decided what to do about our boat problem?"

"Boat problem?" Oliver piped up from behind them.

"Not yet—" But before Nicholas could finish, a nearby clock began to chime half past midnight.

Nicholas, Henri, Oliver, and Hardy began to run toward the wharf.

CHAPTER 39
WHAT HAVE I DONE?

"What is that sound?" Cynthia asked, covering her ears.

Elaina grinned up from the floor where she was laying out the bucket, soap, and towel. "I believe that is your granddaughter Alison."

"And what is it this time?"

"She is under the impression that Dinah took one of her beaus."

Cynthia gave Elaina a sly look. "Did she?"

"Could either of them convince any sane man to marry them? My guess is the fellow found his senses and ran as fast as he could in the other direction. But your daughter is gone to a party, so they might just have to handle this situation themselves."

All of Elaina's mirth disappeared, however, when she removed the old woman's stockings. "Cynthia, when did this happen?" The smell of infection assaulted her as she peered more closely at the contusion on Cynthia's heel.

"Oh, that was a foolish old woman doing what she shouldn't and trying to get out of bed on my own." Cynthia shook her head and made a face. "I tried to put my feet right into my slippers, but they hit a floorboard and scraped a nail instead."

"Cynthia, this had to have happened at least three days ago! Why didn't you tell me? What did Matilda say?"

"I haven't told her."

"And why not?"

"Cinders, I haven't seen my daughter in two weeks."

Elaina stopped examining the foot and stared at Cynthia. "You can't be serious. All that time when I'm working elsewhere, and she hasn't come to see you once?"

"Cinders!" Aspen called through the door. "Are you in there?"

Elaina hopped up from the floor and opened the door, only to have Aspen dart in and slam it shut behind her. Her face glowed until she saw Cynthia. Then she turned ashen.

"Don't mind me," Cynthia said dryly, waving a lazy hand. "If it were up to me, you would all be back where you belong, and you would have taken me with you."

Aspen looked back at Elaina, her eyes wide, so Elaina nodded and smiled.

"She's telling the truth. Now what is it?"

Aspen glanced back at Cynthia and swallowed. "We're leaving."

Elaina stared at her stupidly. "Leaving?"

"Yes. All of us!" Aspen's smile was brighter than Elaina had ever seen. "In half an hour, we're all going to sneak out. Drake says he's stolen a few tools from the stable to deal with Felix and Ivor. He's going to take them by surprise when I bring out their dessert."

Elaina glanced at the window. "At midnight?" It wasn't unusual for her to stay up with Cynthia, as she had to finish her other chores before attending to the old woman, but the other servants were usually long asleep by then.

Aspen shook her head impatiently. "All I have to do is get their attention so he can sneak up on them. When they're unconscious, we'll run to the wharf, where a royal boat is going to take us back to Ashland!"

Elaina blanched. "A royal boat?" She grabbed Aspen by the arms. "Who told you all of this?"

Aspen smiled and quirked an eyebrow. "I'm not supposed to tell. But I can tell you that he's going to take us away. Isn't that wonderful? Now, I must go and make sure Gram is ready!"

As she dashed off, Elaina turned slowly and shut the door again. Was it possible? Was someone going to take them away? But why them? There were other slaves in the land. And why now? Most importantly, who had promised to do such a thing? Did she dare hope that it might be *him?*

Her waking dream ended, however, when she looked at Cynthia's foot once more.

"Cinders," Cynthia said, her voice quite cross, "don't you dare think of turning this down just for me."

Elaina shook her head. "I can't leave you alone."

"You have kept me more company in the last two years than I've had my entire life, even when I was the life of the party."

"But—"

"But nothing. I will not allow you to waste your youth on an old selfish hag like me. I made the choices that led me here, and it's only fair that I now walk this path. You, on the other hand, at no fault of your own, have been abused in the worst way since arriving." She stretched out her hands, and Elaina took them. When Cynthia spoke again, her voice was softer. "You must go." She smiled a little, though Elaina thought she saw sadness, too. "Find that prince. Insist that he explain himself, and I can almost guarantee you Ashland will have a new princess within a month."

Elaina knelt slowly at Cynthia's feet again. "At least . . . at least let me finish tending your foot first."

A few minutes later, the old woman's last embrace ate at Elaina as she hurried with the others out the back door of the manor. Though she was poised and ready to run, her blood thick with fear and energy, she still felt Cynthia's feeble arms encircling her as the old woman said her soft, slightly warbling goodbye.

Only when Drake used one of his tools to knock Felix unconscious and Ivan quickly after, did it dawn on Elaina that they were actually leaving. She was going to be free.

"Should have done that two years ago," Drake muttered as they filed quietly into the streets.

"We didn't have a boat waiting for us in the harbor two years ago," Lilly reminded him.

They didn't talk again until they reached the wharf. Their progress was slow, due to Gram's limited speed, but once they were there, Elaina quickly spotted the little rowboat in the distance. She had passed by this part of the wharf enough while going to the market to know all the boats that did and didn't belong.

"You there! Halt!"

They broke into a run as a man with a torch shouted out at them. Drake swept Gram up into his arms, and Lilly and Jacob held hands. Elaina grabbed Aspen's hand and pulled her along until they were twenty yards from the boat.

As they drew nearer, however, Elaina realized that there was not one man in the boat, but seven. One was standing and frantically beckoning to them, but Elaina felt her heart sink. A boat that small would only seat a dozen people at most. And with her party, there would be thirteen.

She let go of Aspen's hand and looked up at the sky. "What do I do?" she whispered.

Someone needs you.

Cynthia's face flashed in Elaina's mind, and more shouts sounded behind them. No, one person didn't need her. Thirteen people needed her.

"Keep going!" she shouted at Aspen and Lilly, who had turned to see where she was. Whirling around, Elaina ran at top speed back toward one of the larger ships. Scrambling on board, past the sleeping watchman, Elaina leaned over the edge of the bow and strained to see in the light of the full moon.

Sure enough, there were men up the harbor who were pouring oil onto the water. More men were chasing her little group. If the boat didn't get help, they weren't going to make it out of the harbor in time.

Elaina turned and threw open the nearest chest on the deck. It was empty. The second contained rigging, but the third held what she was looking for. Grabbing as many casum balls as she could, Elaina hugged the clods of dirt to her chest and ran back to the bow.

The little group had paused to get settled in the boat, and the men in pursuit were almost upon them. Elaina waved frantically for them to go. When they finally pushed off, she felt her heart simultaneously rise and sink. Never had she thought freedom would be so close, and now it was just out of reach. But then again, no one would be free if they didn't get out of the harbor in time.

The boat was agonizingly slow to begin its journey out to sea, as everyone continued shuffling and squeezing in for a place to sit, often in the rowers' way. She didn't think they would make it at one point, but at just the last moment, the boat left the harbor and reached the open part of the bay, which Elaina guessed held a larger, sturdier ship anchored farther out.

The moment they crossed the threshold, Elaina hurled a casum ball down into the water.

A wall of flame lit the water as the casum ball hit the trail of oil that floated on the surface, cutting the little boat off from all possible pursuit. Elaina pulled her hood off to see better as the flames licked the sky, and she squinted at the boat, praying to at least see who their saviors were inside.

A man seated at the back of the boat turned and stood as they moved slowly into the darkness of the night. Just before the rising flames cut them off completely, however, Elaina felt her heart stop.

She had locked eyes with Nicholas.

CHAPTER 40
WATER AFLAME

J ust as Nicholas was about to dive off the side of the boat, someone grabbed him from behind and yanked him back down.

Nicholas thrashed and fought to break free. "We need to go back! We have to get her!"

"You can't!" Henri shouted. He pressed his forearm into Nicholas's chest. "You'll be killed!"

"We can't leave her!" Nicholas writhed frantically, but Oliver joined Henri in pinning him to the bottom of the boat. "Elaina's back there! We can't just leave her!"

"The water is aflame!" Henri shoved Nicholas hard until he knocked his head on the wood. "You'll kill yourself in the fire before you ever reach her. Then what good would it do her?"

When Nicholas finally focused on Henri, he could see tears running down his friend's face as well.

"Let me up," Nicholas said, shoving at Henri's hand. "I need to see!"

After a long shared look with Oliver, Henri finally let Nicholas sit upright again, but he never let go of Nicholas's arm. Nicholas watched in agony as the whale oil lit up the night, cutting the city off from view. His head hurt and his body ached, but that pain was nothing compared to the turmoil that was his heart.

"Cinders's name is Elaina?" one of the women behind him whispered to another. She sounded surprised.

She had been so close. He should have known who it was when the young woman recognized their problem of too many bodies on such a small boat. Only Elaina would have identified such a challenge from a distance. And yet he hadn't pursued her. Instead, he had watched her set them free.

Nicholas put his head in his hands and cried.

CHAPTER 41
LIKE A COLT

Elaina's knees hit the ground with a crack, but she refused to let the pain show on her face.

"So I was pulled from an important gathering to be told that you chose to play the hero." Matilda's voice was soft. Elaina hated it when her voice was soft. "You helped your friends escape. Congratulations. You just forgot one thing."

The switch bit hard as it came down across Elaina's back. She bit her tongue until it tasted metallic.

"Now you will be the only one here." Matilda leaned in to whisper in Elaina's ear. "I suppose I should rejoice. You've saved me from feeding five extra mouths. And as you don't eat very much, I suppose that will save me quite a bit of coin." Matilda stood and smiled sweetly, patting her dark hair into place.

But Elaina was only half-listening. Worse than the welts, which Elaina could already feel forming on her back, was the bile that threatened to escape from her stomach. She could taste it, sour and bitter in the back of her throat, but she clamped her mouth shut. She would die before allowing Matilda the pleasure of seeing her sick.

But truly, she was sick. Sick to her core, sick to her heart. She had been so close to freedom, only a few dozen yards. Humanity and the dignity of being called by her own name had been just within her grasp. Perhaps she would have been allowed to flee to whatever country had been her original destination of exile.

Below it all, though, even worse than the lost freedom was that she had been so close to him.

The switch came down hard on her back again, jarring Elaina from her thoughts. She briefly considered snatching the stick away and breaking it on her knee. But Ivor and Felix were standing just behind her, and she had no chance of overpowering them both.

"Why did you stay?" Alison asked from the doorway. She looked bored, playing with a curl of her coal-dark hair, her bony fingers pulling the curl to pieces, but something in her question made Elaina burn inside.

Elaina used all of her remaining strength to push herself off the ground. Slowly, shaking, she straightened until she was standing upright.

Matilda's eyes grew round, and she raised the horsewhip again. This time, however, Elaina caught her by the wrist.

"I stayed because the Maker told me to."

Matilda stared at her for a moment before barking out a strange laugh and lowering her hand. Felix and Ivor began to move toward Elaina, but Matilda waved them back, keeping eye contact with Elaina. "You are so special that the Maker speaks to you, does he?"

Elaina clamped her mouth shut tight. She had said too much. And from the look on Matilda's face, they both knew it.

The courtyard was quiet for a few long minutes. Alison looked back and forth between Elaina and their mother before finally going in and hollering to Penelope that she was hungry. Ivor and Felix hovered uneasily behind Elaina. Elaina hoped they were most uncomfortable after having lost the majority of their charges, thanks to Drake's expert use of the heavy tools.

"It's getting harder and harder to smuggle help in," Matilda said, handing the horsewhip to Felix and walking toward the house. "If the Maker himself bade you remain, then remain you shall. You will honor his wishes by making up for your lost friends. Measuring the flour for Penelope, mucking out the horse stalls, washing the bedclothes, mending the laundry, cleaning the fireplace, serving the tea, and going to market, among other things." Matilda paused and then looked at the two guards. "Leave us."

As soon as both men were gone, Matilda stalked back over to Elaina. "When you arrived here two years ago, I told you I would break you. And I guarantee that I will still break you like a colt if it's the last thing I do." She leaned forward. "I swear to that."

CHAPTER 42
LIKE A MAN

Nicholas and Henri were quiet as they slowly made their way up to Nicholas's chambers. Henri's face still had a hint of gray to it, and the bags beneath his eyes only added to Nicholas's guilt.

Guilt like salt in a wound that already burned incessantly. He had been so close to her. So close to saving her from the wretched end Henri had described for him. And yet he'd stood helplessly by, allowing the boat to carry him to safety as he watched them take her, knocking her down against the large ship's deck and tying her like an animal. And the more he remembered the look on her face, the less Henri's argument about the oil on the water mattered. He should have at least tried.

A servant ushered them into Nicholas's receiving room, where he went and stood by his southern window while Henri collapsed onto a low sofa.

"I leave you for one week. And you go to war?"

Nicholas jumped at the sound of the familiar voice, but Henri groaned.

"It wasn't war, Eloy. It was a rescue mission."

"Then why do you look five years older than when I left you?"

Nicholas took a steadying breath and turned to face the man Henri often referred to as his beloved captor.

Of course, Eloy's official title was Bodyguard to the Royal Children of Destin. And that bodyguard was giving him the fiercest glare he had ever seen.

In spite of himself, Nicholas felt a little shiver run down his spine. Henri liked to tell Nicholas of how slight and young his bodyguard had been when he was first asked by King Everard to guard his children. But if he had ever been thin before, Henri saw no sign of it now. Muscle bulged from his bared dark arms like another layer of armor. His only true armor was a breastplate over his clothes, though Nicholas knew Eloy carried at least a dozen weapons on him at any given time. His dark eyes gleamed a little too brightly as they settled on Henri.

"He came to help me," Nicholas said, unwilling to let his friend take the brunt of his bodyguard's wrath. Henri would have enough to deal with from his father alone.

"Of course he did," Eloy snapped. "Now my question is what he did while he was helping you."

Nicholas glanced at Henri.

"I helped him find a young man who had gone missing from the dock several days ago. We found him and now we're back."

"And put yourself in the middle of a war that is not yours!" He turned to Nicholas. "What were you thinking of, putting him in danger like that?"

"Eloy, I wanted to go."

"No." Nicholas shook his head. "He's right. It was irresponsible of me to bring you along. Especially with what I knew of the Shadow." He sighed. "I just didn't expect to see him on this particular mission."

At the mention of the Shadow, Eloy whipped his head around to Henri. His voice was barely above a hiss. "You saw the Shadow?"

"Yes, I did." Henri stood and faced Eloy. "And what I saw chilled me to the bone. There is a darkness in him that must be stopped, or it's going to spread beyond Ashland's borders to every kingdom. Including ours."

Eloy scoffed. "Your parents will stop it if it tries."

"My father is a busy man!" Henri scowled. "I don't see why I can't stop it myself if I need to. Because I did."

Eloy's voice went flat. "What do you mean *you did?*"

Nicholas rubbed his eyes. He had never meant for all of this to happen. "Look, Eloy—"

But Eloy didn't listen. Instead, he grabbed Henri's hand and flipped his palm up. Leaning over, he examined it closely. "Henri, you didn't." This time, his voice was haggard.

Henri didn't answer, just yanked his hand back and turned to stare out the window.

"He saved a man's life," Nicholas said.

"It was the right thing to do," Henri added stubbornly.

"Henri, Sorthileige is not a game!" Eloy grabbed Henri by the arms, his face losing its color. "You could have been killed!"

"You think I don't know that?" Henri shook his head. "Have you forgotten who my real mother was?"

Eloy sighed and put his hand gently on Henri's shoulder. "You don't understand how special you are. How much people would sacrifice to use you."

"I understand when my friends need my help. I understood that it was the right thing to do." Henri looked at Nicholas. "I don't regret a thing."

Eloy shook his head, then reached into the leather pouch he carried at his waist. "Your mother sent me to give you this."

Henri took the parchment and broke the seal. After reading it, he looked up at Nicholas. "My mother wishes for me to come home sooner than I had planned."

"You should go," Nicholas said, mustering up a spent smile. "You might have helped me change the course of the war."

"But Elaina—"

"I know where she is now, and that she's alive, thanks to you."

Henri eyed him suspiciously. "Are you going to go after her yourself."

Nicholas shook his head. "My father has made sure no boat will carry me out of the eastern harbor. Not without his permission, at least. He's already notified the captains that disobedience is punishable by exile." He ran his hand through his hair. "He keeps me on a short rope as it is."

"Then what will you do?"

Nicholas glared at the door. "I'm going to win this war." He turned back to his friend. "Now go. Give your family my best."

After Henri had gathered his things and departed with Eloy, Nicholas took a long drink of spiced wine from the goblet his servants had prepared and left on his bedside table.

Eloy was right. Nicholas had endangered Henri in a way he himself would never be at risk. But if anything was to be learned, it was that Nicholas had been going about this war all wrong. He had been going about it like a boy. It was time he started acting like a man.

"Ask my father to meet me in my study," Nicholas told the servant as he strode out of his chambers. The servant bowed and hurried away to do as he was told. After a long hour of thinking and praying and wishing that the Maker would talk to him through the stars, too, Nicholas had a plan. If only his father would see it as such.

When the servant returned to Nicholas's study, however, he was still alone. "I am sorry, sire," he said, keeping his eyes on the ground. "But your father is . . . otherwise occupied."

Nicholas took a deep breath to keep himself from uttering something that might sound like treason. Then he nodded at the servant. "Very well, then. Summon the admirals. Have those who can meet me here in no less than two hours." If his father wasn't going to take this seriously, he would.

In two hours, the majority of the admirals had convened in Nicholas's study. They spent the rest of the afternoon and most of the night coming up with a strategy Nicholas would never before have considered. But the image of Elaina's thin face and the memory of the gifted stranger writhing on the ground pushed him forward. He was going to end this evil once and for all.

It wasn't until the next day as Nicholas prepared for the magistrates to meet with him that his father arrived.

"So kind of you to grace me with your presence," Nicholas said without looking up from the parchment he was studying.

"I've been waiting for years for you to take this rebellion seriously," his father responded, his good mood unaffected by Nicholas's sarcasm.

"So the dozens of times I went into battle alongside our admirals was what exactly?"

"Son, you were thinking small. Now you're taking charge! And I like that!" He smiled as he pulled random books off the shelves and, after a glance, tossed them to the side.

Nicholas put down the parchment. "Father, you don't even know what I found in Solwhind."

"You brought back Appleby's son. What else is there to know?"

"You need to come with me." Nicholas stood and stalked out the door.

His father followed at a more leisurely pace. When they began descending to the dungeons, however, the king lost his self-satisfied grin. "What are we doing here?"

"I want you to see the young man I brought back with me." Nicholas stopped in front of the last cell.

Inside, a figure skulked in the far corner between the wall and his mat.

The king squinted in the poor light. "Who is that?" The figure inside turned at the sound of the king's voice, and Xander jumped. "That's impossible!" He leaned in a little closer, but the hunched figure inside leapt at the bars, sending the king stumbling back. "How did this happen?"

"You know that *distraction* I've been working on all these years? It appears that our culprit is the Shadow himself."

"Who told you that?"

"Willard, here, before the Sorthileige took his mind during the boat trip back."

His father shook his head. "Sorthileige? I don't understand. What does the Shadow have to do with Sorthileige?"

Nicholas related to his father all that had happened to them while in Solwhind. His father's expressions ranged from outraged to skeptical to horrified to annoyed. "You don't actually believe Henri Fortier. His father is always going on about the dangers of—"

"Do you see this?" Henri pointed at Willard, who was now growling at his own foot. "Would you call that an exaggeration?" When his father didn't answer, he added, "Jackson went mad just over a week after he had received his *gift*." He leaned forward. "Father, we need to stop this. Now. I don't know what this Shadow wants, nor do I understand his actions, but I am confident that if we do not stop this war soon and apprehend him, we'll be seeing an age of darkness we've never seen before."

The king stared into the cell for a long time. When he spoke, his voice was distant. "I looked over the plans you submitted with the admirals last night. It is bold, I'll give you that. But . . ." He scratched his head thoughtfully. "I will sign off on your plans so that the funds may be allocated to the navy. But at the first hint of opportunity for negotiation, we will drop our weapons and agree."

Nicholas shook his head in disbelief. "Negotiate with the same evil that's murdered hundreds and caused a civil war?"

"If that's the fastest way to return to peace, then yes!" Xander started walking toward the dungeon's entrance. Nicholas followed his father back up the steps. They stopped halfway up, however, and Xander took Nicholas by the shoulders. "Look, son. All I have ever wanted from the day you were born was to hand you a kingdom of peace and prosperity." His voice was unusually gentle and his eyes bore into Nicholas's. "But I cannot do that if the country itself is in shambles."

For the first time in a long time, Nicholas looked at his father. Truly looked.

Xander's midsection and neck had grown far thicker than Nicholas could ever remember them being, and his breathing was loud and labored. Even now, he leaned on the foot with less gout, and his eyes had become glassy and red.

"You wouldn't have to worry so much if you took better care of yourself," Nicholas said, swallowing the emotion that threatened to surface. Turning, he continued up the stairs. He didn't have time to feel sorry for his father when it was the man's own fault he was in such poor health.

"That ship sailed long ago." Xander coughed. "So what is the next part of your scheme to stop the Shadow?"

"We ask King Everard to return and help us root out—"

"Over my dead body."

Nicholas turned at the top of the stairs, surprised at the vehemence in his father's voice.

But Xander only growled and shook his head, stomping up ahead of Nicholas.

"Why ever not?"

"That king is one of the most arrogant pompous fools I've ever had the misfortune of dining with. And his continual offers to *save* us are grating on me."

So Henri's father had not been ignoring their state after all. Nicholas groaned. "You mean to tell me that you've been rejecting his offers all this time? Father, how many lives could have been spared on the battlefield?"

"This is my kingdom, and I will see it saved myself!" Xander roared, his words echoing down the halls and making the servants scatter.

"You haven't been there to watch the blood flow!" Nicholas

was shouting now, too. "I have! I have watched hundreds of our people bleed to death while you sit in your—"

"Watch your arrogance now, Nicholas! I'm warning you!"

"You will doom our kingdom if you're too prideful to know when to ask for help!"

"I have heard enough." Xander swerved around a corner, nearly knocking Nicholas over in the process. "You," Xander called to the nearest unfortunate soul he saw. "Have my scribe brought to my study."

"Father, what are you doing?"

But Xander didn't answer. Instead, he marched to his study in silence. Throwing the door open, he went to his desk and sat down in his chair so hard Nicholas thought it might break.

Nicholas leaned over the desk, praying his father would listen to reason before he did something irreversible and foolish. "You said you were letting me take control of the war!"

"You may have all the *Ashlandian* weapons, men, and coins our treasury can offer." His father leaned forward as well. "But you may not involve foreign countries and kings. If you can't win this war on your own, then perhaps you're not ready yet to lead this kingdom. There you are, Wes. What took you so long?"

The palace's head scribe walked in and sat at the little desk in the corner, his hands shaking as he prepared his writing tools.

"Take this down and have it made public."

"Father, don't do this." Nicholas kneeled before his father. "Let your anger at me subside before—"

"Let it be henceforth decreed and known that King Everard Fortier, Queen Isabelle Fortier, their children, and all their military might are henceforth unwelcomed from setting foot in Ashland. If they attempt to breach our borders, they will be escorted out immediately by whatever means necessary."

"You're going to start another war!"

But Xander ignored Nicholas. "Oh, and before you are finished," he told the scribe, "take the Fortiers off our list of invitees for the annual Apple Blossom Gala."

CHAPTER 43
STEPDAUGHTER

E laina had just donned her apron when Matilda stuck her head through the kitchen door. "You're up early," Elaina said in her most chipper voice. In her few short months of lone service to the Winters, Elaina had learned that nothing annoyed Matilda as much as when Elaina was happy.

"We have an important guest coming this afternoon," Matilda said, ignoring Elaina's bait. "You know what that means."

Elaina pulled a piece of stray hair out of her eyes and gave Matilda her sweetest smile. "Yes, Stepmother."

"And you will lose that sarcastic tone and act like a decent daughter. Or I'll make you pay tonight."

Elaina rolled her eyes at the mixing bowl. As soon as Matilda had gone down the hall, Elaina turned to the dog curled up at her feet. "Every time a guest comes, it's the same thing. 'Yes, Stepmother! I love you, too, Stepmother!' 'I apologize for my poor choice of dress today, Stepmother. I really must remember to dress properly.'" She mixed harder. "As though anyone unfortunate enough to witness the spectacle is actually fooled. At least she usually leaves the switch in the stalls where it belongs when others are here, though. I'm not sure if I've finally begun to measure up to her expectations, or if she's simply tired of using the switch. Hitting someone is a lot of work, you know."

Dog didn't answer, just gazed at her trustingly with a hint of begging in his big brown eyes.

Laughing, Elaina dropped a piece of dough on the floor. Though she'd never had the chance to own a pet before, as a life at sea allowed only enough room for cats, which made Elaina sneeze, she had discovered the manor's animals invaluable once all the other slaves had fled. The days grew long and lonely, with only a tired Cynthia at their beginning and end. And talking to the stars was out of the question more than ever, since Matilda, Ivor, and Felix only had watchful eyes for her now.

Particularly Matilda. Though the beatings had indeed grown fewer, and Elaina had somehow found a way to keep the household running, there was something dreadful in the mistress's silence that made Elaina look twice over her shoulder, a gleam in Matilda's eyes that made her shiver. Matilda still intended to try and break her. Elaina was sure of it. The only question was when.

After breakfast had been prepared and served, Elaina grabbed her basket and set out for the market. She looked back at Dog. "Well, are you coming?"

Dog took a leisurely stretch before hopping up and trotting after her through the door.

Elaina smiled to herself as she pushed the gate open and heard a second set of little feet clopping after her. Well, hooves, actually. She held the gate open for the dog and the goat, and once the three of them were out in the street, she let it slam shut.

"Today," she said to the animals, ignoring Felix as he set out behind them, "we have several tasks ahead of us that we absolutely must accomplish or *Stepmother* will be quite angry." She held up her basket and gave it a thump. "First, we need to find a few ripe strawberries at the market. Barker," she looked at the goat, "perhaps you can be of assistance with helping me sniff them out. Just don't eat them like you did last time."

She looked at Dog. "I suppose I should give you an assignment as well, but we both know that you'll just sleep through the whole errand anyway." She smiled down at the dog. "Anyhow, after we visit the market, we need to go to the jeweler." She shook her head. "I'm not sure what the girls think they need new cloak clasps for right now when they can hardly afford the strawberries, but I suppose I must try anyway." She looked down and grinned at the two animals following her. "Can't have the two young mistresses suffering without new brooches now, can we?" Such suffering would most assuredly result in punishment of some sort, and Alison's fingernails had been particularly sharp as of late.

Pickings at the market were sparse, and it showed on the pinched faces of the merchants, but Elaina did her best anyway to wave and smile at those she recognized as she passed. She hardly even noticed that Felix was following her anymore. Despite her attempted escape, he had stopped intervening every time she stopped to converse with strangers. Perhaps it was because he felt sorry for her. Or, the more likely possibility, he had grown bored with his duties and was considering following Penelope's lead and looking for new employment. Trailing a slave girl, a lazy dog, and a mischievous goat seemed hardly the ideal position for anyone with Felix's size or talents. Particularly when one's pay came later and later with each passing week.

After managing to secure five whole strawberries at the market, Elaina moved on to the jeweler's shop where she had to leave her faithful friends outside. After ensuring that Dog wasn't lying where he would be trampled, and then warning Barker not to eat the trouser legs or shoes off any unsuspecting passersby, Elaina went inside to browse the meager selection of brooches.

"Is this really all you have?" Elaina heard a young woman ask the shop owner.

"It's the same thing as I told you last time," an exasperated woman replied. "The king's embargo is letting nothing through but the barest of supplies to keep us fed. It seems the king does not consider jewels as essential as flour, unfortunate for me as it is."

"But I heard that the king's son had a second meeting with a number of our magistrates less than a fortnight ago!" the girl protested.

Elaina tapped her lips with her thumb as she pretended to study the three brooches on the shelf, but she really couldn't have cared less what they looked like.

"Even after all that talk about fealty to the Shadow?" an older customer gasped nearby.

Elaina dared a peek over her shoulder to see the girl shrug. "My father says that many of the magistrates never pledged loyalty to the Shadow in the first place. They only kept silence while he had power. My father thinks they're a bunch of little—"

"Hush now, child!" The owner, a thin woman with graying hair, glanced around her shop. "Someone will hear you. The Shadow still has enough followers that life could be difficult for you and your family if he ever heard such talk."

"But the bailiffs have already returned!" the older customer said. "Surely they will put to rest all this rebellion nonsense soon enough."

The shop owner sent Elaina a direct look, and Elaina turned back to browsing the brooches.

"Unfortunately," the owner said in a softer voice, "I fear that it shall be more than a little longer that some must suffer the repercussions of this rebellion."

Felix cleared his throat loudly. The women quickly moved to discussing an inane piece of gossip, and Elaina felt her cheeks burn. It wasn't as though she hadn't considered going to a bailiff and reporting her kidnapping. She'd spent hours dreaming up such a daring act of defiance. But the bailiffs were still few compared to what they had once been, and Felix never let her walk within twenty feet of one.

And there was still Cynthia.

"I think I will take these," Elaina called in a loud voice.

The shop owner came over and lifted the two brooches Elaina had pointed to. They were both small, hardly larger than her thumb, and an ugly shade of orange, but they looked closest to what Elaina thought her mistress could actually afford.

"I don't suppose that Mrs. Winters has actually sent you with real coin this time?"

Elaina gave her an apologetic smile and shook her head.

The shop owner sighed and looked back at the pins. "I would have cut Mrs. Winters off a long time ago, but I know how difficult that would make things for you." She sent a scathing look up at Felix who was frowning down at them. "But let her know that this is the last time I can extend their credit."

Elaina threw her her deepest look of thanks. As soon as she could, she accepted the two small packages and scurried out the door.

It was the same story everywhere she went. The merchants had long ago begun denying Matilda Winters any credit. Now there was no way to replace the rugs with holes or the girls' fading gowns or the manor's broken windowpanes. And no matter how little Matilda liked the situation, even she knew Elaina couldn't fully restore their manor as it began to fall apart at the seams.

Of course, that didn't mean she had any scruples about bullying Elaina into trying anyway.

The bright blue of the skies, or perhaps it was the lessening of their brown haze, helped bolster Elaina's spirits as she started home. Yes, she was still a slave, but the air smelled sweeter and the sun was clearer than it had been since she'd first come to Solwhind. Studying the faces around her, she realized that despite the pathetic market there was an air of hope that floated among the people as well.

It had only dawned on Elaina after the bailiffs had returned just how little of Solwhind's citizenry seemed to have ever really wanted the rebellion.

Still, questions niggled at her, poking holes in her hope. What kind of power had managed to take control so quickly in the first place? And why was it pulling back now? Yes, Nicholas's war efforts had been successful. She had gleaned that from listening to gossip in the marketplace. But where was the Shadow? And why had he declared himself the leader in the first place if only to hide from the people he claimed to rule?

As she walked, Dog and Barker following her, it struck Elaina that the Shadow's sudden disappearance reminded her greatly of her mistress's silence. Scheming. Patient. Furtive. And she liked none of it.

Elaina put the goat back in his pen when they arrived home, although they both knew that he wouldn't stay there. Then Elaina carried her basket of brooches and strawberries back into the kitchen.

"He's more of a dog than you are, you know," she said to Dog as he curled up at her feet again. "At least Sir Reginald pulls the carriage like a proper horse, and Mrs. McDougal lays eggs like a good chicken should. Sheba chases mice, and Martin steals food and avoids her. But you, Dog, are a terrible excuse for a dog."

Dog just panted and gave Elaina a hopeful doggy grin.

Laughing to herself, Elaina had reached down to rub his head when a familiar voice wafted through the closed door between the kitchen and the hall.

"Who was that?"

"Just my slave girl returning from her errands. Now, do you have my money or not?" Matilda sounded impatient, but Elaina had to remind herself to breathe. For the voice that had spoken first could only belong to one man.

ELAINA HAD to restrain herself from running in and throwing her arms around Alastair. The king's spy was here. In Matilda's manor. Elaina was so close to freedom that she could nearly push the door open and touch it.

Still, if Alastair was here, that meant he must be undercover, and it would be of little use for her to ruin his disguise. So Elaina contented herself with leaning against the wall beside the door and straining to hear everything that was spoken in the hall. To prevent herself from doing anything rash, she rubbed her chipped wooden bracelet between her fingers.

"You said you would have my money paid back with interest by last autumn. *Last autumn!*" Matilda snapped. "And now you're asking for more?"

"The prince has been more aggressive than I thought. I never expected his father to give him so much power to interfere. But war is like that."

"I practically paid you to take half the city! And then I convinced my wealthiest friends to do the same. How, with a third of the combined wealth of Solwhind, are you losing your grasp to a prince hardly old enough to be wed?"

Elaina frowned. If Alastair was undercover, who did Matilda think he was?

"I can't keep control over the military."

"And why not?"

"The gifts I've collected to keep them in line are running low."

Matilda scoffed. "You promised me these gifts were strong. That if I gave you the money for that . . . that liquid darkness or whatever it is, you would be strong enough to control the hired swords."

"The gifts *are* strong! But they only last a little while before they begin to run dry. Besides," he sighed, "I'm having to use more of the Sorthileige on myself now. And Sorthileige is expensive."

Sorthileige? Elaina shivered. She prayed he wasn't telling the truth, that he truly was posing as someone else.

"Well, get more gifted people then, so you can take their . . . whatever you call them . . . *gifts* and end the war once and for all! Then we can try to recover at least some of the money I've lost."

There was a long silence. Finally, he said, "I'm running out of gifted citizens. I've killed too many."

Elaina pressed herself against the wall for support.

"The money the recipients paid was good," he continued, "but the naturally gifted need to be replenished. And don't even suggest using children. Their powers don't solidify for harvesting until they're grown."

Elaina barely suppressed a gag.

"I need more money to pay the hired ships so we can end this war and allow new gifted travelers to come to the city like they used to. People have stopped coming since the prince launched the offensive."

"I still don't understand why these *gifted* people are so important to you," Matilda said. "You'd be better off simply forgetting about them and being content with the taxes of the people you *already* have under your control. I only supported your attempt to harvest the gifts because you said selling the gifts would make good money. I thought it was a means to an end, not some ongoing obsession!"

"Taxes haven't been very lucrative as of late, if you haven't noticed. And the gifts did make a good profit. But I need to purchase more Sorthileige to continue the process, and I need more gifted citizens to harvest. I told you when we began this arrangement that finding the gifted was my objective the whole time. It was your idea to put the city under my control."

"Because fairness and the way gifts are allocated by the Maker are not my concern! My concern is with the fact that we had an arrangement, and now you owe me a great amount of coin. I was supposed to have been made a duchess by now for all my assistance, and you a king!"

Elaina lowered her head between her knees and drew in deep, even breaths. Dread pooled in her stomach and her mouth tasted bitter.

Had she been in the presence of the Shadow from the start?

"Look," Alastair continued in a tired voice, "if I can find this one gifted citizen, all of our troubles will be over. We needn't even retake the city! Hang the war and let the prince retake it. If I can get this one gift, I can go off in search of more gifted citizens, harvest them, and sell the gifts privately. We can then split the money, and no one will ever be the wiser. I just have to find this girl."

"What girl?" Matilda asked.

"The one who talks to the stars."

Elaina's breath was coming in and out too fast.

"Oh please—"

"No, listen! If I can find her and convince her to join me, she can use the stars to tell me where the gifted citizens are—"

"And if she won't?"

"Then I will take her gift. It wouldn't be nearly as productive that way, as the gift would eventually run out without her to host it, but either way, I can find many more of the gifted, harvest them, and then immediately sell their gifts to those who would pay handsomely. If I could get her gift to last even a few years, I could locate the most powerful people in the world. Believe me, people want these gifts. I swear, I will make all your investment back, plus interest. You might not be duchess in the end, but you will be very, very rich."

Matilda's voice was petulant. "I've heard those who buy your gifts seem to have rather interesting endings."

"Their endings wouldn't be so quick if they would just do as I said and—But really, that doesn't matter right now. What matters is that I find this girl so I can repay you."

There was a pause, and Elaina wondered if she might actually faint for the first time in her life.

"And why haven't you found her yet? You've found enough of the others using my money."

"I trailed her for years. Then two and a half years ago, her father practically handed her to me, but the blasted prince kept interfering. And even when I did finally have a way to get her for myself, there was a mix-up in her boats, and I lost her."

Elaina knew it would be wise to leave now and hide in the stable, but a sick, desperate curiosity kept her rooted to the spot.

"If I find this girl," Alastair said, his voice slightly less agitated, "there will be gifts enough for everyone. You will be rich, and equality will finally be grasped by all."

Matilda snorted and said something about caring for proper food and clothes more than equality, but Elaina didn't hear. All she could think about was Nicholas.

Nicholas had followed her like a puppy.

Nicholas had insisted she keep the guards.

Nicholas had stayed by her side whenever he thought her in danger.

You knew, she thought to the Maker. *And despite all my objections, you sent him to protect me.*

After angering and pestering and annoying and betraying Elaina from the day they met to the day he exiled her, it was now blatantly clear that Nicholas was the only reason Elaina was still alive at all.

CHAPTER 44
A PROPOSAL

N icholas, hold on!"

Nicholas was very tempted to keep running, but better judgment won out. He slowed to a jog and motioned to his guards that their morning exercise was over. Reluctantly he turned and walked back to where his father and some of his advisers stood. He was surprised when he got closer, however, to find his mother there as well.

"You could have waited for me inside." Nicholas mopped the sweat off his face with one of his sleeves as he approached them, dropping a quick bow to both of his parents. "I would have finished in ten minutes or so." *You could have given me ten more minutes of peace.* But he knew better.

"You've been avoiding us these last few weeks," his father said. "Your mother and I have tried repeatedly to get your attention for more than five minutes at a time."

He had been avoiding his father, to be specific. Nicholas had spent more than enough time meeting with his mother, planning for this very moment. "I thought you wanted me to run the war. That doesn't leave much time for lounging." He glanced at his mother, who briefly met his eye and looked at the ground. "Very well, then. You've found me. What is it that I must know now?"

"The war is going well. We've practically won," Lord Stiles said in his high nasally tone.

"Meaning . . ." Nicholas looked back at his parents warily.

"Your father," his mother said in a soft voice, "believes it is time you take a wife."

Nicholas did his best to act surprised. He would have been, had she not secretly called him and Alastair together two weeks before to warn them of what his father was planning.

Of course, that didn't make this meeting any more enjoyable. He motioned to a nearby servant carrying a platter of goblets. Only after he had downed an entire cup of wine and had its warm courage rolling around in his belly could he look his father in the eye.

"And I suppose from the crowd here," he gestured at the dozen individuals gathered behind his parents, "that you already have someone in mind."

His mother pursed her lips and sent his father a disapproving look, but the king ignored it.

"That I do."

"Well then?"

Xander nodded at one of the lower magistrates, who pulled out a parchment and skimmed it. "Lady Amelia Seamus."

Nicholas nearly choked on the bread roll he'd just popped in his mouth. "You can't be serious." Not even his mother had antici-pated such a poor choice.

"And why not?" His father scowled.

Nicholas scowled right back. "She's the daughter of one of the Shadow's most ardent supporters!"

"*Was* the daughter of one of the Shadow's most ardent support-ers. It seems that he is willing to not only pledge his allegiance to the crown again if we make this alliance, but also guarantee the loyalty of all those under his influence. Which is many, I can assure you."

"You don't have to tell me about his influence," Nicholas retorted. "I've been to Solwhind. I've seen the consequences of his *influence.*" He shook his head then looked at the small crowd. "I would like a word with my parents. Alone."

Some of the lords sniffed haughtily, but they did as he asked, going to stand a ways off where the grass of the back lawn met the sand.

Nicholas turned back to his parents. "The blockade is working. The bailiffs have returned, and we've taken most of their sea ports, ships, and ammunition." Nicholas threw his hands up and ran them through his hair. "Over half the city has already signed oaths swearing allegiance to the crown, and more are doing so every day, according to Alastair. I cannot believe you would stoop to negotiating with evil, particularly to speed a process that has already begun!"

His mother gave him a nearly invisible nod, but his father scoffed.

"Dale Seamus has promised cooperation from dozens of the local leaders in return for his daughter's hand. It will seal the war's outcome."

"Coercion does not guarantee allegiance. It only means I would be tied to the whims of my father-in-law for the rest of the man's miserable life."

His father rubbed his eyes. When he spoke, his voice was surprisingly kind. "I know this is hard for you. This girl is not Elaina, nor will she ever be. But would you at least give her a chance?"

Nicholas resisted the urge to flinch. Instead, he planted his feet firmly and crossed his arms. "No, I will not. I want to find my own wife."

A small knowing smile lit his mother's face.

Xander, however, snorted. "And just how do you propose to do that?"

Nicholas took a deep breath. Hopefully he could present the idea as well to his father as he had to the mirror that morning. But it was now or never.

"If it is peace and goodwill that you want, then I suggest holding a ball."

"A ball?"

"Yes. Invite not only the nobility and the daughters of our magistrates, but every eligible young lady from every corner of the kingdom. Let them all come as equals so that I may judge for myself, with your blessing, of course, who has the true heart of a queen."

His father scowled, but he didn't immediately refuse, which was encouraging. Alastair had been right. His father could not argue with the wisdom of such a plan, at least not immediately. The question was whether true wisdom would win out over pride in the end. And with his father, Nicholas could never predict which would take the day.

"The marriage most likely won't be of noble blood that way," his father finally said.

"It wouldn't be of noble blood with the alliance you're proposing, either. *Miss* Seamus is only a lady because her father bought the title for her after siding with the Shadow. Everyone knows her father was only a wealthy cattle owner, magistrate or not."

Xander glared at him for a long time. Nicholas could feel the eyes of the advisers and magistrates on his back as well.

"Very well," his father finally growled. "But only on one condition. The ball will be held on your twenty-second birthday, no later. You will be allowed three consecutive balls, which should be more than sufficient to find a suitable bride. But if you cannot find this perfect bride by the end of the third ball, you will marry the girl I choose for you."

Nicholas wanted very much to grin and hug his mother to congratulate her on their success. Instead, he bowed his head. "As you wish, Father."

As long as everything fell into place, three balls should be more than enough time to find the girl who talked to the stars.

CHAPTER 45

INVITED

In the days following Alastair's visit, two distinct sets of voices sounded again and again in Elaina's head.

Someone needs you.

The stars had been right. Because of her, Nicholas and the other captives had rowed to safety. In the two months since their escape, Cynthia had also managed to recover from her foot injury, although it had been several weeks before Elaina was able to breathe more easily about her friend's health.

But there were moments when Elaina wanted nothing more than to simply crack in two. She didn't dare try to talk to or even hear the stars now, not after what Alastair had told Matilda. And she missed them. After a lifetime of having the stars as her constant companions, Elaina felt like a void in her heart had opened and might never be filled again. Was life always going to be like this? Cynthia often told her to take heart, reminding her of the reports of the kingdom's reunification, and she was encouraged by the great numbers of bailiffs returning to the city, but most of the time, none of that mattered. For Elaina was still very much in Matilda's grasp. She proved as much by cutting off Elaina's trips to the market, hiring a local girl to make her runs instead.

The second voice, however, was the one that drove Elaina on

day after day. With every step that made her feet ache and every harsh word from Matilda and her spawn, Elaina rehashed the familiar words in her head.

I am strong enough.

No, Elaina. You're not.

Her father hadn't believed she was strong enough. Matilda was determined that she wouldn't be strong enough. But she was. And Elaina strove every day to prove that. Whether he was dead or not, she was going to prove to her father that she *was* strong enough for the sea in its ancient perilous beauty. Strong enough to survive Matilda.

Today, Elaina's dry hands stung as she put new hay into the horse's stall. "The switchings I can take," she told the little black cat as she wound herself around Elaina's ankles. "It's the games she plays that I can't abide. Oh, come now, Sheba. Be patient. You'll get your milk, but only after I finish filling Sir Reginald's trough. He deserves it after a full day of pulling *them*."

She smiled to herself as she shooed the cat away. She didn't dare talk to the animals whenever Matilda was anywhere nearby. But when Matilda was gone, the animals seemed to tolerate Elaina's idle talk well enough. "And don't go teasing Mrs. McDougal," she continued to the playful little cat, who had moved from being underfoot to pawing at one of the chickens. "I need her to lay an egg for breakfast tomorrow. Dog, come here. Get this little troublemaker away—" She paused, sure she'd heard the pull bell ring at the door.

When the bell rang a second time, Elaina dropped the hay and ran to the house, dusting herself off along the way. While she was hardly proud of the position she held in Matilda's home, it was irksome to appear filthier than most paid servants whenever she greeted someone new at the door.

Whoever was ringing the bell must have been in quite a hurry, for by the time she had pulled the door open, she was just in time to see a blue coattail disappear around the hedge into the street.

She followed him to the gate, which was now the edge of her world.

It was a royal courier.

Her heart sank as she watched him jog on to the next manor. Perhaps, if she had reached the door in time, she might have invited him in for some refreshment and slipped him a message about her predicament. He could have notified the bailiffs at least. But with Felix's eyes heavy on her from his post at the edge of the yard, Elaina could only sigh and start back toward the house.

That's when she saw the letter.

She snatched it up, and her hands shook as she tried to open it. Why would a royal courier be going from house to house? Why would he leave them a letter?

Elaina had just succeeded in breaking the familiar blue seal when the letter was plucked from her hands.

"Reading our messages now, are you?" Matilda scowled at her.

"The royal courier was here!" Elaina explained, wishing she'd taken the letter and run to the stable. "He—"

But Matilda had stopped in her tracks. Her eyes grew so wide they looked like they might roll out of her head. "Girls!" she shrieked. "There is to be a ball!"

"A ball?" Dinah gaped.

"Where?" Alison pulled at her mother's arm.

Matilda shook her off and read the letter aloud.

To the citizens of Ashland,
*   In light of the kingdom's reunification, Crown Prince Nicholas Alexander Calvin Gabriel Whealdmar of Ashland will be hosting three balls. Every eligible woman of marriageable age is invited to attend along with her family, for it shall be there that the prince chooses his bride.*

. . .

ELAINA FELT as though someone had punched her in the stomach. After two and a half years, she hadn't dared hope Nicholas still cared for her, let alone that he might defy his father and wait to find her. Not after he had been the one to exile her. And yet, the realization that he would very soon be wed to another made her want to curl up in a corner and never awaken again.

"When is it, Mother?" Dinah was now as energetic as her sister had been a moment before, bouncing on the toes of her slippers. More of her wild black hair fell out of place every time she jumped.

"In three weeks' time," Matilda said to her daughter, but she was looking closely at Elaina. "Cinders, why do you look ill all of a sudden?"

Elaina tried her best to pull together a smile, but she knew her mistress would see right through it. "I was only thinking of home, Madame. And how much I should long to return for even three nights, just to see the countryside."

Matilda didn't answer, but her eyes took on that devilish gleam of delight.

"Mother, we haven't suitable dresses to wear!"

"What shall we do with our old gowns? They don't fit! We can't be seen by the prince in such rags!"

Matilda refolded the letter calmly. "No need to fret. The neighbor's girl will run to the silk shop and purchase all the new materials, and Cinders shall make you new gowns."

Elaina shook her head. "Beg your pardon, Madame, but the silk merchant said he will no longer extend the family credit."

For one long moment, Matilda looked as though murder might not be beneath her. After a moment, though, she surprised Elaina by turning and smiling kindly at her daughters. "Well then, Cinders will just have to fix up your dresses and make them stunning for the balls as they are. Go pick three each and consider the changes you want made to them."

"Fix their dresses for the ball?" Elaina echoed. "Beg your pardon, but with *what?*"

"That is your problem, Cinders. I just expect it done in time for us to leave in two weeks."

Elaina gaped at her mistress. "Madame! I am capable of many things. I care for your animals, and I cook your food. I serve tea, mend holes, scrub floors, wash your clothes, and care for your aging mother. But of the many things I can do, this is not one of them. Turning old clothes into fine silk?" She shook her head in disbelief. "This is not my gift!"

"Then what is your gift?"

Elaina snapped her mouth shut and glowered at her mistress. "Sweeping cinders, Madame."

Matilda's serpentine eyes swept over Elaina as though seeing her anew. Her subtle smile made Elaina's stomach roll.

"Yes," Matilda said softly. "You certainly look it." She turned and began to head for the parlor but paused without turning at the door. "Gift or not, you will find a way to fix up my daughters' dresses and make them into decent, modern gowns of style, or you will regret it." Elaina could hear a smile in her words. "I have friends in high places . . . or rather, friends in low places who you would not be keen on meeting should you fail."

CHAPTER 46
ALL SHE WANTED

The rest of the day passed in a blur for Elaina. She bounced around between her rekindled anger at Nicholas, anger at his father, anger at Matilda, worry that Matilda had picked up on her slip about her gift, and pain that she tried very hard not to entertain.

For if she let her pain see the light of day, it would consume her.

"What has my daughter done this time?" Cynthia asked.

"I don't know what you mean."

"You've slammed everything you've touched tonight, from the door to my stockings trunk."

Elaina paused and took a deep breath, leaning against a bedpost to compose herself. "Forgive me, Cynthia. I just never knew Matilda's madness could be so far reaching."

"Come here." The old woman patted the edge of her bed. "Tell me what happened."

Elaina knew better than to argue. Cynthia always won such battles. With a wan smile, she did as she was told.

"It appears the reunification of the country is complete," she said, staring at her bruised, calloused hands. "The prince has announced that he's holding a ball in three weeks to find his future bride."

"Ah."

"And that's not the worst of it. Matilda has threatened me with her . . . unsavory friends should I fail to fix the girls' gowns in time for the ball." She shrugged and buried her face in her hands. "I only just learned to mend a torn seam before Gram left. I can't remake gowns that have been tattered for a year now."

"Forgive me for prying, but I hardly think the damaged gowns are your greatest priority right now."

Elaina pulled her face out of her hands and stared at Cynthia. "What do you mean?"

"I mean that you need to see your prince more than anything, or rather, let him see you. If there was ever a time for you to find your freedom, it's now."

Elaina began to shake her head, but then she noticed Cynthia's plate, which had been left on the edge of her bedside table. "You haven't touched your food." She bit the inside of her lip. "You hardly looked at your breakfast either. Are you feeling unwell?"

Cynthia just leaned back into her pillows and gave Elaina a tired smile. "The Maker takes everyone sometime, Cinders. I believe I shall be joining him soon."

"No!" Elaina jumped off the bed and knelt by Cynthia's side. When she took Cynthia's frail hands, however, their papery skin was colder than Elaina had ever felt it. "You have been the one who's helped me get through these years!" She pulled one of those papery hands to her cheek and closed her eyes. "You can't leave me now. Here." She jumped up and grabbed the plate of food. "Just have something to eat, and you'll feel better in the morning! You'll grow strong again, and—"

"Child, I am the reason you stayed behind."

Elaina shook her head, but even as she watched, Cynthia's breaths grew more and more shallow. Or had they been that way this morning, too? Elaina wished she'd paid more attention.

"Go to that chest over there, the blue one." Cynthia pointed a thin hand at a chest beneath the window.

Elaina obeyed. She'd never opened this particular chest before. Inside was a faded blanket covered in moth holes. But upon Cynthia's instruction, she moved the blanket aside. Beneath it was a shiny pile of pink silk. Elaina gasped as she held it up in the light. It was a little out of mode, perhaps, but the material had very clearly been cut and sewn by a superbly talented seamstress. Rosettes of white, pink, and red silk ribbon were sewn into the dusty rose bodice and layered skirts. Miniature pearls and other glittering little gems no larger than seeds had been expertly stitched into the neckline and shoulders.

It was possibly the loveliest gown Elaina had ever seen.

"It's a bit old fashioned, but then, so am I," Cynthia said. "I think it should fit you rather well, though, without needing too many alterations." She reached out and stroked the gown's skirts lovingly. "It was my favorite gown. And now it's yours."

"But Cynthia—"

"Because you are going to the ball."

Elaina shook her head, though for some reason her disobedient arms clutched the dress to her chest. "I highly doubt Matilda will let me go, let alone wear a gown more beautiful than her daughters'. Besides," she sniffed, "who would stay with you?"

Cynthia shook her head and waved her hand dismissively in the air. "Don't you see, Cinders? You sacrificed your life to remain with me. Now the Maker is giving me a chance to go to eternal bliss . . . and you a chance to find a true home. See how merciful he is?"

Still clutching the dress, Elaina ran and threw her arms around the old woman's neck, squeezing her eyes shut to hold in the tears. "I don't want to leave you," she whispered.

"I'm the one that's leaving, you little ninny," Cynthia whispered back. "Now," she pulled back and wiped her own eyes, "stop this nonsense and try on that dress. I want to at least see it on you."

Too heartsick to argue, Elaina shrugged out of the dirty, torn dress that had once been her finest. As she slipped into the pink gown, however, a new feeling of resolution filled her. Or rather, it was a feeling that she had long ago forgotten. Elaina went to the full-length mirror in the corner and turned before it.

A ridiculous longing took hold of her. If only *he* could see her in this dress.

"He won't be able to take his eyes off you, you know." Cynthia said smugly from the corner.

Elaina had to smile as she turned once again, the rosettes at the bottom of the dress billowing out as she did. And as she turned, something within her changed. A familiar fire, almost forgotten, was rekindled. Why *shouldn't* he see her in this dress? She was a young woman of marriageable age, though most women attending the ball would be a few years her junior, closer to Alison's age. And yet, why not?

Matilda wouldn't take her. She was sure of that. But Elaina could still use her extended absence to make her escape. The Winters family always took at least one guard with them when they left. If she put her mind to it, Elaina could find a way to create a distraction and sneak out without Felix noticing.

She would wear the dress on the run if she had to.

But even as Elaina schemed, she was reminded of the frail figure in the bed. Cynthia seemed sure her time was limited, but there had been times in the past where she had said the same thing. Elaina couldn't leave her alone, not while she still breathed.

She turned to ask Cynthia what to do, but by the time she had turned, Cynthia's eyes were closed, a soft smile on her face. Elaina ran over to the old woman.

"Please, Cynthia! Give me a few more days! The ball isn't for three weeks! You needn't go now."

But the old woman, eyes still closed, just shook her head. "You are the most beautiful creature I've ever seen." She drew a deep shuddering breath. "I know the prince will think so, too."

Elaina wasn't sure just how long she sat at Cynthia's side

counting her breaths. Minutes? Hours? She wanted to take the dress off for fear of dirtying it on the rough wooden floor, but removing the dress would cost her precious moments of what little life still clung to the old woman.

Eventually, however, Cynthia let out one breath and didn't draw another in.

The tears fell silently, but for once, Elaina didn't regret letting them fall. Yes, Cynthia had broken through her defenses. Yes, her father might have said that the old woman had made her weak. But Cynthia had been worth it.

ELAINA WASN'T sure what time it was when she finally awakened once again. The sky was still black outside, but the hand that she clutched had finally gone cold. Elaina took the dress off listlessly and put her old clothes back on. Then she placed the dress in the back of one of the broken wardrobes in the attic, behind another moth-eaten coat, before heading to the other side of the house.

"And why are you waking me at this hour?" Matilda grumbled when Elaina entered her darkened room.

"I simply thought you should know that your mother is gone." Was that her voice? It sounded dead.

"Huh." Matilda yawned. "Finally." She rolled over in bed. "I will send for the undertaker tomorrow morning. I expect not to be awakened again before that."

Elaina trudged back across the manor and up the steps to the attic, ignoring the desire to once again enter Cynthia's room. Instead, she pulled the gown from the wardrobe and went to sit beneath the window. How long had it been since she'd talked to the stars other than that one horrid night out on the docks?

As she threw open the shutters, Elaina knew her grief was making her reckless, but for once, she didn't care.

Hello, little one.

413

Elaina closed her eyes and basked in the sound of their voices again. "I missed you," she whispered.

We've been here all along.

"What do you see?" Elaina hugged the dress to her chest and snuggled beneath it like a blanket. "Tell me of the world. Just like you used to."

We saw a woman pass into the Maker's courts of bliss and eternity.

"How did she go?" Elaina held her breath, but she didn't need to. As soon as they spoke, she could hear the smiles in their voices.

She passed knowing she was loved. After a life of riches and admiration, that was all she wanted in the end.

Elaina nodded. She wanted to ask more, but with the dress covering her like a blanket and the comforting lullabies of the stars, she finally let herself drift into the most peaceful sleep she could ever remember keeping.

CHAPTER 47

BROKEN

"C inders! Get up. The grave keeper's boy is here to collect the body."

Elaina managed to catch herself before she tumbled off the window seat where she'd fallen asleep. After another round of Matilda's banging, however, she realized that she was still clutching the dress and the window was still open. She yanked the shutters closed and dashed over to the wardrobe where she stuffed the gown unceremoniously just before Matilda barged in.

"What is taking you so long?" She put her hands on her hips as Elaina rubbed her eyes and yawned. Elaina made sure to blink several times as though surprised before following Matilda into the hall. A young man stood behind her mistress looking quite red in the face, as though he at least had the decency to feel embarrassed about waking a young woman in her personal chamber.

"Take him to the room," Matilda snapped. "And make sure he doesn't steal anything. Fetch me when he's done. I have work for you to do."

Elaina nodded and led the young man to Cynthia's room. She was vaguely aware that Matilda's chores were sure to be horrendous, now Cynthia wasn't there to occupy Elaina's mornings or evenings. But the anticipation of Matilda's evil couldn't compare to the tightness in her chest as she watched him open a long bag and lay it out on the bed beside her friend's body.

"Be careful," she said without thinking. "Please."

When he turned, however, she saw that his eyes were sympathetic, and she gave him a sad, grateful smile. His movements were gentle as he guided the bag over the body. At least someone was showing Cynthia the respect she deserved. Elaina wanted to turn away as he heaved the bag over his shoulder and took it downstairs to the cart that stood out in the yard. She couldn't look away from the window, however, until the bag was in the cart and the cart had rumbled out of sight around the hedge.

Once Cynthia was gone for good, Elaina slowly made her way back up to her room. Perhaps if she was quick enough, she could properly stow the gown away where it wouldn't be found by Matilda or by any pest that might nibble at its fabric. Because one truth was certain:

Now that Cynthia was gone, Elaina was going to escape this house of hell and go to the ball.

As she pushed the attic door open, however, she came to an abrupt halt. Her mouth opened, but no words would come out.

The beautiful rose silk gown lay all over the floor in pieces. In the midst of the pile of pink fabric sat Matilda, looking as composed as ever as she grasped yet another portion of the skirt and pulled it apart at the seam.

"Well done, Cinders," she said with a pleasant smile. "You have done your work quite nicely. This silk will be the perfect addition to my daughters' dresses to make them suitable for the ball."

"You have no right!" Elaina cried out, falling to her knees and gathering a few of the beautiful pieces in her hands.

"I have every right!" Matilda stood, towering over Elaina as she hugged the dress's remains to her chest. "You took something that was in my house, and as everything in my house belongs to me, you're lucky I don't have you arrested for theft!"

"It was a gift!" Elaina screamed.

"A gift she was not in the position to give." Matilda dusted her hands off and began walking toward the door. "I expect you to have those added to my daughters' gowns within the week."

"No."

"I beg your pardon?"

"I said I will not!" Elaina jumped to her feet and threw the shreds on the ground. "I will not be party to this. She would have hated it, and I won't sully her memory that way!"

Matilda only raised her eyebrows a little. "I'm not sure whether you're aware of it or not, but there are many individuals in this city, reunified or not, who would pay a very, very high ransom for a girl who talks to the stars."

Elaina stared at her in horror.

"No need to look so surprised. I've had my suspicions for a while, but your little performance last night thoroughly convinced me. Now believe me when I say that what I have put you through will be like a mother's caress compared to what those people will do to you."

Elaina felt the acid in her stomach move up her throat, and before she could stop herself, had fallen to her knees as she retched up the bile from her empty stomach onto the floor. Through blurred eyes, she saw Matilda close her eyes and sigh as a smile like that of a cat stretched across her face.

"How can you be like this?" Elaina rasped through her burning throat. "How can you stand to be so cruel?"

To her surprise, Matilda pulled a dusty stool out of the clutter and seated herself upon it. "You loved my mother."

Elaina glared at her from the floor, still unable to sit upright.

"I wasn't as deaf to your secret conversations as you might have thought, but that is beside the point for now. I think you ought to know, however, that my mother was not the person she led you to think. No, my mother was every bit as cold and calculating as I am. And it served her well."

"She changed."

Matilda shrugged. "Perhaps. Perhaps not. But that doesn't alter what she did that taught me to be the way . . . the woman I am today." She gave a dark chuckle. "I don't know if you've ever thought yourself in love, but I did once." Her eyes grew distant. "He was the son of a wealthy lord, and he lived several houses down from ours. When my mother learned that I was infatuated with the boy, she told me I needed to seduce him immediately before another girl could take him."

Elaina frowned but said nothing. She wanted to deny Cynthia's ability to suggest such a thing, but by the old woman's own admission, she had done things she regretted. Elaina suddenly didn't want to hear the end to this story. Not when the pain of Cynthia's loss was still so raw.

"I was too shy, though. I was of merely sixteen, maybe seventeen years, and had known the boy only a few weeks when she made the suggestion . . . or edict, rather. When I told her I couldn't, unbeknownst to me she went to one of my friends. Now, this friend also happened to have fallen for the same boy. My mother must have watched us at our frequent parties enough to deduce our admiration."

Elaina studied her bracelet, unwilling to show any interest in such a story.

"She gave my friend the same advice. Unlike me, however, my friend had no scruples about taking my mother's advice. Within a month, there was a wedding." She let out a humorless laugh. "Wouldn't you know it, they had a baby boy nine months later."

"Why?" Elaina hadn't meant to ask the question or even acknowledge her mistress, but the question had popped out of her without her permission.

"Because I needed to learn an important lesson, one that has kept me well and fed and housed ever since." Matilda's voice grew sharp once again. "That I cannot rely on the goodness of others to sustain me." She turned her beady eyes back on Elaina, who still sat upon the floor. "You're not so unlike me, though, you know."

Elaina recoiled. "I'm nothing like you."

"Oh, I beg to differ. You think you're all alone here without the other servants, but has their absence really made a difference?

Even when they were here, you kept them at arm's length. You didn't ask for their help, and you were loath to accept it. Don't look at me like that. Come, you can't tell me you didn't try to refuse my mother's help in such a small gift as that dress, something she would obviously never wear again. You didn't want to be in her debt. Because that would mean you would have to rely on someone else other than yourself. And relying on others creates opportunity for weakness."

Elaina wanted to throw things, to shout that it was all a lie. But the shards of rose-colored gown that surrounded her were like witnesses in a trial. Each lonely piece was a memory. If only she could cover her ears and deny it all.

She had resented the first guard requested by her father. She had pushed Nicholas away when he'd tried to comfort her after her father died. She had ignored her aunt's advice and jumped head-long into danger by attending the meeting. Even after she was enslaved, she'd done just as Matilda had said, wanting to rely on the other servants as little as possible. She had worked to show she was strong and so everyone around her knew it.

But that didn't make her like Matilda.

Did it?

Matilda shrugged and stood. "Not that it matters to me. You will either do as I say and fix up the gowns, or someone will be here to collect you in the morning." She began to walk past Elaina but paused by her side. Lifting the heel of her stylish boot, she brought it down upon the loose part of Elaina's wooden bracelet with a sickening crunch. "I do actually know who you are, in case you were wondering. But I like the name Cinders better. It suits you."

CHAPTER 48
NORTH

The next two weeks flew by in such a blur that Elaina couldn't recall much of what really took place, nor did she care to. For the days were a mix of insults, cruel jokes, and more chores than ever, now that she had ball gowns to sew.

The house itself was a flurry of activity. Men and women came in and out of the home carrying out the old furniture and bringing new pieces in to replace them. Elaina briefly wondered where Matilda had obtained the money for such luxurious pieces. It mattered little to her, though, until the eve of the family's departure, when she found the dresses she had slaved over discarded behind the house.

Dread filled her as she carefully gathered up the tattered remains of the gowns and went into the house to investigate why the gowns had been treated so. When she reached Dinah's room, however, she found both girls dancing around with armfuls of new gowns in every color imaginable.

"Where did these come from?" She dropped the pathetic pile in her arms and entered the room in a daze, daring to pick up a yellow evening gown that had slipped from Dinah's arms during her waltz.

"Don't touch that!" Alison snatched the gown up and threw it behind her on the floor. "You're going to dirty it!"

"But where did you get them? And if you have new gowns, then why did . . ."

"Did you really think Mother would have let you go to the ball?" Dinah tossed her new clothes on the bed and flipped her headful of curls. "Particularly after your infamous betrayal of the crown?" Her green eyes glittered. "We can't have our older sister shaming the family that way now. Suppose they recognized you? Then the prince would never talk to us."

"Really, Cinders." Alison threw her bony arm around her sister's waist. "She's right, you know. Our beloved prince can't be forced to relive such misery—"

Something inside Elaina snapped. She grabbed Alison by the arm and shoved her hard into the wall. Pressing her elbow against the girl's throat, she leaned forward until she was inches from Alison's long pale face. Dinah tried to pull on her arm, but Elaina's anger made her strong, and with one hand she grabbed Dinah's wrist and twisted until Dinah let go with a cry. Then she turned back to Alison.

"You have no right to speak of such treachery," she hissed. "Not when your mother practically funded the rebellion." Alison tried to protest, but Elaina kept her pinned against the wall. "And do not speak of the prince as though he is in any way yours. He is far, far too good for the likes of you!"

"She's in here, Mother! Trying to kill Alison!"

Elaina had a lot more to say to the spoiled brat, but before she could, she was yanked back and thrown to the floor. When her vision cleared, she found herself looking up into the face of a stranger.

"That will be quite enough," Matilda growled, stepping out from behind the strange man. "I leave the house for ten minutes, and this is what I come home to?"

Elaina tried to roll away, but the man grabbed and held her wrist firmly.

Matilda moved so that she could stoop in front of Elaina as the man pinned her arms behind her back and held them there securely.

"I warned you before. If you do not have the strongest will, someone else will impose his will upon you." She patted Elaina on the cheek. "You've served me well, Cinders. You're a strong girl, I'll give you that. But I am stronger. Enjoy your time with the Shadow."

Elaina jerked down as hard as she could, a new sense of urgency filling her muscles. She succeeded in breaking free, but as she scrambled for the door, Dinah closed it. The man caught her again and squeezed her arms so tightly she thought they might pop out of place. This time, he heaved her up onto his shoulder and headed down the stairs. With each step, the stubble on his cheeks rubbed Elaina's arm, and the smell of body odor made her nauseous.

"Come, girls," Matilda called from the bedroom. "We have a boat to catch."

ELAINA CONTINUED to struggle as the stranger hauled her out of the manor, but it was to no avail. Like a sack of flour, he tossed her in a wooden trunk on the back of a cart. Then he slammed the lid shut, imprisoning her in darkness. The only light came from a small keyhole, nearly the size of her eye. Elaina screamed as she kicked and punched the lid, but it was no use. The lid was too heavy. Barks and bleats sounded from the yard as the man clucked at the horse and the cart began to bump along.

Elaina continued to shriek and push against the lid. But no one heard her, and even if they did, no one came to her rescue.

Eventually, her strength gave way to anger and then despair. After more than two years of forced servitude, insults, and loneliness, this was how it was going to end. Elaina would be subject to whatever evils the Shadow had planned for her. Nicholas would find a new wife, and the world would continue on without her. Curling into a little ball, Elaina felt hot tears running down her face.

Never in her life had she longed for something so much. Some-one. But that someone wasn't here, and his arms weren't around her and the safety of his gentle smile would never bless her again. They would be given to another woman, one it seemed, that he was about to choose.

Well, if it was another woman he wanted so much, then he could have her.

Darkness fell as they left the main part of the city to travel up a rough dirt road. There were few other travelers that shared their path. Only the constant clip-clop of the horses marked the passing of evening into night.

"Why?" she whispered through the keyhole as the world fell dark. "Why bring me through all of that just to reach this end?"

Don't despair. You're approaching a rut!

Those were strange words of comfort. Elaina frowned, sure she'd heard the stars wrong.

Before she could ask again, the whole cart jarred, knocking Elaina's head into the side of the chest. Then she understood. Unfortunately, her revelation came too late, and Elaina realized as she rubbed her sore head what they had wanted her to do.

She nearly fell asleep as she waited and listened for more instructions. But when they whispered the same words again, she was ready. Positioning herself as best she could in the bottom of the trunk, she waited for the sound of the front wheels hitting the rut first. Throwing herself against the trunk's side, she felt the world around her begin to spin.

Her landing was painful as the heavy trunk tumbled on top of her before bouncing off and rolling down into a ditch on the side of the road. Elaina lay on the cobblestones, feeling as though all of her bones had been smashed and that she would never walk again.

Get up, Elaina! the stars called out. *Before he sees that you're gone!*

"I can't," she whispered. Aside from the pain of falling off a moving cart and having the trunk land upon her, the effects of hunger, thirst, and being cramped up in the trunk for so long had taken their toll.

Instead of hearing a response from the stars, however, Elaina felt something wet nudge her. Turning, she found a familiar face licking her hand.

"Dog!" she whispered.

At the sound of her voice, he began nuzzling her face and neck. Not to be outdone, however, a familiar bleat sounded to her right. Thanking the Maker, Elaina reached up until she was able to wrap her arms around the dog and goat's neck. By leaning on them, she managed to move from the middle of the road into the bushes at its side. Once there, Elaina stumbled into the soft summer grasses.

"What do I do?" she whispered, as much to the animals as to the stars. "He'll find out I'm gone. He'll come back for me."

Elaina, you must stand.

Elaina squeezed her eyes shut. "I told you, I can't."

Elaina!

But Elaina didn't want to get up. Instead, she curled up into a ball. Sleep. If she could only get some sleep, all would be well.

Elaina, you need to go north.

It was Barker who forced her up in the end, goading her with his short little horns until she'd been bullied into standing.

"Remind me to sell you to the first market we find," she grumbled at him. Her answer was another bump to the backside.

Once she was steady on her feet, she fought for enough balance to make out the constellations above her. Slowly, so slowly, she found north and began to follow it.

How far they walked or for how long she couldn't say. She could only focus on putting one foot in front of the other to the rhythm of the stars' constant chorus of *north*.

When the sky began to gray, however, Elaina couldn't go on.

Her knees buckled, and she tumbled to the ground. The animals pushed and prodded her with their noses and horns. Dog whined and Barker bleated pitifully, but it was no use. Elaina couldn't move another inch.

CHAPTER 49
DETAILS

C onrad, have you seen Alastair?" Nicholas called through the door. As much as he disliked talking to Alastair's assistant, who still remained under close watch, Nicholas was feeling ambitious this morning, and a missing spy was not going to deter him.

"Pool Garden," came Conrad's monotone response.

"Really? What's he doing there?"

"You think he tells me anything anymore?" Conrad's reply was acidic.

Nicholas almost felt pity for the man as he headed downstairs. Two and a half years was a long time to spend in a small set of rooms, only let out under close supervision. It might have been enough to drive Nicholas mad. But the memory of Elaina's face at her trial still kept Nicholas's word firm. Until she was safe once again, Conrad would remain under lock and key.

The morning was lovely, despite the summer heat that sent sweat rolling down his back and the bugs that seemed determined to eat him. The way the yellow sunlight blanketed the earth was a reminder of the dream that still haunted him. If he closed his eyes for even a moment, he could still see her hair covered in the same soft light like dew on a yellow rose.

Focus, Nicholas.

It wasn't a long walk to the Pool Garden. The inn where the Pool Garden was located was just a few streets down the palace's main road. It struck Nicholas as an odd place for Alastair to spend his morning. But then, Nicholas had also used the garden's lush greenery and quiet pools to occasionally escape the madness of the palace, which had far exceeded the level of ludicrousness that his sister's wedding had ever raised. Perhaps Alastair, too, had simply needed time to think without being asked a question about the infernal ball.

Nicholas waved to the innkeepers as he walked in and headed for the back. The old man and his wife, well acquainted with Nicholas by now, simply smiled and waved back. They had long ago stopped asking him how they might be of help. For Nicholas, the escape provided by the exotic red maple trees and tranquil ponds with spotted golden fish was the greatest gift they could give.

But Nicholas wasn't there to relax this morning. The night before, he had made the decision to tell Alastair everything about Elaina. After all, the ball had largely been Alastair's idea, and Nicholas knew this was his last chance at finding her. And for that to happen, Alastair needed to know everything.

Nicholas had just begun down one of the meandering wooden paths when he heard the very voice he'd come in search of. He turned and followed Alastair's voice until he heard a second voice. Then he stopped in his tracks.

There, to his right, he could see Alastair's form, partly hidden behind a group of ferns. With him was a thin woman, though Nicholas couldn't see her face to try and recognize her.

"But I sent you the money!" he was protesting. "Do you know how hard it was to scrape together the hundred thousand gold pounds? And now she isn't even here?"

"You mean in addition to the money you still owe me? Besides, you can't seriously think I would bring her with me," the woman was saying.

Wanting to keep Alastair in view, Nicholas ducked behind a large pine tree.

"This is the daughter of Admiral Baxter Starke," Alastair snapped. "You don't think she's clever enough to escape the moment she sees light the size of a pinhole? Your guards have managed to keep her under control for years now. Why did you think them incapable for a day's journey across the bay?"

"Because I learned that she was just that," the woman retorted. "She never told me her name. I didn't even know who she was until you told me who you were looking for." She huffed. "The girl is clever. She would have found a way to escape if I'd tried to bring her myself on a ship. Isn't that where the wench grew up? At least this way I was able to hire a man who could focus solely on her and not on the safety of myself and my daughters as well."

"You should know, then, that I got a message from your hired hand this morning. Elaina has escaped."

Nicholas couldn't have moved if he'd wanted to. Instead, he dug his fingers into the bark of the tree until they hurt. Elaina was alive, and somehow, she had managed to break free.

And Alastair was all to blame.

Nicholas closed his eyes and leaned his head back against the trunk. He'd been so careful, or so he'd thought. But every move he'd made had been not only seen by the enemy, but handed to him on a silver platter. Nicholas had invited Elaina into Alastair's very company and practically given her to him through the exile. Then it dawned on him with a jolt of horror. Could Alastair be the Shadow? Or was he just a lackey like Conrad?

"This all could have been taken care of if you had simply told me she was in your *home!*" Alastair said.

"I didn't know she could speak to the stars until just recently. And as soon as I did, I hired the mercenary and sent word to you. What more could I have done?" The woman paused. "I'm still not sure why we're even having this discussion. I am not the one in the wrong here. You have yet to deliver on your promised payments."

"You can't demand payment on something you haven't delivered!"

"I gave you the war! Besides," the woman scoffed, "it wasn't my fault that the mercenary couldn't keep track of a tiny, battered, half-starved wench."

At these words, Nicholas was loosed from his shock. Searing anger shot down his spine, and it was all he could do to keep himself from leaping through the ferns and beating them both senseless.

"Really," Alastair said, "I should just have ignored your advice and not started this fruitless war in the first place. I would have had her by now and been free of *you*."

"Don't blame me for all your woes. I was in court the other day to watch some public proceedings. You were quite helpful to the king. You're doing yourself no service, you know, by sharing so much information with him. Why keep up the charade?"

His voice was acidic. "In order to gain information for *your* war, I must be indispensable to the king. And to be indispensable to the king, I must continue providing good leads." He paused. "I told them once that lithorium was a grave concern, but that was the biggest falsehood I dared try. The prince is sharp and starting to reach out to others besides me for information."

"Well, if this girl is as dear to the prince as you claim," the woman continued in a more collected tone, "then she will definitely be at the ball. She had even managed to find a gown the day I discovered her gift. I will know better than anyone else what she looks like, if she shows up. She's changed in the last two years. Even the prince won't know her as well as I do." She paused. "New arrangement. I will help you find her, and you will secure the prince's hand for one of my daughters in return."

Nicholas was wondering if this might be an appropriate situation in which he might gag, but a little voice inside told him not to. That Alastair was the Shadow, he was now absolutely convinced. And the Shadow, as he had seen personally, had powers that Nicholas was rather sure he could not defeat on his own. As much as Nicholas wanted to do to Alastair everything that had been done to Elaina and more, he restrained himself. If he had learned anything from his time at war, it was the value of patience.

"I do have the king's ear," Alastair muttered. "It shouldn't be too hard to turn him toward one of your daughters. This means that while we're at the ball, I will watch the prince, and you will search the crowds for her."

"I will also make sure my daughters are introduced to the—"

"Let me take care of that. Now for goodness sakes, woman, go! Before someone sees us here. You may be a mere woman of business, but I have an image to uphold."

Nicholas stayed pressed against the tree for a long time even after they left. His head was spinning, and he wasn't quite sure he wouldn't look inebriated if he tried to make his way home at that moment.

His initial instinct was to go directly to his father and tell him all he had heard. But as ever, he knew before the thought was complete that his father wouldn't believe him without proof. Over the years, Alastair had become one of the king's favorites, and when he wasn't undercover in Solwhind, he was very rarely away from the king's side.

In fact, it was he that Nicholas had tasked with venturing to Matilda Winters's home as soon as the rebels had surrendered. Only when Alastair had come home empty-handed had Nicholas thrown himself completely into planning this ball, hoping that if she was still alive . . . Rather, if she was still in the vicinity, she would understand his invitation and come.

No, Nicholas would have to find help somewhere else. The guards? Possibly. Nicholas had a good number that he knew would follow him without question, and the soldiers even more. But the more people that knew, the more likely his secret was to get out.

He was going to need someone with unquestionable loyalty not only to him but to Elaina as well.

Almost immediately, the answer was clear even in his muddled

435

head. *Thank you,* he said to the Maker as he headed back into the inn.

"Master Chan?" he called.

The old innkeeper removed his spectacles and gave Nicholas a pleasant smile and a quick bow. "Yes, sire? How may I help you?"

Nicholas pressed a gold coin into the man's hand and closed it before he could protest. "I need a writing desk, quill, ink, and parchment. And I'm going to need to borrow a horse."

If the innkeeper was surprised, he didn't show it. Instead, he only glanced around and then motioned for Nicholas to follow him into the personal chambers the innkeeper shared with his wife.

"No one will bother you here, sire," he said, pulling a little stool out from beneath an old, battered writing desk. "My horse is out in the stall. Her saddle is hanging just beside her. Use her as long as you need."

Nicholas gripped the man's hand tightly, wishing words could properly convey his thanks. As soon as he was alone, he prepared the quill and began his letter, a letter his father would surely order burned if he ever laid eyes on it.

To His Most Excellent Majesty King Everard Fortier of Destin,

I have found her. I think. But I am going to need your help . . .

CHAPTER 50
MY GIFT

Elaina rolled over and snuggled more deeply under the covers. The aroma of fresh bread filled the air, and she even caught a faint whiff of cinnamon. She wanted to sleep forever, but the rumble of her stomach eventually forced her eyes open.

Only then did Elaina realize she had no idea where she was. Someone had placed her in a soft bed and piled upon her quilts of every color and design, which she was still buried beneath despite the late afternoon sun that was creeping in through the windows. Two thick hunks of bread slathered in butter lay on a plate beside her, as well as apple slices sprinkled with cinnamon. A mug of something hot steamed up beside the plate.

Cautiously, Elaina propped herself up on her elbow and looked around. The room she was in seemed to make up the entire cottage, as there were no doors but the two that led outside. The windows were large, though, and covered in colorful curtains of reds, yellows, and blues. The dozens of pillows lying around, the apron hanging on the door, and the quilts she was wrapped up in were made of fabric bits of every shape, color, and size pieced together in mosaics of beauty.

What caught Elaina's attention, however, were the countless

paintings hung on every available inch of the walls. Each painting featured the same girl. In some pictures, she sat quietly with a book or examining a flower. In others, she danced or ran or waited on a dock as she looked out over the ocean. Sometimes she was laughing, pouting, or crying, or wearing a huge toothless grin. But in every single painting, the girl's face was the same.

It was the same face that gazed out from a large painting hanging in the grand entrance of her manor.

It was Elaina's.

A fireplace sat in the far corner of the room, and before it stood a petite woman with her back to the bed. She stirred a large pot over the fire, and Elaina was tempted to ask what was in it. Instead, however, she simply watched and waited, fear and angst and stupid, stupid hope making it hard to breathe.

Then the woman turned around.

"Mama?" Elaina nearly fell out of the bed.

In a moment, Elaina was wrapped in the woman's arms in the tightest embrace she could remember. The woman wept as she touched Elaina's hair, neck, and face over and over again, but all Elaina could do was hold on and remind herself to drink in the almost forgotten scent of apple blossoms and lavender.

"I didn't think you would remember me." The woman pulled back and gave her a trembling smile, her face red from the tears that continued to stream down.

Elaina gingerly lifted her fingers to the woman's face. The shape was familiar. Elaina distinctly remembered having her mother's chin. Gray now streaked through the light brown hair and wrinkles edged her large brown eyes. Still, the longer Elaina stared into the woman's heart-shaped face, the more she knew that her mother was indeed alive.

"But how?" she whispered.

"Didn't your father tell you?" When Elaina shook her head no, the woman's smile fled. "I thought perhaps that was how you had found me . . ."

Elaina's stomach dropped. "Mother . . . Mama, Father's ship

disappeared over two years ago. Just after he left me in the capital."

Elaina hated herself as her mother's face paled.

She stood and began to pace about the small room, wringing her hands. "He was supposed to tell you on your eighteenth birthday," she muttered while she walked. "But when you never appeared, I feared something had happened to you both." She looked at Elaina in amazement. "But if your father didn't tell you, how did you find me?"

"The stars brought me here after I was abducted."

"After *what*?" Her mother's eyes narrowed.

Elaina blanched, not sure even where to begin. But before she could try, her mother rubbed her temples and walked back to the little table where she had prepared the evening meal. "Wait for a moment. I get the feeling I am going to need a bit of wine for this."

Once the wine was poured and her mother was sitting on the edge of her bed again, Elaina took a deep breath and dove into her tale, starting with Davies Tanner announcing her gift in the tavern to advising the king about the rebellion to her enslavement. She chose to skip over certain unnecessary parts, such as Nicholas's constant interference and the way it had felt when they'd danced, but it was still a good hour before she finished to her mother's satisfaction.

They were silent for a long time after Elaina was done. Her mother took Elaina's hand and ran her fingers over Elaina's knuckles, and Elaina closed her eyes, soaking up the love she had yearned for for so long.

"When we staged my death," her mother finally said in a soft voice, "we only wanted to keep you safe. I never thought it would bring you further harm. I just . . . I cannot believe we were in the same city all this time. I could have saved you without a second thought."

Elaina moved until she was snuggled against her mother's side. "How?" she asked, closing her eyes and basking in the moment. It was as if she were five years old again.

"I'll show you later. For now, you need to rest."

Elaina wanted to point out that she had just awakened, but as soon as her head hit the bed, she was unable to argue. Instead, she let herself slip back into the arms of sleep, for arms of love held her tightly as well.

I'm so confused, she thought to the Maker. *But . . . thank you.*

"I THOUGHT YOU WERE TIRED." Elaina's mother yawned as she sat up and rubbed her eyes. "Why are you up so early?"

"I *was* tired." Elaina drew her borrowed shawl closer around her body to keep out the night's chill. "Unfortunately, the stars had other plans." How did sleeping for a whole day still leave one tired?

"What are they saying?"

"Nothing that cannot wait." Elaina turned away from the window and padded back to the bed, but before she could again bury herself in the blankets beside her mother, her mother sat up and shook her head.

"Every time they spoke to you as a child, something important was imminent. Like the time you saved your father's ship from that summer squall. What are they saying this time?"

Elaina rubbed her eyes. "They want me to go to the prince's ball." Even as she uttered the words, she could hear the stars through the open window once again.

Go, Elaina, they whispered. *You must go to the ball.*

"I just got here. I am not leaving my mother. Not now, at least." After two years of slavery and before that, twelve years of thinking her mother dead, Elaina deserved a few days with her mother. Or at the very least, a single night of happy, contented, uninterrupted sleep.

People will die, Elaina.

Elaina groaned and glared up at the fading stars. "Fine then. Suppose I do go. Have you forgotten that I've been exiled, and return is punishable by death? Or that Matilda will be there?" She looked down at the shredded, threadbare gown that had once been blue. "Besides, what would I wear?"

"If your wardrobe and being recognized are what you're concerned about," her mother said, "I can help you there." Even in the light of the dimming moon, her brown eyes sparkled and her mouth was curved into a mischievous smile.

See? The stars sounded smug. *Everything will work out.*

Elaina looked back and forth between the stars and her mother. How could she tell them? How could she voice the fear that drowned out nearly all the rest? Exile and ball gowns were worked around easily enough, it seemed. But no amount of money or power would be able to fix the broken rhythm in her heart that somehow still threatened to overwhelm her.

"Look." Her mother took Elaina by the shoulders and turned her so that they were facing one another. "I've known Nicholas's mother since we were young, younger than you. And I knew Nicholas long enough in his boyhood to know that while he may be a bit..." She looked as though she were suppressing a smile.

"Arrogant? Fickle? Pompous?"

"I was going to say flighty," her mother finished with a shake of the head. "He was never unjust, even as a boy. And I know that his mother would never have allowed him to grow up as such. If we can convince him of the truth . . . if you can *prove* to him that this Alastair betrayed you, then I'm convinced that you will be acquitted of all charges."

Elaina sighed and looked out the window again. The stars had disappeared completely, and the sun was preparing to crest the line of neat little cottages that made up her mother's street. She would never admit it, of course, but her mother was right. Nicholas was many things, but he had never been unjust.

Well, except for that time when he exiled her for a crime she didn't commit.

"If I did go then, how would you get me into the palace

without being seen? And where would we get a dress so late? The ball is in three days."

Her mother's face lit up again. "We'll have our morning meal first. You're too thin and you need to eat. Then," her eyes sparkled, "I will show you *my* gift."

Elaina couldn't turn down the offer of food, so she nodded and followed her mother to the little corner where her mother began to stoke the fireplace embers.

"I don't remember you cooking at home," Elaina said as she pulled up a stool.

Her mother laughed. "You should have seen me when I first moved here. Your father took a week away from work to *bury* me. We found this darling little cottage and he made sure I had all of the necessary items before returning to you. But being a noble-woman by birth, I had absolutely no homemaking skills. Thank the Maker, my neighbors were curious but also kind, and over the years I've learned to keep myself decently, if I do say so myself."

Soon bread and little pats of butter had been served, and Elaina and her mother sat down to eat.

"How did you earn enough to keep so comfortable?" Elaina wondered aloud as they ate.

Her mother leaned back and looked around the cottage. "Well, your father made sure I had a regular sum sent to me every month. But after the money stopped coming . . ." Her mother grew quiet, and Elaina felt her own chest tighten.

"I don't know if you remember," she continued after a moment, "but I had always loved to paint."

"I vaguely remember you trying to teach me."

"One of my favorite memories. I think you got more paint on your face than on the canvas. But anyhow, I learned that people would pay a good deal of money for likenesses to be made of themselves and their loved ones. It's kept me nicely, even with the war going on. People liked to have images of their fathers, husbands, brothers, and sons before they went off to war."

The room grew quiet again, and Elaina couldn't help

studying the dozens of pictures on the walls. There was, of course, the innate desire to be angry with her parents. How many times had she come to port in Solwhind and not known that her most beloved soul in the world was only a few miles inland? But as she studied the portraits, she could see the longing painted into every canvas, no matter what its subject was doing.

"Elaina," her mother said, taking her hand and squeezing it. Her large brown eyes were wide and pleading. "I cannot even begin to describe the agony my soul has suffered every day since leaving you. You won't understand until you're a mother, which I pray one day is your privilege. But once you have a child, your world becomes theirs. Your purpose is to comfort them, to care for them, and to give them everything they might ever need. But the attack changed everything."

"How did you survive?"

Her mother shrugged. "I honestly can't say. A miracle. A gift of the Maker. I recall my attacker standing over me and holding something to my head, and I could feel the power draining from me as he held me there against the ground. Then he slipped. Just slipped without a reason. When he fell, he dropped a little jar he was holding, and it broke. He fled after that, and someone found me and brought me home."

"But if he left, why did you have to leave?"

"Your father and I knew that you wouldn't be safe. We were sure he would return to finish what he'd started. My gift had already been diminished, and we didn't want anything so horrible happening to you." She shuddered. "There are no words for the evil blackness that fills you as he draws the gift out. The best way we could think of to protect you was to send me away and stage my death. It wasn't hard. I was close to death when they found me. If my attacker caught wind of my death, he would not come for me again, which meant he wouldn't see you or the gift that you were beginning to show." She reached out and touched Elaina's face, a sad smile on her own.

"Why can't we stay here?" Elaina whispered. "Why can't we just stay and be happy?"

"Because you have a destiny, my darling. From the first day you told me the stars had spoken to you, I believed your gift was a miracle. And I believe that no less now than I ever did." She stood and brushed the crumbs off her lap. "So if the stars have told you to go to the ball, then go to the ball you shall. And I will do everything in my power to make sure you do."

Elaina frowned. "I've already told you I have nothing to wear."

"And I have already told you that it's time you see my gift. Stand up."

Elaina did as she was told. Her mother directed her to the middle of the room where there was no furniture. Then she reached into her long sleeve and pulled out a smooth wooden stick.

"What is that?"

"This is a little tool that I've found helps me control my gift since part of it was stolen."

"But what does it do?"

Her mother beamed. "Watch." With that, she raised the stick in the air, pointed it at Elaina, and flicked it with her wrist.

Elaina jumped when a small spark popped in the air. Her mother didn't stop, though. She continued to twirl the stick until Elaina felt a cold breeze rushing around her ankles. Then, as the popping grew louder and faster, the tattered hem of her gown began to grow. As it swelled, its holes and tears disappeared, and the color changed from a gray-blue to violet. The violet raced up her skirts, through her bodice, up her shoulders, and down her sleeves.

And everywhere that the color changed, so did the material itself. Violet gossamer and silk of the purest kinds soon covered her body. The gown no longer reached just below her knees but rippled all the way down to her feet. And when she pushed the full skirts out of the way, lovely golden slippers peeked out from underneath. Her arms were draped with gems of all sorts, and her neck hung heavy with amethyst stones of every size and shape.

"How?" Elaina gasped as she lifted one arm and then the other.

"How do you talk to the stars?" Then her mother gave a wistful sigh. "The change used to be permanent, but now it only lasts until midnight of the day I alter it."

"You can do this to any dress?"

"Oh, more than dresses. I can do anything. I could make a squash turn into a carriage. I could make rats turn into steeds. All you need to do is ask."

"So I could wear this to the ball?" Elaina asked.

"As long as you're back by midnight."

Elaina chewed on her cheek thoughtfully as she fingered the airy material. "If I was able to hide from Matilda and Alastair . . ."

"Consider it done." Her mother pulled her in for a tight hug.

"But what about you?" Elaina pulled out of the hug to look her mother in the eye. "You can't go back there. What if Alastair recognizes you? I can't let you do that. Not after I just got you back."

"Now listen here, Elaina Starke." Her mother put her hands on her hips and fixed Elaina with a reproachful stare. "I did not move away and have sailors raise my daughter just to watch you fall into danger because *I* was afraid."

"But—"

"Not buts. I am finished with hiding. If the Maker wants you to go to the ball, then that means that He has a plan. And that is good enough for me. Besides," she gave Elaina a hard smile, "I am your mother, and now that we're together again, I hardly intend to send you into the lions' den alone. You're getting my help whether you want it or not."

CHAPTER 51
GETTING TO WORK

"Can't we just stay at an inn?" Elaina asked as the driver loaded their things from the ship onto their hired carriage. "We'll be less conspicuous that way."

"The inns in Kaylem will all be filled by now." Her mother pulled on the makeshift leash for Dog and handed Barker's rope to Elaina. "Besides, what would we do with these two? No inn would let us keep them."

As it was, the carriage driver was giving Barker a suspicious look and muttering about never having transported a blooming goat before.

"Why are you suddenly so insistent on avoiding your aunt and cousin?" Her mother studied more her closely.

"Because I spoke to the stars again last night, and if I absolutely must attend this ball, I cannot have Lydia interfering. They may or may not be back from the summer manor in time for the ball, but I don't wish to take the chance of them seeing me."

Instead of answering, her mother pursed her lips and gave Elaina a warning glance. They said nothing more until the driver had helped them into their seats and the carriage was bumping down the road.

"I know you're not keen on attending the ball with the prince," her mother finally spoke again in a low voice, "but what does this reluctance have to do with Lydia?"

Elaina watched the countryside pass by through the window but saw nothing. What she wouldn't give to forget that awful day. "I wasn't named a traitor without witnesses."

Her mother frowned. "What do you mean?"

"Alastair's assistant planted the coins and acted as a witness himself, but the other witness . . ." She faltered, knowing that her next words would bring her mother pain.

"Elaina, who was the second witness?"

"Lydia."

For a moment, her mother looked as though she might faint. "Oh. Oh my. But . . . how?"

Elaina shrugged. "There wasn't much to her witness statement really. She spent the whole time weeping."

"Then I would suppose she at least felt guilty about being called."

"I don't know, but I really don't care to know. She was jealous when—" Elaina caught herself. There was very little that her mother needed to know about him, and even less that Elaina wanted her to know.

"When you took your place in the court?" her mother finished.

"I suppose you could say that."

Her mother stared sadly out the window. "One of the hardest parts of our society is the preference given to the eldest. Should Charlotte have been born before me, it would be Lydia who was to inherit the title instead of you. Did your father explain to you that we're one of the few families where women legally hold the title themselves? It must have been so hard for Lydia to give up that rank when you arrived." She leaned back in her seat and played with her earring thoughtfully. "I suppose she would have become used to the position the title gave while they were keeping it ready for you."

Elaina had wondered about this many times before. But when she remembered how excited Lydia had been at her arrival, she was convinced that title had nothing to do with her cousin's jealousy. The jealousy had been all for Nicholas. Still, the drama of her reunion with Lydia paled in comparison with what Elaina had been tasked to do.

"We can sort this all out some other time perhaps," she said, shaking her head. "But as I said, the stars spoke to me again last night, and I know what I need to do. And without knowing Lydia's true allegiance, I cannot take the chance."

Her mother nodded faintly, her eyes still distant. "I think I know a place we can stay. It will be dusty, unless someone has discovered it since I've been gone. But . . . we can try, I suppose." She turned and studied Elaina more closely. "What is it that the stars want you to do?"

"First, I need to sneak into the manor and get something from my old sea chest." Elaina hoped her mother wouldn't ask for any details. To her relief, however, her mother only nodded.

"Very well. I can make you invisible for that."

Elaina sat up straight. "Could you make me invisible for the ball?"

"I'm sorry, but no. It is very difficult, and I can only manage it for short periods of time. Making one object look like another is one thing, but complete invisibility takes nearly more power than I have."

Elaina sat back and sighed. "Very well."

When they disembarked just in front of the manor, where they could peek through the vine-covered fence, Elaina felt a chill go down her back. The front lawn looked as though she had only left the season before, rather than two years. The roses and hedges were just as trim and neat as they had ever been. Elaina wanted to gawk, but she knew they might be easily seen by anyone on the road. She almost broke the silence to ask what they were doing when her mother motioned her over to the side of the house, where she had already put her bags down and pulled the wand from her sleeve.

Holding her finger up to her lips, she waved the wand, and

Elaina looked down to see . . . nothing. She was invisible even to herself.

"Which window was yours?" she whispered to Elaina.

"The one on the end, your room from when you were a girl."

"Good. It's close by. Can you climb the trellis?"

Elaina nodded, then remembered that her mother couldn't see her. "Yes." She turned and tested the trellis. Carefully, wishing she had her old pantaloon petticoats from the ship, Elaina climbed up to her old window. She held her breath as she gave the window a tug.

Perhaps the window had rusted shut. Perhaps someone had taken her chest or gone through it after the trial. Maybe their whole plan was doomed.

It took a few yanks, but eventually, the window popped open and she was able to climb in.

She had to pause for a moment as her eyes adjusted to the dark of the room. As soon as she could see, she began to search. Her heart fell when the chest was not in its usual place. She stepped as lightly as possible to peek around the corner of the attached dressing room. Her heart leapt for joy when she spotted the chest pushed up against another window. Then she froze.

Lydia was indeed back from the summer manor, for she now sat on Elaina's old chair, cradling something in both of her hands, a far-off look on her face. Her gown was lovelier than ever, a yellow silk that gathered at each side and was tied off with little ribbons of red. Lydia didn't look like most of the other girls they had passed earlier on the street, however, excited beyond reason. She only stared at the object in her hands.

The chest in the corner was open, and to Elaina's great relief she could see the glass slippers still inside. She knew she should grab the slippers and get out, but found herself unable to do so. Instead, she crept up to her cousin and peeked at what Lydia held.

It was one of her seashells. Not one that was precious or worth any amount of money. Elaina had simply kept it because she liked how smooth its spirals were. And yet Lydia stroked it as though it were the clearest gem in the world.

"Lydia! Don't forget your mask. It's nearly time to go."

Elaina jumped when Charlotte called from the hall, but if she made a sound, Lydia didn't seem to notice. Her cousin simply sighed and laid the shell back in the chest before closing it and leaving the room.

Knowing better than to tarry any longer, Elaina opened the chest again and snatched the shoes out before tucking them in her skirts and climbing back out the window. She could see her feet beginning to return as she reached the ground, and immediately felt guilty when she saw how drops of sweat had begun to run down her mother's face.

"I'm sorry I took so long, but—"

Her mother held up her hand for silence and picked up her bags. Elaina clutched the shoes and followed her around the garden, through the corn stalks to the stable. Walking around to the back, her mother stopped and glanced around before dropping her bags and disappearing through a little door in the stable wall that Elaina couldn't even see until it was open. She stared at the little door until her mother reappeared, an impish grin on her face.

"It's still here, and it's not even that dusty," she whispered, beckoning to Elaina to bring the bags. "Climb up with me."

Elaina coaxed Barker up the narrow steps easily. Dog was another story. But when she finally did reach the top, Elaina was surprised and delighted to find that an entire section of the stable loft had been walled off from the rest of the stables, creating its own little room. A child-sized bed sat in the corner, along with a table and two chairs beneath a single round window. The ceiling was barely high enough for Elaina to stand up in, but all in all, it was far nicer than her attic in the Winters' manor had ever been.

"What is this place?" she asked.

"My father had this built for me when I was little." Her mother grinned, looking around in obvious satisfaction. "It seems the servants still keep it decently tidy and free of mice."

"They miss you, you know," Elaina said, putting their bags in the corner. "Even when I was there, they spoke of you often."

"I pray we shall soon be reunited." She peered at Elaina. "What took you so long anyway?"

Elaina shook her head and set to unpacking their bags. "Lydia was there. But I got these." She pulled the shoes from her skirts, where she had rolled them up.

"Where did you get those?"

Her mother looked so shocked that Elaina laughed. "King Everard gave them to me."

"Of all people . . . But what do they do?" she asked, taking them from Elaina and examining them more closely.

"I'm not sure. Not even King Everard knew. But he said the Maker had wanted me to have them. He got the feeling I would need them one day. And last night, the stars told me to get them." She took the shoes back and hugged them to her chest. Having them back was like a nod from the Maker himself, a promise that hers wasn't a hopeless mission after all, painful as it might be. "So what do we do now?"

"We get to work."

HER MOTHER SLOWLY CIRCLED HER, and Elaina did her best not to slouch, despite having to slightly bend her head while standing upright in the small loft.

"Aren't you coming with me?" she asked hopefully. "Can't we do this on the way?"

"I wish, my darling, but no."

Elaina felt her face fall, but her mother smiled and touched her cheek. "As far as the court knows, I've been dead for fifteen years. Having me there would bring unwanted attention. Besides," she reached down to finger Elaina's threadbare skirt, "I won't just be keeping you adorned, so to speak. I'll also be hiding you from others. That way that horrible woman and her daughters won't recognize you."

"What about Alastair?"

Her mother tugged on her skirts and pursed her lips thoughtfully. "I cannot say for sure. My disguise will hide you from those who might casually notice, but if someone is looking for you specifically, they might see you after all." She sighed. "I also didn't expect to need to hide you from your aunt and cousin. That will complicate things a bit. The more people I need to disguise you from, the thinner your disguise will be from any."

Elaina nodded glumly. A small ridiculous part of her had considered chancing one dance with Nicholas just to see if he truly had changed. But if there was a chance he might recognize her, a dance was out of the question entirely. Then she remembered something.

"I did hear Aunt Charlotte tell Lydia to get her mask," she said hopefully. "Wouldn't that help?"

"It surely will help, but it won't be enough to protect you from every prying eye. No, I will just have to stay here where I can concentrate without distraction. Now, let's see about your transportation."

Elaina stared at her in confusion as her mother walked over to another wall, the one the bed sat against. She felt around the seams in the wood until another compartment revealed itself, and she pried a second door open. She motioned to Elaina, and Elaina joined her at the little door as they peeked down upon the animals below.

"Oh, thank the Maker," her mother breathed. "The main carriage has gone. That means Charlotte and Lydia are already on their way." She climbed out into the open loft, which was filled with bales of hay.

"Where did you learn to do all of this?" Elaina asked as she followed.

"You would be amazed at how creative one gets when one isn't living as a noble. Now then, I think this shall do nicely."

Elaina laughed when she saw the pathetic object her mother was looking at. "Aunt would die of shame if she knew I was taking this to the palace. Paolo uses it for garden work, particularly for gathering pumpkins."

"It won't look like a pumpkin cart when I'm through with it." Elaina's mother pushed up her sleeves and pulled out her wand. "Close the stable doors so no one sees us."

Elaina hurried to obey, but when she turned around, she couldn't believe her eyes. The sun-bleached hay cart was popping and crackling as it swelled into the most elegant coach she had ever seen. The orange stains that had painted its insides were no longer blotchy but had colored the entire coach the subtlest shade of peach. Pearls vertically lined the ridges that had formerly been wooden planks, and the entire coach rounded out so it wasn't rectangular in the slightest.

"Mother!" she exclaimed, creeping forward to touch it. "How did you even imagine all of this?"

Her mother gazed at her masterpiece. "Your father used to say that I saw the world with a purple sky, blue grass, and a pink sun. I daresay he was right. I suppose my gift only made sense with a mind like mine. But now we need to finish your escort. Let's see. We'll need a coachman, footman, and at least four horses." She looked around, tapping her chin with her finger as she thought. Just then, the goat let out a bleat.

With two flicks of her wrist, the dog and goat had lost their tails and fur. Instead, each sported a handsome uniform of bronze over his fully human figure. Without prompting, as soon as they were steady on their two legs, each immediately took his place on the coach.

"We need some horses. Any ideas?"

"I . . . I think some dormice used to live in the tree just outside the stable," Elaina said, still staring in awe at the two men before them who acted as if nothing were amiss.

Without answering, her mother slipped outside and was back in less than a minute. In her hands, she held four fat rodents. With four little jabs of the wand, each dormouse lost its fine, soft fur and began to whinny as it pawed anxiously at the ground.

Elaina walked around them as if in a daze. When she turned back to her mother, she found herself being studied with a thoughtful frown.

"You can't mean there's more."

"Well, I can't have you going to the ball dressed like that. I should have found a way to hem at least one of my gowns before we left." Her mother grimaced. "Spin."

Unable to come up with more questions, Elaina simply obeyed. As she slowly turned, she felt the icy breeze start at the top of her head and make its way down her shoulders, chest, stomach, and legs. When she opened her eyes, she looked down to find herself swathed in a sea of pearl pink silk and lace.

"There," her mother panted. "All done. There's an old mirror that should be hanging on the back door of the stable. My father's stable hand always used it to keep an eye on the front doors when he was busy in the back. Go look and tell me what you think."

Elaina turned and made her way to the dusty old mirror, walking on her toes so the fine skirt wouldn't be dragged through the dirt. She disliked the sensation of having dirty feet while wearing such a glamorous gown. But when she reached the mirror, all thoughts of disdain dissipated in a cloud of awe.

The gown was not only the color of a rare pink pearl, but where the bodice met the skirt was lined with dozens of actual little pink pearls. Little bits of sea glass had been woven into the bodice in crisscrosses and swirls, and when she moved at all, the whole gown shimmered in the light. Its thin shoulders hung off her own, and a delicate pearl necklace adorned her neck with a single white gem the size of a small seashell. Her hair had been pulled up on top of her head into an intricate braid, also woven with strings of pearls. Little white gems shaped like the one on her necklace hung from her ears. The most lovely and reassuring part of the whole ensemble, however, was the delicate pearl-edged mask that was perched securely on the top of her nose.

"There are only two things missing."

Elaina turned around to see her mother holding the glass slippers.

"Do you know how long I've yearned to do this?" her mother asked, her voice catching at the end, brown eyes shining in the light of the stable's torches. "All my life, I've wanted to give my little girl the gown she deserved. And now the Maker's given me the chance. If I died today, I would be satisfied."

Elaina ran into her mother's arms and held her as tightly as she could. All too soon, however, her mother pushed her away. Kneeling down, she held out the shoes so Elaina could slip her feet inside.

As soon as she touched the glass, Elaina's breath caught and her heart beat faster. Power, like a tidal wave, washed over her entire body, encasing her like a shell that encompassed her every move. King Everard had been right. Whatever it was that they could do, these slippers were not to be used lightly.

"I don't know what to say." Elaina smiled as she tried to find her voice, looking down once again at everything that had appeared out of thin air.

"You don't need to say anything." Her mother pulled her in for a kiss. "Just stay safe, do your job . . . and try to have some fun. Did the stars tell you yet what it is that you need to find?"

Elaina nodded and did her best to smile, but felt her spirits sink as her new footman handed her up into the coach. She didn't dare tell her mother what it was that the stars had sent her to look for. She didn't want to frighten her.

CHAPTER 52
A BALL OF GLIMMERS

E laina struggled to don the cool mask of repose she had practiced so often on her ship. But as she stepped out of the coach, the memories came flooding back. Most poignant was Sophia's wedding and the dream that had almost been. The realization that Elaina was later than she'd thought only made her rush of emotions stronger.

She didn't have long to linger in the memories of what should have been, however, for the guards were opening the doors as she approached the top of the steps. Her heart skipped a beat as one of them leaned down. Would he recognize her? Was her mask too small?

It only turned out to be a bow, however, and Elaina breathed a sigh of relief as she continued on through the grand entrance unaccosted.

The pathway that led toward the ballroom was easily marked, but Elaina had no plans to follow it. Feigning a cough as a servant walked by, she stepped deftly off the long blue carpet and into the shadows. Then she waited until the servant was distracted, which didn't take long, and took off down a darkened hall until she found the door she had been looking for.

For the first time in a long time, Elaina was thankful for all of the walks she and Nicholas had taken during his longer lessons when Master Dustin had fallen asleep, for it was during one such walk that he had shown her the secret servants' entrance to the highest balustrade overlooking the ballroom.

"They use this particular balcony to watch the guests and make sure nothing is amiss," he'd said as he'd opened the secret door. "It's so high that few actually notice it from below." Now Elaina prayed that would be the case as she crept through the darkened hallway and cautiously opened the balcony door.

The stars had said to find the Dagger of Power, whatever that was. It was in the palace, they had said, but where it would be when she arrived, they didn't know. And though Elaina might have gone mad trying to imagine all the places a dagger might be hidden in the sprawling palace, she had a sneaking suspicion that Alastair would know exactly where to find it. She was also fairly sure that Alastair would have his sticky paws on all the goings-on at the ball.

The height nearly made her dizzy. She was higher than even her old crow's nest had been. Elaina gripped the edges of the banister for good measure as she gazed down. Hundreds, possibly over a thousand people mingled below. Her stomach tightened as she scanned the crowd for the familiar figures of Alastair, the Winters family, and her aunt and cousin. There were too many people, though, and Elaina couldn't identify a single one. Disappointment set in. She would have to mingle in order to find the spy. As she was turning back to the door, however, another familiar figure caught her eye.

Elaina's breath left her as she stared down at Nicholas. The military uniform he wore, white with blue trim and dark trousers, made his shoulders look noticeably wider than they had before. A silver rope hung from his shoulder, and various military awards decorated his chest. And though she couldn't see the details of his face, the silver circlet on his brow made him look much older than the boy she remembered.

Elaina knew that she should go, but she couldn't tear herself away from looking at him. And despite the self-loathing she harbored for simply admitting it, a small but desperate piece of her heart longed for what she knew she couldn't have.

Maybe you don't have to avoid him after all. Perhaps he could help, a small voice inside her whispered. And for one brief moment, she considered it.

But no. This was her mission. Her responsibility. If the Maker had wanted him involved, the stars would have told her. And as it stood, she was already breaking the law by being back in the kingdom without his permission. Besides, once she had laid eyes on the prince, Alastair's form was easy to spot where it hovered nearby. As long as her mother's disguise held, she might be able to talk him into giving something away. She didn't need to talk to Nicholas at all.

But as she turned back to the door, a hush came over the crowd. Too late, Elaina realized that one by one, they were all staring up at her.

MANY POINTED, and the murmurs began to buzz where loud, lighthearted laughter had dominated before.

A glimmer at the bottom of her vision caught her eye, and Elaina looked down to see her gown shimmering as though her mother had embedded not pearls but the stars themselves into the material.

She would have to have a word with her mother about knowing when too much was too much. Too much attention. Too many people. And too much Nicholas. For as she gazed down, she briefly locked eyes with the prince.

Elaina bolted back through the servants' door. Without waiting to see whether someone came for her, she ducked into another door in the servants' hallway, nearly stumbling down a flight of stairs. But her glass slippers were surprisingly sturdy, and she somehow made it to the bottom in one piece.

After a long journey through a winding maze of servants' halls, more staircases, and an extensive walk through the kitchens, Elaina finally found a side door that opened up to the ballroom. Thanking the Maker, she slipped in quietly and hid behind the throng of proud parents and ambitious, hopeful girls fluttering their fans nervously at the edge of the dance floor.

Elaina decided to use them as a shield to search for Alastair, but as she did, a whiff of raspberry pastry caught her attention. Only then did she realize how ravenously hungry she was. After all, it wouldn't hurt to get a bite to eat while she looked. Sliding over to one of the dozens of refreshment tables, she began to fill one of the small plates set out when someone bumped her from the side.

Elaina turned to apologize but froze when she found herself face-to-face with Matilda.

"I beg your pardon," Matilda said in a silky voice. "I didn't see —" When she made eye contact with Elaina, however, she stopped. Her brow faintly creased, and Elaina waited for the onslaught of foul words that were sure to begin. To her surprise, however, they didn't. Matilda only tilted her head a bit and then dropped a quick curtsy. "I didn't see you, my lady."

Elaina balked, unsure whether or not her voice would be disguised as well as her face, but was saved from answering when someone else touched her on the elbow.

"My lady." A young man bowed, probably a good three years younger than Elaina. She had to hide a smile at the hope in his young face. "Would you do me the honor of joining me in this dance?"

Elaina was about to decline his offer until she realized what a good view she might have from the dance floor. Also, she would be saved from speaking with Matilda.

Sending up a quick prayer that she might remember the dances Nicholas had taught her and that none had been added in her absence, she nodded politely back at Matilda and turned to the young man.

"It would be my pleasure, sir."

She didn't have time to bask in her relief. For though the dance floor certainly had a better view than her previous hiding spot, Elaina found that the dances were much faster than she remembered. She scarcely had time to reorient herself between tunes, and every time she tried, another young man would come asking her for a dance.

It was after a dozen or so tunes that Elaina decided dancing had not been her brightest idea. Just as she finished curtsying to her partner and managing to excuse herself, however, she found herself held securely in the arms of someone new.

"Most beautiful lady. I am the prince's official emissary for this particular event, and it would be a great honor if I might speak with you for a moment about dancing with the prince himself." Alastair's request was phrased politely enough and probably would have pleased most young women into fainting, but the firmness with which he took her arms for the dance made it obvious that his wasn't a request at all.

And the look in his eyes was far less hesitant than Matilda's had been.

Elaina's first instinct was to run. And yet she stayed put. This might be her best opportunity to search for the dagger, or to at least get a sense of where it might be. Though she had no idea as to how she would actually get it from him should she find it, Elaina gave him a practiced smile and curtsied deeply. She doubted he would try anything too bold in public, particularly with the king nearby. At least, that's what she hoped.

As the dance began and Elaina carried out the customary skirt swishes from side to side, she studied her partner. His hair, tied behind his neck neatly with a black ribbon, was no more gray than it had been the first time she'd met him. His pale eyes glittered as he watched her back, his excitement making him look younger than she knew him to be. It also made him look hungry.

"What is your name, fine lady?" he asked as they moved in a slow spin.

Briefly, she panicked and said the first name she could think of. "Cinderlaina."

He cocked his head. "That's an odd name."

"Pardon me, sir, but that is not a very gracious thing to say." She batted her eyes through her mask and pretended to be affronted.

"You are quite right. Please forgive me. It is simply . . . unique. And I'm sure the prince will agree. Where does it originate from?"

Elaina berated herself for not planning better with the finer details. Cinderlaina was possibly the dullest name she could have come up with, but it had been all that came to mind. Now, as she struggled to remain calm, she felt as though she were playing a dangerous game, the kind where a predator toyed with its prey. And unfortunately, she was fast becoming the prey rather than the predator she had hoped to be.

The dance finished, and Elaina was no closer to finding the location of the dagger. Feeling the need to escape and recover before trying again, Elaina began to curtsy, but Alastair's long thin fingers never loosened their grip on hers. Instead, they tightened, and as they did, Elaina felt a surge of power and nearly gasped.

The surge was similar to that which she had felt years before when meeting King Everard. But this touch was different. It felt sour, as though something within him had spoiled. Rather than the pure, pulsing light she had felt from the king, Alastair's grip moved through her, chaotic and turbulent, like an erratic set of explosions rather than a steady flame.

Elaina could no longer bring herself to smile as he touched her. She could only stare at him as a small triumphant smile touched the corners of his mouth. The others were clearing from the dance floor, yet he held her firmly in place.

This had been a terrible idea.

Just as she was getting ready to cause a scene, however, another hand placed itself firmly on Alastair's shoulder.

"Alastair, my friend, thank you for helping me find such a lovely creature as this lady. I think I shall enjoy this next dance immensely."

Elaina tore her gaze from Alastair's sudden look of hate to find herself staring into a pair of ice blue eyes.

It was the prince.

ALASTAIR WAS SLOWER to obey than Elaina had ever seen him, but he finally let go of her hand and put a thin smile on his face as he bowed to his prince and then Elaina. She felt dual waves of relief and disappointment as he stepped away and Nicholas took his place. She felt safer with Nicholas at her side, even with his threat of execution in mind, but she still hadn't found the dagger.

"My lady." He bowed. "I don't believe I've ever seen you in my court." His voice rumbled even deeper than Elaina remembered it, and it sent a traitorous ripple of nerves through her body.

"That is because I did not grow up here, sire."

"Where did you grow up?"

"A variety of places." She shrugged as the musicians signaled for the next dance to begin. "Mostly in Solwhind." Truly, she felt as though she had aged eons during her time in the eastern city.

To her surprise, he did not smile. Instead, he started to dance as stiffly as a guard might change his position at the turn of the hour. "Are your parents here?"

"I hope I do not seem at all rude, sire," she laughed, "but is it customary in the capital to interrogate one's dance partner on the first dance?"

He bowed his head as much as the dance allowed. "Of course not. I apologize, my lady. I hope you will forgive me. I simply do not have the time to make small talk the way I once did."

Elaina gawked up at him, unable to conceal her surprise. Who was this stranger? Yes, the eyes were Nicholas's, and the dark unruly hair that even now tried to stick out in different directions despite its newer shorter cut, was surely his. But the carefree laugh and the dramatic gestures were nowhere to be found. Was the Nicholas she knew gone completely?

In his place stood a man with the unmistakable mannerisms of a soldier. His shoulders and arms were indeed wider than they had been the last time she had seen them, and his face had lost any of the soft boyish lines it might have held the last time they'd met. Instead, his face was far more angular. Stress lines, nearly invisible, edged his eyes and mouth, and a scar puckered on the lower right side of his jaw.

For some inexplicable reason, Elaina had a strong urge to reach up and touch the scar, but thankfully, the dance kept her hands busy. She tried not to shiver as his hands encircled her waist.

"Have you been to the palace before?" he asked. His voice was friendlier this time, but the intensity of his gaze didn't waver as they stayed trained on her face.

"As I said, I grew up mostly in Solwhind, sire. Why do you ask?"

For the first time, he looked as though he might smile. "You certainly know how to make an entrance."

She laughed, but butterflies flew in frenzies around her stomach. "Surely I am not the first girl to take a wrong turn."

He conceded this with a nod, but she could see the curiosity burn even more brightly in his eyes.

With Nicholas, Elaina didn't feel at risk as she had with Alastair, but still she found herself running, evading each question the same way she moved in time to the music. A twirl here, a dip there, anything to avoid being caught. She wasn't sure if he truly recognized her through her mother's disguise, but she was confident that he was suspicious.

That small, annoying voice of reason reminded her that she needed to be looking for the dagger, but every time she looked up, Alastair was there, watching them intently from the side of the dance floor. And whenever she looked at the other side, Conrad

Fuller was waiting as well, though he was mostly hidden behind a wide pillar.

She needed to get on with her mission. But the cowardly part of her was more than glad to have Nicholas by her side. As they moved on to a second dance and then another, there was also a ridiculous, naive part of her that silently pleaded for him not to let go. The familiar warmth of his hands on hers was intoxicating, and she felt herself slipping as her anger, frustration, sorrow, and longing all began colliding once again.

"Tongue tied in a sheet bend?" the prince asked casually.

Elaina laughed. "Precisely."

As soon she spoke it, though, Elaina knew it was the wrong thing to say. An average girl should not have known what a sheet bend knot was. But there was no way to take it back. And from the sudden brightness of his eyes, Nicholas knew that, too. She had walked right into his trap.

"You wouldn't happen to know," Elaina felt herself grasping for words, air, anything to help her speak again, "what hour it is? I'm afraid I cannot hear the bells toll from here."

"Half past the eleventh hour." He drew closer. "Is there somewhere you need to be?"

She extracted her hands from his and dropped into a clumsy curtsy. "I am afraid I need to refresh myself in the powder room. Where would I find that?"

He frowned, but pointed her in the right direction.

"Thank you!" she called over her shoulder as she lifted her skirts and fairly ran. Once she was in the powder room amongst the other ladies, she leaned against the wall and put a hand up to her face. Her cheeks were flushed and far warmer than usual. She should never have given him so much time. Once again, her foolish infatuation had won out over reason, and she had wasted an entire night of searching for the dagger because of it.

After several minutes in the powder room, avoiding the annoyed glares from the women who apparently recognized her as the prince's dance partner, Elaina peeked outside. As soon as she saw that the prince was engaged in a conversation with another gentleman, she turned and ran toward the entrance.

Only to run smack into Lydia.

Elaina quickly curtsied. "Pardon me, my lady."

"Of course. The . . ."

They stared at each other for what felt like eternity. Elaina's blood drained from her face as she waited for her cousin to make the announcement, to tell everyone that the traitor had returned, or at least to demand to know what Elaina was doing at the ball or even in Ashland for that matter.

To her surprise, however, Lydia finally looked at the ground and smoothed her dress nervously. "The fault was mine." Lydia spoke politely, but the way her brows furrowed betrayed her suspicions.

Elaina didn't wait to see what conclusion her cousin reached. She darted out to the main entrance and down the many white steps to the drive where her unusual coach was waiting. She fairly leapt inside, and not a moment too soon. As soon as the door was closed behind her, the coach took off at a frantic pace, down the drive toward the city.

Elaina leaned back against the cushions and tried to catch her breath. That had been too close. Midnight was only minutes away, and she was no nearer to finding the dagger. To make matters worse, however, Elaina was dangerously close to losing both her cover, it seemed, and her heart.

CHAPTER 53
A BALL OF GAMES

So who was that beauty you were dancing with all last night?" Nicholas's father slapped him on the back, making Nicholas lose his grip on the absurdly small button of his uniform's sleeve that he had spent the last five minutes trying to close. "You know we have servants to help with such things." Xander waved a servant over.

Nicholas yielded his sleeve to the servant. "Habit, I suppose," he said tersely. "No one buttons your sleeves for you on a warship."

"No changing the topic. Who was the girl?"

"I danced with many women, Father."

"Surely you can't be that absentminded. I'm talking about the one you only spent four dances in a row with."

"I didn't get her name." He didn't need to, but he wasn't about to tell his father that.

His father shook his head. "Boy, what good is it to let you choose your own wife when you're too dim to even get their names?"

His sleeves properly buttoned, Nicholas tugged his uniform into place. "It was only the first ball, Father. I have two more to make my decision."

His father began to respond, but the trumpets announced the

beginning of the second night, much to Nicholas's relief. He waited until his father had gone to collect his mother, however, before he exited his chambers to make his own way down to the ballroom.

It was moments like this that he missed Henri most acutely. If his friend had been allowed back to the palace for the ball, Nicholas would have told him how he was certain that he had found Elaina. Or nearly certain, at least.

Had Henri been there, he would have said something about how daft Nicholas was for doubting her, and Nicholas would have had to agree. But there was no Henri to talk such sense into him, so Nicholas did his best on his own.

He had singled her out too much the night before. If she returned tonight, he would need to be more careful in interspersing their meetings. Her reluctance to dance with him had been obvious at first, something he couldn't deny that he deserved. Actually, he deserved far worse than simple reluctance. After pronouncing her exile and decreeing her future execution should she disobey him, and then failing to save her from the life of enslavement he had inadvertently sentenced her to, Nicholas deserved little more than her wrath and hatred.

And yet, he dared to hope.

But if she hated him so much and was so reluctant to be seen with him, why was she at the ball to begin with? And how in the depths had she escaped that woman's mercenary and found such a glamorous gown?

How did one girl get more mysterious the longer one knew her?

He didn't have time to ponder this, though, because the palace steward was waving him up onto the dais. Straightening his jacket one more time, Nicholas took a deep breath and left the shadows to face the crowd.

"I want to begin by thanking you for coming out for another night of celebration," he said when all the trumpets had died down. "This is turning out to be the grandest birthday celebration anyone could ask for, much less your humble prince. As with last night, please enjoy the refreshments, the wine, and as much dancing as you can manage."

As he continued to babble on, Nicholas scanned the crowd for her. But there were too many faces, and his heart sank as he made a final bow and turned to pay his respects to his parents sitting on their thrones behind him.

Self-doubt continued to fester as girl after girl was introduced to him, and he was forced to dance with them all. And even worse was the necessity of making conversation with hidden faces behind ridiculous masks. He had introduced the concept of a masquerade at the last minute after overhearing Alastair's conversation with the woman in the garden. He had hoped that a mask would make it harder for Alastair or the woman to recognize Elaina, should she come. But now he wasn't so sure it wasn't making it more difficult for him to find her, too.

Last night he had been certain it was Elaina. She had even fallen for his question about the sailor's knot. And several times, her thumb had moved up to worry her lip. But in all honesty, more than two years had passed since he had seen her in decent light without a fire roaring between them. Was she really so different as the woman in the garden claimed she would be?

"Your Highness, are you looking for someone?"

Nicholas jumped when Alastair spoke. Why did the infernal little man have to get so close to speak with him? Nicholas bowed politely to his partner and let her go, ignoring the pout she gave him as he thanked her for the dance. Turning to Alastair, he tried to make his voice cheerful. "I am looking for my future wife, am I not?"

Alastair chuckled. "But more specifically, sire, are you not looking for a certain girl from last night? Everyone was rather sure you had favored that little sparkling beauty above all the others."

How Nicholas had ever found Alastair anything but annoying was beyond him. *I would favor you not breathing down my neck,* he wanted to snap. Instead, he said, "I would appreciate some wine, if you would be so kind. All of this dancing has made me thirsty."

He didn't miss Alastair's hint of a frown before he bowed and left. Relieved to have a moment to himself, Nicholas had turned back to the crowd when a flash of green caught his eye.

"Your Highness," a chubby man bowed and shoved a young woman forward, "my name is Bret Tanner of the southern border. Allow me to introduce my daughter—"

"I do sincerely apologize," Nicholas said, trying to see into the corner of the room where he had glimpsed the flash of green. "But I fear I have something pressing I must attend to."

The man gaped like a fish as Nicholas walked past them, but Nicholas didn't have time to make amends. He only knew he needed to find her.

Sure enough, a girl in a dazzling blue-green gown was standing just behind a pastry tower. She looked like Elaina, petite with honey-colored hair, and she kept touching her thumb to her lip. He stopped before approaching her, however, and studied her from a distance. She was squinting as she peered out from behind the treats, a half-eaten scone in her hand. What was she looking for?

Nicholas gathered his courage and prepared himself for ultimate rejection as he strode over to stand behind her.

"If you told me what you were looking for, I might be able to help," he said, wishing she would hear the true meaning behind his words.

She started a little at the sound of his voice. Turning, she stared at him for a long moment before swallowing the bite she had just taken. The quick sideways glance she gave the crowd gave Nicholas the feeling that she wanted to dart. He would just have to pounce first.

"Would you do me the honor of giving me this dance? Of course, unless you are already otherwise engaged."

Still, she hesitated.

He hated himself for the sentence he uttered next. "I know you were raised mostly in Solwhind, but is it customary there to deny a prince his request?"

A brief fire flashed in her eyes, and Nicholas almost smiled at her indignation. Yes, that question surely would have angered Elaina.

Before he could inquire further, however, she finally gave him a stiff smile and curtsied. "Very well, Your Highness. This dance is all yours."

Despite his triumph, Nicholas felt a bit deflated as he led her out onto the dance floor, the crowd parting for them as they moved. Whatever she was looking for, it certainly wasn't him.

The next dance began, a little reel that was just slow enough for light conversation.

"I apologize, but I don't believe I got your name last night."

"Cinderlaina."

"And my name is Jack."

She smiled, a real smile this time, though he could tell she was trying not to. "Well played." She nodded. "But I fear I shan't be able to give you my name just now."

"And why would that be?"

She hesitated. "I am not supposed to be here."

Thanks to his royal dictate. Still, Nicholas played dumb.

"And who doesn't find a royal decree an acceptable reason for a young woman to attend a ball?"

"The woman I call Stepmother, I'm afraid. If she finds out I am here, I shall face dire consequences."

Nicholas frowned, confused. "If you would only tell me your situation, I would try my best to help you. Are you looking for something?"

She was staring over his shoulder again, but this time, she looked back up at him with a mischievous grin. Suspicion warred with adoration as he watched her eyes spark. "Yes, actually. I wish to introduce you to someone."

Surprised, Nicholas could only nod and allow her to lead him from the dance floor as soon as the reel was done. She pulled him over to a gaggle of girls who all became fluttery as he approached.

"Sire," she said, taking her arm from his, much to his dislike. "I would like to introduce you to Dinah Winters."

Dinah Winters, a tall, stocky girl with coal-black hair and far too much rouge, looked just as confused as Nicholas felt, but the moment Elaina pulled their arms together, Dinah's snake-green eyes locked onto Nicholas, and she clung to him like a barnacle to the side of a ship. The girl was unusually strong.

"Dinah loves to dance, Your Highness." Elaina told him, a victorious gleam in her eyes and an unrepentant smile on her face. "As does her sister, Alison." She looked back up at Dinah and gave a small curtsy. "I hope you enjoy yourselves."

So *that* was her game.

Nicholas shook his head as he watched her dart off into the crowd again. It had to be Elaina, for there could only be one girl in the entire world so infuriating and so devious. Society would collapse were there any more in existence.

Dinah dragged him back out to the dance floor, and Nicholas resigned himself to the slow serenade that had begun to play, possibly the longest dance in all of the musicians' repertoire.

"Do you know that woman? The one who introduced us?" he asked as the dance began.

She shook her head without breaking eye contact. "No, but I feel as though I've known you my entire life."

Nicholas must have looked surprised, for the young woman brought her face closer to his, her impossibly wide smile growing even wider.

"Perhaps your sister knows her then?" he asked, trying to widen the gap between them.

She only stepped closer again. "Maybe. But sire, don't you think you might like to know me?"

He spotted the shimmering gown of blue-green again out of the corner of his eye. There she was on the other side of the crowd. Her shoulders were shaking and she held one of her small hands over her mouth. Not only did she have the audacity to watch him suffer, but she was laughing at him as well.

Nicholas counted it as the most agonizing dance he had ever endured with the world's dullest ninny. Hours passed, it seemed, before the dance was over, and when Nicholas finally tried to make his escape, Elaina was nowhere to be seen.

But Dinah's sister was, and the thin, fierce girl pounced as soon as Nicholas thought he was free. He nearly put her off until he glanced at his father, who was watching him intently. Inwardly groaning, Nicholas allowed himself to be pulled back to the dance floor. Elaina owed him for this. Not only was he enduring another dance against his will in order to keep her hidden from his father's notice, but this partner was somehow even more insufferable than the last.

Nicholas finally caught sight of Elaina again as the dance was ending. Only this time, she was accepting the outstretched hand of none other but Alastair himself. What was wrong with her? Did the girl have a death wish? Nicholas's muscles tensed as he watched her delicate form whirl around in the arms of the man who was hunting her. He ached to stride over and whisk her out of the villain's arms. Did she have any idea how much danger she was putting herself in?

A wry voice inside told Nicholas that she did indeed. As the two couples brushed by one another, he caught the same look in her eyes that she wore whenever she was discussing strategy, her pretty pink lips set in a thin line and her eyes ferocious and bright.

As soon as the dance finished, the annoying girl . . . Alison was her name . . . clung to him and begged for another dance. As he tried to extract his arm from her, however, panic boiled like acid in his stomach. Elaina and Alastair were no longer on the dance floor. Instead, arm in arm, they were heading up a set of stairs toward an upper balcony that looked out over the kingdom.

Abandoning all attempts at politeness, Nicholas peeled Alison off his arm and strode after them, taking the steps two at a time. He caught them just as they reached the top of the stairs.

"I hope you don't mind too much, Bladsmuth, but I'll be stealing this one back now."

Elaina looked incensed, but her ire was nothing compared to the pure loathing in Alastair's face. For a long moment, Nicholas and the spy stared one another down. As they did, an eerie feeling moved through Nicholas like an ill wind, and he had to resist the urge to shudder.

That his opponent had the ability to hurt him, Nicholas had no doubt, but from his two years at war, Nicholas had learned that while the Shadow had declared war, Alastair Bladsmuth was not the kind of man to make his war openly. He preferred back alleys and dark shadows. Here, there were guards and witnesses everywhere, and unless he had a way to silence them all, his secret would be revealed.

At least, that's what Nicholas was gambling on.

After an eternal moment, Alastair did indeed bow in concession, but there was no accommodating smile this time, nor did he offer a gracious reply. Instead, he simply shoved Elaina's arm toward Nicholas before stomping out to the balcony.

"Why did you do that?" she asked testily as they made their way back down the stairs. "Can't a lady spend the evening with whom she chooses?"

"She can," Nicholas snapped, "as long as she knows what she is doing."

That she was scheming against the Shadow, not trying to marry him, was obvious. Still, jealousy colored the edges of Nicholas's mind. "It would be a travesty," he tried to make his voice smooth again, "for you to waste such a beautiful evening up on the dark balcony when you could be down dancing in the light."

The annoyance fled her face, and she looked startled. "What hour is it?"

"Do you have somewhere better to be?"

She opened her mouth and closed it again. Then, glancing about the room, she finally said, "I need to get home to my mother before it's too late. She worries if I'm not home before midnight."

"The balls are designed to last until dawn."

"That may be so, but my mother is very adamant I be home early."

He brought them to a halt at the fringe of the crowd. Letting go of her arm, he smirked and folded his arms across his chest. "I thought your *stepmother* had forbidden you to come at all."

Her eyes widened.

Nicholas nearly laughed as he realized he had struck the great Elaina Starke speechless. As she stood there, touching her thumb to her lips and struggling for words, he also realized that his attraction to her had only increased in her absence.

She was a bit too thin, perhaps, but her gentle curves of girlhood had settled into the steadier lines of a woman. Her chin was held as defiantly as ever, even in her temporary confusion, and her stormy blue-green eyes still flashed like lightning over the ocean. It took every ounce of self-control in him not to reach out and pull her tightly against his chest, where he could wrap his arms around her and protect her from any evil that might even think of looking her way. He hadn't been able to protect her from the evil that Alastair had brought upon them all before, but she was here now where he could see and touch and breathe in the painfully familiar fragrance of her skin and hair.

Why is she pushing me away? He pleaded silently with the Maker. *What am I supposed to do?*

"It is a quarter after the eleventh hour," he finally said in a quiet voice. "If you will not stay, would you at least allow me to escort you to your carriage?

He was sure she would say no, but to his surprise, after a moment, she merely nodded and sighed, hanging her head as she placed her arm on his.

Nicholas fairly sprinted out the main entrance, determined to get her alone before she could change her mind. Pausing at the doors, he whispered to one of the guards,

"I wish to have a private word with this young woman. We are not to be disturbed."

The guard saluted, and Nicholas continued down the steps,

relishing the way each step felt with her arm on his. He stopped, however, when they were nearly at the bottom. Before them was a carriage, but it was the oddest and most . . . dramatic coach he had ever seen in his life.

Sea green, just like her dress, the coach looked as though it had been made from one gigantic seashell. Pearls the size of his fist dotted its edges, and the four horses at its head were harnessed by what looked like reins of kelp.

"A bit ostentatious, isn't it?"

He looked down to see her wearing a small indulgent smile, as though she was no longer even trying to pretend. That was a step in the right direction. "But she just couldn't help herself." Then she sighed.

A prickle on the back of his neck warned Nicholas that there were eyes watching them from above. Of course, Alastair would be watching them if he couldn't be with her. So Nicholas handed her up into the coach, turning his back so that it faced the palace.

"Go," Elaina called out through the window, but Nicholas put one boot in the coach and shook his head at the somewhat odd-looking driver.

"You're playing a dangerous game," he said in a low voice.

She looked at the floor. "You think I don't know that?"

He took a deep breath. "Meet me tomorrow night on the outer lower balcony, the one on the west side of the ballroom."

This time, she looked him in the eyes, and the sadness in her face pierced him to the heart. "What about tomorrow will be any different from this evening? Or the last? Or," she added in a whisper, "the last few years?"

"Everything," he whispered back, daring to cup her chin in his hand.

"How can you promise that?"

"Because this time," he said, forcing himself to let go of her, "I have a plan."

CHAPTER 54
UNNERVED

Nicholas had to keep his feet from charging after her carriage as it sped away. He considered calling for his horse and making chase, but he knew that would only give Alastair an excuse to follow under the guise of accompanying the prince. No, it was best to stay here where he could keep an eye on Alastair, the way he had the night before.

Still, Nicholas felt cautiously ecstatic as he retraced his way up the steps. She hadn't refused him outright. And if she did meet him as he had requested, his plan might actually work.

Nicholas stopped to address the guard again before going back in. "Notify Captain Oliver that Alastair Bladsmuth is not to leave the palace, and if he tries I am to be informed immediately." The guard saluted and sprinted off. Nicholas took a deep breath before returning to the gala inside.

The thousands of candles that lit the ballroom made his head hurt when he returned from the dark of the outside. By now his parents would be wondering where he was and what he was doing, but Nicholas was too tired to care. He motioned for his steward to join him.

"Let the guests continue uninterrupted, but if my parents ask about my whereabouts, I've been called away by something important."

Nicholas didn't get more than two hallways away from the ballroom, however, before there were footsteps behind him. Closing his eyes, he turned. "I know I have a duty to the kingdom, but I have no wish to—"

"And I don't wish you to," came his mother's calm reply.

Nicholas opened his eyes. "I'm sorry. I thought you were Father."

"I suspected. Come, I'll walk you to your chambers." She took his arm. "Now tell me, what's troubling you?"

He gave her a wry grin. "Is it that obvious?"

"I told you, I'm your mother. I know everything."

Nicholas chuckled. "Well if you know everything, then you shouldn't have to ask now, should you?"

"You didn't get much sleep last night."

He shook his head. "It's more than that. I'm tired of war. I'm tired of being spied on in my own home. I'm tired of . . ." But he didn't finish that thought. He couldn't. Letting his doubts get the better of him now would only make him more unfocused.

They walked in silence, the echoes of their footsteps the only sounds in the polished stone halls. When they reached his chambers, she surprised him by following him inside rather than returning to the ball. As soon as the door was closed, she folded her arms and looked at him expectantly.

"I don't know who that girl is, but I have my suspicions."

Nicholas began the aggravating battle of unbuttoning his uniform at the collar.

"I do know, however," she continued, "that your father is determined to see you betrothed sometime tomorrow night. So if you cannot convince your mystery girl to say yes by the end of tomorrow's ball, he is more than ready to have the heralds declare your betrothal to Amelia Seamus."

Nicholas scowled. "Thank you for the encouragement."

"Don't get impertinent with me. I'm trying to help."

"I don't know what to do!" Finally free, Nicholas flung his jacket on the bed. "Father thinks the war is over, but I'm caught up in its most vicious battle yet."

She stepped closer and took his right hand. Turning it over, she gently touched the scars that crisscrossed from his elbow to his fingers. "Are you sure about that?" she asked softly.

"Mother, Alastair is the Shadow."

For the first time in his life, Nicholas saw his mother freeze. When she was finally able to look at him, her eyes were huge.

"Why haven't you told your father?"

"I've tried! But he never listens!" Nicholas leaned heavily on his dresser. "And to make matters worse, Elaina's courting danger. She's seeking him out at every turn, and I cannot for the life of me understand why."

There was a long pause before his mother spoke again, and when she did, her voice was faint. "You are sure it's her?"

Nicholas nodded.

"Well." She drew a deep breath. "Tell me what I need to do."

Nicholas closed his eyes and hung his head, but he couldn't help smiling a little. "Do you really wish to get caught up in this? Father would be angry if he knew."

She snorted. "Do you think I don't know how to manage your father by now? And really, if someone as dull as Amelia Seamus takes my place after your father passes, I might just lose my mind."

Nicholas shivered then straightened. "I need Father distracted when the guests arrive tomorrow evening."

"I can't stop the heralds from making announcements. That would be too obvious."

He shook his head. "This one won't be announced. I just need to make sure he stays unseen."

She smoothed down his rebellious hair. "Nicholas, you have plotted and planned your entire life, organizing everyone and everything to make sure it is just as you want it. I knew you had some sort of scheme already in place. See? Everything will work out just fine." She turned to leave but paused at the door. "Do you remember when you came to me several years ago and said you wanted to be a new kind of man?"

Nicholas nodded.

"Today you've become that man." She smiled sadly.

"Mother?"

She paused once more. "Yes?"

"I have one more thing I need you to do."

"And what would that be?"

"Pray."

"I do every night. What would this prayer be about?"

He sat on a chest and leaned his elbows on his knees. "Pray that she listens to me, and that all would go well tomorrow. And," he swallowed, "that she would forgive me."

CHAPTER 55
LAST CHANCE

Elaina closed her eyes as the familiar rush of cold air encircled her. When she opened them and looked in the mirror, she gasped.

This gown was the most beautiful by far.

In a way, it was simpler than the others. Blue gauzy material the same color as Nicholas's eyes hugged her torso then waterfalled all the way to the ground, pooling out past her feet. White rosebuds encircled her waist, and her bodice was embroidered with swirls of grain-sized sapphires sewn with silver threads. And though the skirt was blue, it glinted when she moved, shimmering like a rainbow. On her head was a tiara of thin milky glass adorned with miniature glass roses. A simple string of pearls encircled her neck with a single large sapphire lying at the top of her chest.

"What do you think?" Her mother put her wand down and smiled triumphantly.

"It's breathtaking," Elaina said. "But might the train be a bit much?"

"No gown is complete without a train."

"There is a decent chance that I just might have to run."

Her mother rolled her eyes, but with a flick of her wand, the dress's excess material disappeared and the skirt's hem ended just at Elaina's ankles.

"Thank you."

Her mother frowned. "You're not smiling. What's wrong? I'll fix it now."

"It's not the gown." Elaina stroked her skirts reverently. "The gown is perfect."

"Then what is it?"

Elaina touched her thumb to her lip and rubbed it there for a moment as she considered her answer. "I have only one night left to do what the stars told me. The first two nights were complete wastes of time. And these slippers are beautiful, but they haven't done a thing to help."

Her mother put the wand back in her sleeve and came to take Elaina's hands. "I may have missed much of your life," her voice was soft, "but I think there's more to this ball than you're telling me." Elaina still didn't answer, so her mother nudged her. "Tell me or I'll send you to the ball in something truly ostentatious."

Elaina quirked an eyebrow. She wasn't sure how one could get more ostentatious. But if anyone could do it, it would be her mother. "Fine then. Prince Nicholas won't leave me alone, and that's exactly what I need him to do."

"I see. And why do I get the feeling that you haven't told me everything there is to know about you and the prince?"

Elaina found a stick on the ground. Picking it up, she tossed it, remembering too late that her driver and footman might chase after it.

But Elaina's mother ignored the panting carriage escorts as they caught and fought over the stick. "You're not just annoyed at the man's attention, Elaina. Something here runs deeper."

"But that's just the problem!" Elaina began to pace back and forth in short, quick steps. "He refuses to be lost! He keeps getting in the way, and whenever I have the chance to search, he intervenes! As though I don't know what I'm doing!"

Her mother gave her a doubtful look. "Can you wield a weapon?"

"What?"

"You heard me. Can you wield a weapon? Sword? Dagger? Crossbow even?"

"No, but—"

"Well, if the prince is any sort of man, and it seems he is, do you think he would be comfortable knowing you're seeking out danger without some method of defending yourself? It seems he's come to the conclusion that you're pursuing something dangerous, and he's attempting to help."

"Mother, the Maker told the stars to send me on this mission! The Maker wouldn't have told me to do something if he hadn't thought I could do it! If he wanted Nicholas involved, the stars would have told me so." She marched over to where her driver and footman were still tussling over the stick and yanked it away from both of them. "Besides, that is not what I'm upset about."

"What is it then?"

"He has the gall to act as though his boyish infatuation could be something real!" Elaina exploded. "As though he ever truly did care!"

This time, her mother's voice was soft. "You love him, don't you?"

To her horror, Elaina burst into tears.

Her mother gathered her in her arms and held her tightly as Elaina sobbed into her shirt.

"I want to get him out of my head . . . my heart. But he just won't leave!" She swiped at the tears, but they continued to fall. "I can't let him in again. Not like last time. There's too much at stake!"

Her mother pulled her wand out again and began meticulously arranging Elaina's hair on her head, tucking this or that lock away and pulling others free to hang down. "How long ago was it that Nicholas supposedly believed himself in love with you?"

Elaina looked down at her hands. "Not quite three years."

Her mother frowned and paused. "I don't know what you know of the war, but did you know that the prince led the majority of the war efforts himself? He even fought in many of the battles alongside his men." She paused. "Rumor had it that the prince was searching for a girl the entire time."

"He just didn't want me to reveal national secrets." Elaina sniffed.

"Oh come now. Don't you think you're being a bit ungracious?" Her mother took her by the shoulders and forced her to stand still. "I truly don't know how much of this is true, but won't you regret it forever if you don't give him the chance? Because it seems to me that he's doing everything in his power to find you and right the wrongs of the past."

Elaina took a deep breath and tried to wipe away the rest of her tears, but when she put her hands up to her face, it was already dry. So she straightened her shoulders and allowed her footman to help her up into the carriage. Before the door shut, however, her mother stuck her head in.

"Even if you decide not to accept his affection, there is one thing you might want to consider."

"And that would be?" Elaina was suddenly itching to leave.

"The Maker did give you this mission, but he never specified that you had to complete it on your own, did he?"

Elaina huffed. "No."

"From what you've told me, I think that if you asked your prince for help, he would readily give it."

With horrifying clarity, her conversation with Matilda sprang to mind.

You're not so unlike me, you know.

Matilda had been right, though it killed Elaina to admit it. Relying on Nicholas had made her weak once. And as much as she wanted to rely on him now, as much as she yearned to, the pain he had caused was still too sharp to allow her the freedom to choose. He had broken her before, and she couldn't bear that kind of betrayal again. Not now, with the security of the entire kingdom hanging in the balance.

Her mother reached up to touch her face. "The stars may have given you direction, but that doesn't mean you must make the journey on your own."

"I really don't know how to do it any other way," Elaina whispered, shaking her head sadly.

"Then why don't you let him show you?"

HER MOTHER'S words echoed in Elaina's head as the horses galloped toward the palace for the last time.

What if she did let him in?

Part of her wanted to believe him so badly that her chest ached. Though she had tried to kill all of her lingering desire for him, for his companionship, in the core of her heart there had always been a sliver of hope that it had all been a mistake, that he had never wanted to send her away, and that he had been searching for her all this time.

But another voice, one that sounded, to Elaina's annoyance, much like Matilda's, wondered why the most eligible prince in the land, and probably its most accomplished flirt, would part with his old ways just to chase her down. The warring thoughts made her head spin, and she tried desperately to steady herself as the carriage came to a stop.

Undesirous of theatrics today, Elaina made her way through the servants' halls until she reached the lower door that opened up to the ballroom from the kitchens. Should she meet him on the balcony? Or should she sneak off alone and begin searching every room of the palace for the dagger? There were certainly enough rooms to keep her busy for the night.

As she surveyed the crowd, however, Elaina realized she didn't need to even bother with hiding as she made her decision. For this time, the prince was not dancing with anyone else. He was standing at the back of the crowd near the opening to the western balcony.

Beside him was a very large man in a dark cloak and mask. The large man leaned over to say something to the prince, but the prince didn't respond.

He was looking directly at her.

CHAPTER 56
A BALL OF GLASS

"I t was so gracious of your father to invite me to such a splendid gala," King Everard muttered from beneath his mask, which covered far more of his face than those worn by most of the other guests. "Where is he anyway?"

Nicholas kept his eyes on the crowd, but he couldn't help smiling. "My mother has endeavored to keep him occupied while you're here." He glanced over at the man beside him. "Thank you, though, for coming. I can't tell you how horrified I was at my father's arrogance, but nothing I said would change his mind. It only made him more stubborn, if anything."

"Why does that not surprise me?" The king's mouth turned down even more. "Still, inviting a forbidden guest to your engagement ball? I'm impressed. Most young men of your age wouldn't dream of defying their fathers so."

"That makes it sound *so* much better."

"Doesn't it?"

They stood just at the edge of the crowd, and for that, Nicholas was grateful. The breeze could be felt coming through the open balcony behind him, making the heat of the crowded room more bearable. Though he had no idea how his mother had kept his father occupied thus far, or how Oliver had managed to keep the giddy young women at bay, he was grateful. Their efforts had allowed the palace steward to open the ceremony so that Nicholas could slip in through a side door with his visitor, unannounced. Now if only they could find Elaina before someone noticed him.

"So where is Henri?" Nicholas asked.

"After hearing of your opponent's appetite for gifts, I thought it best that he stay out of this one."

Nicholas nodded unhappily as guilt and unease gnawed at his stomach. If this villain had even King Everard on edge, what could Nicholas hope to do against such darkness? Having the king beside him allowed Nicholas to breathe easier . . . for now. But was one night long enough to end an evil that had been thriving for decades?

"I have to say," Nicholas pitched his voice a bit lower as he continued to search the sea of faces, "I am grateful that you've come. If the stakes had been anything less, I wouldn't have—"

"Nicholas." King Everard turned and looked directly at Nicholas for the first time that night. The blue fire in his gray eyes was a bit unnerving, but Nicholas managed to hold his gaze. "Let me make one thing clear. Not a day goes by that my wife and I don't regret not going after her ourselves, order or no order by your father."

Out of the corner of his eye, Nicholas could see a thin wisp of blue flame swirling around the king's powerful hands even as he spoke.

"The way we see it, your invitation to this ball was a gift of the Maker, a chance to set things right," King Everard continued in a growl. "If that girl truly is here, I am willing to use any means necessary to find her and keep her safe." He turned back to the crowd. "It only irritates me that I have just one night to assist you."

Nicholas shook his head grimly. "My father would notice anything more. No, your help tonight will be more than enough."

"So where is that monstrous little spy?"

"Alastair mysteriously disappeared as soon as you appeared.

I'm sure he's still on the premises somewhere, particularly since he knows she will most likely be here."

"I dislike sitting and waiting for him to pop up."

But then Nicholas saw her, and he could form no coherent response.

She was a vision. Arrayed in a dress that looked as though it were made of a million blue topaz stones sewn together, she stood silently at the far edge of the crowd. How the entire court wasn't staring at her, Nicholas couldn't understand, but it seemed all he could do was gawk. Her heart-shaped face was drawn into a focused frown, and she brought her thumb to her lip as she carefully studied the room. Even from afar, she managed to fill him with hopes and dreams and longings that he had never felt for another soul. When she finally met his gaze, all the pieces of his broken world finally fell into place.

"Well, what are you waiting for?" King Everard's gruff voice came from behind him. "Go get your girl before *he* shows up again."

He was right, but that didn't make Nicholas feel any less slow or clumsy as he tried to stride purposefully out onto the balcony, praying she would follow.

When she appeared, it was as though the heavens had opened up and a sliver of eternal bliss was shining down on him. Just behind his feelings of joy, however, came panic. She had been so hesitant last night. What could he say or do that might change her mind now?

Give me words, he prayed silently as he walked toward her. Gently taking her hand, he drew her out to the middle of the large balcony. Out of the corner of his eye, he saw King Everard station himself at its entrance. For a few moments at least, they were alone. Or as close to it as they might get.

"Dance with me?" he asked.

She quirked an eyebrow above the very small mask that just managed to outline her eyes.

"My mother is trying to keep my father busy," Nicholas hurried to explain, feeling like an idiot, "but should he find us, we need an excuse so that he thinks I'm appropriately occupied."

She thought for a moment then nodded.

Taking her hand in one of his and her waist in the other, they slowly began to move in circles. As they turned, Nicholas tried desperately to think of something . . . anything to say that might actually break down her walls. For they seemed higher now than they had ever been. So he was caught off guard when she spoke first.

"Is that King Everard standing over there?"

"It is." Nicholas dared a smile. "I asked him for a favor."

"What for?"

"To help me find you. What else?"

She stopped dancing, and Nicholas wanted to groan as she pulled her hand from his and took a step back. "I don't understand," she said, shaking her head.

"Don't understand what?"

"Why you would work so hard to find me after you banished me in the first place?" Her voice trembled. "You knew I wasn't guilty. And you still sent me away." She swallowed. "Was it because I turned you down?"

Nicholas closed his eyes.

She thought he had wanted her gone. No wonder she rebuffed him again and again. She not only blamed him for failing to save her, but all this time she had believed he had ordered her sent to Solwhind.

"Elaina," he croaked in a haggard, broken whisper, stepping closer so he could take her hands in his again. "The magistrates . . . they were going to put you to death. When I couldn't convince them to set you free, I convinced them to let me banish you."

"And that was better how?"

"You were supposed to go to Destin!" He squeezed her hands as though he could will her to understand. "Something happened on the docks that day, but I never found out what it was or why you were moved to another ship." He pulled her hands closer to his chest. "Since then, I have spent every waking moment trying to find you." He gestured toward the ballroom. "This night . . . the three balls. It was all for you."

Her mouth fell open a little, and her eyes were as large as chestnuts. She made no sound, but beneath the mask, the wet shine in her eyes reflected the moonlight. Slowly, she brought up one hand and traced the scar on his jaw. Her touch was like that of a butterfly.

And it was intoxicating.

"What is this from?" she asked breathlessly.

He nearly laughed with relief. She was talking to him again. He turned his right arm and pulled up the sleeve. He could hear her sharp intake of breath as the moonlight caught the raised scars and gave them shadows.

"Never think you're faster than a casum ball," he said wryly as he rolled his sleeve back down. "Particularly when you're on a moving ship."

"So you really did go to battle."

"Far too often." He leaned his head forward until it touched the top of hers. "Now won't you tell me what you're doing?"

She looked down and shook her head.

"And why not?"

"The entire kingdom depends on your survival. It's too dangerous. My fate holds very little weight comparatively. This is my duty and my duty alone."

Something inside Nicholas snapped, and he took her by the shoulders and leaned down until they were face-to-face. "There are two things you need to understand about me," he said in a tone he had never used with her before. But he was too angry to care. "First of all, my safety is not your decision to make."

Her eyes widened, and for the first time, uncertainty flashed in their blue-green depths, but Nicholas wasn't finished.

"Second," he said, "an entire world rests on your fate."

"What world?" she breathed.

"Mine." And before he could think better of it, Nicholas pulled her against him until his lips found hers.

If asked, Nicholas wouldn't have been able to count the number of kisses he'd shared before finding Elaina. The gesture had been fun and exciting, each one doled out with little value or consequence. He would have thought nothing of it if a passing pretty girl had asked him for a peck or even something more. But no kiss he had ever given or received had ever felt like this.

Because the girl he had searched and prayed and longed for, the one he had never deserved but wanted more than life itself, was kissing him back.

The gentle curves of her lips were like rose petals in full bloom, soft and pure in their innocence. He ran the backs of his fingers down her temple, cheek, and jaw before cupping her face in his hands and pulling her closer.

Trembling under his touch, she wrapped her small hands around his wrists and held them tightly, and the relief they brought made Nicholas want to weep.

She was here.

She was safe.

She was in his arms.

She was kissing him, too.

"I hate to interrupt the moment, but I'm afraid I see something," King Everard called in a low voice. When Nicholas and Elaina turned to look at him, he was peering into the trees below the balcony, his sword already drawn. He looked pointedly at Elaina. "Don't leave his side."

As soon as the king had climbed over the edge of the balcony into one of the trees below, Nicholas turned back to Elaina. "I need you to tell me what you're looking for. We can look together, but we need to do it before my father returns."

Still trembling, she nodded, a half smile still on her face, and Nicholas couldn't help reaching out to touch her once more.

"The stars have told me to find something called the Dagger of Power."

Nicholas felt the blood drain from his face as he recalled the orbed dagger he'd witnessed in Solwhind. "Are they telling you where?" he whispered.

She looked up at the nearest palace tower. "Up."

"I'm coming with you."

"But we'll find it faster if we look separately." The old stubbornness had returned to her eyes.

"While you were in Solwhind, did you happen to learn how to use a sword?" He folded his arms and cocked his head.

Her shoulders stiffened.

"Because if you did, I might actually believe that you have a plan to get the dagger from the Shadow once you find it."

She huffed and crossed her arms. "Fine." Then her voice fell. "But I only have until midnight. So we need to search fast."

Nicholas and Elaina slipped back into the ballroom, and Nicholas prayed that no one would notice them. To his surprise, few even spared them a glance as they moved along the edge of the room.

"I'm surprised no one has recognized you yet," Nicholas whispered as loudly as he dared.

"My mother created a sort of . . . disguise for me. Only those really looking for me and who know me well should be able to recognize me, at least until midnight."

"Wait, your *mother*?"

"A long story for a later day. Let's focus on finding the dagger for now."

They had just started up a set of winding steps and rounded the first turn when Nicholas heard a dreaded sound.

"Nicholas!"

They both froze, Elaina hidden in the shadows ahead of him. Glancing over his shoulder, he saw his father walking toward the stairs as though he intended to follow them up. A young woman and her parents were right on his heels.

Wait for me, Nicholas mouthed to Elaina.

"Please," she whispered, shaking her head. "Don't go."

He swallowed hard, holding her gaze for a second longer. On her face was a mixture of dread, pain, and fear.

"Nicholas!" His father called him again.

Nicholas gave her hand a quick squeeze before turning and running back down the stairs. He hoped she would understand. He couldn't risk his father seeing her again. Not now when they were on the brink of escape.

"What are you doing sneaking around at your own ball?" his father asked as he approached Nicholas at the foot of the steps. "I threw this ball for you to find your future wife, not hide from her."

"I was actually—"

"Let me introduce you to the special guests I told you about," his father boomed, gesturing to the man, woman, and girl behind him. "This is Lord Seamus, his wife, Lady Seamus, and their daughter, Lady Amelia."

Nicholas glanced back up into the darkness of the stairs. As his father continued to drone on, and Nicholas tried to think of a way to get out of his predicament, he got the sinking feeling in his gut that he should have never left Elaina alone.

CHAPTER 57

LOST

Elaina's heart fell as she listened to the king introduce Nicholas to Lady Amelia Seamus, whoever that was, and the old anger flared inside her chest. This scene was too familiar, and she was short on time. Another minute she waited, listening to them talk with indistinct words. Then two minutes. And still Nicholas did not return.

I'm trying, she told the Maker as traitorous tears threatened to come to her eyes once more. *I'm trying to let him help.*

Her mind was made up, however, when she peeked around the marble column to see him bowing to the girl and her parents. The girl's hand was in his.

No. She wasn't going to relive that horrid moment. Rather than watching him choose another woman again, she would just proceed the way she had planned all along. By herself.

Because with King Everard gone, apparently she was the only person she could count on.

All wistful thoughts dissolved when she reached the top of the staircase. There were so many rooms. A dagger could be hidden anywhere. Elaina ran to the nearest window and pulled until it creaked open. She stuck her head out as far as it would go.

"Is it on the second level?" she whispered.

Up, the stars called back.

And so Elaina continued to climb the palace, pausing at each level to find a window and consult the stars. It wasn't until she had reached the fourth level that the stars stopped answering. Unfortunately, Elaina realized as she looked around, the fourth level was where the personal chambers began. There would be more places than ever to look here.

To her relief, however, very few of the rooms were locked, and those that were often opened with a little shove. If she somehow survived this, Elaina decided she would leave a note for Nicholas telling him to get the palace locks repaired, if not for his sake, then for the sake of the kingdom's security.

There were few servants and guards around to see her as she slipped in and out of the rooms, and that was a good thing, as her progress was slow. Every little space that might possibly contain a dagger had to be searched. Curtains, beds, drawers, wardrobes, chests, and even misshapen rugs had to be examined.

Not only was the work monotonous, Elaina also found herself often distracted by the buzz of feelings running amok in her head and heart. Anger and awe warred and interrupted her focus.

As frustrated as she was, she couldn't suppress the wonder that bubbled inside her chest. Nicholas had always walked with a swagger, but there was a new confidence in the way he carried himself, the same kind of stern assurance her father had always worn like a medal. And Nicholas's dizzying new height and the impressive breadth of his shoulders made her legs feel like sea foam. The way his hands had caressed her face as blue eyes had searched her soul made her heart ache from within. His hands had grown hard and calloused over the years. She could only guess it was from all the fighting, but that had simply served to heighten her admiration for him. His touch had been so tender, and yet so full of yearning that it had made her wonder how she ever could have doubted him. She had wanted him to pull her closer so she could hide in his chest forever.

Then he had been offered another woman. Again. And as she

continued to pause and listen for steps every few minutes during her search, hoping he had followed, her heart cracked a little more each time she heard nothing.

Elaina slammed a drawer shut just a little too hard. This was like searching the waves for a lost boot in the middle of the sea. Why couldn't the stars just tell her where it was? Why did the Maker have to be so cryptic?

"Can I be of help, my lady?"

Elaina jerked upright to see a young servant girl standing in the doorway.

Elaina tried desperately to think of a good explanation as to what she was doing so far away from the ball in some stranger's room. "I . . . am looking for something that was lost . . . last time I was visiting the palace."

"In the duke's visiting chamber?" The girl looked blankly around the room.

"I'm afraid it's not mine. It belongs to someone else. They knew the area of the palace, but not the actual room." Elaina prayed the servant girl wouldn't report her straight to the guards.

"If it's something lost, I might be able to help." The girl twisted a strand of blonde hair between her fingers. "My mother wouldn't like me taking strangers around the palace, but since she's serving at the ball . . ." She bit her lip then gave Elaina a small smile. "If you want, I'll take you."

Elaina hesitated. She had been searching for a long time already. How much time did she have left? As if answering her unspoken question, the bells tolled eleven times. Elaina looked at the girl and nodded. She was getting nowhere this way. And the stars had said to go up. Perhaps this girl was the answer to her prayers.

"Thank you for helping me," Elaina called ahead of her as they left the chamber and headed toward the northwestern part of the palace. "I wouldn't have bothered, but I'm afraid I will not be returning to the palace for quite some time after this."

"Not to worry, my lady," the girl called back. "We have a pile of lost objects we keep in one of the upper towers. It just sits there gathering dust really. Won't be doing any harm by just looking at it."

The pile of objects turned out to be more than just a little way up. Up into the tower they climbed, passing level after level, Elaina's nerves growing with each step they took. Just as she was about to find a way to excuse herself and go back down, however, they reached a little round room with windows going all the way around and a door on each side that opened up to a narrow balcony.

Elaina moved over to the window and stared out at the scattered lights in the valley below. When she turned her head to look back at the girl, the girl gestured to a pile of varied objects in the center of the room. "Sorry for the long climb, my lady. Still, maybe you'll find what you're looking for here."

But Elaina couldn't answer. There, in the middle of the pile, lay a short, twisted dagger. And at the end of its hilt was a glowing little orb smaller than a plum. As she ran to the pile to examine the dagger more closely, Elaina wondered how the servant hadn't noticed it as well, or at least thought it out of place. Surely anyone who had seen the weapon wouldn't have left something so suspicious sitting out in the open.

"Have you ever seen this dagger before—" Elaina started to ask, but as she turned around, the servant girl began to melt away.

And in her place stood Alistair.

CHAPTER 58
LIGHT THE COLOR OF BLOOD

Alistair smiled and folded his hands in front of him. "I really do wish I could convey to you how much I appreciate your mother's gift. I only regret that I wasn't able to gather it all. Most gifts I sell in order to maintain a natural balance, you see. But hers was one I couldn't bear to give up. Her death was such a shame." He gave her a beatific smile. "But was it really? Now, I suggest you give me that knife."

"And if I don't?" Elaina wrapped her hand securely around the dagger's hilt and pulled it close to her chest.

"You see this?" He held up a long tube of red clay with a small bit of string hanging out of its end. "I'm not sure if your father ever took you to the far east, but even if he didn't you might recognize this. You see, if I light a fire to this string," he struck a match and held it beside the string, "all I have to do is throw it high in the air. My assistant, whom I'm sure you remember, will see it, and he will leave his hiding place outside your aunt's home and truly end your mother's life."

"How do you know about my mother?"

"Well, her attempt at veiling you from me was sweet but rather foolish, considering I possess what's left of her power." He frowned. "I know exactly what such power looks like. Besides, I

515

have it on good word that an unusual carriage was seen heading toward your aunt's home last night."

Don't listen to him, the stars warned Elaina through the open balcony, but Elaina stood frozen, still holding the knife to her chest. *No matter what the cost, you cannot let him have that dagger.*

"I have no choice," she whispered.

"They're talking to you now, aren't they?" He took a step closer, his eyes half closed and his voice nearly inaudible. "What a spiritual thrill that must be. I can't wait . . ." He shook his head. "I'm afraid I'm getting ahead of myself." He held his hand out. "The dagger, please."

Elaina felt as though she no longer occupied her own body. The part of her mind that still made sense screamed at her not to do it, but the thought of her mother dead and cold, all alone in a barn, seemed to have taken control of her faculties. And as soon as she handed him the dagger, she knew she had made a dreadful mistake.

Where was Nicholas?

Elaina backed up until she was leaning against the railing of the balcony. As she did, Alistair pulled a little clay jar from his cloak. Elaina tried to bolt past him to the stairs, but he caught her by the arm and yanked her back so hard she fell to the ground, smacking her head against the stone. As the world tilted around her, she could feel his hands on her shoulders. She was pushed up onto a chair, and despite her attempts at kicking him and freeing herself, he managed to bind her firmly to it.

"I truly am sorry for the rope and everything. If I had some sort of guarantee that you would just listen to me . . . give me a fair chance, I wouldn't have to begin our conversation this way."

Elaina wanted to shout that she knew his designs already and would never join him. But getting him talking would give Nicholas . . . King Everard . . . *anyone* more time to find her. So she played dumb. "What do you want from me?"

"Not from." He gripped the arms of her chair and leaned in toward her. "I want you to join me!"

"Doing what?"

"Don't look so disgusted now. You and I were fair friends once, weren't we? I have to say, you were one of the most impressive young ladies I'd ever met, and that's still true to this day."

"You haven't answered my question."

He sat back on his haunches. "I told you the truth when I said that my friend was murdered, the gifted one who served in the king's court. But I'm afraid I didn't tell you the whole truth. What I didn't tell you was the kind of villain my friend became as he began to explore his powers. In just a few years, he was able to fool and extort nearly everyone in the court while blinding them with his natural charm.

"After several years as his personal assistant, I realized that if I didn't stop him, he would end up more powerful than the king."

She searched his face for regret, for any sign of remorse. "You killed him, didn't you?"

His voice shook for the first time. "I might have killed my friend, but we are better for it. If I hadn't, our dear Prince Nicholas would never have been born."

"What does this have to do with me?"

He held up the dagger again, studying its pulsing orb closely. "I need you to help me spread equality."

"What?"

"Before you say no, think about it. I know you well enough to know that you won't be content to stay here in Kaylem. You want to travel the world! Well, come with me, and we'll do just that!"

"Doing *what*?" she cried.

He leaned in again. "Making sure everyone has access to wonderful gifts such as your kind has been given."

"You mean kill the gifted."

"Look." He shook his head as though explaining something simple to a small child. "After my friend's death, I went searching, hating myself for what I'd done. It became such a burden that I nearly ended my own life as I wandered. But I found my salvation when an enchanter discovered me and taught me how to see beyond my pain."

His voice was nearly a whisper. "They taught me to see the truth, that if my friend had not been the only gifted one in the court, someone might have stopped him. So, yes, there is a bit of blood involved, but think about it! We'll redistribute the wealth so all have access to such strengths!"

"So you want me to find the gifted so you can take their gifts." Elaina's patience was wearing thin. "I could never partake in such darkness."

"I once thought so, too. But," his eyes gleamed, "the enchanter taught me that once you learn to empty yourself of all your shackles, the burdens of restraint that weigh you down, there is room for so much more power!"

"You mean Sorthileige!" She glared at him. "That's how you steal their gifts, isn't it!" She looked down at the dagger he still held. "That's how you control it . . . all of it!"

"You needn't be afraid!" He brushed her hair back with his hand, ignoring her flinch. "I can teach you just as the enchanters taught me! It's really not as frightening as it seems! You see, when you learn to empty yourself of all your preconceived notions, as I did, you can also learn how to control the gifts, putting them in here," he held up the knife, "and taking them out again."

"Sorthileige is the poison of evil."

"Poison to those who haven't created room for true knowledge inside them. But the more you empty yourself to partake of it, the easier it becomes!"

"And the more you need." Elaina leaned as far back as she could. "If you truly knew me as well as you claim, you would know that I would never ask the stars to help me spread such violence . . . such insult to the Maker who gives the gifts in the first place!"

"I thought you might say that." Alistair looked quite sorrowful as he raised the knife to Elaina's temple. He moved its sharp tip slowly, his eyes trained on her temple with a thoughtful frown as though searching for a particular spot. "Believe me, this is quite difficult for me to do. Your gift is the most beautiful I've ever seen."

Elaina felt a sharp pain in her temple, followed by a warm trickle down her cheek. She cried out, but he only hushed her and gently wiped away the blood with a handkerchief. Then he pulled a little clay bottle from his belt and uncorked it and placed it on the floor. "And you're sure you don't wish to come with me instead? To make available such gifts to others as you've been given yourself?"

Elaina had nearly worked off the knot that held her wrists tightly behind the chair, but she was struggling to get the final twist. "Available to everyone with money, you mean," she snapped.

He shrugged and began to run the tip of the knife along her temple again. "You see that clay jar on the floor?"

Elaina stopped struggling for a moment to peer down at the jar, but she couldn't see its contents.

"Sorthileige isn't cheap. Once I discovered how to remove and interchange gifts, I had to sell everything I owned to purchase my first few drops."

Elaina's blood ran cold when she realized what darkness sat just inches from her feet. *Send King Everard,* she begged the Maker. But even as she finished her prayer, Alistair's knife tip seemed to have found its place. She cried out again as he made another cut to the side of her face.

"If you plan on taking my gift to get information from the stars," she panted, leaning her head as far from his knife as she could, "you should know that it doesn't work like that. The stars tell me what the Maker wants me to hear! Not what I want to hear!"

Something whizzed past Elaina's face, just missing her cheek. Alastair jumped, and his dagger clattered to the ground. He let out a curse as he dove after it, knocking Elaina's chair on its side.

Elaina tried desperately to loosen the last part of the knot, but before she could finish, Nicholas was standing over her. He cut her wrists and ankles free with one hand while holding his sword up with the other. Elaina rolled out of the chair and onto the ground.

"Run!" he shouted.

Elaina began to obey, but then she realized that Alastair still had the dagger. Spinning around, she found Nicholas and Alastair facing one another. Alastair held his dagger high, but Nicholas blocked his view of Elaina, his sword held defensively as he crouched down before them.

"Give it up," Nicholas said in a low voice. "King Everard will be here any moment to put an end to that evil you carry. I've already told him exactly how you use it."

"King Everard isn't near at all," Alastair spat out. "He's off chasing Conrad. In fact, I'm assuming he's met the ambush by now."

Elaina's heart stopped.

"It wasn't that hard to find a number of individuals with a grudge against the good king."

Nicholas lunged, but Alastair ducked.

"Nicholas, the jar!" Elaina shrieked.

Nicholas was able to avoid stepping on the lethal jar, but the jerk caused him to stumble. As he did, Elaina watched helplessly as Alastair dipped the tip of the knife into the little jar on the floor, sliced his own palm with the dagger, then grasped the orb with his bloodied hand.

As Nicholas righted himself, Alastair began to change. His body grew translucent like a cloud. And like a cloud, he rose up off the ground and began to float toward Elaina. Elaina ducked and covered her head, but in the time it took for Nicholas to reach her, Alastair had thickened again on the other side of the room, cutting her off from the door.

This time, he began to shrink. Nicholas was forced to bend in order to meet Alastair's vicious attack from below. Then, without warning, Alastair grew to twice his usual height. He shoved Nicholas into the wall as he did, and it was all Elaina could do to scramble out of the way as the two men engaged again. And again. And again.

Even in her fear, Elaina marveled. Nicholas was the most adept swordsman she had ever seen. He bent and rolled and attacked and parried in smooth, elegant moves.

In spite of his skill, however, Alastair's continual tricks kept Nicholas and Elaina running around the small circular room, barely managing to stay unwounded.

"What do we do?" Elaina shouted out to the stars as she neared the open balcony.

Watch, the stars replied.

Elaina wanted to retort that such advice was unhelpful when she realized that Alastair had begun to flicker. Only then did she understand.

His powers were beginning to fade.

Nicholas seemed to realize this as well, for he began to back Alastair into one of the walls. As he did, Alastair held the dagger up to his palm, but before he could draw more blood, Nicholas threw his own knife. With expert aim, it pinned Alastair's arm to the wall. Alastair let out a cry of rage and pain, and with his other hand, released a cloud of smoke that filled the room.

Nicholas fell to his knees as he made choking sounds, and Elaina began to cough as well. Still, she could see through the smoke well enough to spot the orbed dagger on the ground. She got on her hands and knees and began to crawl toward it, but as the smoke cleared, she realized that the orb's glass had broken. A sphere of light the color of blood rose slowly into the air and hovered before her. Elaina stood and took a step toward it.

"Don't touch that!" Alastair screeched. "Don't touch it!"

"Elaina, wait." Nicholas choked. "You don't know what that will do!"

But Elaina was unable to look away. In the circle of red light, she could see exactly what Alastair was going to do.

He would use every bit of power on himself, even if it drained his stores of gifts and Sorthileige in the process. Then he would gather more and continue to hunt until he died. She could hear echoes of her father's men as a cloud of darkness enveloped their ship. She could hear her mother's scream and hundreds more like it. Beside her, she could still hear Nicholas gasping for breath.

Unopposed, Alastair would never stop. He would kill and kill and kill again.

Elaina reached her hands up in the air and clasped them over the sphere of floating red light.

CHAPTER 59
GOOD FOR NOTHING

A strange pulsing filled Elaina's body. The world around her began to change, its colors separating as though her surroundings all lay swathed in a rainbow. Alastair's screaming grew so loud that it threatened to make her ears bleed, yet at the same time she could hear the music from the ball below floating up to them as if on a cloud. One of the flutists was horribly flat. The smell of the fat someone had thrown in the garden near the kitchens made Elaina dreadfully nauseous, and the floor beneath her seemed to tilt. Breathing grew difficult for the thick water floating in the air around her.

On the back of her tongue, Elaina could taste metallic smoke. She fought the urge to fly, disappear, and dream all at the same time. All kinds of impossible actions and sensations were at the tips of her fingers, and Elaina stared at them in wonder. Had her hands always been that shade of blue?

She was going to explode into a million tiny pieces.

Ignoring Nicholas's pleas and Alastair's furious shrieks, Elaina fled. Down the winding stairs she ran in a daze, stumbling and tripping in her mad attempt to make it down. She had to get to the ocean. She had to quench the fire that was now burning in her blood. Her whole body felt as though it had been set aflame. Only the parts of her feet that touched the slippers were cool, and Elaina prayed through the fog in her head that the ocean water might bring the same kind of relief as the glass.

As she ran, the thousands of sounds that had overwhelmed her at first were drowned out by the sound of her own heart pounding and the toll of the midnight bells. She came to a halt at the bottom of the tower stairs and slumped against the cool stone wall. In an attempt to focus, she scrunched her eyes shut only to realize that she could still see even with her eyes closed. What was happening to her?

The burning intensified, and Elaina took off again. Somehow, she managed to make it down to the ballroom. She ignored the cries of disdain and surprise as she shoved her way through the crowd. She did notice that her magnificent gown had disappeared and she was once again wearing her old tattered one in its place. But that was the least of her worries as she fought her way to the entrance.

Before she reached the doors, however, a hand grasped her wrist and yanked her back, throwing her to the ground. She found herself on her back, staring up into a face that she should have known but couldn't place.

"My master's been looking for you." He sneered.

Elaina frowned up at him, but couldn't remember how to make her feet move.

But just as he reached down for her with his other hand, another figure shoved the first aside. A flash of golden hair.

"Run, Elaina! Run!"

The sound of Lydia's voice brought Elaina enough focus that she was able to push herself to her feet and stumble out into the night air. In the distance, the moon glittered on the ocean's dark waves. She was almost free.

As she ran down the steps, however, she tripped, and her right slipper fell off. As soon as it was gone, her right foot grew as hot as the rest of her body. Elaina turned to search for it, but blurry figures at the top of the steps appeared. Rather than face them, whoever they were, she continued down the grand steps in her frenzy to reach the water.

But running in one shoe was difficult. Once she hit the gravel and began to sink into the stones, Elaina gave up and yanked the other slipper off. Squeezing it to her chest and gritting her teeth against the added burning in her feet, she continued on toward the water.

Just as she was about to reach the prince's private dock, she was again flung to the ground. Hands pressed her against the grass.

"Quick, get her feet."

Why was that voice so familiar?

"Look at her shoe!" another familiar voice gasped.

"I want that."

"Dinah, I saw it first!"

"Girls!" The first familiar voice spoke again in its cutting tone. "Keep her arms down and do something right for once in your lives! Now, what do we do with her?"

"We'll take her back to your house. The crown doesn't keep watch over borrowed land, so she should be well hidden there."

There was that voice again. A man, the one who had grabbed her in the hall.

"And you're certain that your master wants it this way?"

"Alastair wouldn't have rented the house for you if he didn't," the man snapped.

Someone stretched an arm out toward her. Just as Elaina felt a tug on the shoe that she still clutched, the would-be thief cried out and cradled her hand. "It burned me!"

"Let her keep it," the man said as he lifted Elaina into the air. He tossed her onto the floor of what looked like a carriage, but Elaina still couldn't concentrate enough to be sure. "She's good for nothing in this state as it is."

Such a comment should be upsetting. She should set him straight and tell him exactly how useful she thought he was. But it was all she could do to simply curl into a ball on the carriage floor and hold on tightly as the carriage began to bounce along.

CHAPTER 60
THE ONE WHO FITS THE SLIPPER

C aptain, send birds ordering all the dock keepers and patrols to close down the borders. Shut down the roads as well. I want all travel stopped!" Nicholas shouted, running toward the entrance. Cries of dismay rang out as he barged through the ballroom, but he didn't care.

"Sire." His captain joined him at the top of the entrance steps. "What has happened?"

"A terrific question," Everard's deep voice boomed as he joined them.

Nicholas was glad to see the king had survived Alastair's ambush, but he had no time to rejoice. "Alastair's orb broke, the one on his dagger. Elaina somehow . . ." Nicholas shook his head, searching for the right words. "Absorbed it. Then she took off, and as I turned to chase her, Alastair disappeared."

"You mean he escaped."

"I assume so. But as I turned to chase after Elaina, he literally vanished."

"What's this about Alastair disappearing?"

Nicholas turned to see his father behind him, glaring at Everard.

"And what is *he* doing in *my* kingdom at *my* palace?"

531

"Doing what you should have done years ago," Everard growled.

Nicholas's father began to reply, but Nicholas didn't have time for bickering.

"Father, Alastair is the Shadow!"

"You keep saying that—"

"I have seen him with my own eyes! All along, we've been harboring the enemy in our own court and feeding him our most precious secrets." Nicholas rubbed his eyes. "And now Elaina's gone."

His father shook his head. "Elaina Starke? I don't understand. Elaina's been gone for years. And I'll have you know that you've offended the Seamus family. I don't even know if they'll have you now after running out on them the way you did!"

Nicholas rolled his eyes and turned back to Everard. As he did, however, a gleam caught his eye.

Shining like a beacon in the light of the moon, a single glass slipper lay at the bottom of the steps. Nicholas hurtled down and picked it up. As he held it higher to inspect it more closely, he heard Everard groan.

"You know what this is?" He turned to the king.

Everard nodded and closed his eyes. "It's one of the glass slippers I gave to Elaina the first time I met her, back on her father's ship." He took the shoe. "Its power has been awakened." Turning back to Nicholas, he said, "tell me exactly what kind of power Elaina absorbed back in that tower."

As Nicholas explained what had happened with the dagger, the king's face darkened. When he was done, Everard held up the shoe. "She needs this. Without it, that amount of power will kill her."

At this statement, even Nicholas's grumbling father grew silent.

"How do I find her?" Nicholas asked, struggling to maintain some sort of composure. "They might try to disguise her."

"It's possible. But the Maker chose her to have the shoes."

Everard took a deep breath. "We will simply have to trust that they will fit only her."

"What are you going to do?" Xander asked incredulously. "Try the slipper on every girl in the kingdom?" He sounded near hysteria.

Despite his father's derision, Nicholas met Everard's eyes and nodded. "That is exactly what I am going to do. And I can only assume that wherever Elaina is, Alastair will be also."

"Now that his dagger is broken, he might not have the ability to take her gift just yet," Everard added.

"You're right," Nicholas said. "That might buy us some time. He won't kill her until he has her gift."

"You cannot be serious!" Xander sputtered. "Searching the entire kingdom for a girl with only a shoe?"

"Xander."

Everyone turned to see Nicholas's mother join them. Her face was unusually white, even in the moonlight. "Don't do this."

"I am busy right now, wife. Nicholas, this is impossible. You need to send out the guards instead."

Nicholas's mother didn't flinch at his rudeness. "Xander, don't put our son through the kind of pain you had to endure."

"What do you mean?"

"Our son has found his true love." She paused and drew a deep breath. "Don't make him lose her the way you lost Kendra. Let him go. Let him find her."

Nicholas could feel his mother's pain from where he stood, but for the first time that Nicholas could recall, Xander seemed touched by it as well. He tried to speak several times, but failed as he held his wife's injured gaze. Finally, he simply nodded.

"Very well."

They stood together on the steps for the better part of an hour, Nicholas, Oliver, and Xander planning together as to how the rescue should be made. Nicholas didn't miss, however, when Everard slipped away and disappeared into the palace.

He didn't reappear until it had been agreed that Nicholas

would travel with a small contingent of soldiers throughout the surrounding neighborhoods. Oliver would accompany him, and soldiers would be stationed throughout the city and on the roads to make sure travel was halted. Once they were finished, Everard pulled him aside.

His eyes had deep dark bags beneath them that hadn't been there before, and he looked more spent than Nicholas had ever seen him. "I have made sure the Sorthileige that was spilled during the fight is gone."

"Are you—"

"Don't worry about me. A few days, and I'll be good as new." He pressed his lips together. "I only regret that I cannot join you in your search. I received a message just before the ball that I am needed at home. It is a rather delicate situation, I'm afraid. One that must be dealt with immediately."

"I understand. What shall I do if I discover more Sorthileige?"

"Do what you must to keep Elaina safe, but at all costs, try not to engage with the Sorthileige or anyone who wields it directly." A shiver moved across the king's large shoulders. "As much as you can, let it be and wait for me to finish it off as soon as I can return."

Excusing himself from the others, Nicholas walked the king to his horse. "I'm just grateful that you would answer a call from your son's reckless old friend. We're not exactly neighbors with an easy distance to travel between us." He paused. "And I've not always been the most considerate of friends to Henri."

The king put his big hand on Nicholas's shoulder, and despite Everard's obvious exhaustion, Nicholas felt a slight tingle of power flowing through it. "I may not always agree with your methods, but you have heart, Nicholas. You will make a good king, and I am glad my son will have you as an ally one day." He nudged his horse forward.

"How did you survive the ambush?" Nicholas called out after him. "Alastair said he had all sorts of men in wait for you."

Everard scowled. "I may have some gray hairs, but I'm not *that* old." As if to prove it, he drew his sword and held it up. Blue flame engulfed the blade, and Nicholas grinned.

His grin disappeared as the king rode away and Nicholas walked back up the steps, his grip tightening on the glass slipper as he did. Part of him knew he should be afraid, but there was no time for fear. Elaina was probably alone with Alastair as he attempted to get his beloved gifts back from her.

You've given me a second chance, Nicholas told the Maker. *Now I need your help to find the one who fits the slipper. And if I do, I'll never let her go.*

CHAPTER 61
VESSEL

Elaina scrunched her eyes shut in an attempt to block out the casum balls exploding all around her. How long their barrage had gone on, she couldn't say, but at some point, whether that was ten years or ten minutes after she had been thrown into the carriage, another sound broke through the chaos. This sound was a familiar one. Did that mean the explosions were growing farther away? Shaking, she slowly lowered her hands from her ears.

When she forced her eyes open, however, there weren't any casum balls at all, nor was she in the carriage. She was alone in a room with a single window and no furniture. The floorboards beneath her were beginning to rot, and through the haze clouding her eyes, she could barely make out thick trees rising up like serpents outside the window.

She rubbed her eyes, trying to recall how she had come to be there and why the world seemed so incredibly loud.

Though she couldn't recall where she was or even what she had been doing before the assault, an instinct told Elaina that she needed to leave. Wherever she was, it wasn't safe. So she rolled over and tested her strength. She was able to push up onto her hands and knees and rock a few times, but when she tried to stand, her ankles collapsed, and she hit the floor hard.

She couldn't do it. She couldn't crawl, let alone walk. Every part of her body felt as though it were wilting. Her skin was as hot as the glowing lava she had seen once on a deserted island in the middle of the sea. Her senses still screamed that every touch, smell, taste, color, and sound were too heavy, too painful to fully comprehend. Whatever relentless force had invaded her body, it was killing her slowly, for her blood and skin and bones strained unnaturally to contain it as it raced about. It would only be so long before the foreign power burst through everything in order to get free. And as it fought for freedom, pressing out all the while, death was creeping in to take its place.

As she lay there, panting, Elaina realized that if nothing else, the death that was seeping into her bones was quieting the chaos enough to hear. Voices, individual ones rather than buzzes or rings, were coming from downstairs.

"Did you hear that?" a woman's voice said.

"She's awake," replied a man.

"I'll go up."

"No, we had an arrangement. She's mine now." Footsteps followed, and her door opened then closed.

She could sense someone beside her, but Elaina decided to keep her eyes shut.

"I would have killed you already if I knew how to get my gifts back. Unfortunately, your little show spilled what was left of my Sorthileige, which means I cannot retrieve my gifts from you until I get more."

Elaina winced as he grabbed a fistful of hair and yanked her head so she would face him, but she refused to open her eyes. Alastair. That was his name. And he had tried to kill Nicholas.

"I know you can hear me, so pay heed. If you decide to disobey me, I know exactly where your mother, aunt, and cousin live. Cross me, and I will kill them even after you are dead. And then I will kill the prince, and I will make sure his death is even more creative than theirs."

He shook her again, and her arm bumped against something beneath her. It was freezing. But as its shocking cold moved through her, the entire previous night came back, and Elaina's eyes snapped open. Holding his gaze, she glowered at him with as much rebellion as she could muster.

He let go of her hair and her head hit the ground, making the pounding in her ears even worse as he stomped out.

"I did what you wanted," Elaina whispered as soon as he was gone, rolling over to stare up at the crumbling ceiling. "I kept him from getting the dagger." She paused, licking her cracked lips. "So why are you letting him win?"

The stars didn't answer, of course, for it was day. The Maker didn't give her any other sign, either. All she could do was wait as hours passed and her pain turned more and more to a still quiet that began to slow the beating of her heart. Conrad came up once with a cup of water, but he only allowed her enough to wet her mouth before taking it back again.

Several times, Elaina tried to call for help, but her voice was nearly gone. She could feel her strength and sense of control slipping away as the raging sensations and urges and abilities inside her warred for dominance over the ever-encroaching death.

"They will be here any minute." Matilda's voice rang out from below. "Go get ready!"

Shrieks sounded, mostly likely from Alison. "They're on the bridge! The prince is almost here!" she squealed.

If only Elaina could see what they were talking about. Then it came to her. Maybe she could. Of all the conflicting desires churning inside her, Elaina found that invisibility was one of them. She had never tried to become invisible before, but perhaps now was the time to listen to the sudden urge that made her want to. Pushing against the floor until beads of sweat had formed on her brow, Elaina rolled over, put the slipper in her apron pocket, and began to crawl to the door. Conrad must have thought her completely immobile, for he had forgotten to close it.

As she inched toward the banister, she could hear Matilda again from below. But this time, Elaina's heightened hearing picked up even the woman's whispers.

"I made good on my word to help you catch her. Now you need to make one of my girls fit the shoe!"

"I don't have much power left!" Alastair retorted. "Whatever I use now will be gone forever. If we don't get her out of here, we'll all be imprisoned or worse, whether the slipper fits or not!"

"Maybe not."

Elaina let herself roll onto her side and rest for a moment. The thoughtfulness in Matilda's voice made her nervous, and she prayed for the strength to run, should she get the chance.

"If the prince thinks he has his bride, he'll lift the border blockade. We can all leave. You can take the brat wherever you want, and I will have a daughter on the throne. By the time he realizes he's got the wrong one, they'll be wed and it will be too late."

"Madame, I fear you overestimate my abilities."

"Make sure I don't, or the prince and King Everard will find you, if it's the last thing I do."

He paused. When he spoke again, his voice was weary. "What do you want me to do?"

"Make Alison look like Elaina. And make sure her feet are the right size. That girl has absurdly small feet."

"I told you, I don't know that I can make the illusion last—"

"Just do it. Or you'll never see another penny from me again!"

Alastair huffed. "You then, come here."

Elaina watched as he moved into her line of sight. Taking Alison's hand, he closed his eyes. His hand trembled so hard that her arm began to shake as well. Before Alison could protest, though, her eyes grew wide and she let out a yelp as her face began to contort. Slowly, familiar features began to take shape, and Elaina found herself peering down at an exact double of herself.

Just as the transformation was finished, someone rang the

door pull. Its song echoed through the house like a wail from a tomb. For a long second, everyone stared at the entrance. Matilda was the first to fly into a fit as she arranged the girls in the nearly empty drawing room, and Alastair bounded up the stairs. Elaina must have forgotten to stay invisible, because he grabbed her by the arm then dragged her down the stairs and out a side door that led into a dilapidated stable built against the side of the house. In it were two horses.

"You and I are going to ride to the nearest port." He hauled her up onto one of the horses. "Then we're going to hire a ship to take us away from here as soon as the borders are open again. And you are not going to say a single word to a single soul."

Elaina slowly pushed herself halfway into a sitting position while he thrashed around, throwing random objects into a sack.

"I'm going to die," she whispered.

"Yes, you are." He didn't pause in his work.

"There's too much power." She looked down at her hands. They were beginning to flicker. Orange, blue, pink, yellow, green. Her horse stamped nervously as she clenched her fists, trying to pull the power back in. "People will die."

He didn't respond.

Elaina had heard the stars for as long as she could remember, but the danger she felt boiling in her blood now didn't need their warning. If she disobeyed Alastair, her mother, aunt, cousin, and Nicholas would die. But if she didn't, they would still all die. So would hundreds of other people. For the powers within her that were fighting to get out were far too great for any one human to contain. They needed vessels, bodies to course through. And though she wasn't sure how she knew it, Elaina understood that such powers would be dangerous if unleashed from a body. When they killed her and made their escape, everyone around her . . . everyone in Kaylem, possibly, would pay.

Praying for one last burst of strength, Elaina pulled the glass slipper from her apron and stuck it on her foot. Then she yanked the rope from the hook where Alastair had hung it. She clung tightly to the horse's mane as she reached out far enough to shove Alastair to the ground. Her hands flickered again, and the horse whinnied, but this time Elaina didn't try to rein him in.

"Go!" she shouted.

The horse took off like a dart fish into the evening sky. Elaina held on with all her might, leaning into the horse's neck for support. Though she didn't know where exactly they were, she knew that her greatest hope lay within the ocean. So she pointed the horse to the west and closed her eyes.

Nothing in the world would have been more welcomed than sleep. But every time she started to drift off, the glass slipper would shoot the sensation of frost up her leg to jolt her awake, as persistent as the stars had ever been.

Hold it in a little longer, it seemed to say. *You're almost to the ocean.*

Once there, Elaina would be free to die in peace. And no one would be coming with her.

CHAPTER 62
LYING EYES

Nicholas stared doubtfully up at the house before them. Calling it a house was generous, really. Holes dotted its roof, and most of the windows were broken or missing completely. Dense weeds sprawled across the lawn, and the large tree stooped over the entrance as though to eat its guests.

They would never have even made the trek out to such a place if there hadn't been a note in the treasury from a local landowner that the house had been let for the ball.

"You're sure you wish to waste time here, sire?" Oliver made a face at the house. "No one seems to be home. They're not answering the bell."

"Try again." Nicholas had sworn that he would try every house in the land. And if that meant searching dilapidated messes like this one, then that was what he was going to do. He would never forgive himself if he missed her because he wasn't in the mood to search an ugly house.

This time, the door opened.

"His Royal Highness Crown Prince Nicholas Whealdmar has decreed that every maiden of marriageable age in the land is to try on the glass slipper," Nicholas's page called out.

Drawing a deep breath and willing himself to go through the

motions for the hundredth time that day, Nicholas prepared himself for another disappointment.

"Sire," Oliver called from the porch. "You're not going to believe this."

Nicholas hurried to the door. His men moved so he could walk through, but as soon as he did, he froze.

There, sitting in a fine, albeit ugly gown of green silk, was Elaina.

As Oliver proceeded to explain the rules of the slipper fitting, Nicholas studied the young women before him. The girl beside Elaina looked vaguely familiar, but in his exhaustion, he couldn't place her face. As his captain finished the explanations, though, Nicholas realized she was one of the girls Elaina had dumped him with at the second ball. But where was her sister? And why did she look so disgruntled?

Elaina's smug expression changed to confusion as Nicholas turned his back on her and began to walk about the room, examining the empty halls. Why was she staying here when her aunt was so close? When he had questioned Lydia that morning as he made his rounds, both she and her aunt had denied that Elaina was staying with them, or that they had even seen her since she was exiled.

He stepped closer to study the girl that looked like Elaina. Everard had warned him not to trust his eyes, but in this instance, they were telling him everything he needed to know. Elaina would not have been sitting there calmly, mooning over him as the older woman looked on in silence. She would have been glaring at *someone*, though whom her anger might have been directed at more, he didn't know.

And Elaina's eyes were blue.

Nicholas's heart pounded as he realized just how close he had come. This girl certainly wasn't Elaina. But if she was using the Shadow's powers to impersonate her, that meant Elaina was close.

Still, Nicholas allowed each girl to try on the glass slipper as he struggled to come up with a strategy. The sister tried on the shoe first, but her foot was too wide. The imposter tried it on next. Her foot was small, like Elaina's, and for a moment he was sure it might fit. But the longer she tried to shove her foot inside, the larger her own foot seemed to grow. She looked up at the woman, whose expression went from shock to outrage when Oliver declared that the shoe simply wouldn't fit.

"Come back!"

Everyone jumped at the shout. It had come from the west side of the house. Nicholas sprinted down the hall toward the sound. He burst through a door just in time to see the silhouette of a woman slumped against a horse's neck as it galloped away from the house. Nicholas sprinted back to his horse, slowing only to claim the glass slipper from his captain.

"Arrest that woman and her daughters," he yelled to Oliver as he mounted his horse. "And anyone else who is with them!"

The sun began to set as Nicholas chased her through sandy hills of wild grass. He should have caught her easily, but he was heavier, and the sand slowed his mount's chase. By the time he crested the final hill, they had come to the ocean. He was still several hundred yards behind, however, when she came to a stop at the edge of a deserted dock.

The girl got off the horse, though her dismount was more like a collapse. She pushed herself up just enough to roll off the pier and into a large fishing boat. She looked on the point of fainting, but she managed to untie the rope that held the boat in place and weakly shoved off using one of the oars.

Nicholas's horse hadn't even come to a full stop when he flung himself from the saddle. Keeping his momentum, he gathered his strength and made a flying leap into the water. Somehow, he landed in the boat as it floated out to sea.

She was trying to row, but the oars hardly moved as she pushed them. She was half-lying, half-sitting on the boat's floorboards, using the bench to prop herself up. A single glass slipper already rested on one of her feet. The other foot was bare. Her eyes were mostly closed as her arms struggled to move the oars.

Strange flickers of light were beginning to spark all around her, but Nicholas was beyond fear of strange magic.

"I know you're not one to listen to anything I say." He made his way over to the bench across from hers. "But I believe my order was that *every* maiden was to try this slipper." He reached for her one bare foot. When he touched her skin, though, blistering heat seared his fingers, even through his leather gloves. Her skin was hot enough to set a wick on fire. Clenching his jaw, he reached down again and worked to ignore it. Slowly, he placed the slipper upon her foot.

The shoe fit as though it had been made for her.

She closed her eyes and let her head fall back. "Thank you," she breathed. Then she jerked upright and her eyes opened wide. "You have to get out of here. The power inside me is too much." She shook her head and gulped more air. "It's going to kill me, and when it does, you can't be here." The corners of her eyes glistened. "I have to get away so I don't hurt anyone."

Nicholas stood and moved to the bench she leaned against. Lifting her off the boat's floor and placing her on the bench beside him, he held her tightly against his side.

"Do you know how many awful women I had to endure today?" he asked, cupping her face in his hand.

"But you like women." Petulance might have been on her face if she hadn't looked so exhausted.

He tweaked her nose. "Not in general, not anymore. Trying this ridiculous shoe on a hundred feet has cured me of my desire for any woman but one."

"But Nicholas, the power—"

"Is something we'll face together. I've been chasing you in one way or another for nearly three years, Elaina Starke. I'm not about to leave you now." He bent down to kiss her, but stopped halfway to her lips.

The boat rocked. Something cold and sharp was placed against his neck.

"Gently back away from the good prince, and I might not kill him right in front of you."

"Alastair," Nicholas growled, but the knife was only pressed more tightly against his skin.

"You give a decent chase, Elaina," Alastair said, "but I must thank you for making this incredibly easy for me. Now I can kill you both at once."

In his peripheral vision, Nicholas could see Alastair just off his shoulder, dripping wet, and Nicholas hated himself for it. In his excitement to see Elaina, he had forgotten to be vigilant. Some soldier he was.

Let her know how sorry I am . . . for everything, Nicholas prayed as he looked into Elaina's wide eyes for the last time. *And I beg you, keep her safe!*

CHAPTER 63
LAST SURRENDER

In the changing colors of the twilight sky, a single star glimmered above them as Elaina, Nicholas, and Alastair remained frozen in their places.

What should I do? she prayed. As she thought the words, in one fluid motion, Nicholas had thrown his head back to smash Alastair's nose while he shoved Elaina to the back of the boat.

She watched in a stupefied daze as Nicholas and Alastair fought, rocking the boat so hard she had to grip its sides so she wasn't thrown out. The cold glass against her feet kept her focused just enough to hear the star's reply.

Let go.

Elaina fought to understand as the boat bobbed dangerously around. Let go? Let go of what? The boat? If she did, she would fall into the ocean and drown. Of course, that might keep her approaching death from harming anyone else . . .

Even as she considered such a morbid thought, though, Nicholas's words from long before echoed in her mind.

It is only human not to be strong all the time. You don't have to bear every burden all alone.

And yet, that was exactly what she had tried to do. What she was still trying to do. Every time sorrow or pain befell her, Elaina welcomed the added weight upon her shoulders. Rejecting every offer of help, she had fought every uphill battle on her own. Just like she was doing now.

The men continued to fight, but unable to sit any longer Elaina did her best to stand. When she was upright, she looked down at the glass slippers. They had begun to glow, rainbow spirals ribboning out as the heat within her increased. Even now, she was trying to contain all the power on her own. The slippers were trying to pull it from her, but she was trying to deny it from even them. She was holding back. But why? What did she have to lose? Pride like Matilda? A squabble with her dead father?

Nicholas's life.

Matilda had been wrong. Elaina's strength wasn't just about pride, nor was it only about proving herself right. Elaina needed to be strong to save those she loved.

But what if she wasn't strong enough? What if she hurt him?

Elaina closed her eyes and tested the world around her. Sure enough, she could feel power emanating from the slippers themselves. And from the front of the boat, she could feel strength as cool and confident as steel. So much strength she had tried to push away over her lifetime. Her father and her mother. Her aunt. Her cousin. Cynthia. And Nicholas. So much from Nicholas.

"Very well," she whispered to the sky. "I will try."

The burning inside her had heated to a heavy boil, sending her defenses hissing into nothingness like steam. Elaina closed her eyes and tried to focus as she unwound her body, like unwinding a spring. Removing her own walls would have been difficult enough on any day, but now it was nearly impossible. She began to shake as she worked to loosen her muscles one at a time. The process took so long that she began to wonder if she would ever succeed, when blood-red light filled her vision.

Elaina screamed as the hundreds of gifts were torn from her body. The abilities that had raged inside for the last day now seemed to cling to her soul as she struggled to set them free. Forcing her eyes to stay open, Elaina looked down and realized that the red light was seeping from her veins and into the air, where it was sucked into the vortex that now swirled around her feet.

Alastair's cry tore through the dusk as well. When Elaina pulled her gaze from her slippers to look up, he and Nicholas were no longer fighting. Instead, Alastair had fallen to his knees. Red light was being sucked from him as well, its long tail snaking across the boat and into the vortex.

Elaina's heart sped even faster. Far too fast. Clutching her chest, she doubled over. She had let some of her walls fall, but they weren't enough. She had yet to stop fighting. But she didn't know how. And she couldn't hold on much longer.

Then Nicholas was at her side, leaning forward against the blood-red gales. "I'm here!" he shouted over the chaos. "You can do this!"

"I'm trying," she whimpered.

"Don't try." He placed a cool hand on her searing cheek. "Just let go."

"But if I let go, you'll die."

"And if that's the Maker's will, nothing will change it."

Elaina pried her eyes open to stare into his. Where she thought she might see fear, there was none. Bright blue, they were melded to hers, and in them was only determination.

"I want to let go . . ." She shook her head. "But I can't—"

"For once, would you stop fighting?" he shouted, pressing himself forward until his face was inches from hers. "For once, just let me love you!"

Then his lips were on hers. Pulling her close, he buried one hand in her hair and the other held her tightly against him at the small of her back.

Elaina's first reaction was to push away. He didn't understand the danger. He couldn't.

Yet he didn't let go.

She couldn't recall the last time she had felt so secure. His words from the balcony came back to her.

My safety is not your decision to make.

Nicholas was a man. A soldier. A prince. He had seen war and death, and he had come face-to-face with pure evil. All for her. He had made his decision. And with that in mind, Elaina made hers. In the comfort and safety of his arms, she felt the rest of her defenses fall.

She surrendered.

A new kind of heat rolled down her body, starting in her lips and rushing down into her feet. She gasped at the sensation, looking down just in time to see the glass slippers glowing red and blue, so bright they were nearly blinding.

You've done your part, the stars called. *Now let them go.*

Leaning on Nicholas for support, Elaina stepped out of the slippers. "Go!" she cried. He pulled her to the center of the boat, between the shoes and where Alastair lay face down on the boat's floor. She clung to Nicholas as they watched the shoes radiate brighter and brighter before bursting into flame.

Elaina and Nicholas ducked as a heat wave rolled out, and a great cracking echoed across the water.

When they opened their eyes again, the slippers were no more. All that was left of the shoes were two glowing embers surrounded by small piles of ash.

CHAPTER 64
A STRANGE GIFT

"I think we had better go," Nicholas said as they stared at the thickening smoke rising from the embers. He grabbed Elaina's hand and she let him pull her into the water. They surfaced just in time to see the entire boat go up in flames.

Nicholas continued to float at the surface with ease, but Elaina slipped beneath the waves. She tried to swim, but her arms were devoid of any strength.

As she sank, one of Nicholas's strong arms shot out and wrapped around her waist. Pulling her up against his shoulder, he began the slow swim back to shore.

The distance between shore and where Elaina had rowed to hadn't seemed so far until he had to haul them back. Elaina's conscience scolded her for allowing him to do so much physical work on her behalf, but for the first time in a long time, she ignored it and simply let him carry her.

When they finally reached the dock, Nicholas used one arm to pull himself up out of the water then turned and hauled her up after him. This should have brought relief, except that she began shivering violently as soon as she was out. The heat of the day was gone, and the shock of what she had just survived made her feel as though her bones might simply shatter against each other.

Nicholas carried her to the edge of the dock and set her down gently on a low stone wall before striding to a nearby storage shack. He gave the door several hard shoves with his shoulder. When it opened, he disappeared briefly before returning with a large wool blanket. Lifting her like a small sick child, he wrapped the blanket around both of them until all that was left uncovered were their heads. Once they were wrapped in the blanket together, he set her in his lap and pulled her tightly against him and began rubbing her back in rapid circles.

"W . . . w . . . what are y . . . you doing?" Elaina's mind was far from clear, but even in her muddled state, she knew that their current situation was far from proper.

He didn't stop. Instead he began rubbing her arms. "You just survived dark enchantment, abduction, hunger, and drowning. I'm not about to lose you to the cold."

Elaina was too cold to argue, and the heat and strength of his hands were comforting, so she said nothing more.

They sat that way for a long time, her leaning against him and him fighting to keep her warm. He had to get new blankets from the shed twice before her shivering slowed enough that she could talk without her teeth chattering.

When she was finally warm enough to sit on her own beside him, he allowed it, but he insisted on keeping the blanket wrapped around them both to trap the heat. That was fine with her. Despite his shirt being soaked, she could feel the warmth of his skin through the material, and somewhere beneath her fear and exhaustion, girlish delight squealed silently inside as he wrapped his muscled arms around her.

"Shouldn't we find someone to tell our families we're well?" she finally wondered aloud.

He shook his head. "My men will eventually find us. And you're in no shape to walk anywhere. We'll be best off if we wait here and keep you warm."

Bolstered by the heat that was finally seeping back into her body, Elaina examined the deserted dock more closely. "I don't believe I've been to this dock before."

"Probably not. We're quite a bit south of Kaylem. Only fishermen use this area much." He squinted down at her. "Are you all right?"

Knowing he was asking about more than her temperature, Elaina leaned against his shoulder. "No." Then she gave him a tired smile. "But I will be."

He brushed his fingers against her right temple where Alastair's knife had made its marks, Nicholas's dark brows knitting together.

"They'll heal," she said softly, catching his hand and pulling it away. Then she gave a rueful laugh. "I might be horribly disfigured from now on, but I'll survive."

"Nothing could disfigure you." He leaned down and kissed her temple.

Elaina closed her eyes and soaked in the way his lips felt against her skin. "In most noble circles, facial scars aren't exactly en vogue with the ladies." She opened her hands and examined her palms. "Of course, neither are callouses."

"Elaina." He pulled away so he could look her straight in the eye. "I want you to tell me truthfully. What did those people do to you?"

She looked away. "Last night? Or in Solwhind?"

"Does it matter?"

Elaina hesitated. The bruises were gone. Matilda would never again whip her, nor would Dinah or Alison mock her or strike her or throw food at her. She was free. Still, a single tear coursed down her cheek.

Nicholas wiped it away with his thumb and pulled her into his chest. She tucked her head beneath his chin and attempted to steady her breathing. "I tried to be strong."

"They will pay for this." His deep voice resonated in his chest.

But Elaina pushed away and looked him in the eyes. His angled face looked as though it had been chiseled from stone, unmoving and full of wrath.

"According to the law, Nicholas. Justice, not revenge."

"Nothing the law can do will be enough to satisfy their debt." For the first time, his voice shook. "Elaina, you can't understand what it was like lying there every night, agonizing over all the ways you might be suffering. Starving, beaten, or even worse, if some degenerate excuse of a man had found you . . ." He shook his head and tightened his arms around her. "Some nights I thought I might go mad. And even worse was knowing it was my fault."

"It wasn't your fault." She sighed. "I can only imagine Benedict's glee upon hearing the charges." She tried to smile. "If I couldn't be here, though, Destin would have been what I wanted as well." She paused for a moment, remembering the conversation she'd overheard between Alastair and Matilda. "Alastair was behind my switch in ships, but even his plans were thwarted when I was placed on the wrong one."

"And I'm supposed to be *thankful* for that?"

Elaina thought for a moment and nodded. "I might have been made a slave in Matilda's house, but if Alastair had gotten his way, I would have been his as soon as we left port."

Nicholas grunted. "She's still going to pay for what she did. They all are."

"There's been too much bloodshed already." Elaina stared up at the stars that were softly serenading them from above. The melody was peaceful, and the events of the last few years seemed a million miles away.

He was silent for a moment. When he answered, his voice was softer, almost a whisper. "You're right. There has been too much blood." He gently pushed her off his arm and pulled a small pouch from where it hung around his neck beneath his shirt. "I want to show you something. It got me through the war." He pulled the pouch open and held it upside down. Something small and shiny fell into his hand.

"I've carried this with me since the day we had our first dance practice," he said quietly, staring at the object in his palm. "You were the first thing I ever saw that I understood I truly needed." He held his hand up so Elaina could see.

Glinting in the moonlight, two silver bands were melded together by a swirling silver filigree. A round blue stone sat between the two bands, the same clear blue as Nicholas's eyes. Other smaller stones, every color of the rainbow, dotted the filigree around the rest of the ring.

"It's wondrous," Elaina breathed, her heart skipping a beat. Then she looked up at Nicholas. "You've really been carrying it around all this time?"

He pulled the ring closer and peered at it in the light of the moon. "This ring got me through battles lost, injuries, dying men, and even the battles won, knowing I was taking the lives of my own people." He swallowed and cleared his throat.

"I hated it at first after you left. It reminded me of all the ways I'd mistreated and taken you for granted. I nearly tossed it into the ocean once." He shook his head. "But as the darkness began to close in, it reminded me too much of you. When blood ran red, its shine was still pure." He met Elaina's eyes and held her gaze miserably. "Just like you."

Elaina couldn't have looked away if she'd wanted to. So many nights she'd languished over this man, sure he had found someone new. Sure he no longer cared for her and that she had lost him forever, particularly considering the cruel words she had left him with on the palace steps, refusing to forgive the wrong he so desperately needed to be released from.

"What is it?" he asked. "You're not usually this quiet."

"You're so different," she whispered.

He gave her a tired smile. "Must be the uniform."

She cautiously reached up and ran her finger along the scar on his face. He closed his eyes and exhaled as she did. "It's something more," she said. "You were a boy when I left."

"Don't remind me."

"But the man you've become . . ." She gave a little laugh. "I feel like I hardly know you. Of course," she fingered one of the buttons on his shirt, "the uniform certainly doesn't hurt. I've always liked a man in uniform."

Before she knew it, his lips were on hers and he was pulling her closer. She leaned in willingly, hungrily as he kissed her. And as he did, the remaining ropes that had held her heart down were loosed. Her heart soared, beating freely for the first time in years.

"Elaina Starke," he broke away, breathing heavily as he placed his forehead against hers. "I'll never be able to atone for the man I was when we met, but I can beg your permission to try for the rest of my life."

Elaina choked out a laugh as tears ran freely down her face.

"Elaina, will you marry me?"

"Yes. Yes, yes, yes!" She placed her hands on his neck and pulled him down for another kiss. As they kissed, Nicholas found her hand with his and slid the ring down her fourth finger.

How long they sat that way, kissing, laughing, and weeping, Elaina couldn't tell nor did she wish to. Eventually, however, she began to feel hungry, realizing with a shock how long it had been since her last meal.

"I know you wish to wait for your men, but would it hurt to help them find us by at least reaching a road of some sort?"

"Can you ride your horse without falling off?" He looked at her with concern.

"I think so."

"Very well. But let me know if you need me to carry you."

She smiled up at him as he stood. "I will."

His eyes widened. "Is that Elaina Starke I'm hearing? Did she actually just agree to let me help her?"

Elaina laughed and gave his arm a weak swat as they made their way to the horses. "I'm afraid you're not the only one who needs to make an apology."

"Oh really?"

She leaned into him as they walked. "I was so determined to be in control . . . to prove my father wrong, really, that I pushed away everyone and everything that might have helped me. Including you." She looked up at him. "If *I* have learned anything during my time in Solwhind . . . and our return, it's that I am not in control of the world. Nor should I be." She chuckled. "Perhaps that's why the stars are always so cryptic."

"It would have been nice if they had been a little more specific about the dagger. Or Alastair, for that matter."

"The Maker has spoken to me my whole life through the stars," she said, "but I could never understand why they wouldn't simply tell me everything. Instead, they were often vague or only told me enough to get a certain job done. I've begun to wonder, however, if the Maker perhaps isn't simply desirous for each job's completion, but that he's also concerned with *how* I approach each job he gives me. Not telling me everything forces me to trust and rely on him and others." She felt strangely shy as she peeked up at him. "I think I've finally learned that complete control will never be mine. Nor should it be."

He gave her a sly smile. "And when did you learn that?"

"Tonight." She pulled him down for another kiss. "I also have learned tonight that relinquishing control can be nice."

"Unfortunately," he smirked, "if you plan on marrying the prince of Ashland, I get the feeling you shall need to take control sometimes whether you want to or not." His eyes glinted wickedly as he grinned down at her.

"And why is that?"

"I'm told the prince of Ashland is rather stubborn sometimes. Much like a mule. The princess, whomever she may be, will probably be charged by the king with keeping him in line."

BRITTANY FICHTER

"Be careful with that kind of talk. Give me too much freedom, and I'll make you into a respectable prince."

He let out a belly laugh. "Now where is the fun in that?"

EPILOGUE
GETTING STARTED

Elaina recovered quickly once they were discovered by Nicholas's guards and whisked back to the palace, where her mother was brought and Elaina was attended to by the best physicians in the land. Nicholas visited her numerous times each day, often having to be chased away by both their mothers and ordered to eat.

The reunion between the queen and Theresa was one full of tears and many, many embraces. Elaina even spotted the king shedding a tear of his own, but when he met her eye he cleared his throat and busied himself with a book.

Matilda, her daughters, and Conrad were charged with a number of wrongdoings including slavery, contract keeping with a criminal, and theft. When their manor was searched, records were found showing that Matilda had practically handed Alastair her entire fortune under contract that he would gain it back for her with interest. Despite the hundred thousand gold pounds he'd stolen for Matilda when she'd traded him Elaina's secret, the majority of her debts had never been repaid, and all their possessions were sold in order to make payments on the three years' taxes that were due.

Elaina saw to it, however, that Barker and Dog were reunited with their other animal friends at Rosington, where Dog took to following Theresa wherever she went, and Barker grew happy and fat.

The reunion with Lydia and Charlotte was not one Elaina looked forward to as she recovered, but she knew that getting it over with as soon as possible would allow her to heal faster. So when she was well enough, she was moved to the sitting room in her new personal chambers at the palace. There, she waited with her mother as Charlotte and Lydia were shown in.

Elaina tried to sit straight as she waited, but all she wanted to do was crawl beneath the sofa and wait for them to leave. The only thought that kept her in her seat was the knowledge that Lydia had kept her secret at the ball.

A short knock sounded at the door. Elaina gripped the bottom of her seat as her cousin and aunt walked in. For a long moment, they all froze and simply stared. Then, in a rush of tears, Lydia threw herself at Elaina.

"I didn't want to testify! I didn't even mean to tell them anything, but Alastair asked me if there was a place you kept your special things, and I didn't—"

"Lydia!" Elaina took her cousin's face and held it in her hands. "I believe you."

Lydia sniveled and looked up at Elaina through red eyes. "You do?"

Elaina nodded. "Alastair and Conrad used us all. Even me and Nicholas." She got off the sofa and knelt beside Lydia to hug her. "I've missed you."

This brought on a whole new round of weeping, but as Elaina held Lydia, she realized that she had truly missed her cousin. Many moments between them had been strained and even unkind, but after her years of solitude in Solwhind, Elaina knew she wanted and needed her cousin. She needed a friend she could lean on.

568

ON THE MORNING that marked a week until the wedding, Nicholas disappeared, and no one could tell her where he had gone or why, only assure her that he was quite safe and had taken his captain and a few soldiers and headed out before dawn.

One day passed, then two, then four, and though Elaina trusted him with all of her heart, she couldn't help being a bit peeved that he had felt the need to run such an errand right before their wedding. The last thing she wanted was another reason to worry. Not now, when life was perfect.

All of her frustration went up in smoke two days before the wedding, however, when she walked into her chambers one evening to find her father sitting beside her mother, their hands clasped as they leaned eagerly toward one another. Their conversation was so deep that they didn't notice her entrance until, in her shock, she dropped the teacup she'd been carrying and it smashed on the floor.

"So what do you think of your wedding gift?"

Elaina jumped as Nicholas walked up behind her and wrapped his arms around her shoulders.

"Wh . . . where?" she sputtered, looking back and forth between Nicholas and her father. "How?"

Her father stood, looking uncharacteristically nervous. "The Shadow did something to the weather and drew us into a storm. When the storm broke, we found ourselves stranded on a deserted island with no way to escape until Prince Nicholas here found us."

"It turns out they were on an island only five miles north of Solwhind," Nicholas added. "But because of Alastair's power, they were trapped on the island. I left as soon as I got news that a number of ships thought missing had reappeared."

"Why didn't you tell me?" Elaina gasped.

"I was afraid of getting your hopes up and then disappointing you again." Nicholas turned her to look at him. "You're not angry, are you? That I didn't take you along?"

In reply, Elaina flung herself at her father. And though he'd never been one for embraces, he held her just as tightly, stroking her hair soothingly as she sobbed into his shirt.

"The prince told me everything that happened," he whispered into her hair. "And I . . . Can you ever forgive me?" He paused. "For doubting you?"

Elaina only cried harder.

ELAINA'S WEDDING gown was just as beautiful as the one her mother had imagined, or so her mother claimed, but as Elaina gasped over it in front of the mirror, her mother assured her that this gown wouldn't be disappearing at midnight.

"I drew it," she said proudly as she placed a circlet of rosebuds on Elaina's head, "but five seamstresses are responsible for its existence."

Elaina ran her fingers over the thousands of clear diamonds embedded into the skirt. It looked like hills and valleys of snow glittering in the sun. Her white sleeves were long but sheer, dotted with little round gems of every color, and the bodice was embroidered with silver and blue roses. Her slippers, though not glass, were still beautiful. They were also practical enough for dancing.

Theresa pulled Elaina from her fawning attendants just as the bells began to toll.

"Elaina," she said, pausing to touch the curl that had escaped Elaina's complicated hair twist, "I want you to know I couldn't be happier for you. You're marrying a man who adores the very ground you walk on."

Elaina laughed. "How do you know that?"

Her mother's eyes gleamed. "I could see it in his eyes the day you put a tadpole in his tea."

"You remember that, too? Am I the only one who doesn't?"

"Let me finish. Marriage is hard work. You will only be happy as long as you work to put the Maker first and one another before yourselves." She smiled. "You're so much like your father. Independent, duty driven. Keep in mind that loving him is just as important, if not more important than always finishing your task, whatever that may be. And you'll have many as you begin to inherit the responsibilities of the queen."

Elaina nodded seriously. She had considered this. Putting a war-torn country back together again would be no easy task.

"But Elaina?"

"Yes?"

"Most importantly, for goodness's sake, have fun! Live a little, and don't let duty steal your joy."

Theresa's words echoed in Elaina's mind as her father took her by the arm and led her to the back of the chapel. She had to breathe through her mouth a few times to calm her racing heart.

As soon as the doors were opened and the melody floated out to them, however, her mother's words made sense. There he was, standing tall and confident in his white uniform edged with blue and silver, saber at his side and his hands clasped behind his back. His dark hair, though combed, was as wild as ever, and for the first time since the war, the gleam of boyish mischief was back in his eyes.

As she and her father began the slow walk down the aisle, Elaina vowed then and there never to let duty blind her to the gift of Nicholas again. For he truly was a gift. The Maker had managed to give her the one man who could teach her to let go. And somehow, in her often rigid, overbearing self, that man seemed to have found the same thing.

She would have it no other way.

The thousands of flower petals that floated down upon them from the chapel ceiling created a shower of pink rain as she and her father reached the foot of the dais. And as Elaina stared up at the man before her, she saw her own joy reflected on his face.

Though she would never know exactly how, she somehow managed to repeat all of the holy man's words. At least, she assumed she did, for no one said otherwise. All she was aware of was the feel of Nicholas's rough, warm hands on hers and the bright blue of his eyes peering back into her soul.

But eventually the wait was over, and she heard the holy man utter the final words.

"My prince. Let this wedded kiss be the first of its kind, and may you never know its last until the day the Maker ushers you into his eternal bliss."

Slowly, almost fearfully, he took her face in one of his hands and her waist in his other. When he brought her face up to his and pressed his lips against hers, Elaina closed her eyes and basked in the fierce joy of his kiss.

For in it was determination.

Vulnerability.

Desperation.

Faith.

Hope.

Love.

Oh how she loved this man.

When he finally let go, Elaina turned to see the holy man now holding a delicate circlet of rose gold scattered with little pink gem rosebuds.

"Kneel," he said kindly.

Letting go of Nicholas's hand, Elaina sank to her knees. As she did, her heart began to hammer in her chest. He removed the roses her mother had placed on her head and put them to the side.

"Elaina Hope Whealdmar, daughter of Admiral Baxter Starke and Marchioness Theresa Starke, do you swear to love and honor Ashland, working for its good and seeking its welfare in the Maker's name?"

"I do."

"Do you accept the honor, privilege, and burdens that come with the crown?"

"I do."

"Do you swear to serve as crown princess, and when the time is declared, queen, until your duty is lifted from you, accepting and striving to fulfill the duties that are named in our ancient texts?"

"I do."

"Then," he smiled so widely his eyes crinkled as he lifted the gold circlet high before placing it on her head, "I hereby anoint you Elaina Hope Whealdmar, Crown Princess of Ashland."

A roar erupted from the crowd behind her as Elaina stood and took Nicholas's hand again. And though he still stood like a soldier, the smile on his face radiated the unbridled joy of a small boy.

THE WEDDING CELEBRATION was even more extravagant than Princess Sophia's had been, though Elaina had had very little to do with any of its plans. Still, it was magical. Garlands of roses, lilies, and peonies were strung together and hung from the vaulted ceilings. Tables were piled high with every kind of delicacy from all over the world, and the wine was more abundant than even the food.

And for the first time since moving to Kaylem, Elaina spotted King Xander holding his wife's hand.

The celebration itself was everything any bride could have hoped for, but Elaina felt her heart flutter as Nicholas led her out to the dance floor. A sense of familiarity hit her as he pulled her close. The music began, and Elaina closed her eyes.

In that moment, it was only the two of them again. Young and naive, she and Nicholas danced alone in an empty ballroom as he called the steps over and over. That's when it hit her.

"You've really wanted to marry me since that first dance?" She opened her eyes and looked at him in wonder. "How did you know?"

He shook his head and grinned. "I knew the moment you put that tadpole in my tea. I simply got a bit . . . distracted along the way."

Elaina laughed as he twirled her around and then back into his arms.

The rest of the celebrations flew by in a blur, though Elaina couldn't quite contain her excitement when the Fortiers walked up to give their congratulations. Queen Isabelle was every bit as brilliant and wise as rumor said, and Elaina nearly died of elation when she extended an invitation for Elaina to visit their legendary Fortress and become better acquainted.

After finally meeting Queen Isabelle and thanking King Everard once again for his help, however, Elaina found herself longing for an end to the day. And though the day seemed to last a week, Nicholas eventually took her by the hand and held his finger to his lips. The music still played behind them as they stole away, but Elaina was ready.

"I hope you don't mind, but we'll be staying in my chambers tonight," Nicholas said in a low voice as they started up the stairs.

Elaina's stomach did a flip as he opened the door and she stepped inside. The room was dripping with rose petals. Goblets of wine had been set beside the enormous canopied bed, and a low fire was burning in the large hearth across from the open balcony.

"Your nightdress is over there on the chair," Nicholas said quietly, nodding at a large chair by the fire. He shoved his hands in his trouser pockets and shifted, moving his gaze to the floor. "I'll give you some space to get changed." Then he headed into the next room over and shut the door.

Elaina could only nod, grateful that he was giving her so much room to get ready. Her heart suddenly thundered in her throat, and she drank half a goblet of wine in an effort to calm herself. She undressed as slowly as possible, but pulling on the nightdress still took far too little time.

When he came back in, she was standing on the balcony overlooking the waves that gently lapped at the beach below. She heard him enter but didn't turn, only hugged his arms when he wrapped them around her and laid his chin on her head.

"Why me?" she asked softly.

"What do you mean?"

She turned and looked up at him. "Why me, when you could have had any woman in the world? They all wanted you, but I didn't, and you still chose me. Even after years of being apart."

"I suppose you could turn the question around. Why did you decide to put up with a scoundrel like me?"

She nudged him and smiled wryly. "You didn't give me much choice."

He laughed and shook his head. "You wouldn't have had a boy you didn't want, and you know it." He sobered then and brought her hand up to his face, rubbing the back of her hand against his cheek. "I told you, growing up in my family was anything but steady. My father was inconsistent and wandering. My mother, heaven-sent as she is, was often withdrawn. My sisters rarely gave me the time of day. I was loved but spoiled, and when you get everything you want, the world can feel as though it moves with the wind." He shrugged. "You didn't."

She took his hands and traced his knuckles with the tips of her fingers. "You asked me once what I wanted. Now I need to know. What is it that you want?"

"I want *you*." He nuzzled her ear. His breath was hot against the side of her face. "What else could a living, breathing man want on his wedding night?"

Elaina laughed. "I mean for the future."

He hesitated, playing idly with her hair. "I want my kingdom to prosper and for justice to prevail, of course. I want my people to heal and be united again." He poked her. "I'm determined to get a ride on your father's ship once it's repaired, now that he's been found and all."

Then he whispered in her ear, "I want to see you happy. I cannot wait to see what you do for our people." Laying his hand on her belly, he added, "I want to see you healthy and glowing as you carry our daughter."

"Our daughter." Elaina chuckled, though shivers of happiness ran up her spine. "That's rather specific."

"Call it a hunch." He took her hand and twirled her around once. "I want to dance with you out here under the stars when the children are all tucked in bed. I want your face to be the last thing I see before I leave to meet the Maker.

Elaina, the stars called.

Elaina paused, tilted her head, and listened, a smile coming to her face as she did, and perhaps just a bit of blushing.

"What are they saying?" he asked.

She turned around and wrapped her arms around him, leaning in for a kiss. "They say that's a long list."

He laughed and crouched down. In one smooth motion, he'd tucked his arms beneath her knees, lifted her in the air, and twirled her in a circle. "Well then, we had better get started."

A Curse of Gems

A Clean Fantasy Fairy Tale Retelling of Toads and Diamonds

JAELLE NEARLY FELL several times as she ran home. Her muscles, unused to running long distances, cried out for her to stop, but she ignored them. By the time she reached the cottage, she could barely put one foot in front of the other. Panting, she made it into the house, only to realize that neither Selina nor Chiara was home. This was a great blessing, as Jaelle was still spewing diamonds whenever she spoke. But Jaelle didn't stop looking until she'd spotted her sister sitting on the bank of a nearby creek, her legs dangling off the edge and over the water.

Jaelle called her name several times on the way over, but Selina didn't turn. Finally, only after Jaelle had climbed down the embankment and seated herself on one of the larger rocks right beside the creek, did Selina even acknowledge her with a short nod.

Though the creek wasn't deep, the embankment that surrounded the creek was, and it was possible to sit down inside and stick one's toes in the water without being visible from above. The natural comforts of the day, however, no longer captivated Jaelle.

"You did this, didn't you?"

Selina just stared into the water as it bubbled.

For a long time, neither said anything, partially because Jaelle wasn't sure what to say, and partially because she wasn't sure how many jewels she could fit into her pockets if they continued to come. She didn't want to lose any and make vagabonds or wandering gentlemen suspicious. Or Chiara. Chiara would be the worst.

"Selina—" Out tumbled a diamond the color of blood.

Selina held up her hand, her face red and puffy, like she'd been crying. But for once, Jaelle didn't care.

"Selina, what have you done?" As if being a young unmarried woman in Terrefantome wasn't enough, now she was producing what were considered to be the most valuable forms of currency and the best weapons in the land. Jaelle folded her arms and sat straighter. "Selina, I am going to hound you and hound you," she said, diamonds pouring from her mouth like a thin waterfall, "and I'm not going to let you rest until—"

"Gifts come at a cost."

"Gifts?" Jaelle echoed. Two blue stones, a green stone, and six little red stones clinked into her hand. She pocketed them and continued. "What *gifts*? And why?"

Selina still refused to look at her. "Because I hired her."

"You...?" Two white stones. But before Jaelle could examine them, she saw something else out of the corner of her eyes and in her shock, stumbled backward and fell off her rock. She missed hitting her head by inches, and her back hurt, but those were the least of her concerns as she watched twin snakes slither out of her sister's mouth.

"Selina, what..." she shrieked, but Selina just looked at her.

"I know," she said when the snakes had finished their escape.

Jaelle watched in horror as a slimy toad poked its way between her sister's lips and then plopped onto her lap.

"You..." Jaelle stared up at her. "Selina, what did you do?" she whispered.

Soon it was agreed that Jaelle would sit perched on a very tall boulder six feet away while she listened to Selina tell her story. Their seating arrangement was Selina's idea, but after watching two black adders make their way out of Selina's mouth, which also made Selina's speech very difficult to understand, Jaelle was forced to admit that she did indeed need to back up, if only for her safety.

"Balbina is a Taistille witch," Selina began, watching two toads make their way down her clothes.

"You hate the Taistille."

"I hate what the Taistille do. But we all have our uses from time to time. Anyhow, when you told me what Mother was threatening you with, I realized she was never going to let you go. She lets me go my own way, as long as I contribute. But you're too useful. You know her trade, and her bad hand and stiff leg would make it impossible for her to work without you." She paused. "My mother is concocting a fear in you now that she can leverage for the rest of her life."

Jaelle's heart fell as she listened. She'd known all of this, of course, but hearing it from Selina only made it more real.

"So as soon as I realized how miserable she was determined to make you, I knew my time was limited."

Jaelle was too horrified to say anything. So Selina went on.

"I found Balbina. Balbina doesn't travel with any of the Taistille troops nearby, so she was rather difficult to locate."

"Why?"

"Why what?" Selina asked, this time producing a rattlesnake.

Jaelle swallowed. "Why doesn't she travel with the others?"

Selina didn't even blink. "They say she's too dangerous."

"Well, that's a surprise," Jaelle muttered.

"Will you just let me finish?" Selina rolled her eyes, and Jaelle nodded, so she continued. "When I told her I wanted a way for you to buy your freedom, she became curious."

"How much money did you give her?"

Selina gave Jaelle a funny look. "None." Then her jaw went taut, and she looked up at the sky.

"Well, how did you pay her? The Taistille never work for less than a steep price."

"It doesn't matter," Selina said quietly. Three red and blue frogs hopped down her dress to the water.

"Yes it does!" Jaelle put her hand over her mouth, nearly choking herself in the process as two of the smaller gems tried to roll back down her throat. She had to wait for a moment before trying again. "Masks are one thing," she rasped. "But Taistille witches use dark—"

"You think I don't know that?" Selina snapped, and two of her snakes hissed. Then she sighed. "You know that I lived in Maricanta's capital city before Mother and I moved here, correct?"

Jaelle froze as Selina paused to allow a large rat snake out. Only when it had made its way down Selina's leg, did Jaelle remember to nod.

"Our queen, Drina, was—and to my knowledge still is—greedy. She loves wealth and glory and beauty. And as she has two sons, I paid a few bribes to have a message delivered to her."

Jaelle paused. "Wait, you wrote to a *queen*? And how in the blazes did you get a message over the wall?"

Before she could answer, Jaelle's stomach growled, and for the first time, Selina seemed to notice the hour of the day. She looked around at the gray sky and gave a little start. "What time is it?" she asked, somewhat breathlessly.

"The clock tolled the tenth hour a few minutes ago." Jaelle paused. "Why?"

Selina turned and shook her head. "Look, we don't have much time, so you need to listen fast."

"But—"

"She'll be coming by soon to fetch you, so you need to pay attention."

Panic fought with anger as Jaelle stared at her sister.

"Why?" She tried to keep her voice from breaking as a few warty toads hopped out of her sister's mouth. "Why would you do this?" Tears began to stream down her face. This was ten times, a hundred times worse than what Chiara had planned to do. "You've made a deal with darkness," she whispered. "Don't you understand that this is more than snakes or jewels or money?" Jaelle leaned forward. "We can find another way to escape, but not one that will cost you everything!"

Selina gave her a sad smile. "You've always been so good to me, even when my mother did everything in her power to break you."

"But you've been good to me, too. You're not like her!"

"Maybe I wasn't at one point. But I've given far too much of myself to this place now to live unaffected on the other side of the wall. I've done...things that wouldn't make you proud. You, however," she wiped away a tear. "You have always belonged to another place." Selina paused, her ear cocked. "Mother is calling for me." Then she gave a dark chuckle. "If nothing else, I shouldn't have trouble with men from now on."

"No. No!" Jaelle shook her head emphatically. "We're going to find a way to get you out of this!" She racked her mind for some way...any way to pierce the darkness her sister had involved them in. "The other side!" She hopped up and moved closer to her sister. "I've heard there are people who can break this kind of curse! I've heard stories in the village! There...there's a king." What was his name? "Evergone. Everand. Everard! That's it. We'll find a way to get to the other side of the wall, and we'll find him! He destroys things like this. I've heard enough stories from people from all over that mention him."

Selina hopped off her rock and walked toward Jaelle.

"And that," she said, a little garden snake wiggling its way out of her nose, "is where you're wrong." She glanced at the road again. "The queen is coming to fetch you any minute. She's going to take you back to Maricanta."

"I'm not going to Maricanta without you."

"I've already drawn up some guardianship papers myself and signed Mother's name, so if the queen mentions those, pretend they're part of our usual traditions here."

Jaelle gaped. "Guardianship papers? What does that even mean?"

"Nothing, really. They're just papers I've written myself stating that Mother has relinquished guardianship of you and that you'll be traveling under the queen's protection with the intention of marrying Lucas. But they're important because they'll make the queen think Mother has given you up legally, and they'll make the royal betrothal papers faster to draw up in Maricantan courts."

"Selina, who is Lucas? Now you're talking nonsense."

Selina rolled her eyes.

"Shut up and listen. You're going to get married, and you're going to get away from this place forever." Her mouth quirked slightly, despite the tears in her eyes. "Just don't fall for him too hard. He's still a man, and even on the other side of the wall, men do as they please."

Before Jaelle could respond, Selina held a wet rag over Jaelle's face. Jaelle began to cough and sputter. She recognized the faint scent of cotton musk. She broke free of her sister's grasp and tried to run to the river to wash it off. But she'd only succeeded in taking three staggering steps when Selina caught her again and wrapped her in a tight embrace.

"Let me go." Jaelle fought weakly, barely able to keep her eyes open. "Don't put me to sleep. We can fix this." But already her words were slurring, and her legs buckled beneath her.

"Goodbye, sister," Selina whispered just before Jaelle fell asleep.

Find out what happens to Jaelle, Lucas, and Selina in A Curse of

Gems: A Clean Fantasy Fairy Tale Retelling of Toads and Diamonds.

Dear Reader,
Thank you for reading Cinders, Stars, and Glass Slippers! *Cinderella is my favorite fairy tale, and I hope you loved reading it as much as I loved writing it.*

If you'd like more (free) happily-ever-afters, visit BrittanyFichterFiction.com, *where my subscribers get bonus stories, sneak peeks at books before they're published, book coupon codes, and much more.*

Sign up today!

Also, if you enjoyed this book, please consider leaving a rating or review on your favorite ebook retailer or Goodreads.com to help other readers find it as well!

ABOUT THE AUTHOR

Brittany lives with her Prince Charming, their little fairy, and their little prince in a ~~sparkling~~ (decently clean) castle in whatever kingdom the Air Force has most recently placed them. When she's not writing, Brittany can be found chasing her kids around with a DSLR and belting it in the church choir.

Connect with Brittany:

Subscribe: BrittanyFichterFiction.com
Email: BrittanyFichterFiction@gmail.com
Facebook: Facebook.com/BFichterFiction
Instagram: @BrittanyFichterFiction